'Nay!' she whispered, but her own heart contradicted her, thumping deceitfully with excitement. His lean head dipped down, his lips seeking hers.

'Aye,' he replied, a rough certainty threading his voice.

Hunger kindled in her belly, a hunger she had never before experienced—yearning, craving… for what? As the sensuous curve of his mouth brushed hers, she wanted to scream out loud with joy at the exquisite touch.

Cursing her traitorous limbs as they curved sinuously into his muscular frame, she seemed incapable of resisting, her body melting to a burning pool of liquid beneath his touch. The heady smell of him enveloped her: a sensual delight of horse and woodsmoke that plucked at her senses, promising more, much more.

Meriel Fuller lives in a quiet corner of rural Devon with her husband and two children. Her early career was in advertising, with a bit of creative writing on the side. Now, with a family to look after, writing has become her passion… A keen interest in literature, the arts and history, particularly the early medieval period, makes writing historical novels a pleasure. The Devon countryside, a landscape rich in medieval sites, holds many clues to the past, and has made her research a special treat.

Recent novels by the same author:

CONQUEST BRIDE
THE DAMSEL'S DEFIANCE

THE WARRIOR'S PRINCESS BRIDE

Meriel Fuller

MILLS & BOON®
Pure reading pleasure™

First published in Great Britain 2008
Harlequin Mills & Boon Limited,
Eton House, 18-24 Paradise Road, Richmond, Surrey TW9 1SR

© Meriel Fuller 2008

ISBN: 978 0 263 86284 3

Set in Times Roman 10½ on 12¼ pt.
04-1008-88682

Printed and bound in Spain
by Litografia Rosés S.A., Barcelona

THE WARRIOR'S
PRINCESS BRIDE

Chapter One

Dunswick, Scottish Borders, AD 1157

'God preserve us! They're coming again! Run and save your souls!'

Tavia of Mowerby wheeled around in astonishment as frightened screams broke from the far side of the market square.

'Keep going, Tavia!' Noticing her lack of movement, her father growled at her, the fleshy lines of his face mottled purple in the early morning light. 'We'll not make any coin if the cloth is still in the cart!'

He had woken her before the sun had risen, shaking her shoulder roughly before pulling her up from her wooden pallet, glowering at her as she stirred the embers to life, put on the pot to boil the water. He was never in the best of moods on market day, especially as her mother had been too ill to make the journey into the city this week.

'But…what is happening…?' Tavia's fingers stilled once more on the smooth nap of the material before she caught her father's scowl. She lifted the bolt of cloth hurriedly from the ox-cart on to the trestle table, the brilliant hues of blue, purple and green glowing in the sunshine. She still remained awed by the process that turned the matted coats of their humble collection of sheep into such beautiful cloth. Pulling a length of the roll out across the trestle, she allowed it to fall in gentle pleats in order to show the cloth's drape to the best advantage. Her father nodded grimly at her actions; it was the closest he would come to approval.

Glancing up, high up to the thick stone walls that encircled the city, Tavia could see the soldiers of King Malcolm, resplendent in their green-and-gold surcoats as they fanned out along the walkway, or crouched in the turrets of the gate-house, arms bent back as they drew their bows. A *frisson* of fear shot along her veins. Something was not right.

Her father answered the worried look in her wide blue eyes with a brisk shake of his head. 'It's nothing, it'll be another false alarm, just like all the others,' he grumbled. 'Ever since Henry took the English throne, this town has run scared. Bunch of lily-livered mice, the whole lot of them!'

'It's no secret that King Henry wants these lands back...'

'And what would you know of it, girl?' Coughing roughly, Dunstan spat on the greasy cobbles. 'Malcolm has promised that Northumbria will remain in Scottish hands. We have nothing to worry about.'

Tavia eyed the hunched positions of the soldiers between the grey stone battlements, her eye dropping down to follow the scurrying townspeople as they nipped down alleyways, flicked behind shut doors. Usually at this hour, the market-place would be crowded with people, merchants and trades-man, eager to do business with the people of Dunswick. Carts would jostle for space, merchants would argue over the best places to sell their wares, and the sound of music and laughter would fill the air. Now all she could hear were warning shouts, shouts renting the tense hush of fear.

Tavia made a determined effort to draw some strength from the waxy solidity of her father's face. At nearly sixteen winters, the young king of Scotland, Malcolm, had done little to inspire his people, people who had been used to the wise and powerful hand of King David. It had fallen to Ferchar, earl of Strathearn and regent to Malcolm, to assure the people that the border lands with England were safe.

An arrow, lit with flame, hissing and spitting, thumped into the pile of woven fabric. 'Sweet Jesu!' Dunstan hauled himself up on the table, grabbing at the arrow with his bare hands. 'Save the fabric!' he bellowed at Tavia. She grabbed at the top layers to pull it into a heap on the ground, watching the beautiful colours shrivel and scorch on the cobbles. What a shame. All her mother's hard work disappearing in a moment. She caught her father's arm. 'We need to leave, 'tis not safe.'

'Nonsense, I'm not going to pass up an opportunity to make coin, my girl. We need every penny we can get.'

'Aye, but with no custom, 'tis hard to make anything at all.'

Her father's eyes reddened with anger. 'Just watch your lip, maid, or you'll see the side of my hand.'

'At least let me go and see what's happening.'

Dunstan shrugged his shoulders. 'If you must,' he agreed, grudgingly, grunting heavily as he reached down to gather up the ruined, singed fabric from the cobbles.

The smell of burning filled her nostrils as she ran towards the gatehouse, past town houses where the shutters had been closed. Out of the corner of her eye, she could see the thatched roofs on a row of cottages, alight, flaming, thick, charring smoke flowering into the sky. The sturdy leather of the soles of her boots gripped decisively on the slippery cobbles, as she leaped over the street's central ditch stinking with dirty water. At this time of year, as the weather started warming up to summer, the city began to reek with the foul smells of so many people living in one place. How different it was to her family's simple cottage on the hillside, a few miles outside Dunswick. There, she could breathe in the sweet, fresh air, hear the lambs bleating on the fells behind her and drink the sparkling cold water from the stream.

Reaching the walls of the gatehouse, she placed one hand against the cool stone to catch her breath, leaning over slightly. Shouts above her drew her gaze upwards, and she backed away, panic slicing her innards. Sweet Jesu!

Starkly delineated against the pale blue of the sky, the white frothy cloud, the hulking figures of the enemy could be seen, climbing over the tops of the walls. The red-and-gold surcoats of Henry II, the English king, flashed menacingly as more and more of his men piled over the battlements. Swords clashed, echoing in her ears; men grunted with exertion as they fought for their lives. She jumped backwards, horrified, as a soldier's body landed with a tremendous thump, inches from her feet, blood seeping through the metallic skin of his chainmail as he sprawled across the ground, arms and legs at hideous angles. A dragging weakness invaded her legs, and she swayed slightly, a sick taste in her mouth, before dropping to her knees beside the man, wondering how she could help him, touching the cold metal of his hauberk gingerly.

'Get out of here, maid! 'Tis not safe!' Another soldier jerked her up by her shoulder and shoved her back in the direction of the marketplace. 'Save yourself, maid. It will not be long before they're in here. Save yourself!'

'But this man…' She gestured at the soldier on the ground.

'Was dead before he fell,' the man replied bluntly. 'We're no match for these English devils. Now make haste!'

She ran then, sheer panic forcing her to move her limbs, to head for a place of safety. Too late to run home, the city was surrounded. Her breath came in great gasps as she fled along the narrow city streets, urging her muscles to work harder, faster. No time to warn her father; she just hoped he had managed to hide himself. Too bad her crossbow was still in the cart in which they had travelled to town; she had only thrown it in at the last moment, as another form of protection on their journey. If only she had it with her, then she could find a high spot and pick these barbarians off one by one.

The shouts at her back were gaining on her, intermingled with the distinctive thump of a battering ram on the solid wooden gates. Twisting her head back, she almost screamed out loud at the sight of the red-and-gold garbed soldiers, mounted on huge gleaming destriers, cramming into the other end of the narrow lane. They must have come in from another entrance!

'God have mercy on me!' Tavia whispered, ducking away to the right. Blood pumped uncontrollably behind her ears, in her brain. She bolted down an alleyway, hoping her direction would lead her away from the English, would yield up some place she could hide, could creep into until this nightmare was over.

And then she saw it. Her sanctuary, rising up before her, the one building that no enemy would dare to attack or desecrate with their barbarous ways. The church. Sobbing, half with relief, half with the effort of running so fast, she stumbled up the smooth, level steps, her toe tangling in the long hem of her *bliaut*. She wrenched the bulk of her gown away, her movements jerky with agitation, and climbed higher. The church would be her salvation. The great door of coarse oak yielded under her slight weight, and she fell into the dark haven, breathing in the heady smells of incense and balsam. Running along the aisle, she fell on her knees at the simple wooden altar and prayed for her life.

Behind her, the door swung back violently on its hinges, the harsh noise bouncing menacingly through the high vaulted spaces of the building. Sweat slicked Tavia's palms as she clasped her hands tightly in prayer, her eyes closed. Every muscle in her body stretched with trepidation, with fear. If she didn't look around, then it wouldn't be real, it would all be a horrible dream.

A boot in her back kicked her prostrate on the altar steps. The pain radiated out from her spine, bruising her delicate skin. Shocked, aghast, scrabbling on her hands and knees, she tried scrambling to her feet, only to be kicked back down again, harder this time. She bit her lip, wanting to cry out at this brutal treatment, not wanting to give them the satisfaction. How dare they treat her so!

Still prone, she twisted her head. Five or six English soldiers stood over her, faces shadowed by metal helmets, the long nose-pieces obscuring their features. The memory of the soldier falling to her feet at the gatehouse shot through her mind. Rage, boiling rage, rose in her gut. 'How dare you!' she hissed, pushing one flat palm against the stone floor to lever herself up. 'How dare you defile the sanctity of this church!' The soldiers exchanged mock-innocent, wide-eyed looks, and guffawed. One leaned down and grabbed a fistful of her *bliaut* at her waist. Through the fabric, his knuckles ground into her flesh as her head jerked back with the ferocity of the movement.

'Only if we kill you,' the soldier ground out, the warm stench of his breath wafting over her face. 'And we have no intention of doing that…yet.' He threw her back, her head knocking against the side of the altar. 'Geraint, you first.' He gestured to the younger soldier at the back. 'And make it quick…the rest of us want a piece, too.'

Geraint frowned at the older soldier, his manner hesitant. 'But…le Vallieres said…'

'He'll never know…' the older man snarled back, scratching absentmindedly at a day's growth of beard. 'Don't you think we deserve it?'

Tavia began to shake, her body trembling all over. Her mind jumped and stuttered as she fought to make sense of what was happening. Never before had she felt so completely violated, so vulnerable. As the nominated soldier stepped forward, she forced her brain to think coherently, to think of a way out! Her fingers clung to the side of the altar, a thick, carved oak chest, covered with a linen cloth and, on the top, a heavy silver cross, ornately carved with an intricate filigreed design. As the soldier approached, she propelled her frightened body upwards, making a desperate grab for it. A blade hissed as her fingers curled around the weighty silver, as she swung it round with all her strength, aiming for the soldier's head. He ducked and the cross sailed past the man's helmet, landing with a deafening crash on the flagstones.

'Feisty wench,' a soldier muttered.

'You might need some help with that one!' another teased.

The young soldier grabbed the thick rope of her hair at the back of her neck, yanking her head back. The cold point of his dagger pushed at the delicate skin covering her windpipe.

'We can do this one of two ways, maid.' His narrow face gleamed with runnels of sweat, the filth of battle. 'The easy way or the difficult way. Either way, the outcome will be the same. Your city burns around you, your townspeople have fled. There is no one to save you.'

'I would rather lose my life than lie with the likes of you!' Tavia spat out. But nerves made her voice quaver with fear.

'Enough!' Incensed, the soldier dropped the dagger, jabbing the toe of his boot into the back of one of her knees to send her flying backwards on to the stone. Her head thumped against the floor. Momentarily dazed, she watched as he lifted the hem of his mailcoat, ripping off his leather gauntlets to fumble with the belt of his trousers. Nausea rose in her stomach as she closed her eyes. Was this really to be her fate? To be raped by English soldiers and left for dead?

From the top of his chestnut destrier, Benois le Vallieres surveyed the devastation around him with a dispassionate eye. His men had done their job well. The reeking smell of burning thatch filled the air, air that moments previously had been filled with soldiers' screams and shouts. Now the streets were empty, the townspeople trembling behind their flimsy doors, watching, wondering what the English would do next. Few had been killed in this attack; Henry's intention was merely to frighten the young King Malcolm into some form of discussion about the ownership of these border counties. And, of course, Henry had hired his most trusted mercenary to carry out the mission, and would pay Benois well if the young Scottish king agreed to a meeting.

Benois rolled his huge shoulders forward, trying to ease the tension that pulled along the back of his neck. He couldn't remember the last time he had slept in a soft bed, or laid his head on a linen pillow stuffed with sweet-smelling herbs. At night he slept under canvas, alongside Henry's soldiers; his meals were lukewarm and often unpalatable, if there was food at all depending on whether the supplies had reached the soldiers. But these hardships mattered not to him. He relished this relentless way of life: the remorseless pace of the marching; the continual harassing of the northern counties that fired his blood, and drove away those darker thoughts that he tried so desperately to forget.

A scream rent the air. Fingers gloved in leather curled around the reins as the stallion beneath him skittered on the cobbles. Benois pushed his toes against the stirrups, raising himself in the saddle to pivot his long, lean body this way and that, trying to locate the source of the sound. He had believed all his soldiers to be out of the city by now, but he could hear guttural shouting, the noises of a scuffle coming from over to his left. He dismounted in a single, stealthy movement, dropping to his feet with barely a sound, leading his horse along a narrow, shadowed passageway to a church. Loosening his hold on the reins, he strode up the steps, pushing one large fist against the iron-studded door to throw it open.

The ribald laughter hushed immediately. His men, Geraint, Arnaud, Jean-Paul, gaped back at him, jaws dropping open, forming a mute tableau of surprise. And below them, spread-eagled on the floor, a maid. His heart jerked in shock, in anger.

'Let her go.' His order, sharp and commanding, rapped out from the doorway. The young soldier's hands fell away from his belt. His dagger slipped from nerveless fingers, its blade clattering against the stone floor. Silence, laced with thickening guilt, cloaked the church. Benois's frame filled the doorway, a giant silhouette against the daylight, his broad shoulders almost touching the sides of the arch, long legs spread wide across the threshold.

'Get out.' Benois stepped to one side, folding his arms impassively over his chest.

The soldier closest to Tavia bent down to pick up his knife. 'You'd better say your prayers now, virgin,' he whispered. The soldiers scuttled out, heads hanging, shamefaced as they passed their commander.

As he turned to follow his men out of the church, his mouth taut and white with rage, Benois glanced back at the maid lying under the north window. In the dim light, filtered through the narrow arched slits, he could just make out the slender figure crumpled up against the altar, the stark whiteness of her face like a ghost against the grey backdrop of stone. Although her eyes were open, she made no move to scramble for cover, or to hide. Benois frowned, irritated by his own uncustomary behaviour. He didn't have time for this now, but if his soldiers had gone too far…?

His men were descending the steps, blinking in the bright sunshine, their guilt evident by their shuffling steps, their mumbled excuses. Instinct told Benois to leave the maid; he had already given the order to retreat, and his soldiers would be gathering beyond the gates of the city, ready to ride back to Chester. And yet it was he who had given the command for no bloodshed in this attack on the city, no raping and pillaging. There was something in that still, pale face that made him hesitate, causing him to spin on his heel and stride up the aisle, pulling his gloves off decisively as he approached the altar steps.

The maid was of peasant stock, judging from her clothes. Her booted feet stuck out from a *bliaut* ragged with patched-up holes. The dress bagged around her thin frame like a sack; it had obviously been made for someone far larger than herself. The linen scarf that covered her hair had fallen back in the scuffle with his men to reveal her dark wine-red hair.

Her light blue eyes stared past him, unfocused, as he bent over her, unsure what to do. Since fighting for Henry, he had tended to avoid the company of women, finding physical pleasure only in his swift visits to whores, and now, he, Benois, most feared commander of Henry's northern battalions, had no idea what to do next.

He patted her on the cheek. Nothing. Seizing her by one shoulder with his great hand, he shook her, not gently. No reaction. He began to shake her a little more. Suddenly she began screaming hysterically, like a wild woman, a banshee—a high-pitched screeching like an animal howling in pain. He winced, pulling back slightly, trying to retreat from the noise that threatened to blow his eardrum.

'Get away from me...you...barbarian!' she stuttered the words out, a piercing wail, jerking upwards from her prone state to shove her hands up towards his chest, trying to push him away. She struggled against him, throwing her shoulders back and forth, trying to dislodge his hold. He dropped his grip on her shoulder immediately, sitting back abruptly on to his heels.

'Easy, maid. I have no wish to hurt you,' he muttered, amazed by the luminous quality of her skin, the beauty of her face, set in a perfect oval.

She focused on him then, shaking with horror, her wide cerulean eyes lit with fear. Tears welled in the corners, threatening to spill over, and her hands flew to her face, as if she couldn't bear to look at him. Tears bubbled through her fingers, dripping over the fine bones of her hands, splashing to the floor in great, dark spots.

Benois shifted uncomfortably. His calf muscles began to cramp in this crouched position. She seemed to be in one piece; maybe he should just go.

'You're inhuman,' the maid blubbed out. She jabbed a finger in the direction of the door. 'Those men...were inhuman!' Her whole body quivered with terror.

'Did they hurt you?' Benois frowned. Scanning her neat figure, he could find no evidence of attack, no reason why this maid should weep so much. The noise of her crying made him feel graceless, inept. It was a long time since he had offered a woman comfort, sympathy, and he wasn't about to start now.

'Nay.'

The single word was enough for him. Benois sprung to his feet, eager to leave, his huge, bear-like frame towering over the forlorn, seated figure. He was reluctant to spend time dabbling in pleasantries with a peasant girl. At his movement, she turned her large, aquamarine eyes up to him. The glossy wings of her hair parted over her forehead, forming a shining auburn frame to her terrified expression. 'They hurt me,' she added, 'but not in the way you imply.'

'Good.' He nodded curtly, his tone matter-of-fact, abrupt. 'Then, as you appear to be recovered, I will bid you good day.'

Tavia's eyes widened, chips of sapphire staring at him in puzzlement, as if unable to comprehend his words. *'Recovered...?'* Her voice rose a couple of notches as she struggled to speak. 'Are you completely insane?' She tilted her head back, pointing at the thin line of blood trickling down her neck with one grimy hand. Her pink fingernail quivered against her pale skin.

Benois shrugged his shoulders. 'I've seen worse.' He clamped his lips together in a furious line. His soldiers were trained, professional men; men who should have known better.

Tavia viewed the man in astonishment, unbelieving as to his remorseless words. He stood before her, this barbarian of a man, without a hint of apology for his men's actions. In the half-light, she could decipher no hint of his visage, except for his mouth, clamped firmly into a cruel, thin line. The silver metal of his helmet covered his head, the glittering skin of his hauberk shone out from beneath a short cloak of ermine, lined with red silk. The fine wool of his tunic bore the colours of Henry II, two lions embroidered in heavy gold thread across the breadth of his chest.

She folded her hands together in her lap, trying to still their trembling. Her voice, when it emerged, was a low whisper of condemnation. 'So you don't care one jot that your soldiers chased a woman into a church, kicked her down to the floor and threatened to rape her at knifepoint?'

No, he didn't care. 'Those men will be punished.' His answer was terse. Why did he even offer this woman an explanation?

'I thought I would be safe here,' she murmured. Tavia tipped her head back, the cut on her throat smeared red across the graceful line of her neck. 'But they followed me, pursued me, like I was their quarry…' Her voice wavered as she fought back fresh tears, fighting to maintain some sort of composure. 'Your men are animals.'

The lick of contempt in her tone squeezed his chest. 'Aye, they are,' he replied grimly. The tiny metal loops of his chain-mail glittered as he reached down from his lofty height to help her up. His extended hand loomed before her, tanned and sinewy, the fingers surprisingly fine and tapered for such an oaf of a man. She didn't want to accept his help, but the strength had run from her legs like water.

'Come on,' he said, irritated. 'I haven't got all day.'

The curtness of his tone stung her and she sneered at his hand as if it was a piece of rotting meat. 'I don't need your help,' she lobbed back at him. 'Just leave me!'

With a grunt of annoyance, he seized her wrist, hauling her roughly to her feet, before turning on his heel, and sweeping out of the church.

Tavia leaned shakily against the altar, blood pumping furiously through her veins. She closed her eyes for a moment, shuddering with relief, tracing her palm tentatively. Her skin still burnt with the force of the man's grasp, the imprint of his hand. But something was amiss. His palm had not been smooth against her own, but ridged and dented as if the skin had been through a mangle. A touch she would never forget.

Chapter Two

Tavia jerked awake, her heart banging out a jittered rhythm. Through the hazy layers of consciousness, soldiers continued to chase her through the church, a pair of ferocious slate-grey eyes leading the pursuit. She blinked rapidly, trying to dispel the frightening image, peering into the gloom of the cottage that was her home. Reaching out to touch the cool, gritty dampness of the stone wall beside her, her fingers shook with the comfort that she was finally safe. Her journey northwards from the city had been beset with anxiety, her muscles tensing at every creak from the trees, every sighing whisper through the grass, her mouth dry with the thought that the English would return. Once dark had fallen, she had crept through the narrow alleyways and side streets before running swiftly over the rough moorland to the farmstead.

A low moan from the pallet on the other side of the cottage drew her attention. The straw in the linen pillow rustled beneath her hair as she turned her head from the wall to look over at the huddled form. All she could see of her mother was a strand of silvered hair coiling out from the top of the blanket, the rest of her slender figure hidden by the covers.

Tavia chewed on her lip, fervently hoping her mother would be better this morning. She had awoken many times in the night to the sound of her mother thrashing about on the mattress. When Tavia had gone over to try to settle her again, her mother had pinned her with a wild, disorientated gaze, scarcely recognising her own daughter.

'What! Still lying a-bed, chit?!' Her father pushed himself through the doorway, scattering raindrops as he pulled off his hat. He strode over to Tavia's pallet in the corner, grabbing at her shoulder through the thin stuff of her linen chemise, wrenching her upwards. 'Time you had the pot on!'

Tavia shifted into a sitting position. She hunched her knees upwards, drawing the frayed woollen blanket up to her chest, clutching her arms about her calves. She rubbed her face with her hands, trying to eradicate the tiredness around her eyes. 'I'm sorry, Father.' She murmured an apology, having no wish to argue with him while her mother still slept. Normally, she rose with the dawn, lighting the cooking fire in the middle of the cottage, and starting to make the big cauldron of porridge for when her father came in from the fields.

'If you don't rise now, I'll give you something to be sorry for,' Dunstan growled. Leaning over, he pulled sharply on her long braid that fell like a glossy dark red rope down the centre of her slim back.

'Ouch!' She rubbed her scalp, turning wide eyes up to him.

'Up!' Dunstan spoke abrasively, jerking his thumb in the direction of the unlit, blackened hearth.

Tavia shook her head, trying to clear her mind and concentrate on her chores. Throwing back the covers, she swung her feet to the floor, pushing her toes into leather slippers. The toggle had broken off the right-hand shoe, making it difficult to walk in. She fumbled for her underdress, folded neatly on a stool beside her bed, silently thanking her mother for saving the fine piece of wool to make the garment. It was the one item Tavia owned that came close to luxury, and she relished the feel of the soft wool against her skin. Wearing this underdress, her *bliaut*, made of a cheap, coarse weave, did not aggravate her skin. She dragged the heavy gown over her head, fastening it on each side with leather lacings.

'Where did you run to yesterday?' her father asked gruffly, as Tavia finally placed a steaming bowl of porridge before him. She folded her arms over her chest, unwilling to tell him the full events, unwilling to hear on her own lips that she had never been more frightened in her whole life.

'I went to the church,' she muttered. 'I thought it would be the safest place.' Her top teeth nibbled at the rounded fullness of her bottom lip.

'Well, you could have thought to come back and help me with the ox-cart.' Her father shovelled a spoonful of porridge into his mouth, his beady, red-rimmed eyes roving over her slim frame, almost with disgust. 'I had a devil of a time trying to reach home on my own.'

'I wanted to make sure it was safe before I left the church,' she explained hurriedly. She turned back to the fire to hide the fear in her eyes, remembering how she had stared as the wide oak door had closed behind the soldier, that giant of a man, and how she had stood, frozen, unable to move, for a long, long time.

'More,' Dunstan commanded, shoving the empty, porridge-spattered bowl over the uneven planks of the table. She ladled the white, sloppy mess into the bowl and handed it back to him, grateful for the small routine chores that made her feel normal again, grateful for her father's familiar rough treatment of her.

'We'll travel to Kelso on the morrow, take the wool there,' her father announced suddenly, belching. 'I made no coin yesterday because of the attack.' His eyes narrowed. 'And I expect you to stay with me this time.'

Tavia whirled around, the spoon in her hand spattering white gobs of porridge on to the brown earth floor. 'But, Father, it's not safe!' She quailed at the thought of travelling to town again. 'All these attacks!'

Dunstan brought his fist crashing down onto the bare, worn planks. 'You'll do as I say, girl! I always knew you were lily-livered, just like that useless piece of womanhood lying over there.' He poked a finger at her mother's limp form on the pallet.

Tavia jutted her chin in the air, placing the spoon carefully down on the table and moving to her mother's side, resenting her father's accusation. She touched her mother's forehead; the icy coolness of the skin came as a shock after her mother's high temperature in the night. Tavia frowned. What was the matter with her? Suddenly her mother lurched upwards, her body snapping wildly from one side to the other, as she crossed her arms over her chest to claw at her shoulders with desperate fingers. 'Get them off me! Get them off me!'

'Shh! Calm down!' Tavia whispered, sitting down on the side of the pallet and trying to draw her mother's body into the circle of her arms.

'My whole body is itching, it's on fire,' Mary moaned. Tears gathered in the corners of her wide blue eyes, as she concentrated on her daughter. 'Help me, Tavia, please.'

Tavia jumped up, shocked at the deterioration in her mother's condition and whirled around. 'She needs a physician, Father. She can't go on like this.'

'Costs money,' Dunstan spat out through a mouthful of

porridge. 'And coin is one thing we do not possess.' He glared at her, the flesh on his face pinched and blotchy. 'If only you had made more effort with Lord Greaves, then all our troubles would be over. We'd be living the life of a noble family if only you'd wedded him.'

Lord Greaves! Tavia recalled the bent, arthritic creature at least twice her age, eyeing her covertly in the marketplace on several occasions. He had been the last in a long line of potential husbands lined up by her father, rich woollen merchants who visited the stall on a regular basis, men who showed an interest in the weaver's daughter.

'He didn't like the colour of my hair,' Tavia replied, sweeping her father's dirty bowl and spoon from the table, and plunging them in a pail of cold water to wash them. She scrubbed viciously at the clots of sticky porridge, the icy water stinging her hands.

'And not just that,' Duncan added. 'Just look at you, so thin, scrawny. Men want women with a bit of flesh on them; they want sons, all of them. You don't look fit to breed, girl.'

Tavia's eyes darted to the gloomy corner as her mother moaned, restless on her pallet. 'Surely we must have a few coins saved?' She turned to her father in despair, the cloth between her fingers dripping on to the packed earth floor.

'Nay! I told you! Can't you use some of your herbs on her?'

'Nothing is working.' Tavia shook her head, thinking of all the different tisanes and poultices she had made up for her mother over the past few days. 'Nothing works.'

'Slut can die for all I care,' Dunstan muttered into his beard.

'What did you say?' Tavia gaped at him, incredulous, unbelieving at the savage words she had just heard. Tossing the cloth into the pail, she stepped over to the table, thumping it with her small wet fist to get her father's attention. 'How dare you speak about my mother…your wife…in such a way? We need money, Father, and we need to send for a physician… now…today.'

Her father smiled, a narrow, mean curling of his lips. His pale, watery eyes were blank. 'You'll get nothing from me. Either of you.'

Tavia leaned her head against the ridged, nubbled back of a tree, and sobbed, hopelessness ripping through her chest like a knife blade. Speechless with anger at her father's words, she had fled the cottage, seizing up her crossbow from behind the door before heading for the small thicket of trees in the corner of the sheep pasture. How dare he! How dare he treat them both like this? Refusing to lend her the coin to fetch a skilled physician that her mother so desperately needed! She took a deep, shuddering breath, trying to think practically, fingers curling around the smooth stock of her bow as it rested upon the ground. There must be another way.

Needing to steady her anger, she unwound the white veil from her hair, tying the cloth around the tree trunk. Firing her crossbow had always calmed her, channelling her vision on the target in front, slowing her breathing. Oft-times, when she found her father's temper too much to bear, she had come out to these woods, sending arrow upon arrow into the trees; constantly honing her skill made her feel more secure. Indeed, it was because of her father's behaviour that she had learned to shoot; the urge to protect her mother, and defend herself, had become paramount in her life. She had never needed to use the bow against him…not yet, anyway.

Placing the knot in the centre of the trunk to form a make-shift bull's eye, she paced back over the open ground, away from the thicket, her wide skirts flaring over short, sheep-nibbled grass. Determination clouded her delicate features, small lines of strain etched around her mouth. Yesterday, she had felt so useless, so unable to defend herself in the face of those English barbarians; she couldn't let something like that happen again. Her chest constricted with the memory. How stupid she had been to leave her bow in her father' cart; if the weapon had been at her side, she could have picked them off, one by one, including him, that barbarian leader, the man with midnight eyes.

From the leather satchel slung diagonally across her back, she drew out one arrow, tipped with white goose feathers. She placed the crossbow on the ground, upending it so the curve of the weapon faced downwards. Putting her toes either side of the stock kept the weapon steady, so she could draw back the sinew cord and hook it over a notch at the top of the bow.

Slotting the arrow into the central groove, Tavia raised the bow to eye level, willing herself to concentrate, to focus on the target. Her sight narrowed on the knot, the tied ends of the veil fluttering either side of it. Her fingers sought the lever underneath the bow, the lever that would lower the notch and release the cord, which would in turn send the quarrel into the target. Taking one deep breath, she squeezed.

The arrow flew straight, its iron tip landing in the middle of the knot with a dull thud. In a moment, she had re-armed the weapon, sending another, then another arrow straight to the centre of the target.

'When you're done with wasting your time out here, mayhap you'd get your backside in the house, girl! There's work to be done!' Tavia jumped as her father's strident tones cut through the stiffening breeze as he lumbered over the field. Her shoulder muscles tensed as she lowered the crossbow and turned.

Dunstan eyed the three arrows in the target, then spat derisively on the ground, his face ugly with lines of hostility. 'Wasting your time out here with that damned thing!' His mouth curled down with miserable resentment.

'It's no waste if it saves my life one day,' she replied mutinously, resisting the inclination to take a step back from her father's scowl, 'or the life of another.'

'It's no use unless you're a man,' her father cackled. 'With a skill like that you'd earn good money.' He nodded towards the arrows pinning the linen knot to the bark.

Behind her, a slight breeze sighed through the treetops, like water running over stones. 'What are you saying?' Tavia asked, her tone careful.

Dunstan laughed nastily. 'King Malcolm's worried. He'll pay anything for good marksmen. With these attacks from the English, he's losing longbow men every day. Soldiers armed with a crossbow are far more effective.'

'So how does one become a bowman for the King?' She made a huge effort to keep her voice level, calm.

Her father peered at her suspiciously. 'He holds a weekly contest. Any competent marksmen can turn up and have a go. If the King and his commanders think anyone is any good, they'll sign you up immediately.'

'And how much does he pay?'

'Nine pence a day.'

Tavia's eyes widened. 'A small fortune!' Her heart began to pound.

'One that we'll never have if we stand here prattling all day,' Dunstan said roughly. 'Come, girl, there's work to be done.'

The imposing walls of Dunswick Castle stretched up high from a craggy promontory of basalt rock, towering above the patterned roofs of the town. The thick buttresses, constructed of huge square blocks of stone larger than a man, seemed to grow up out of the rock on which the castle perched to form an intimidating, impressive defence.

Shielding her eyes against the bright April sunlight, Tavia followed the wheeling flight of the crows as they circled in the air currents above one of the four corner towers. The screeching of the birds, a sad and lamenting lilt, did little to boost her confidence. Hesitating on the main bridge that led into the town, she swallowed, her throat tightening with an unusual dryness. She picked unsteadily at a loose patch of pale green lichen on the flat stone that topped the bridge wall.

When she had arisen that morning, long before dawn had spread its faint light through the hills and dales, she had felt composed, beset with iron-clad determination about the task she intended to undertake. Dressing hastily in some of her father's cast-off clothes, discovered at the bottom of an oak coffer, she had started the fire and porridge so as not to draw her father's anger. As long as he was warm and could fill his belly, then he would not think to question his daughter's whereabouts. Planting a light, farewell kiss on her mother's brow had only served to strengthen her resolve; with dismay, she noticed the skin on her mother's hands had erupted into savage blisters.

Now, as she yanked the hood low over her delicate features, she wondered about the success of her proposed endeavour. When her father had spoken about the contest to find more crossbow men for the King, he had no knowledge that his words, spoken with derision, had given her a solution to finding the money to pay for a physician's visit to her mother. She would enter the competition, disguised as a young boy, and hopefully be picked as a good shot. Once in the service of the King, she would earn enough in a sennight to hire a competent physician. Only then would she leave and return to her home in the hills.

The outer bailey thronged with people, a profusion of noise and colour. Green-and-gold tunics clashed with ladies dressed in sumptuous gowns glowing in a vivid array of colours. Rich cloaks of fox, ermine and bear contrasted strangely with the drab hues of the peasant clothes, some not more than rags hanging off a thin frame. Backing into the wall of the bailey, Tavia spotted a set of steps to her left and she leaped up, grateful for the easy vantage point. From here she could see the raised platform, tented with a heavily embroidered linen, on which the nobility sat. The fresh-faced King Malcolm, his bright red hair glinting in the sunlight, sat next to his regent, Ferchar of Strathearn. Tavia remembered the outcry when Malcolm's father, Earl Henry, younger brother to King David of Scotland, had died before he could succeed to the Scottish throne. Luckily, King David had arranged for Ferchar to manage the affairs of the state until Malcolm reached an age when he could take full responsibility.

A huge, round archery target had been set up in front of the dais, and already men were taking their place behind the rope line, lifting their bows and shooting. Some attempts drew guffaws of derisive laughter from the crowd of onlookers; others received cheers of admiration. Tavia sprung down from the steps, relishing the comforting bump of her crossbow slung over her back, and started to make her way through the mêlée, heading for the straggling queue that had formed behind one of the castle soldiers.

'Name?' the soldier asked, scarcely looking at her when she had finally shuffled her way to the front of the queue.

'William of Saxonby,' she lied, trying to keep her voice as low and as gruff as possible.

'Bit young, aren't you?' The soldier laughed, showing a full set of rotten teeth. 'Does your mother know where you are?'

Tavia chose to ignore the soldier's taunt, pretending to turn her full attention to the contestant about to shoot. The man, wearing a coarse woollen tunic of dull grey over a pair of well-worn braies, stood well over six foot; an impressive figure despite his tattered garments. Handsome, too, Tavia decided, studying his side profile covertly. As the man raised his bow, pulling back the arrow with ease, the hood of his tunic fell back slightly, revealing chestnut hair as sleek as sable. Angular cheekbones highlighted the raw beauty of his face, the proud, straight ridge of his nose, the up-tilted corner of his mouth.

A rose tint of embarrassment flooded her cheeks, and she ducked her head guiltily, ashamed at her overt perusal of the man. She needed to remember why she was here, not become entranced by another contestant! Besides, she usually showed no interest in the opposite sex, or, rather, they showed no interest in her. Despite her father's obvious attempts to marry her off to some rich suitor, the initial attraction of her physical beauty was quickly overshadowed by her wilful, de-termined manner. Inwardly, she cared not one jot. It bemused her completely that anyone should be enamoured of her, let alone want to marry her; men oft regarded her flagrant red hair as a curse, or even the sign of a harlot, and her scrawny frame was just too lean for most men's tastes.

The man released his arrow, letting it fly towards the target, where it landed, a few inches wide of the bull's-eye. Hah! He might appear to be a masterful shot, she thought, but I would best him any day. She watched as he pulled his hood sharply over his head once more, striding over to pull his arrow out of the target. Tavia frowned. Was there something familiar about the man? Surely she would remember meeting someone who was quite so huge? A debilitating weakness swept through her knees as the man turned back, heading straight for her. His massive frame drew alongside, and, in a hazy bubble of disbelief, she studied the slippery cobbles intently, willing him to pass by, to ignore her.

'Good fortune, young man.' The giant grabbed her hand to shake it. 'I hope you have better luck than me.'

In that fleeting, terrifying moment as he had turned back from the target she had known who he was. His grip had served only to confirm his identity. The noise that surrounded her receded, as his hand curled around hers, the furrowed scarring on his palm scorching her own. Tipping her chin, she sought his face within the woollen shadows of his hood, the glint of those feral slate eyes, the forbidding mouth.

'Nay,' she whispered. 'Not you.'

The hold on her fingers tensed at the sound of her voice, then tightened like a vice.

'Come on, lad! There's plenty more waiting to shoot. Get a move on!' The soldier behind her shoved her forward.

She yanked her hand sharply downwards, releasing his grip. What in Heaven's name was he doing here? He, the enemy, showing his face at the royal Scottish court? She wanted to shout and scream, declare his identity to the whole castle, but if she did that, her own true identity as a woman would be discovered, and her chance to enter the contest would be lost.

His right hand shot out, wrenching at the material of her sleeve, pulling her back, whipping her around to face him. His voice, low and melodious, reverberated around her—a threat. 'I know you.'

Chapter Three

෴

His words, clipped and toneless, sent a freezing chill of terror through Tavia's veins. Her heart pounded against the wall of her chest as she jolted round to face the blunt features of the soldier who had urged her on. 'Guard!' Her voice emerged as a pathetic squeak as she squirmed uselessly against the man's fierce grip. The wavering tone of her speech did little to attract the soldier's attention, especially as the crowd had become restless, bored with waiting for the next contestant. Clearing her throat, she tried once more. 'Guard! Arrest this man! He is an enemy of...oomph!'

A muscled arm squeezed the end of her sentence away, as it swept around her midriff and lugged her backwards, crushing her into a solid length of body. Before she had time to even consider fighting back, the man had spun her around so violently that she almost lost her balance, her head crushed into the massive wall of his chest.

'I think my little friend is jesting with you!' The calm, measured tones floated over her, sending a flicker of anger propelling through her veins.

'Ugh...!' she growled into the coarse fabric of his tunic.

A heady scent of earth mingled with horse rose from his torso, the heat from his skin penetrating the loose weave easily, warming the skin on her face.

'Can't take any sort of competition, I'm afraid,' the man was explaining. 'I'll take him home.'

The brazen insolence of the man! Her fear began to drop away, to be replaced with a wild, boiling rage. She swivelled her shoulders ineffectually within the powerful hold of his arms, first left, then right, desperate to break the imprisonment, but to no avail. Lifting one foot, she stamped down hard, feeling a small sense of gratification as she made contact with a set of toes.

'Enough!' he ordered, releasing the clamp of his hand on the back of her head.

'Let me go!' she stuttered out against his chest. 'I can't breathe!'

In reply, he swung her off her feet, throwing her over his shoulder carelessly, like a sack of grain. One hand crushed into the back of her knees, preventing any movement of her lower body while her head bumped painfully against the breadth of his shoulders. The blood rushed to her head, prickling uncomfortably behind her eyes, as she heard the crowd laugh and chortle, thinking they were witnessing some long-standing argument between friends. How could she convince them that he was not who he seemed? That he would probably slay them all in their beds if given the chance! The rapid pace of his stride prevented her from even lifting her head to scream out, her head bouncing against his spine like a wooden puppet.

At his back, the man carried three arrows stuck into his wide leather belt, the feather ends of which threatened to tickle her nose. In a moment, she realised her opportunity. As the man ducked slightly, as if avoiding a low lintel, she tugged on one of the arrows, very, very slowly.

'Now,' he murmured, 'who in God's name are you?' He bent down, sliding her slender frame back over his shoulder to set Tavia on her feet, as she tucked the arrow that she had pulled from his belt behind her back. The scent of hay filled the air, a fragrant aroma of summer grass mingling with the more acrid, earthier smell of horse manure. He had brought her into the castle stables! In the half-light, the shadowed angles of his face appeared dangerous, menacing, his rapier-like gaze shining like chips of ice as he studied her. Though her legs trembled, a volatile mixture of fear and anger bubbled inside her, driving her on.

'How could you forget?' she shrieked at him like a banshee, bringing the arrow around from her back to drive it into his shoulder.

The iron point, glinting dully in the sepulchral gloom, never touched his flesh. With astonishing speed honed from years of fighting, he wrenched the weapon from her hand, casting it away into a heap of straw. She felt herself gripped, twisted violently, her right arm pushed up into the small of her back.

'You're hurting me!'

'Tell me who you are!'

'My name is Tavia of Mowerby—now will you let me go?'

The hands dropped immediately, his gruff voice genuinely surprised at the high, lilting tones. 'You're a maid?'

He shoved the hood from her face, his lean fingers grazing the soft red sheen of her hair. The pale marble of her skin gleamed with an angelic luminosity, the ethereal nature of her features emphasised by the low-grade wool of the hood that now gathered in heavy folds about her neck. Her eyes, huge orbs of sapphire, threatened to drown him in those deep pools of blue. He sucked in his breath, feeling the weight of guilt descend on his chest. It was she. The maid from the church. The maid who had haunted his dreams for the past sennight, the image of that slender wraith sprawled before the altar pricking his hardened conscience with spirals of concern. More than once he had caught himself wondering what had happened to her.

'Do you know me now?' Her voice held a low challenge, but he could tell from her rigid stance that she was afraid of him. Why did she want to goad him so much? It made him want to laugh. The top of her shining head barely reached his shoulder, and, he reckoned, casting a swift glance over her sylph-like frame, that his body weight was nearly twice hers.

'Aye, mistress, I do remember you, more's the pity. What in God's name are you doing here?'

'I should be asking you that,' she replied, looping her arms defensively across her chest.

'And dressed as a lad.' The flint grey of his eyes narrowed. 'Why?'

'None of your business, soldier.'

'It became my business when you almost shouted my identity to the whole castle.'

'Well, it serves you right. You didn't reckon on me being here, did you? Sorry if I've managed to scupper your plans.' Tavia jabbed the words back to him, annoyance fuelling her speech. 'What were you planning to do? Murder our king in cold blood?'

Her impassioned speech seemed to roll off his shoulders. 'Since when did you become the King's personal body-guard?' He smiled, the well-defined edges of his lips tilting upwards, making him appear younger.

A tiny *frisson* of excitement threaded through her veins. She shifted uncomfortably, not wanting to experience such strange feelings when she was trying to appear confident and in control. But without his helmet, the intimidating coat of chainmail, all those hideous trappings of war, he appeared softer somehow. She chewed at the corner of her lip, shaking her head slightly. What was the matter with her? Mother of Mary, this man was English, the enemy! She needed to alert the castle guard, have him arrested… But how, when his huge frame blocked the only way in and out of the stables?

'Since people like you started attacking our towns, firing our houses, raping our women.' Her condemning tones pulsated around the stable in answer to his goading question. 'Who in the hell are you?'

'My name is Benois le Vallieres, at your service.' He nodded his head briefly, a scant interpretation of the more formal bow.

'I have heard that name before,' Tavia replied slowly, as-tonished, the beat of her heart starting to race. One hand flew self-consciously to the nick at her throat, nervous fingers touching the small cut.

He shrugged his shoulders, his eyes narrowing as he followed her movement. 'No doubt. I am the Commander of the North. For King Henry's soldiers.'

'Then what are you doing here?' she uttered, her voice shrill. An icy clamminess invaded her palms. God in Heaven! Benois le Vallieres! One of the most feared soldiers in the country. She had heard her father, and other townspeople, talk about him. Not just a soldier, she remembered them saying, but one of the Brabanters, notorious mercenaries who showed no loyalty, but fought for anyone who would pay the most.

He raked one hand through his brown, feathery locks. The cloth of his tunic strained over the bunched muscles in his shoulder. 'Just having a look,' he replied.

'Just having a look!' she squeaked back at him. 'You expect me to believe that!'

'Aye—' he took one step closer to her '—I do.'

'Don't you threaten me,' she warned. 'Move back!' She placed one hand on his chest, trying to force him backwards. He didn't budge.

A roar rose up from the crowd outside, followed by excited cheering. Tavia knew her opportunity to enter the contest was slipping away, and the longer that this soldier, this Benois le Vallieres, kept her in these stables, the less likely she would be able to take her turn.

'Let me go,' she pleaded. 'You don't need me.'

His eyes glittered over her, frankly assessing, sweeping sensually down from her curiously coloured hair to the rounded toes of her leather boots. A slow-burning coil of delight ignited in her stomach, but she quashed it away smartly.

'Oh, what a surprise!' she taunted him, trying to appear confident, although reedlike fear quaked her voice. 'I suppose I should expect nothing less from the likes of you! Have you come to finish what your soldiers started?!'

Benois glared at her in disbelief, then threw back his head and roared with laughter. 'You think I'm interested in bedding the likes of you? A common wench from the fields with barely an ounce of padding on her? You couldn't be more wrong!' He surveyed her coolly, tucking the arrow she had filched back into his belt. 'I was merely thinking that, if I let you go, the first thing you'll do is run out there and tell them who I am!'

'Oh!' Tavia's face reddened slightly as she smarted from his insult. Taking a deep breath, she tried to recover her equilibrium. 'Nay, you're wrong. I'll just carry on as if nothing has happened.' She nibbled on a nail.

'You expect me to believe that?' he countered wryly.

'You have to.' Tavia took one pace closer to him. 'You see, I have to take part in that contest.'

'Why?' he demanded, his attention snared by the rounded slenderness of her hips emphasised by the narrow fit of her braies. How could he ever have mistaken this maid for a lad?

'Because I need to become a crossbow man for the King's army,' she replied, exasperated. 'And if you don't let me go now, I'll miss my chance!'

Amusement bubbled in his chest at the severity of her expression, and he sighed deeply, narrowing his eyes to scrutinise her slim frame. Did the maid really think she could get away with something like this? That she could best a man in a contest? 'Then I suppose I'll have to trust you,' he said. 'But you'll have to promise that you won't give the game away.'

Tavia was already nodding. 'I swear.'

'You'd better put this back on, then.' He reached around to pull her hood back over her head, his fingers grazing her cheek with a touch of fire. 'It might increase your fortune.' He didn't sound hopeful.

'I don't need fortune,' she shot back. 'I rely on my skill.'

He raised one dark brown eyebrow at her boast. 'I'm glad you hold yourself in such high esteem,' he murmured. Hands on her shoulders, he pushed her gently out of the stables. She blinked in the daylight.

'And remember, if you break your promise,' he whispered softly in her ear, his breath caressing her skin, 'you'll have me to deal with. And believe me, it would not be a pleasant experience.'

Hands still shaking from her encounter with that barbarian, Tavia took her place once more in the queue shuffling slowly forward over the damp, slippery cobbles. She deliberately kept her head lowered, staring resolutely at the toes of her leather boots, unwilling to give Benois le Vallieres, should he still be watching her, any reason that she would give him away. She prayed ardently that the Scottish guards would have enough intelligence to stop him at the gate, and question him as to his identity, but, with a sinking heart, she knew Benois le Vallieres would outwit them.

When her turn came, she strode up to the rope line, slinging her crossbow forwards from the back of her shoulders, and pulling an arrow from the leather satchel at her waist. Placing one arrow carefully in the central groove of the bow, she raised the sights to the target, trying to keep her breathing slow and steady. Releasing the catch underneath with a slow squeeze of her fingers, the arrow flew straight and true, hitting the red circle painted in the centre of the target. The crowd cheered; there had not been many that morning who had managed to shoot so well.

Tavia glanced up at the dais, searching for some sign of approval from the royal observers, and saw the young King clapping, smiling at her. Lord Ferchar, the regent, rose to his feet, motioning for her to go and stand with the other men who had come through this first contest. As she nodded at him, she realised with a jolt that he meant for her to come and join him on the dais. Fetching her arrow and climbing the few wooden steps on to the platform, she hoped that Benois le Vallieres was not watching. He might think that she was about to break her promise to him.

'You shoot well, young man.' Ferchar, his grey hair grizzled and straggling, came forwards, as Tavia bowed low to the royal party.

'Thank you, my lord,' Tavia said hesitantly, unsure whether she was allowed to speak or whether she had to wait until someone asked her a direct question.

Ferchar curled his lips into a tight smile, and continued. 'Unfortunately, what has escaped most people's notice has not escaped mine.' A sharp gust of wind sent the colourful flags that decorated the dais flapping erratically. Tavia wrapped her arms about her as an icy coldness engulfed her body.

'Oh?' Her voice emerged as a croak.

'The fact that you're a maid,' replied Ferchar, reaching up with gnarled fingers to flip her hood back. King Malcolm gasped audibly, half-rising from his wooden chair, all thoughts of watching the contest forgotten.

'Look! Ferchar, she looks just like…' The end of Malcolm's sentence trailed into insignificance as he appraised Tavia's slender proportions.

'I know,' Ferchar replied.

Tavia remained silent. She hadn't the faintest idea what they were talking about.

'It's your hair,' Ferchar continued. 'Well, there are other things as well, but it's mainly your hair.'

'I can cut it off,' she gabbled in response. 'I'll blend in with the soldiers; they won't even suspect that I'm a maid.' She couldn't let her mother die!

'Why would you want to do that?' Ferchar rapped out. 'Nay, you mistake me, girl. There's something I'd like to ask you. A favour, if you will.'

Tavia nodded, wanting him to continue. Malcolm, his round face jovial, smiled encouragingly at her, although it was obvious that he had no more idea than she about what Lord Ferchar would say next.

'As a maid, you could never be in the King's army, you know that.'

Tavia shuffled uncomfortably.

'But there is something you could do for us.' Ferchar raked his arrogant gaze over the threadbare state of her clothes. ' And we would pay you handsomely, more than a humble bowman.'

'Tell me,' she whispered, a flicker of hope springing to her breast. Maybe it wasn't such a bad thing that she had been discovered after all.

'First of all, who was that man who carried you off?' Ferchar glanced down into the bailey, as if trying to catch sight of him. 'Was he your husband?'

'Aye,' she lied easily. 'He didn't want me to go ahead with the contest.'

Ferchar laughed, the smile not quite reaching his eyes. 'Quite right. A man should assert his marital rights. But if he hadn't caused such a diversion I might not have noticed you.'

She clasped her hands together. 'What would you have me do?'

'Have you noticed your likeness to the King's sister, Ada?'

'In truth, I have never met her, my lord.'

'Then follow me.'

Ferchar leaned over the front rail of the platform and ordered the soldiers to hold the proceedings, before striding off the platform in the direction of the main castle building. Hesitating slightly, before catching the more encouraging, friendly face of King Malcolm, she darted after the flowing cloak of the regent.

After the brightness of the day outside, the great hall of the castle seemed wreathed in gloom. A fire smouldered listlessly in the huge fireplace, sending out great gasps of smoke across the hall, which was deserted apart from one figure sitting at the top table. Tavia blinked her eyes, trying to accustom them to the dim interior.

Still walking forwards, Ferchar raised his hand, gesturing towards the girl who nibbled at a piece of bread. 'Ada of Huntington,' he intoned, by way of introduction. 'The King's older sister.'

They had reached the dais. 'Come over here, my lady, if you please,' Ferchar addressed Ada, as he climbed the steps, indicating that Tavia should follow him. 'There's someone I wish you to meet.'

With regal poise, Ada swivelled around in the carved oak chair before rising gracefully. She lifted one hand to adjust the veil of diaphanous silk, anchored with a heavy golden circlet, pulling it away from her face. Her *bliaut*, sewn with exquisite precision to flatter her slender figure, was of pale green silk, elaborately embroidered about the hem with an intricate design of flowers and leaves. Self-consciously, Tavia smoothed her grubby hands down the front of her tunic before tucking them behind her back.

'Now, do you see what I see?' Ferchar addressed her. 'Just look at the princess!'

Tavia frowned. See what? 'She's very beautiful,' Tavia admitted as Ada approached them, and smiled.

'She looks just like you,' Ferchar said, exasperated, ignoring her whispered admiration. 'Once we clean you up and put some decent clothes on you, I doubt anyone could tell you apart.'

'But why would you want to do that?' Tavia replied, aghast, sceptical that anyone should compare her to this breathtaking beauty.

Ferchar reached out to grasp Ada's hand, his manner soothing as he patted her white fingers. 'The Princess is in danger,' he explained. 'We've had information that the English plan to kidnap and hold her to ransom in exchange for Northumbria and Cumbria. We need to take her to a safe place and in order to do that we need to create a diversion. You, my dear, will be the diversion. You need to lure the English spies away from this castle long enough for us to smuggle Ada out of here.'

'But…' So that's what le Vallieres was doing here! Was he planning to kidnap Ada right in front of their noses?

'It's obvious you can defend yourself—' Ferchar's tone held an ingratiating lilt '—and we would pay you hand-somely.'

An image of her mother, lying frail and listless on a grubby mattress, entered her mind. 'I'll do it,' she agreed.

Chapter Four

'Thank you for helping us like this,' Ada's lithe figure sprang lightly up the stone stairs that spiralled up inside one of the castle turrets. 'Ferchar's been afraid for my safety for some time, but, with all the English watching the castle, he couldn't work out a way of carrying me to safety.' Tavia caught the note of admiration in the princess's voice when she talked about Ferchar and wondered at it—was there more to their relationship than at first appeared? She felt slightly ashamed; Ada made it sound as if Tavia were helping them out of the kindness of her heart, as a friendly favour, but the grim reality was that she needed the money, and she needed it fast.

'I'm just pleased that I could be in the right place at the right time,' she replied, cautiously, following the princess's graceful ascent. Beside Ada's delicate beauty, she felt every inch the peasant that she was, especially dressed in these shabby boy's clothes. 'But I'm not certain you will be able to make me look like you.' Tavia eyed Ada's elegant lines dubiously, the seductive sway of her gown, the glittering jewels at her slim throat.

Stopping on a wide, curving landing, Ada swung round, the fine twirling embroidery on her bodice catching the light from the flame of a single torch, slung into an iron bracket on the wall. The shadowed space highlighted the deep red of her hair, drawn into two braids that fell either side of her head. 'You really have no idea, do you, Tavia?' she questioned, laughing. 'I will find a piece of silvered glass, and we will put our faces side by side, and then you will see how alike we are. Once you are bathed and dressed, I would challenge anyone to notice the difference.' Placing one hand against the uneven planks of an oak-studded door, Ada pressed inwards. Light flooded out into the gloomy stairwell, illuminating the shrouds of cobwebs draping from the angled ceiling. Following the princess into the brightness, Tavia almost gasped in delight.

The southernmost tower of Dunswick Castle housed the women's solar, where the ladies of the royal court, wives of the high-ranking soldiers who had sworn fealty to King Malcolm, spent their days. After the drab grey stone of the castle bailey and the stairs, the room swelled with rainbows of bright fabric and laughing chatter. Everywhere Tavia looked, the bright, jewel-like colours of the ladies' gowns filled her senses.

In one corner, a lady sat at a loom, fingers busy as she pushed her wooden shuttle back and forth through the many-stranded warping threads, weaving a fine cloth resplendent with muted hues of purple and green. Other women held drop spindles, almost hidden in the voluminous folds of their skirts, drawing single threads from fluffy pieces of woollen fleece bunched in their hands.

As the ladies noticed Ada's presence, they rose and curtsied one by one, each murmuring 'my lady' before resuming their work. If they noticed the similarity between the grubby boy in scruffy peasant garb and the luminous beauty of their princess, then they made no comment, displayed no change in their expressions.

'My ladies,' Ada introduced the group of women to Tavia with a wide sweep of her hand. Heads bowed respectfully towards Tavia, and she smiled back, somehow glad of their silent discretion. She had entered a world totally unknown to her, a world of luxury and riches, so completely at odds with the harsh minutiae of her own daily life, that the temptation to be completely absorbed by the fine details of this noble lifestyle nudged strongly at her heart. She was here for the coin, she reminded herself sternly, coin that she would earn, and then escape, to run back to her cold, dry little life in the hills.

'Beatrice will find you some suitable clothes.' Ada indicated an older woman, who placed her embroidery in the willow basket at her feet, before looking Tavia up and down, assessing her size, her frame. 'She needs to look like a princess…like me,' Ada stated, as Beatrice sighed, rising to her feet, her bones creaking with the effort.

'She's shorter than you, my lady,' Beatrice muttered in a guttural accent, before limping off through an open doorway. 'But I'll see what I can do.'

'And a bath as well, please, Beatrice,' Ada called after the woman, flashing a quick half-smile of apology at Tavia. 'She grumbles, but she has a heart of gold,' Ada excused Beatrice's gruff behaviour. 'She looked after me as a child.'

'I must look dreadful,' Tavia tried to excuse her own appearance. 'I daubed mud on my face before the archery competition. To make myself look more like a boy,' she added, catching Ada's bemused expression.

'You're very brave,' Ada whispered. 'I don't think I'd ever have the nerve to do something like that.'

Tavia shook her head, remembering the nauseous churning in her stomach that she had experienced before walking through the castle gates. 'I don't consider myself to be brave. Sometimes circumstances force you to do these things.'

'But your husband…?'

'I have no—' Tavia stopped suddenly, remembering the lies she had told Ferchar, that the English soldier, Benois le Vallieres, was her husband. 'Ah, yes,' she muttered, lamely.

'He didn't look too happy when he led you away.' Ada linked her arm through Tavia's and led her towards the window embrasure, away from the knot of industrious ladies. 'What did you say to him to change his mind?'

'I beg your pardon, my lady?' Confused, Tavia scrabbled to make some sense of the princess's words. How in Heaven's name did she know all this?

Ada laughed. 'I watched everything from an upstairs window; he's a handsome fellow, your husband.'

'Aye, and very lenient, once you know how to handle him.' Tavia smiled, hoping that she would never have to 'handle' that man again. Two encounters had been more than enough for her.

'Then I hope I am as lucky as you seem to be in your marriage.' A secretive coyness spread across Ada's face. Her voice dropped to a whisper. 'Which may be sooner than everyone thinks.'

'Oh?' Tavia replied, vaguely.

'I feel like I can tell you this, Tavia,' Ada spoke in a hurried undertone, excitement making her stumble over some of the words. 'You're a stranger, yet I know we will be friends, and I know I can count on your discretion…?'

The question hung on the princess's lips, warranting some sort of answer. Tavia felt awkward, unwilling to be drawn so quickly into the princess's confidence. Aye, at this first meeting, she liked the maid, but friends? It was too soon to make that judgement. A quiet desperation lurked around Ada's eyes, her neediness like an empty bucket that Tavia doubted she could fill. Not knowing how to reply, Tavia smiled lightly.

'Ferchar will be my husband. He loves me, dotes on me…and I love him.'

'I'm happy for you.' Ada's words meant nothing to her.

'He's so strong, so decisive, a natural leader.' Ada's voice rose a notch, hissing slightly with undisguised elation. 'Why, he even picked out this gown for me this morning!' She smoothed her hand over the soft wool of her skirt.

'He makes a good regent,' Tavia agreed, startled by Ada's curious dependence on Ferchar.

'He'd make an even better king!' Ada blurted out, then clapped a hand over her mouth, before clutching weakly at Tavia's sleeve. 'I've said too much. Forget my words, Tavia!' She glanced hurriedly around the room, checking to see if they had been overheard.

So that explained Ferchar's over-protectiveness of the Princess Ada, thought Tavia. He wanted the maid for himself, for a wife, and wanted to keep her safe. He had obviously already gained Ada's undeniable loyalty; the girl appeared infatuated with him, despite him being at least twenty winters older than her.

'Your words are forgotten, my lady,' Tavia replied brightly. 'Do not think on it again.'

Underneath the magnificent wooden arches of the great hall at Langley Castle, Benois stabbed his jewelled eating knife into a piece of cured ham and put it between his lips, chewing thoughtfully. Below him, in the main body of the hall, his soldiers ate alongside the peasants that worked in the castle fields, hungrily devouring the huge platters of food that seemed to emerge continually from the kitchens.

'Ah, Benois, back already!' Lord Langley, a well-known supporter of King Henry, bounced up the stairs to the top table. 'How are you enjoying our hospitality?' He slapped his friend companionably on the back.

'It's much appreciated, Langley.' Benois leant back in his chair. 'After all those nights spent in cold tents with less than agreeable food, I thank the Lord that you are on our side.'

'And fortunate that I own a castle on the English side of the border that's not many miles from Dunswick.' Langley grinned, lifting a slice of chicken on to his plate.

'That, too.' Benois laughed, the taut skin of his face stretching over his high cheekbones.

'So, what did you find out? They obviously didn't realise who you were.'

'Hmm! I was lucky. Although one person did recognise me.'

'Who on earth? No one knows you in Scotland!'

'No one, it seems, apart from one completely annoying, interfering, god-forsaken maid!' Benois replied. A pair of blue eyes shining from a luminous, pearl-like face swam into his memory. 'She nearly wrecked the whole plan!'

'But how in God's name did she know you?'

Benois sighed, breaking off a chunk of bread from the round loaf on the table. 'The maid was captured by my men in our earlier raid on Dunswick. I caught them just in time. She remembered me from then.'

'Unlucky,' Langley surmised. 'But you still managed to avoid being caught.'

'Aye, although the wench nearly stabbed me with one of my own arrows. The woman is a termagant!'

Langley tipped his head back and roared with laughter. 'I

like it. The magnificent Brabanter mercenary floored by a woman.'

'Nearly,' Benois corrected, smiling. He remembered the supple feel of the girl's body against his own as he had wrenched the arrow from her hand, crushing her easily into him, stopping her struggles.

Langley observed him closely. 'From your expression it seems the encounter was not entirely unpleasant.'

'It was certainly surprising.' Benois grimaced. 'It's not every day you find a woman wanting to become a royal bowman.' He tucked his eating knife back into his belt. 'Or boasting of her expertise as if she were a skilled marksman.' He wondered how she had fared in the contest.

'She sounds perfectly intriguing,' Langley replied. 'I should like to meet her.'

'Unlikely. Once they discover she's a woman, she'll be sent packing.' Why did he even care? He pushed his plate away, annoyance creasing his brow. Why did the infuriating chit suffuse his thoughts so?

'So what did you find out?' Having loaded his plate while standing up, Langley flung his rather portly frame into the carved oak chair next to Benois, grabbing a hunk of bread to chew ravenously. 'Lord! I'm starving.' Crumbs of bread scattered over his chin and down the front of his tunic.

Benois traced one fingertip along the polished wood of the table. 'The Scots intend to spirit Princess Ada away from Dunswick tomorrow morning, so that we have no chance of kidnapping her.'

'And your plan is…'

'To be there before they leave.' Benois's lips curved up into a slight smile. 'The King and his regent were discussing the plan right above me, as I was waiting to shoot.' He shook his head, 'You'd think they would be more careful.'

'Do you think the plan will work?'

Benois angled his head on one side. 'I'll get the Princess, if that's what you mean. But whether it will persuade Malcolm to hand over the lands…well, I'm not so sure.'

'King Henry has ordered it…and the young Malcolm adores his older sister. I swear he would so anything for that maid.' Langley picked up a pewter jug of honeyed mead.

'That may be so…' Benois watched the shiny liquid slide into Langley's goblet, then shrugged his shoulders. 'We'll just have to wait and see. But I, for one, see no joy in looking after a weeping, pathetic princess for weeks on end.'

'It won't come to that.' Langley hefted the jug in Benois' direction. 'Do you want some mead?'

'Nay…thank you.' Benois placed his extended palm over the top of his pewter goblet. 'I have water to drink.'

Langley thrust a hand through his wayward blond hair. 'You intrigue me, Benois. In all the time I've known you, I've never seen you touch a drop of drink. Are you a monk, or something?'

Benois's fingers stiffened imperceptibly around the stem of his engraved goblet. A muscle jumped in the tanned skin of his cheek. 'It's a long story,' he replied at last, letting out his breath from his lungs slowly. He picked up the goblet and took a long, cool gulp. 'There's just one thing I need you to do for me, Langley.'

'Name it.'

'You need to come with me and my men to kidnap the princess. I have no idea what she looks like.'

Away to the east of Dunswick, the land rolled away as a mass of undulating hills topped with purple heather and smooth slopes, a much gentler contrast to the high, barren crags and windswept moorland to the north of the city. Fast-flowing rivers, the water leaping and twisting around jagged rocks and stones, intersected the velvet green of the hills. Red deer roamed the countryside, seeking shelter in the forests of oak and birch, before fleeing as a herd across pastureland at the slightest scent of danger.

The day was warm, holding the promise of summer within the cloudless blue sky. Above Tavia's head, sunlight shafted through the pale green canopy of the trees, highlighting the dark sentinels of trunks below. Gritting her teeth, Tavia balanced precariously atop the docile roan mare, clutching ineffectively at the bunch of reins at the horse's neck, trying to concentrate on the soft, rhythmic plodding of the horses' hooves in the spongy vegetation beneath. Her thigh muscles ached already, and they had only been travelling for a short time.

Ferchar had insisted that she rode. Princess Ada was well known for her excellent horsemanship, and it would look strange if she rode in an ox-cart, or was carried in a covered litter. Luckily, her horse seemed happy just to follow the horse in front. It seemed as if once she had agreed to Ferchar's proposal, he had insisted on a great deal of things. In the past day, he had schooled her in the ways of being a Scottish princess, reeling off strings of facts and family members that he obviously expected her to remember.

Tavia sighed, taking in a deep breath of the pure forest air. At least she appeared as a princess, although she felt awkwardly formal in the Princess Ada's clothes. Next to her skin, she had been allowed to wear her own threadbare linen chemise; apart from that, everything else had been replaced. Her stockings, spun from the finest silk thread, caressed her legs as she wiggled her toes in shoes of the softest, most pliable leather. She thought of the thick, unyielding leather of her old boots, boots that let in the cold and water when she plodded through the hillsides after her father, tending to the sheep or working in the garden. Her underdress was of wool, dyed a lichen green, and fitted her body like a second skin, the tight sleeves emphasising the fragility of her arms. The *bliaut*, laced tightly with leather strings on each side of her waist, was dyed a darker green with long, teardrop-shaped sleeves that hung to the ground. It was these sleeves that would be her undoing, Tavia decided. Unused to such trailing appendages, she continually tripped over them, much to the amusement of King Malcolm and his sister, and to the disgust of Ferchar.

The soldier in front raised his arm, halting the entourage. He leaned forward, dismounting clumsily, as if he, too, were suffering from being in the saddle too long. Tavia frowned. Ferchar had obviously picked the most incompetent soldiers to accompany her on her journey to nowhere, to give the enemy more chance of kidnapping her. The situation would have been laughable if she hadn't been so scared.

'Let's rest a while here,' the soldier announced gruffly.

Tavia's horse plodded gracefully to a halt, without her needing to do anything. She was about to slither down from the back of the animal, when another soldier appeared at her side to help her down. She had almost forgotten—she was a princess. Her legs nearly collapsed beneath her as her feet touched the ground, and she clutched on to the soldier for a moment, before sinking gleefully down on to a cloak that had been spread out over the damp earth.

'How many?' Langley whispered, his broad, affable features obscured by his steel helmet.

Supporting the rangy length of his body against the ribbed bark of a trunk, Benois flung himself back against the tree before answering, 'Four, maybe five.' He held a finger to his lips. Somewhere, high above them, the distinctive sound of a cuckoo resounded through the forest. Moving swiftly and decisively, Benois climbed back to where Langley and the rest of the English soldiers waited in the trees. The harsh lines of his face lightened into a smile.

'I had no need of you after all, Langley. My apologics for dragging you out. The princess sits amongst those rough soldiers like a rose amongst the thorns. She should be easy to pluck.'

'Then let me have the honour of escorting her,' Langley requested. 'You are not renowned for your chivalry around the fairer sex.'

Benois agreed without hesitation. 'I grant you that, Langley. Though why you spend your days in courtly inanities is beyond me.'

'Because it's enjoyable, maybe?' Langley raised an eyebrow. 'You're so caught up in your missions for Henry, that you don't give yourself time to relax, indulge in banter with the ladies, or give yourself any time to think.'

'That's just the way I like it.' Benois's voice held a guarded quality.

Langley shook his head, uncomprehending. His friend was so different from him; the decisive mind, the quick restless energy that drove Benois to accept more and more assignments from the English King, sat in complete contrast to his own more relaxed behaviour.

'You know me, Benois,' he said, looping his fingers into the reins to steady his horse as the animal pawed the loose ground beneath its hooves, 'much prefer the fireside to the saddle.'

'Then let's get this over with,' Benois suggested, vaulting on to his horse, and beginning to urge his black stallion down the narrow path that led to the bottom of the valley, and the

glade where the princess sat. 'And remember, you take the
princess and ride with her back to your castle. My men and I
will hold off the soldiers, to give you time to flee with our
prize.'

As the bloodcurdling shouts reverberated up and down the
valley, Tavia threw the leather flagon to the ground and
sprung to her feet. This was it! Her heart began to pound with
anticipation, nerves, she knew not what. The distinctive red-
and-gold surcoats of the English soldiers flashed in the
sunlight as they careered haphazardly down the slopes,
nostrils flaring on the horses as the animals snorted with excitement. Instinct told Tavia to run, but she stopped herself,
remembering Ferchar's words. Act like a princess, a lady, he
had urged her. Act like a simpering fool, more like, she sput-
tered under her breath. What normal person wouldn't want
to bolt when faced with barbarians such as these?

'Get behind us, my lady!' begged the older soldier who
led the party. Tavia moved back dutifully, amazed that the
soldiers who escorted her had no idea that she was not the
princess. She felt almost sorry for them as she watched them
draw their swords, the metal blades winking as they braced
themselves for the attack.

And then she saw him. Oh, mother of Mary. Not him.

Benois le Vallieres charged full tilt at their small group,
his body lying flat against the back of his galloping horse as
its hooves sent clods flicking up from the spongy grass. She
would know him anywhere now: the defiant cleft on his chin,
those high, slanted cheekbones, that burly frame that dwarfed
all the men around him. Fear knotted her stomach and she
clenched her hands together, her palms slick with sudden
sweat. He would know her, she was certain of it. There was
no doubting the man's intelligence. He would see through her

disguise, and return immediately to Dunswick in the hope of kidnapping the real princess. And Tavia knew that Ferchar needed at least a day to take Ada to safety. She would lose the coin that he had promised her. Unless…

Dragging the heavy encumbrance of her cloak from her shoulders, Tavia backed away slowly, before turning to sprint off into the darkness of the forest.

Benois's sword clashed heavily against the sword of his Scottish opponent with an ugly ringing sound. He hefted the weapon into the air once more, thrusting forwards with the great blade, slashing with a diagonal motion, first left, then right, moving with the skill and grace of a man honed by years of fighting. In contrast to the cumbersome movements of the soldier he fought, every manoeuvre he made appeared precise, using the least amount of energy to produce the greatest effect. In a few moments, Benois had reduced his opponent to a sweating, frightened animal.

'Langley! Leave him to me!' he shouted, aware that his friend was embroiled in a swordfight on his right. 'Fetch the princess!' Benois's sword snared his opponent's weapon, whipping it away into the undergrowth. Breathing heavily, the soldier sank to his knees, raising his hands up limply. Poking him with the point of his sword, Benois indicated the soldier should join his fellow countrymen, who sat huddled miserably on the ground, heads bowed, defeated. In a few moments, Langley's opponent also surrendered, scurrying away on his hands and knees to join the group.

Sheathing his sword, Benois pulled irritably at his leather chin-strap, which anchored his helmet to his head, before glancing about him. Suddenly, Langley burst out from the forest, an expression of complete bafflement on his face.

'Where is she?' Benois said slowly, his voice grim.

'I swear she was here…just a moment ago.' Langley panted heavily, a sheen of sweat breaking out on his face. 'But I just can't find her!'

Benois cursed. 'Probably snivelling behind a tree somewhere. She can't have gone far. Langley, you'd better sit down before you fall down.' He unbuckled the strap of his helmet and threw it for his friend to catch, feeling the breeze sift through the strands of his hair. 'I shan't be needing this, thank God.' He laughed, glad to be rid of the restrictive head gear. 'I doubt one simpering princess will be much of a threat.'

Her whole frame shaking from exertion, Tavia willed her legs to work harder, to take longer strides over the uneven ground. With every step, the bouncy mess of earth and decomposing vegetation dragged at her pace, slowing her, pulling on the delicate leather slippers that afforded little protection against the pools of stagnant water that she splashed through, the hidden branches over which she tripped. Brambles tore into the fine wool of her *bliaut*, leaving angry scratches across her exposed face and hands, as she plunged through the almost impenetrable thickets. Low-hanging branches plucked at her veil, snagging and ripping into it. In frustration, she tore it off, almost crying out in pain as the gold securing pins ripped against her scalp. Why had he, of all people, been sent to kidnap the princess? Why did it have to be him? Tavia prayed that some bumbling soldier would be sent after her, someone who she could lead on a merry dance through the forest, and delay the English from discovering the truth of her identity.

Breaking through the thicket, tripping over one long unwieldy sleeve, Tavia's feet teetered on the edge of a huge natural bowl cut into the forest floor, a pool slick with foul mud at its base. Clutching on to a branch, she fought for balance, listening to the shallow, irregular sound of her own breathing. And then she heard it. A tiny, infinitesimal sound. The crack of a twig. Someone was coming after her. Fear focused her mind with rapier-sharp precision. A bird chirruped in the canopy above and at once she knew her plan.

Setting her feet on the low branches of the pine tree, Tavia began to pull herself up, swiftly, higher and higher. They would never reach her up here, especially as she weighed considerably less than the average soldier. Up here, in the high branches of the tree, her true identity would be safe from detection, and she would be able to delay them a little longer.

'Princess Ada?'

Her fingers stilled briefly at his voice. Refusing to drop her gaze, she pushed her chin defiantly upwards, willing the aching muscles in her arms to haul herself higher.

'Princess Ada? I suggest that you come down now.' Benois's voice held the raw edge of formality, and something else—irritation.

She reached up for the next branch and pulled, levering up her full weight. The branch cracked off suddenly, sending shots of adrenalin lancing through her veins as her feet scrabbled for a foothold, and the branch, weak and rotten, fell to the ground. Sickness crawled through her belly, and she closed her eyes, wanting to cry, not yet willing to admit that she was a fool to climb any higher.

'Princess Ada! May I suggest that you don't climb any higher?' Surprisingly, Benois's voice held concern, but she supposed it wouldn't be good for Anglo-English relations if they managed to kill a Scottish princess.

Her rigid fingers scrabbled at the bark of the trunk, trying to find a more secure hold, as she tip-toed in a circle over the flimsy branch on which she stood, so she could look down cautiously. Her head swam, dizzy with vertigo, as she peered down at the ground, far, far away. And there was that man, his face stern, implacable, his chestnut hair ruffled by the wind. Clamping her eyes shut, she struggled to stop the crazy whirling in her head. She couldn't believe how far she had climbed!

'Princess Ada.' His tone had adopted a more patient, resigned air, as if he were dealing with a naughty child. 'You have nothing to fear from us. Just come down.'

Tavia frowned, concentrating resolutely on the etched bark before her. 'Er…I can't,' she wailed. Her limbs were frozen in fear; if she moved, she would certainly fall to her death.

'I beg your pardon?' Irritation changed to outright contempt.

'I said, "I can't climb down!"' she shouted. The muscles in her throat strained under her panic.

She heard a grunt of annoyance, then a thrashing and cursing, as thin branches snapped under his weight. He was coming after her! In a moment, a warm, large hand curled over her foot. The urge to collapse with relief was overwhelming.

'Don't move,' he warned, as if he sensed the sag, the release of tension in her body. 'I don't have a safe hold of you yet.'

Tavia sighed. This wasn't how the plan was supposed to work. She wondered if she could stall for longer, but she wanted, more than anything, to escape from this stupid situation she had climbed into, even if it meant being rescued by the enemy.

'You need to drop down, my lady, and I'll catch you.' Cool persuasion laced his voice.

'Nay, I cannot,' Tavia replied frantically. 'I just can't

move.' The wind whipped beneath the hem of her *bliaut*, blowing the wide hem outwards.

'Then why did you climb so high, if you're so frightened of heights?' Benois rapped out, exasperated, trying to avert his eyes from the tantalising glimpses of her slim calves, her rounded thighs clad in the finest silk stockings, afforded by her billowing hemline. Why did women also have to make every situation so infernally complicated? No wonder he preferred a life in the field of battle to a life of castles and chivalry.

'I didn't know I was,' she admitted ruefully.

'I can't climb any higher, my lady. The branches will not support my weight.' Benois still held tightly on to the princess's slender ankle. From where he had braced himself against the main trunk, the maid's position appeared extremely precarious. Mud smeared over his hand from her slippers; the fine leather had been scratched and her stockings were torn over her slim calves, affording him delectable glimpses of the lady's smooth white skin where the silk had ripped. The temptation to place his fingertip over the holes, to test the alluring softness of her flesh, took him by surprise. Benois couldn't remember the last time he had wanted to do such a thing. Women meant nothing to him, other than for physical release; they represented a constant source of annoyance, of inconvenience. Curling his scarred hand slowly, a vague sense of unease coiled stealthily in his mind.

Through the lacy fretwork of criss-crossing branches, the sun began to descend. Early sunsets still marked these first days of spring; the warmth leaching from the air as the skies darkened. Benois's stomach growled with hunger. He and his men had forgone their mid-day meal in order to kidnap the princess and now he was starving.

Impatience made him tug irritably at the chit's ankle; he

had no intention of spending any longer in this tree! Langley's advice on how to treat a royal princess was beginning to grate on his nerves; this current situation just proved that courtly manners simply did not work on some occasions!

Resisting the pull on her foot, Tavia wrapped both her arms even more firmly around the branch conveniently located near her chest. She had worked out that the longer she stayed up here, out of Benois's reach, then the less chance he would have of recognising her, of leaving to kidnap the real princess. 'If you go down,' she suggested lightly, 'then I'll follow.'

'I thought you said you couldn't!' His gaze swept over her fragile figure, clinging like a wisp of lace to the tree. Really, this royal maid seemed to contradict herself with every sentence! Did she not know her own mind?

'I feel better now,' she replied. 'I think I'll be able to come down on my own.'

'No chance!' he countered bluntly. 'I, for one, have had enough of being stuck up a tree. I can't wait all day, and all night for that matter, for you to make up your mind. You're coming down now!'

Stretching his big body upwards, he thrust one hand over her calf, fastened his fingers around the crook of her knee, and pulled, hard. Her feet teetered precariously.

'Nay! What are you doing?' she protested, as he began to haul her body downwards. Her fingers scrabbled violently at the branch that had become her security, trying to cling on, but his grip was too powerful. Slithering downwards, she became acutely aware of the touch of his hands over her hips, her backside and, finally, the sensitive curve of her waist. He held her wrapped against him, her feet flailing uselessly in the air.

'It's almost as if you don't want to come down.' His warm

breath skimmed her ear intimately. 'Now, why would that be?'

'Because I don't want to go with you!' she shouted into the soft wool of the tunic that covered his chainmail, furious at his rough manhandling. Steel-clad arms braced her waist, making any escape attempt impossible. 'Let me go!' she ordered, imperiously.

'If I let you go, then you will fall straight out of the tree,' he advised her quietly. 'I am the only thing holding you at the moment.' The mellow timbre of his words had a curious effect on her, generating a weird fluttering sensation in her belly.

'You push the boundaries of common decency,' she threw back waspishly. 'This is no way to treat a princess! Even captured knights are treated better than this. Just wait until I tell King Malcolm about you!'

Laughter rumbled deep in his chest; the vibrations pushing the muscled breadth of his torso against her own softer curves. Holding her with one arm, he yanked the curling end of her braid sharply, bringing tears to her eyes as he forced her to lift her chin, to look at him.

'You're no more a princess than I am,' he announced, the smoke-grey of his eyes grimly assessing.

Tavia licked her lips nervously, a dryness scouring her throat. Her heart hammered in her chest. Was he going to kill her?

'Are you?' he said again, jerking the end of her braid once more.

'Of course I am,' she replied. Her voice echoed lamely.

The breeze ruffled through the sable smoothness of his hair, hair that gleamed like the polished skin of a hazelnut. A few strands fell across his forehead, softening the raw-boned angularity of his features.

'So I've never met you before.'

'Correct.'

'Liar.'

He would know the maid anywhere: the proud, defiant tilt of her chin, the huge eyes of cobalt blue and that hair, her beautiful wine-dark hair that proclaimed her identity like a flag.

'How did you ever think you would pass as a princess?' His tone mocked her.

To admit her true identity would be to fail. And she was not about to do that! This man had to believe her! For the sake of her mother, for this whole plan to work, she had to convince him! Sticking her chin imperiously in the air, Tavia addressed him in prim tones, trying to ignore the proximity of his big body pressed up against her own soft curves.

'Because I am a princess, you fool!'

His eyes narrowed, sparkling chips of granite. 'Oh, so it's usual practice for a princess to run around her own city dressed in peasant clothes; it's usual practice for a princess to shoot a crossbow with unerring accuracy?' He lifted one dark eyebrow. 'Credit me with some intelligence, my lady!'

One finger picked nervously at the nail on her thumb squashed into her side by his big arm. This wasn't going to be easy. 'I admit that my behaviour is unusual for a lady of rank,' she ventured, refusing to let his mocking stare intimidate her, 'but Malcolm taught me to shoot from an early age, and sitting in the woman's solar all day is boring! It's fun going around the town dressed in peasant clothes.'

'Not so fun when you're nearly raped by English soldiers, I suspect.' A stinging wryness entered his tone.

She shuddered slightly at the memory, heart thrilling at the note of doubt creeping into his voice. Benois sighed, momentarily allowing himself to enjoy the maid's soft curves against his own hard frame. He stared at her intently, drinking in the lush, perfect oval of her face, trying to read her mind. What if the maid spoke the truth?

Tavia schooled her features into an expression of stern chastisement. 'Mayhap we could discuss this further on the ground?' She tilted her head in question. 'I don't feel entirely safe up here.' Without thinking, she flicked her blue, long-lashed eyes up to his, trying to impress on him the need to descend, willing herself to ignore the strange, flickering excitement that jolted upwards through her belly and chest at the alluring proximity of his body.

Benois's arms tightened imperceptibly around her; it was a long time since he had held a woman thus. With lurching awareness, he realised his own body's physical response to the maid's nearness: fierce, hungry, demanding. The peach-like lustre of her flushed skin drew him, the pretty curve of her mouth drew him in…she lured him, like a siren singing far out to sea. A predatory glow moderated his flinty gaze; Tavia saw it, and knew at once his intention. 'Stop! I command you to stop!' she cried, pushing futilely at the punishing lock of his arms. 'You mustn't do this! I am the princess!'

'I don't care!' he growled, his voice husky with desire.

As his lips descended, he told himself he had earned this kiss. The maid had teased and taunted him, caused him to miss his lunch and no doubt his supper as well. There was nothing in the least that attracted him to her; the maid was slender and short, her arms thin and wiry, completely opposite to the type of women he sought for physical solace. Henry's camp women, who accompanied the royal court and its entourage of soldiers in the hope of making ready coin, were normally tall and buxom, their beauty often spoiled by the tawdry nature of their business.

The sweetness of her lips stunned him; in that first, fleeting touch, all conscious thought, all logic, fled, to be replaced by a raging thirst to discover more, to plunder further, deeper. The brace of his arms shifted slightly, hauling her closer to him, thigh to thigh, hip to hip. At the intimate contact, she gasped against his mouth. He groaned, bringing one hand up to cup the back of her head, to tangle his fingers in the silk of her hair, to bring her lips closer to him.

Tavia began to struggle against him, ramming her toes into his shins, pushing her small hands against his chest.

'Nay…' He lifted his head, his grey irises lit with silvered threads, passion unbalancing him. 'My lady…for God's sake…don't struggle!' The innate strength in that waif-like body caught him unawares, and, with horrible realisation, he felt her sliding towards the ground. In a moment he had reached down to grab a fistful of cloth at her waist, catching her, but the fierce movement threw him off balance, and they crashed down through the branches together to land in a tangle of limbs below.

The fall winded him slightly, but luckily the branches had broken much of the impact. Although he had managed to twist slightly as he landed, he feared the maid had caught at least half his weight on impact. He lifted himself up on his arms, assessing her, searching her pale face for some sign of life.

Langley burst into the clearing, closely followed by his own soldiers. 'Good God, man, what have you done to her?'

Chapter Five

Pushing himself off the maid, and on to his knees beside her, Benois sat back on his heels, baffled by her unconsciousness. From their position on the tree, the drop had not been above the height of two men, and the dense carpet of rotting woodland vegetation had softened their landing. But, touching a finger to his throbbing temple, Benois realised that their heads had knocked together on impact. A huge purplish bruise had begun to develop above the maid's left eye, marring the polished marble of her skin.

Lying there, sprawled beside him, the girl appeared as a fallen angel, so ethereal, so fragile that Benois could scarce believe she was the same chit who had antagonised him just moments before. The silken folds of her *bliaut* spread around her, revealing the slender curve of her tiny waist; the tear-shaped sleeves had fallen back, revealing the delicate bones of her wrists, deathly white against the earthy leaves. He frowned. Angel, indeed! What in Heaven's name had given him such a fanciful idea? At best, this girl, this Tavia of Mowerby, was an unwelcome nuisance, one he intended to be rid of, as quickly as possible.

'Have you killed her?' Langley wrung his hands together. 'Have you killed the Princess?' He lurked at the edge of the clearing, as if unwilling to come forward to witness the dreadful sight. Above them, leaves rustled, the breeze through the trees began to strengthen with the onset of evening. Benois contemplated the barely perceptible rise and fall of Tavia's chest, then reached his fingers to the side of her neck; a strong, steady pulse confirmed what he already knew. On instinct, his thumb moved fractionally to trace the corner of her mouth, a mouth that still bore the blush of his kiss. He snatched his fingers away, springing to his feet. Was he completely mad? How had this fey creature managed to slip beneath his guard? His self-control had been the one thing he could rely on since…since *that time*.

'Nay, the girl's not dead,' Benois bit back, his slate eyes tracing Langley's lumpy profile in the twilight. 'And, if you look a little closer, Langley, you will see that we have been well and truly duped. This maid is *not* the Princess Ada.'

'Don't be a fool, of course it's the Princess!' Langley came forward, stumbling over an unseen tree root. 'God in Heaven, there will be hell to pay if Henry finds out how we've treated her!'

'The girl has brought it all upon herself,' Benois returned curtly. 'When was the last time you witnessed a princess sprinting off like a hare, and climbing a tree with the grace and agility of a cat?'

Langley shrugged. 'I admit, it is unusual.' He moved to crouch down next to Tavia's prone figure. 'She certainly has the Princess's hair.' He touched his fingers lightly to Tavia's head. 'As far as I know, only members of Scottish royalty possess such an amazing colour. Malcolm and his dead father, Earl Henry, and, of course, King David.' Langley frowned, his eyes sweeping the length of Tavia's figure. 'But you are right, Benois, this maid is not tall enough to be Ada. How high does she stand?'

'Up to here.' Benois indicated the place below the curve of his shoulder.

Langley nodded. 'And there's less of her, too. Just see how this dress hangs about her. She wears the clothes of the Princess…'

'But she is not the Princess,' Benois concluded.

'The question is…' Langley surveyed his friend '…what do we do with her now?'

Through the flimsy layers separating consciousness, the deep timbre of male voices penetrated Tavia's brain. Where was she? Cold seeped disagreeably through the material of her clothes…her back felt wet as she lay on the damp ground. Pieces of memory came floating back, at first slowly, and then in a rush, fitting together neatly to form coherent pictures in her brain. The chase through the forest. Climbing the tree. The kiss. Reality smashed into her as she suddenly remembered. Forcing herself to keep her breathing low and steady, she kept her eyes firmly shut. She could hear Benois's voice, and another man also talking. Why were they still here?

She shivered, the cold beginning to freeze her bones.

'She's awake,' a voice announced.

Pressing her hands flat against the soggy leaves, Tavia pushed herself up, raising one hand to smooth her hair from her eyes. Benois towered above her, scowling, a dark and brooding presence that made her want to scramble to her feet and run once more. He radiated a dynamic energy, an energy that made every inch of his body spark with vitality. He made her feel vulnerable, weak, so she dragged her gaze to the man beside him, a smaller man, also in English colours, who smiled at her courteously. She fixed on his ruffled blond hair and genial features with relief.

'Are you well, my lady?' the blond man asked.

'Aye, no thanks to him!' Tavia grumbled, jabbing a finger in Benois's direction. 'Why did you have to land on top of me, you big oaf!' Why did you have to kiss me? The words were left unsaid.

His mouth curled. 'Ah, Langley, I don't believe you have met the charming Tavia of Mowerby?' Derision laced his tone, as he viewed her bedraggled figure.

'Delighted.' Langley stepped forward. 'Allow me, my lady.' He stuck out his gloved hand, and, taking hers, pulled her up easily from the ground. She swayed a little, her head aching, unwilling to allow any weakness to show before these two men.

'I must go,' she announced. She had performed her task for Ferchar; now all she needed to do was to ride back to Dunswick, claim her reward and find a physician for her mother.

Benois folded his arms across his chest, the metal scales of his chainmail sleeves glinting in the last rays of sunlight that filtered through the trees.

'Go where, exactly?' She flinched at the hollowness of his tone.

'Why, go back to Dunswick!'

'You, mistress, are going nowhere.'

'You can't keep me here!' she remonstrated, brushing impatiently at a twig clinging to the fabric of her dress.

'I've no intention of *keeping* you here,' Benois replied patiently. 'God forbid that I should have to put up with any more of your infernal prattle...'

'Go easy, Benois.' Langley frowned. 'You're frightening the maid.'

'Hah!' Benois scoffed. 'I doubt it very much.' His eyes glittered silver, precious metal sewn through granite.

'It's for your own good,' Langley explained, his modulated tones calm and composed in comparison to Benois's husky cadence. 'It has grown too dark for us to travel safely. We must make camp tonight and travel on the morrow.'

A hollowness churned in her stomach. Tavia stared in dismay at the two men, half-shaking her head. 'But I must return,' she whispered, the memory of her mother lying ill and defenceless on her pallet bed clawing at her brain. 'I must.'

'You should have thought of that before you undertook this deception,' Benois rounded on her callously. 'I suppose it was Ferchar's little scheme. He must have thought it was his lucky day when you walked into Dunswick Castle with your crossbow, and the double of Princess Ada.'

'But you don't need me any more,' Tavia protested, 'I'm not worth anything to you, now that you know who I am. Why not let me go? Just give me a horse and you'll never see me again.'

'If we let you go now, mistress, then no one will ever see you again,' Benois commented starkly. 'You really think you would arrive back in Dunswick in one piece?'

'Of course,' she stated boldly. 'I have my crossbow; I can defend myself.'

'Like you did with my soldiers,' he reminded her.

'That was different…' She faltered as Benois began to shake his head.

'No different, Tavia.' He curled his fingers around the top of her arm. 'Come on, we must make camp while we can still see.'

Tavia had no choice but to accompany the men back to the clearing where the initial attack had taken place. Following Langley's stocky frame, she struggled to walk in her sodden, ill-fitting slippers; her toes aching from scrunching to keep the leather attached to her feet. What could she do? Short of stealing a horse and pointing it roughly in the direction on Dunswick, she had no idea of which route to follow, or, indeed, if she could stay on the wretched animal. Langley had already announced that he had sent the soldiers who had accompanied her back to Dunswick, so she had no hope of securing their escort.

Tavia stopped abruptly, whipping around. At her back, Benois cursed, ceasing his stride immediately, to avoid cannoning into her.

'What now?' he asked brusquely, aware that his hands had risen instinctively to steady her. He dropped them to his sides, his fingers curiously bereft. 'Can't we even take two steps without protest from you?'

'It's not a protest, more a request.' Her wide eyes implored him. 'Benois, I need you to take me back to Dunswick tonight. You must!' she pleaded, tormented by the recurring images of her mother.

'I must?' he replied slowly, astounded that this impudent chit still found the capacity to give orders. Idly, he wondered at the anguish in her wide, light-blue eyes.

'Lord Ferchar would reward you handsomely if you took me back.'

Benois grabbed her chin roughly between thumb and forefinger, so close that an enticing smell of leather mixed with woodsmoke arose from him. 'I wasn't aware you were that important to him,' he responded heartlessly. 'I presumed you were a peasant.'

His words rankled her; she straightened her spine, drawing herself up. 'I'm a farmer's daughter,' she announced.

'My mistake,' he ground out unpleasantly, indicating by his

tone that he still considered her to be ill bred, of the lowest stock.

'I'll reward you,' she said desperately.

His lips clamped into a thin line. 'Be careful, mistress.'

She gulped. 'I said, I'll reward you, if you take me back.'

'How?' He tipped his head to one side, considering her—nay, challenging her.

Was it her imagination or had he stepped a little closer? 'I'll pay you,' she stuttered, wondering how on earth she would achieve that.

Benois laughed, the sound hollow and raw. 'I have coin enough. Try again.'

She squeezed her eyes together, wretched, anticipating his rejection before she even spoke the words. But she would do anything to save her mother's life.

'Not in coin,' her voice fluttered. A cold, sick feeling rose in her stomach, humbling her. Glancing upwards, the rigid lines around his mouth portrayed his utter fury, his condemnation at her words. She had made a mistake.

'You want to offer me your body?' His voice mocked her, cruelly teasing, shredding her confidence. 'You must really be desperate if you wish to prostitute yourself with me.'

''Tis all I have,' she replied meekly, wanting to crawl away into the undergrowth and weep.

The steel-grey of his eyes hardened, the stance of his body at once condemning and judgemental. Somewhere above them, an owl hooted, the unearthly note echoing hauntingly through the trees.

'Then keep it. Keep it for someone more deserving than myself.' He stuck his hand through his hair; the silky spikes fell down rakishly over his forehead. 'Hear me, Mistress of Mowerby, and hear me well. I don't care if you rip off all your clothes in front of me, and run about stark naked, you will not convince me to change my mind. We are not travelling until tomorrow, do you understand?'

In reply, she nodded jerkily, misery gathering about her like a cloak.

Sleep evaded her. The woodland glade, the ground of which had appeared so cushioned and inviting when she had first ridden into it with the Scottish soldiers, was riddled with sharp stones. Every way she turned, rocky corners jabbed her flesh, poking into the rounded curve of her hips, the small of her back. Despite retrieving her cloak, and wrapping herself securely in it, she was still cold, her feet like lumps of ice, her head aching each time the breeze lifted her hair.

On one side, Langley snored comfortably. On her other side, mere inches from her, Benois had stretched himself out, and was now breathing evenly. His nearness made her feel awkward, uncomfortable. She held herself rigid, every muscle held in constant check, just in case she might touch him inadvertently. One of the horses pawed the ground behind her as she followed the alluring line of his profile, highlighted by the waning moon: the straight, proud line of his nose, the enticing curve of his full top lip, the jut of his chin.

Benois turned his head swiftly, eyes twinkling in the soft light, catching her staring at him. Surprised, she gasped, clutching the sides of her cloak to her breast.

'I thought you'd be fast asleep by now,' he murmured. His breath emerged in misty white puffs of air into the cool night. The velvet rasp of his voice spiralled around her like silken thread, drawing her in. 'Not still trying to plan your escape, are you?'

Heat suffused her body, spreading traitorously along her limbs. 'Nay,' she whispered back. 'I wouldn't dare.'

He trapped her gaze, and smiled.

Without thinking, she grinned back.

'We both know that's a lie,' Benois replied mildly, a hint of admiration in his tone. Unexpectedly, his expression hardened, became alert, predatory. In a creak of leather, he had raised himself on one elbow, a finger to his lips. He tilted his head upwards, listening intently for a moment, before crouching over her, lips tickling her ear.

'Come with me,' he whispered. 'We have visitors.'

Her senses quickened at the closeness of his body. Powerful arms drew her upwards, one hand at her back as he pushed her towards the dark mass of the forest. 'Stay out of sight,' he nodded, indicating that she could go further in, 'and you'll be safe.'

'But what is it?' Tavia halted abruptly, turning in the circle of his arm. 'I can't hear anything.' She craned her neck, trying to look over the broad curve of his shoulder, but he pushed her onwards into the cover of the trees.

'Just stay here,' he ordered. His broad palm slid along her back, down her arm, igniting a line of fire around her waist, her hips. Tavia captured his hand, feeling the rough scar of his palm against her own, staying him. The warmth, the vitality of his fingers sparked through her veins.

'Let me fetch my crossbow,' she urged, her eyes huge orbs of diamond in the gloom. 'I might be of some use.'

'There's not above a few.' He glanced at the pale oval of her face, gossamer white in the rays of moonlight filtering through the branches. 'We'll finish them quickly if they attack. Mayhap they'll just pass by.'

Reluctantly, she nodded, toeing the soft ground, watching his dark shape return to crouch down and waken the sleeping Langley, and the other soldiers, before taking cover around the clearing. One of the soldiers led the horses deeper under the cover of the trees. And still, she hadn't heard a sound, just the frantic beating of her heart thumping against her ribcage.

The sound of chinking bridles, of bits ringing between the horses' teeth, could be heard long before the steady thumping of the animals' hooves. Benois lifted one arm, a signal for his men to stay down as long as possible, to remain hidden. With growing anxiety, Tavia watched the group of men approach, not above ten in number; a fierce-looking bunch with trailing, matted hair, eyes wild and desperate and swords already held on high. With a bloodcurdling war-cry, the leader reined in his horse with one rapid, violent wrench so that the animal lifted its front hooves into the air, clawing frantically.

'Come on out, you nobles!' the leader shouted, his speech thickly slurred and guttural. 'We know you're in there! Come out or we'll kill you where you stand!'

Nobody moved. Tavia held her breath. Did these men think they were still the royal party?

A moment passed, then two.

'So that's the way you want to play it, eh?' the leader shouted, his head darting one way, then another, trying to discern the human shapes within the undergrowth. 'Ye Gods, let's be having you then!'

As he and his men charged forward into the bushes, Benois and the other soldiers rose up, stealthily, drawing their swords. For a moment, the brigand leader appeared astonished; he obviously had not been expecting to deal with a group of English soldiers, but it was too late to call his men away. Already swords clashed against each other, the steel flashing through the trees, grunts of pain emerging as a sword sliced through skin, or a dagger found its mark. With her back against the tree trunk, all Tavia could hear was the terrible noise of men fighting. Nervous tension strung her body tight, and she peered frantically through the trees, trying to spot their horses, to find her crossbow. Thank the Lord someone had possessed the foresight to transfer her weapon and satchel to the English horses. She couldn't stand by and watch these men be slaughtered, she had to help. Gliding back through the woodland, she crept over to the horses, feeling along the high glossy backs of the animals until she came to the smooth wooden arc of her crossbow. Her hands shook as she drew the bridle of sinew back to arm the weapon, reaching for a quarrel from the round leather satchel, to fit it along the groove. Pulling the hood of her cloak sharply over her bright hair, hair that gleamed like a burnished coin under the thready light of the moon, she tiptoed back to the edge of the clearing to take up a position. Slinking around the curving girth of a tree, she screwed up her eyes, focusing intently on the scene before her.

Benois, his large rangy form moving with an animal grace, fought easily, the sword moving as if it were merely an extension of his body, slashing one way, then the other. His feet danced across the ground, no ounce of spare energy wasted, each step executed with the precision and skill of a master swordsman. Glancing quickly around the clearing, Tavia noticed with relief that all the other English soldiers, including Langley, seemed to still be standing. Her hands relaxed their relentless grip around the crossbow. They didn't need her…or did they?

Her eyes flicked to a dark spot to the right of Benois; someone was moving, creeping along in the shadows. She raised her bow, setting her sights on the shifting area of darkness, waiting for one shadow to pull away. She drew breath, honing her gaze, as the leader of the barbarians emerged from the darkness, the menacing curved blade of a falchion winking at Benois's back.

As she squeezed the trigger, the man's blade slashed down, intended for Benois's neck. The point of Tavia's arrow drove straight through his ragged clothes, straight into his heart. Benois whipped around, staring in astonishment as the barbarian crumpled to the ground, a dark stain spreading across his threadbare tunic.

The crossbow dropped uselessly from her numb fingers; bewilderment fogging her brain, stifling her. She backed slowly away, struggling to breathe, huge, rounding waves of sorrow rising up to overwhelm her. What had she done? In that single appalling moment, she had lost all sense of control, or responsibility; she had killed a man. She sank to the ground, a pitiful heap, burying her head in her hands.

'Tavia.'

She felt the warmth of Benois's hands in her own. 'It's over,' he said, hunkering down at her feet, staring in puzzlement at the tears washing over her face, dripping down from the bottom of her chin. 'They were vicious, I grant you that,' he admitted carefully. He pulled lightly on her hands, not understanding her tears. 'But we got them in the end.' He laughed. 'Thanks to you.'

Her face turned up to him, tears streaking the milk-white skin of her cheeks. She shook her head. 'How can you laugh?' Her voice stung him, an accusation. 'At least ten men lie out there, dead, all dead, and we did it!'

His eyes narrowed, dangerous cuts of sparkling granite. 'They deserved it, Tavia. They attacked us, remember?' Coldness invaded his voice, crushing her. 'If we hadn't killed them, then they would have killed us…or maybe you would have preferred that? They were going to kill us, Tavia. And I would be dead…' she jumped as his fingers grazed her cheek '…if it hadn't been for that deadly shot.'

The air in her lungs shuddered as she took a deep breath.

'I'm not proud of it,' she returned shakily. She hung her head, shame rolling over her.

'You saved my life.' His fingers tipped her chin upwards, forcing her to meet his gaze. 'I know it's hard to see something like this, when you're not used to it. There's no place for feelings, for emotion, when you're fighting for your life.'

'Is that why you do it?' she blurted out. 'Is that why you laugh when men lie dying around you; why you dismiss killing with such ease? Because you have no feelings? Is it?' She wanted to goad him, provoke him into some reaction.

His face was stony, grim under her verbal attack. 'You've said enough, mistress.'

'I'm right, aren't I?'

He grabbed at her shoulders, wanting to shake her, wanting to stop her mouth with a kiss. His hands rounded on her small shoulders, fingers splayed over the delicate bones beneath. 'Aye,' he admitted ruefully. 'You are right. The best soldiers have no feelings at all. Otherwise all that they witness in battle would make them go mad.'

The soft grey of his eyes pierced hers, and she bit her lip nervously. 'I couldn't do it. And I don't know how you can.' Tavia swept her eyes back over the clearing. 'I feel so guilty,' she whispered, finally.

He released her chin, sprung to his feet, eyes aflame. His caustic tone tore at her rattled senses. 'You don't know the meaning of the word,' he ground out.

Chapter Six

Mist veiled the river valley: shifting diaphanous fingers of white draped lengthways across the clearing like shrouds for the dead. Heavy dew coated the undulating mounds of grass, at first thick white, then changing to a sparkling net of diamonds as the sun began to rise. Through the trees, with slow onset of light, birds began to chirrup merrily, the sweet song of the blackbird mingling with the more humanlike call of the jay. The bodies of the brigands, cold and lifeless, were scattered over the ground, a grim reminder of the events of the previous night.

Gruesome, relentless images harrowed Tavia's brain; in her dreams, she had reached out to touch people, and they dropped at her feet, dead, blood seeping from their limbs. Anguished, she had twisted her head from side to side, trying to rid herself of the appalling images, but only succeeded in waking herself up. She had fallen asleep, exhausted, half-propped against the tree, and at some time during the night had slipped sideways to lie in a more comfortable, horizontal position. Now, as the layers of foggy sleep receded, her limbs ached from sleeping on the lumpy ground in such a miserable, scrunched-up position. She rubbed the back of her neck, trying to relieve the tension in the knotted muscles.

'Try to go back to sleep,' a familiar tone barged into her thoughts. Too close! Her spine tingled beneath the deep vibration of his voice. Cursing her aching muscles, she rolled over abruptly, and found herself mere inches from Benois!

'What are you doing here?' She sucked in her breath, stung with shock, holding her body stiffly away from him. Benois lay flat on his back, the lean length of his legs crossed at the ankles, one arm folded behind his head.

'I *was* sleeping,' he replied. His eyes, in the faint light, had muted to the soft grey-green of old stone. 'Until your shuffling woke me up.'

'You deliberately misunderstand me!' she hissed back, aware that Langley and the other soldiers still snored beneath their cloaks just a few feet away. 'I mean that you are too close!'

The leather cords cross-gartering the bottom of Benois's braies strained slightly as he flexed one foot, then the other. 'You seemed upset last night,' he said, after a long pause.

'That's no reason for you to sleep almost on top of me!'

He quirked one eyebrow, his silvered expression gently teasing. 'You could have chosen a less provocative turn of phrase.'

'Oh!' Incensed, she pushed herself into a seated position, her numb muscles protesting. 'You know what I mean!'

'I know. I also know that your desire to return to Dunswick might have been greater than your desire to sleep.'

'So you're guarding me?'

'Precisely.' He rolled one shoulder forwards, trying to ease the discomfort gained from sleeping in chainmail. 'And…you did seem upset.'

'And you would be the one to provide comfort? How

would you know how to do that?' she taunted him. 'You, the man who feels nothing!' The auburn silk of her hair fell in a gentle curve across her forehead, the amazing rippling colour accenting the exquisite pearl lustre of her skin. Her sky-blue eyes, wide with accusation, provoked him.

She was wrong. Shock walloped him in the guts with the force of a cannon ball. He did feel something, but it wasn't for those men who had brutally attacked them. It was for her. This woman. This ethereal, fey creature who had burst into his life from nowhere, who continually defied him, saved him and surrounded him with energy, and spirit, and light. He couldn't define this fleeting, newborn feeling, but it was there. He liked it not.

Damn it! The woman was making him soft! 'I told you before,' he replied between gritted teeth, 'a soldier becomes accustomed to the fighting, the bloodshed.' He contemplated the interlacing of branches above him, new green leaves beginning to frill along the branches, heralding spring. It was the fighting, the battles that kept him from the memories, and held them prisoner in the depths of his thoughts. He knew they were there, and, if he wasn't careful, those memories would rise to the surface, the flotsam and jetsam of his brain, and he would remember, God help him. Without thought, he rubbed the scar on his hand.

'How did you do that?' Tavia asked suddenly.

His gaze flared over her, burning, incisive. She saw a whisker of agony trace across his features, before his expression shuttered, blank. He looked as if he wanted to kill her.

'I'm sorry,' she whispered hurriedly. 'I didn't mean to pry.'

'Then don't,' he muttered rudely, aware of her luminous gaze sparkling over him. Her lips had parted a fraction, revealing small white teeth, the tip of her pink tongue.

Tavia studied his closed face, aware that she had trespassed through a barrier that he was not willing to reveal. Instinctively, she raised her fingers to his cheek, savouring the rough prickle of his jaw against her palm. He didn't draw away. Rising to her knees before him, her other hand rose, curving around his other cheek so that she held his face within her hands. She wanted to erase that pain in his eyes, smooth away the hurt, whatever it was.

His eyes flicked up to hers, smouldering.

She lowered her mouth, touched her lips to his cheek. A chaste kiss of comfort. That was all it was meant to be.

Benois groaned, the sound, deep in his chest, low and primitive. In a fraction of a movement, he adjusted the angle of his cheek, sealing his lips to hers. Desire ignited deep within her, bursting forth in a shower of sparks. A huge shudder coursed through his frame; his hands seized her waist, looping her body within his powerful arms, dragging her across him. Her hands trembled as she pushed her fingers up to his head, relishing the sifting, silken feel of his hair. Flames tore at her flesh, incandescent, blood hurtling through her veins so fast that she thought she might faint at the enormity of the feeling. She clung to him, aware that reality had been left far behind as she descended into a heaving, churning whirlpool of passion.

Abruptly, Benois shoved her away, hands at her waist, dumping her unceremoniously in a heap beside him. She touched a finger to her mouth, lips burning from the searing taste of his kiss, aghast, astounded. Beneath his furious, outraged perusal, she coloured hotly, the blush seeping from the nape of her neck to the top of her head, embarrassed at how he had made her feel. What had she been thinking of? It had been his expression, his expression of utter pain that had made her do it. The expression that he had tried so hard to hide. But he had made his sentiments perfectly clear. She was of no interest to him. Why should she be? As all those suitors that her father had unwillingly dragged before her had told her, she was too short, too lean, and the colour of her hair could only lead to trouble. This man, like all men, was her enemy, and not just her enemy, but the enemy of her country. And her mother lay dying as she was kissing.

Traitorous flesh thrumming from the impact of his mouth, she jumped to her feet, wiping a hand viciously across her lips. Rejection sluiced over her; she chewed on her bottom lip angrily. What an utter fool she had been!

'Why did you do it?' Ragged anger edged Benois's tone.

She heaved a great sigh, forced herself to meet his gaze with huge eyes. 'For a moment…back then…you looked so sad.'

'And is that your usual practice? To kiss a stranger if they look sad?' His tone barked at her, a brutal rebuke. 'You need to guard yourself better than that, maid. God knows where it could lead.'

'How dare you?' She planted her feet just inches from where he still lay on the ground—she wanted to stamp on him! 'How dare you chastise me?' she railed down at him, temper igniting in her breast. 'You started it…you turned it into—' She broke off abruptly, unable to find the words to describe his kiss.

Wanting to frighten her, to stop her speech, Benois sprang upwards, unbalancing her momentarily as he towered over her. Tavia gulped, startled. Heels scuffing the ground, she backed away, away from his fury, away from his obvious displeasure at being anywhere near her.

'I'm sorry,' she mumbled.

His brows drew together in a heavy frown, seeing the fear chase across her angelic features. He was being mean, and well he knew it. She had given the kiss in good faith, and he had warped her innocent gesture, transforming it into something far darker, far hungrier than he cared to admit. She had apologised, yet it was his fault.

One of Langley's soldiers had collected a huddle of damp twigs and managed to light a fire. As the smoke hazed languorously upwards through the trees, the other soldiers gathered around the heat, mumbling to each other in quiet voices, passing around leather flagons of mead, and chewing on day-old hunks of bread.

'Come, mistress.' Langley, still resplendent in his red-and-gold surcoat, his full-length cloak of mink, beckoned to Tavia. She stood on the outskirts of the group, a forlorn figure, unsure whether to join in, or sit alone. After her apology, Benois had marched off without a word, but, witnessing the grim set of his features, she realised some forbidden boundary had been crossed.

She stepped forwards, hauling the long, drooping sleeves of her gown upwards, conscious that, as well as losing her veil, she had also lost the golden circlet that belonged to the princess. Smiling widely, Langley handed her a chunk of bread, apologising for its staleness. He balanced a lump of cheese on top with his thumb, and she smiled gratefully as she reached out for the parcel of food with two hands. With an elaborate, courtly gesture, Langley unfastened the brooch that held the two sides of his cloak together and laid it flat on the damp ground.

'Please sit, my lady.'

'Thank you.' Tavia sank down, aware that her legs still trembled from the heated encounter with Benois. Langley sat down companionably beside her, pushing his stocky legs out before him.

'Good God!' he groaned. 'I'm not cut out for sleeping on the ground. The sooner I return to the luxury of my castle, the better. I can only hope that you fared more favourably than I last night, my lady.'

'I slept very well,' she admitted, unwilling to admit that waking up had been a shock. She swallowed a mouthful of bread. 'But, my lord, you don't need to keep addressing me as "my lady". I do not own such a title.'

'Forgive me,' Langley replied. 'But you are so similar to the princess that I cannot stop myself. I keep thinking that you are her.' He tilted his leather flagon to his lips and took a deep gulp. 'Have you never wondered about it?'

Tavia chewed on her bread thoughtfully. 'Nay, I only met her for the first time just after Ferchar asked me to help them.'

'Then believe me when I say, you are the spit of her.'

'Maybe her mother has a secret.' Benois strode into the clearing, brandishing a quarrel, which he cleaned with a lump of grass.

Eyes darkening, Tavia pursed her lips together, determined not to retaliate. She continued eating her bread, watching the flames hiss and lick around the wood in the fire.

Benois chucked the bloodied grass into a thicket behind him, and handed the arrow to Tavia.

'Your quarrel.'

She stared at the fatal tip, glinting in the morning light. 'I don't want it,' she murmured, thinking again of the man dropping dead before her eyes.

Benois studied the quarrel. 'It's a shame; the bolt's well made. You'd be a fool to throw it away, mistress.'

'I don't want it!' she repeated, clambering to her feet. 'You can bury it with him for all I care.'

'No time for that,' Benois said brusquely. 'We need to go.'

'Who?' Tavia said suspiciously.

'Why, you and me, of course.' Benois's eyes flicked over her. 'If you wish to return to Dunswick before dark, then we need to go now.'

'Oh, but…' Tavia looked frantically at the rounded, shorter figure of Langley, before returning to Benois's leaner profile. 'So you'll take me back?'

'I said so, didn't I?' he replied impatiently.

'I assumed Langley would take me,' she responded, a hint of desperation in her voice.

'I'm afraid I cannot, my lady,' Langley chipped into the conversation, clapping one hand to his left shoulder. 'I took a slice in the arm from one of those brigands yestereve. I would be unable to defend you.'

'Oh.'

Benois raised his eyebrows, sensing her reluctance. 'Believe me, mistress, escorting you is the last thing I want to do.'

Tavia fiddled with the long ties of her cloak. 'If you point me in the right direction, I'll probably be all right on my own,' she uttered with more confidence than she felt. 'I have my crossbow…' She saw the light flare in Benois's eyes, and trailed off.

'Which you shoot with admirable precision, my lady,' Langley complimented her. 'Why, if it hadn't been for you—'

'Mother of Mary, don't give the chit ideas, Langley,' Benois cut him off forcibly. 'If it wasn't for this girl, none of us would be here in the first place. Now, you bury these bodies, and I'll take her back to Dunswick.'

And God help us both, Tavia thought.

Sticking his booted foot into the metal stirrup, Benois swung himself gracefully on to his horse. The leather in the saddle creaked as he adjusted his weight, bunching the reins into one hand as the horse skittered with excitement, ready to go. His cloak spread in gleaming folds across the horse's rump as he looked over at Langley.

'Give the maid a leg up, Langley.'

In reply, Langley adopted a sorrowful expression, patting his injured shoulder.

Benois shot a glance heavenwards. 'Ah! I forgot.' Realising the rest of the soldiers were busy digging shallow graves for the bodies, his razor-sharp gaze honed in on Tavia. 'Can you climb up yourself, maid? We're running out of time.'

Looking up at the high saddle of the horse, Tavia sincerely doubted it, but she would try.

'Just jump up,' Benois commanded arrogantly. 'Put your foot in the stirrup, then throw the other leg over!'

He made it sound so easy, thought Tavia, grimacing as she tried to hook her toe into the high stirrup. But, despite Langley holding the animal's head, the horse shuffled slightly, and she was left bouncing around with one leg on the ground, with the other foot trapped in the stirrup.

'Oh, help! Help!' she called out. Langley released the bridle and came round, supporting her back so she could disentangle her foot.

'Come on!' Benois ordered. He hadn't seen her display of complete ineptitude, as he waited impatiently on the other side of her horse. 'Langley, stop faffing around, and come and hold her horse's head.'

Tavia marched around to Benois, hands on hips. 'Will you just give me a chance, and stop ordering me around like one of your foot-soldiers. It's really difficult!'

Benois chuckled, watching her cheeks burn with a becoming rose colour. 'It is for some people, obviously!' He jumped down from his horse, grabbing her waist firmly, and set her in the saddle with an easy movement. His hand rested on the pommel, vigorous strands of chestnut hair on a level with her waist. 'Have you ever ridden before?' he asked curiously.

'What do you think?' she answered grumpily, the reins slack between her unknowing fingers.

'Just try to keep up,' he muttered, before swinging away.

In the afternoon, the white strands of cloud began to swell, billowing in front of the sun. Tavia shivered, her hands tightening instinctively on the reins with the involuntary movement, every muscle in her body straining with the effort of keeping up with Benois. Her hip and thigh muscles ached from the unfamiliar position; her knees shook from clamping them either side of the leather saddle. It seemed like they had ridden for hours, Tavia's eyes riveted on Benois's broad straight back, the swishing rump of his horse, but she knew it was not past noon. She should have welcomed Benois's relentless pace; like her, it was obvious that he wanted nothing more than to be rid of her, and wanted this journey to be over as soon as possible, but a tiny part of her wished to plead for a rest.

The horses followed a path alongside a shallow, fast-flowing brook that meandered, glistening, at the bottom of a gently sloped valley. The running, gurgling water provided a melodious backdrop to their ride, and Tavia was thankful that the horses had to slow to a walk in order to pick their way amongst the stones that littered the green valley floor. Further up the slope, the landscape took a harsher profile, with great grey carbuncles of granite growing out of the valley sides until they flattened off into moorland above.

A huge spot of rain splashed down on to Tavia's hand. The water slid off her pale flesh to stain the faded leather of the reins. Then another spot. And another. In a moment, the gathering clouds darkened significantly, and the rain surged down, shining needles of water. The rain sluiced over Tavia's face, trickling down beneath the rounded collar of her gown, the damp wool at her throat itching uncomfortably.

Benois whirled his horse around, yanking at the sides of his cloak to try to shield himself from the worst of the rain. Already his hair was plastered seal-like to his head, emphasising the raw beauty of his features, the high angularity of his cheekbones, shadowed and dangerous.

'We must find shelter!' he yelled at her. 'Come on!' He wheeled his animal away from her with an assured, practised hand, jabbing his heels into the horse's flank to set it into a gallop.

How inconsiderate, thought Tavia. She knew that he meant her to follow him, but at a gallop? Her horse continued to plod steadily onwards and she hadn't the faintest idea how to encourage the animal to go any faster.

Several yards ahead, Benois glanced around. Tavia sensed rather than heard his groan of disgust at her woefully lethargic pace. He galloped back, his horse kicking up clods of soggy earth, before dragging on the reins to halt beside her. 'Will you come on!' he bellowed down at her. 'We'll be wet through at this rate!'

Tavia was already wet through, but she thought now was not the time to mention it. 'I would if I knew how!' she shouted back, her aquamarine eyes challenging him through the stinging rain.

'I cannot believe you never learned to ride,' he muttered, edging his animal round so that his horse was parallel to hers. He leaned over and grabbed her reins. 'Now, hang on!'

Her direction became uncertain after that; all she did know was that the animal beneath her turned into a see-sawing, unpredictable ride. She clung on to the reins, the stringy mane, the saddle, anything to stop her toppling to the ground. Her hips slipped from the left to the right; one of her feet fell from the stirrup and she lurched forwards, the pommel digging into her stomach. When, finally, the horse stopped abruptly, she lay forward over the animal's back, exhausted, her fingers interlaced with the mane, trying to control her rapid, frightened breathing.

'We'll stop here!' Benois declared autocratically. He had already dismounted, appearing at the side of her horse. 'Look, there's some shelter over there.' Lifting her head wearily, peering through the incessant rain, Tavia followed his pointing finger towards a dark hole in the side of a granite escarpment. A cave, she thought. Well, anything was preferable to staying on this horse. Leaning forwards, she managed to swing her leg over the back of the horse, slither down its side shakily, reluctant to accept any more help from Benois. As her feet touched the ground, she clutched on to the saddle for a moment, trying to regain her balance.

Through the dismal, sluicing rain, she appeared as a bedraggled waif, her elfin features pale and luminous. One of her braids had become hooked around the pommel, tugging at her head as she took a step towards the cave and she shrank back as he reached forwards to gently detach the curling end. The silky softness of her hair made his fingers linger; suddenly he longed to see her with her hair free and unbound, with no veil, no ribbons confining its glorious colour.

Her frowning expression jolted him back to reality, and he released the end of her braid as if it stung him. Pulling her by the top of her arm, he dragged her towards the cave and into its dim, damp interior, annoyed that her beauty lured him so, made him forget his true purpose. He released her shoulder abruptly, wanting to push her away, to punish her for attracting him so, and she stood there, fixed to the spot, limp and trembling. 'Are you all right?' he asked gruffly, no hint of concern in his voice.

'Am I all right?' she repeated his words, astounded, scrabbling behind her for some sort of handhold in the rock. 'Nay! I am not. Not only do you chide me for not being able to mount my own horse, you also start galloping at a tremendous pace when I cannot even ride, before pulling me off the horse like a sack of grain and dragging me in here!'

'We needed to shelter from the rain!' he responded. 'And you dismounted on your own, if I remember rightly.'

'Only because I knew you were about to pull me off,' she replied defensively. 'I've had enough, Benois!' Eyes bruised with tiredness, she slumped against the rock behind her.

She's exhausted, thought Benois, suddenly. Her cloak had fallen back over her shoulders, the ornate brooch that fastened the two sides together digging into the skin at her throat. Beneath its cloying folds, the elegant lines of her *bliaut* were revealed, the fabric clinging wetly to her svelte figure. His breath caught, his eye tracing the soft round of her bosom, an elaborate girdle embracing the indentation of her waist. Her complaint was justified: the maid was half the size of him, yet he had pushed the pace this morning, covering the same distance as if he had been riding with a group of experienced soldiers. And, until now, she had not uttered one murmur of complaint, or failed to keep up.

He ran the flat of his palm over his face. 'I am sorry,' he admitted, ruefully. 'I'm used to riding with soldiers, not escorting ladies.'

Tavia nodded jerkily. 'At least you have the courtesy to apologise.' Her voice, prim and formal, echoed around the cave. Fatigue washed over her as she leant back against the rock, a natural ledge supporting her weight.

Benois moved around the space, treading with the minimal grace of a cat, to gather an armful of the dry sticks that littered the floor of the cave. Reaching for the pouch at his belt, he drew out a sharp flint, and a piece of metal, glinting dully. Crouching down over a bunch of dried moss and grass, Benois struck down on the metal, producing a shower of sparks. A tiny curl of smoke appeared from the kindling. Benois fed the fire quickly, building it up, so that soon the heart of the wood burned strongly. The occasional raindrop, blown in on the breeze, hissed into the flames. Tavia's eyelids began to droop.

'We need to dry our clothes,' Benois stood up sharply, almost cracking his skull on the low roof of the cave.

Tavia's eyes shot open. 'My clothes are fine,' she lied, testing the sopping wetness of her skirts between thumb and forefinger.

Benois smiled faintly. 'Well, I am soaked through, so I suspect you must be, too. This weather looks set to stay for the day. We'll not travel any further.'

A huge sob rose in her throat; despair clouded her features. 'Then I'll be too late,' she whispered.

Chapter Seven

The sorrow of her expression plucked uncomfortably at the strings of Benois's heart; feelings ignored by him for the past few years came coiling to the surface. He knew that with his next question, an uncertain involvement in this maid's life would begin; an involvement that a few days earlier he would have rejected without question. He teetered on the edge, between frozen reserve and compassion.

'Too late? Too late for what?' The words pushed him into the abyss.

'For my mother, Benois. She's the reason I did all this in the first place.'

'Tell me,' he urged.

'My mother needs a physician. We…we have not the coin to afford such an expense. When Ferchar saw me at the contest, he offered me a great deal of coin to impersonate the princess. I need to return to Dunswick as soon as possible to secure a physician…before my mother dies.' Her eyes, huge and imploring, searched his face for some sense of understanding.

'Have you no other family members who could help you?'

'Nay, my father…' she picked at a loose thread in her girdle, dropping her eyes to the floor '…didn't have the money.' How could she tell Benois of her father's bullying ways? She wanted him to respect her, not pity her.

'Then we must go.' Benois eyed his glowing fire ruefully. 'So much for drying out.' He frowned out at the slanting rain, then at Tavia's wilting figure. 'Are you sure you can make it?'

'Of course,' she replied. 'I must.' Her heart leaped, despite the prospect of the grim journey ahead. She stepped over Benois, her movements wooden and jerky with the cold. 'Thank you, Benois. Thank you for doing this.'

He threw her a brief, curt nod in reply, not wanting her gratitude. 'It will be faster if we leave your horse here, and you ride up before me.' Benois raised his foot, stamping the fire out with his heavy leather boot.

When the familiar walls of Dunswick town rose up out of the mist later on that day, Tavia wanted to shout for joy. Benois's powerful war-horse had carried the pair of them effortlessly, despite him losing patience with her at the start of the journey. Tavia had refused to lean back into him, her awkward position confusing the animal's gait and slowing him down. In exasperation, Benois pulled on his arm that circled her waist, and hauled her against the flat muscled expanse of his chest, ignoring her squeak of protest. 'Relax,' he had grumbled in her ear. At the hypnotic vibration of his voice rippling against the small bones of her back, she had shivered. Why did this man, a hated enemy, draw her so?

'I cannot enter the city dressed as I am.' Benois pulled on the reins, nudging the horse to a halt beneath the green canopy of a small copse. 'They would shoot me in a moment for the colours that I wear.' His voice rumbled against her ear; a ripple of excitement lanced her flesh. 'I need to trade clothes with someone; maybe a peasant or a pilgrim so I can accompany you. I don't want to be noticed...like the last time.' He chuckled.

His strong, sinewy hand held the bunched reins laced across her stomach. That brief touch of his fingers sent spirals of warmth through her belly 'I wouldn't want you to take that risk...for me,' she muttered faintly. 'For a start, I doubt we could find clothes big enough...'

'Are you saying I am fat?' he teased.

She twisted rapidly in the saddle to face him, swiftly regretting the move. His grey eyes scorched her, the dark spiky lashes framing the wide ovals of his eyes. His mouth sat just inches from her own. 'Nay,' she tried to explain, 'you're tall, that's all!'

His arm tightened fractionally around her waist, a protective gesture to prevent her falling. Unable to hold his gaze, she dropped her eyes, focusing on the jewelled brooch that fastened his cloak at his throat. 'And furthermore,' she said, hoping to sound capable and efficient, 'I'll be fine on my own from now on.'

'So you're dismissing me?' he questioned sardonically. Was he still teasing? She didn't dare look up, for if she did, she would surely drown in the slate whirlpool of his eyes. In truth, she would miss his fierce, restless ways, his protective strength. She curled her lip slightly; never before had she relied on a man, and she wasn't about to start now. That way made you vulnerable.

'Don't tell me you're not overjoyed?' Tavia focused on the intricate silverwork that bound the agate stones of Benois's brooch. 'Now you'll be rid of me quicker!'

Nay, he was not overjoyed. For some curious reason, he didn't want to let her go. She snapped her eyes up, snaring his fierce glance. 'You're the one at risk, here, Benois, not I.'

He released the reins, snagging her delicate chin between thumb and forefinger. 'I didn't know you cared,' he replied sarcastically. The warmth flowed from his fingers, suffusing her face with a soft blush.

'I don't!' She tried to wrench her chin away, but found herself inextricably bound. 'Let me go!'

'Gladly.' His hand fell away.

Heart closing with unexpected sadness, Tavia slithered clumsily from the horse, ignoring the way her back bumped painfully against the saddle. 'What will you do now?' she couldn't resist asking, smoothing the long sleeves of her gown back into place, trying to appear unconcerned.

Benois's hands rested lightly on the pommel, as he concentrated on some point in the trees. 'Ride back and tell Henry we failed in the mission, I suppose.' A wry smile lightened his expression, contrasting with his flat, bland tone. He baulked at sending the maid back into Dunswick on her own, his senses at once suspicious and alert. From what he knew and had heard about Ferchar, the man was not to be trusted, and Benois was certain that the regent's scheming had only just begun.

'You don't seem thrilled by the prospect,' Tavia ventured. She hesitated over her departure, torn between the need to help her mother, and the wish to stay here, to talk, to discover more about this man. 'Will Henry punish you because you haven't kidnapped the princess?'

Benois looked sharply at her, almost in disbelief, then he threw back his head and laughed. 'Nay, lass, Henry and I go back too far for him to punish me.' His face shuttered suddenly then, as if he had said too much. He resented the way that this maid, this complete stranger, seemed to possess an unnerving ability to read his mind. He wanted to resist, yet, in truth, he knew this contact with her, however brief, had changed him. Whereas before he had thrived on the thrill of battle, the lure of an attack, now he began to question it. This woman was making him think, and thinking took him over shifting, unsteady ground. He didn't want to think.

'Get thee gone, maid,' he said roughly, squeezing his powerful thighs against the horse's flanks in order to set the animal in motion.

Huge aquamarine eyes berated him, made him pause in his escape. 'You could at least have the common decency to bid me "adieu" properly,' she chastised him. 'I did save your life, remember.'

Guilt washed over him. 'No doubt it will be something you'll remind me about on a regular basis,' he grimaced. The horse's hooves made a rustling noise as it sidestepped, excited, over the fallen leaves on the ground.

'As I have no intention of ever seeing you again, that will not be a problem for you,' she replied crossly, realising from his mute, closed features that he would not say any more. She must have been mad to want to stay a moment longer in his presence! 'But you could at least say "goodbye".'

'Goodbye,' he intoned, scathingly, sweeping low in his saddle in a mocking bow.

Tavia's mouth quirked into a smile. 'I bid you *adieu*, my lord,' she replied formally, refusing to be daunted by his derisive behaviour. And then she was away, in a flurry of skirts, pacing decisively along the track towards Dunswick, the glowing fall of her hair forming a startling contrast against the greens and browns of the surrounding vegetation.

As Benois watched the elegant line of her figure step quietly, purposefully, through the trees and away from him, the urge to kick his horse into a trot and follow her threatened to overwhelm him. In surprise, he realised that her nurturing presence, the sweet ferocity of her nature, had begun to loosen the iron bonds that held fast to the clot of pain within his heart. Was there a way through? he wondered. Was there hope after all?

Ferchar chewed voraciously on a roasted chicken leg, throwing a stripped bone down to one of the dogs trotting expectantly around the great hall. Wiping his sleeve along the greasy smear coating his lips, he feasted his eyes on the spread of food along the table, wondering whether to have the poached trout or a floury bread roll.

'King Henry should have sent a messenger by now.' Ferchar's long, thin fingers, sparkling with heavy rings, finally selected a bread roll. He studied it moodily, before ripping a piece off sideways with his teeth.

'It's not been above a day,' Malcolm tried to reassure him, pursing his lips in concentration as he stabbed his eating knife into a slice of roast venison. 'And you said yourself, that peasant chit can take care of herself.'

'I don't give a fig about her,' Ferchar replied nastily. 'But Henry would have sent a ransom note as soon as the princess was seized. It's not like him to miss an opportunity to push us into a corner.'

'At least Ada is safe now,' Malcolm murmured.

Ferchar burped loudly, his eyes following the movements of a comely serving wench as she made her way with a full jug of mead along the top table. 'I wish I could be there when Henry realises he has the wrong maid! What a delight that would be!' Ferchar slumped back in the oak chair, throwing the half-eaten roll back on to his plate, as if bored by it. He stared dolefully down from the dais, watching as a puff of smoke belched out from the carved stone fireplace, enveloping those near it in a choking fog.

Nothing seemed to be going to plan at the moment, and when things didn't go according to plan, he liked it not. True, Ada was safe from the English, but the stupid chit still couldn't remember anything about the message her father, Earl Henry, had told her, despite Ferchar's constant questioning. Ferchar knew that Earl Henry had left a fortune on his death, and, if the information given to him by the old servant who attended him was correct, Earl Henry had told his daughter where the fortune was hidden. If only Ada could remember!

At the opposite end of the great hall to the high dais, the iron-studded oak door swung inwards, grating noisily on its rusting hinges. A Scottish soldier walked in first, closely followed by Tavia, stepping proudly, head held high. The eyes of the peasants and soldiers all eating their midday meal at the trestle tables set in lines below the high platform followed the slender girl as she made her way across the hall. Some whispered to their neighbours how similar she appeared in looks to the Princess Ada, and some mistakenly rose in their seats, bowing their heads deferentially as she passed.

Ferchar thumped his fist heavily on the oak table, causing the platters to jump, the pewter goblets to spill droplets of wine. 'What in God's name are you doing here?' he shouted irritably, half-rising from his seat. 'You're supposed to be locked up on English soil!'

Innards quaking, Tavia dutifully followed the soldier up the steps to the high dais. Her toe, encased in a soft leather slipper, snagged on the top step, causing her to stumble momentarily. Regaining her balance, she drew herself upright, tilting her chin defiantly, refusing to be intimidated by these nobles. She had only come to claim her dues, after all.

Ferchar lurched out from the table, pushing back his chair tetchily, his thick-set physique made to appear heavier by the thick robes that he wore. Malcolm remained seated, a tentative smile across his rounded, boyish features.

'What happened?' Ferchar's breath fanned over her, foul with the stench of alcohol. He stopped a couple of feet away from her, rings glittering as he raised one hand to stroke the sparse hair of his long beard.

Tavia forced herself not to recoil—to show weakness would be the way of a fool. 'The English did catch me,' she admitted. 'But they realised soon enough that I was not Princess Ada!'

'You gave the game away, you stupid bitch!' A gob of spittle appeared on Ferchar's lips, as his pale eyes flicked angrily over her. 'What did you do?'

Malcolm rose uncertainly, a faint note of remonstration in his voice. 'Er…Ferchar, don't you think—?'

'Sit down!' Ferchar lashed back at him. 'When I need your opinion I'll ask for it.' Malcolm sank down into his chair once more, white and silent.

Pale and trembling, Tavia stood her ground, almost unbelieving as to the way this man was treating her. All the courteous manners and charm she had witnessed on the last occasion had slipped away, to be replaced by this brutal rudeness. King Malcolm appeared to have lost all authority, Ferchar treating him with the utmost disrespect. A cold, sliding fear scraped along her veins; the smallest part of her wishing for the strong figure of Benois at her side. Inwardly, she reeled. What was she thinking? When had she ever asked a man to fight her battles for her? She had stood up to her bullying father for all these years, and how different was Ferchar to him? Her encounter with Benois had made her soft, pulled at her independence, her will.

'You dull-witted wench!' Ferchar berated her. 'I suppose you blurted out the truth the moment they caught you in their hot little hands!' His fleshy jowls wobbled. 'Why couldn't you have kept your mouth shut, you stupid guttersnipe?'

Rage reared up in her breast and she took a step forward, blue eyes blazing. 'I don't have to take this from you,' she said, breathing deeply to keep her voice low, threatening. 'Ada is safe, isn't she? You've got what you wanted. Now give me what you owe me, and I will leave.'

The blow came from nowhere, the square cut of a sparkling gemstone ripping into the side of her cheek, lacerating her flesh. Her head jerked back under the surprising force of Ferchar's fist; in shock, she clutched her palm to the side of her face, sucking in her breath, cradling the injury. On the wall opposite, the intricate patterns of the tapestry blurred and swam as her eyes watered under the impact of the blow.

'I gave you no permission to speak,' Ferchar hissed, pushing one of the rings more securely on to his index finger. In horror, she realised that Malcolm had disappeared, no doubt not wishing to witness any further violence. A hum of chatter, of people eating and laughing, of pewter plates occasionally knocking together rose as background hubbub from the lower part of the great hall, but, despite this, a gripping band of panic tightened around her chest—she felt totally alone. There was no one to help her, no one to spring to her defence, but she was used to that; and she would make this man give her the money if it were the last thing on earth that she did.

'You only speak if I ask you a direct question,' Ferchar explained slowly, rubbing his hands distastefully, as if he couldn't quite bear the touch of her base-born skin. 'Now listen to me, wench, and listen to me well. I am not going to give you any money. You did not carry out my plan exactly.

I wanted the satisfaction of my enemy, King Henry, knowing that he had been duped good and proper. And you failed to provide that satisfaction, so you lose. Now begone…' He dismissed her, turning away to sit down once more.

'You don't frighten me,' Tavia announced boldly, walking nearer to him. Standing by his chair, Ferchar was only half a head taller than herself, yet his burly physique was twice the width of her own.

Ferchar laughed. 'Think you to intimidate me, wench? You're a bold one, I'll give you that.' He smoothed down the front of his tunic, picking at a tiny speck of grease, fixing her with his colourless eyes. 'Get thee gone, maid—'

'Nay, I will not—'

'Ah, there you are, dearling,' a voice boomed out across the great hall. 'I've been looking for you everywhere!'

Astonished, Tavia whirled about, heart leaping involuntarily at the familiar deep voice. Struggling to isolate the broad figure of Benois amongst the crowd in the hall, she failed to notice the tall man mount the steps to the dais, a peasant wearing braies fashioned from a crude uneven weave and a drab, threadbare tunic. Over his head and shoulders he wore a hood and cape, constructed as a single garment from thin grey wool that stretched tautly across the muscular width of his shoulders.

'Who are you?' Ferchar demanded, nervous fingers pouncing to his sword hilt. Only a single soldier remained on the high dais to protect him, and he suspected most of the castle guards were too drunk to come to his aid, should he wish it. This man appeared rather too large and powerful for comfort; a fighter, Ferchar thought, judging from the way he moved, and not someone he would care to tangle with. 'What do you want?' he challenged, as the peasant approached with a light tread.

'Forgive me, my lord Ferchar.' The man bowed low. Ferchar frowned slightly: there was an unusual catch to the man's voice, an accent he couldn't quite place. 'I have come to take my wife home.'

The words rapped into Tavia's consciousness like an icy raft of hailstones, her jaw dropping in surprise as one lean, cool hand wrapped about her wrist—a warning. As awareness stole through her veins at his touch, she tried to pull away, irritated by her response to him, annoyed as to the reason that he was here. She didn't need him fighting her battles for her!

'Thank God!' Ferchar breathed a sigh of relief, smoothing a white hand across his lined forehead, back over his wispy grey hair. 'Take the wretched woman away and keep a closer eye on her next time!'

'I'm not leaving until I receive the coin owing to me!' Tavia's voice rang out firmly as, furtively, she attempted to drag her hand out from Benois's punishing grip. Her mouth set in a stubborn line—what did Benois hope to achieve by this?

'I should heed your husband, maid,' Ferchar advised slowly, yawning. This whole affair began to bore him; he glanced longingly at his full cup of mead on the table. 'If he's got any sense, he'll take a strap to you for your disobedience.'

'He's *not* my—!' Benois spun her around, effectively shutting off her speech, hauling her against his side in a huge bearlike hug. Teeth rattling at the swift violence of the movement, Tavia found her mouth pressed up against the supple leather of his borrowed jerkin, unable to protest any further.

'You heard the regent, *sweetling*.' Benois laid great emphasis on the term of endearment, making her want to punch him. His eyes swung dispassionately over the bluish weal that marked her cheek.

'Go away,' she hissed up at him, lifting her face away from the constricting press of his chest. 'This is none of your affair!'

Benois ignored her words, dropping his head to plant an affectionate kiss on her nose. 'You've become a little over-wrought, *dearling*.' He shot a withering glance at Ferchar, as if he had the weight of the world on his shoulders. Tavia wanted to kill him!

'You drew the short straw with that one,' Ferchar sympathised, collapsing back into his chair, and raising a pewter goblet to his lips. 'I don't envy you!'

'Can't let you out of my sight for a moment, can I?' Benois said in a loud, patronising voice as he hauled her down from the high dais. His hold on her was such that her feet danced rather than walked over the stone flagstones of the hall.

'Let me go!' Tavia shrieked, realising his intention. Kicking out, she began to struggle within his hold. She coloured hotly under his churlish treatment off her, hating her own weakness, her inability to push him away. Watching their exit, Ferchar guffawed loudly, smug with the glory of his own achievement.

Benois refused to let go of her until they had left the castle, marching her out ruthlessly through the inner bailey, the outer bailey and finally over the drawbridge. He refused to talk to her, not responding to her tirade of insults, her pleading to take her back inside, her occasional, ineffectual jabs at his chest with her free hand. At last he stopped in the sepulchral shadows of an alleyway, almost flinging her back against the wall, one strapping arm pressed up against the stone on either side of her, effectively blocking her in.

'You have no idea what you have just done.' She glared at Benois hotly, anger bubbling in her breast. Furious, she ducked down quickly, her back bumping against the damp stone, intending to escape under his arm. But he seized her shoulder before she had even moved a couple of inches, forcing it back against the wall.

'I know exactly what I am doing.' He towered over her, eyes glittering in the shadowy gloom, a foreboding figure. Above his tawny head, the sky was a cloudless, brilliant blue.

'Nay!' She punched him in the chest. 'You have completely undermined me! Ferchar was about to give me the coin! I just needed a few more moments with him!' Emotion wavered in her voice; she wanted to cry at the futility of it all. All those risks she had taken…and for what? To see her mother die?

Benois grasped her attacking fingers, holding them fast against his chest. Under her hand, his heart beat steadily, a reassuring beat. 'You just don't know when to stop, do you, Tavia? I heard you in there—' he jerked his head in the direction of the castle '—berating the regent like he was some lowly serving boy, demanding your money. If you had pushed him any further, he would have strangled your pretty neck with his bare hands.' The ugly mark on her cheek drew his gaze, and he lifted his fingers, scuffing the cut lightly. 'In fact, it looks as if he had already made a start.'

Pain seared through her cheekbone; she sucked in her breath sharply, wincing, trying to control her reaction, trying to forget the sickening crunch of Ferchar's fist that seemed to constantly replay in her memory. Willing herself not to collapse before him, not to show any weakness, she drew herself upwards. 'I don't need you to fight my battles for me,' she said slowly. 'I can take care of myself.'

'Then you're an even bigger fool than I thought you were,' he grumbled. His hood had fallen back, and now he stuck a frustrated hand through his hair, sending the chestnut strands awry.

'I'm going back in there,' she announced suddenly.

'Like hell you are!' he growled.

'You can't stop me!'

She had the briefest impression of silvery eyes, alight with desire, looming close. His arms scooped around her sides as he leaned into her, melding the long lean hardness of his bigger body against her own fragile curves.

'Nay!' she whispered, but her own heart contradicted her, thumping deceitfully with excitement. His lean head dipped down, his lips seeking hers.

'Aye,' he replied, a rough certainty threading his voice. Hunger kindled in her belly, a hunger she had never before experienced, yearning, craving…for what? As the sensuous curve of his mouth brushed hers, she wanted to scream out loud with joy at the exquisite touch. Cursing her traitorous limbs as they curved sinuously into his muscular frame, she seemed incapable of resisting, her body melting to a burning pool of liquid beneath his touch. The heady smell of him enveloped her, a sensual delight of horse and woodsmoke that plucked at her senses, promising more, much more.

She arched into him as he deepened the kiss, his tongue questing along the seam of her lips, demanding entrance. He groaned, a passionate animal sound, as she opened her lips to him, clawing at his shoulders. Locked together in hungry embrace, reality faded away, to be replaced by a glistening bubble of scorching, intense enchantment. Whereas moments before Tavia had tried to push him away, now she clung to him, almost sobbing with the beauty of his thrilling caress.

And then it ended.

Wrenching his lips away, Benois staggered back, astounded, his heart beating unsteadily. Blood whipped through his veins, desire pulsing through his body. Anger flooded through him—what had he been thinking? He had accused the maid of being foolish, but who was the greater fool now? Her indomitable will, her stubbornness, had made him want to punish her, but, instead, he had kissed her. And it wasn't the sort of kiss he had bargained for.

'Sorry,' he muttered, jerkily. He dropped his hands away from her, taking a step back. 'I should not have done that.'

Heart still racing from the impact of his kiss, her lips burning and bruised, Tavia fought to maintain her balance, her hands seeking the gritty stone behind her for support. Sunlight, beginning to shaft into the deeper recesses of the alleyway, caught the bright gleam of her hair as she shook her head, amazed, loathe to admit how much his kiss had moved her.

'You think a mere kiss can stop me?' Tavia fought to keep the tremble from her voice. 'How dare you use such an underhand trick? Mind you,' she continued, a hint of contempt in her voice, 'I suppose I should expect nothing less from one such as you.'

His big body crowded in around her, although he touched her not. 'Don't push me, Tavia.' His voice carried a warning.

'Why?' she taunted. 'What else do you intend to do to me?'

An image sprung into his mind; he quashed it swiftly, a *frisson* of desire bubbling in his loins. 'Let's get out of here,' he muttered, beginning to pull her down the alley, feeling her resistance. He turned back to her, witnessing her set mouth, her mutinous features. 'For Christ's sake, woman, if it's money you're after, then I will give you some. You are not going back into the castle, and that is an end to it.'

Chapter Eight

Lifting his pewter goblet to his lips, allowing the honeyed mead to slip delectably down his throat, Ferchar sank back against his ornately carved chair and closed his eyes. It would be a shame when the young King Malcolm came of age, he thought ruefully, for he could become used to being in charge. But Malcolm was not yet sixteen, he thought idly, and showed none of the leadership prowess that his uncle, King David I, had been renowned for. At the moment, the young king was easy to control, easy to influence, a situation that gave Ferchar immense satisfaction.

The fire burned low in the grate, a heap of smouldering embers that spit and crackled occasionally. Many of the castle occupants had gone to sleep; those with no chamber allocated to them rolled up in their cloaks on the floor of the great hall. Cleared of food and dirty plates, the long trestle tables had been scrubbed down and pushed back against the walls to gain more floor space. Every now and again, a cough broke the silence, or the wavering rumble of a snore.

Malcolm stuck his head around the side door leading from the dais. 'What happened?' he enquired querulously.

Ferchar opened one eye, looked over to him in irritation. The open door had caused a troublesome draught to sneak in, to whirl around his ankles. 'Aha! How like you to re-emerge when all the unpleasantness is over!' he chided sarcastically. 'Come in, will you, my feet are freezing!'

Malcolm slid in, closing the door behind him. 'I couldn't go to sleep until I knew you were safe,' he offered in his defence.

'How noble of you,' Ferchar jeered. 'You didn't think to send the castle guard to my aid when that woman was threatening me, did you?'

Malcolm remained silent, not wanting to antagonise Ferchar. The regent had obviously drank a few cups of mead, judging from his movements, which seemed loose and uncoordinated. As he approached the table, his leather boot kicked against something that protruded out from the chairs. Puzzled, Malcolm bent down to pick up the item, a worn leather satchel, from the dusty wooden floorboards.

'What is it?' Ferchar rapped out as he studied Malcolm's expression. His eyes alighted on the scuffed bag between the young King's fair hands. 'That stupid fool maid must have left it…nay, dropped it after her husband dragged her out of here.' His lip curled into a smirk at the amusing memory. He wondered what punishment the husband would mete out to his wife; she certainly deserved a sound hiding for her bold, challenging behaviour.

'I'll leave it at the gatehouse,' Malcolm said. 'Mayhap she will return to claim it.'

'Give it here first.' Ferchar held out his hand. 'Let's have a look.'

'Should we?' Malcolm held the satchel primly against his chest.

'Don't be such a ninny! The woman's a peasant. It will

be amusing to see what rubbish she carries around in her bag.'

Ferchar's drunken fingers fumbled with the leather straps and buckles, finally tearing open the leather flap, upending the bag and dumping the contents on to the polished oak planks of the table. He poked about through the meagre contents, the corners of his thin mouth turning downwards.

'Hmm! Nothing much here. A handkerchief, a flagon of water...hey, what this?' His fingers seized on a small, jewelled dagger. 'Looks like an expensive piece for a peasant.'

He rotated the knife between his hands, seemingly transfixed by the way the honed metal blade caught the light. The stones winked and flashed, beautiful gems of diamond and sapphire studding the hilt. Ferchar smoothed one fingertip over the ornate engraving that looped and twirled its way up the blade, a delicate tracing of flowers and trailing vines. He flipped the blade, studying an inscription in Latin on the other side. A lump formed suddenly in his throat, his chest, a burning excitement coiling through his veins.

'I've seen this knife before, Malcolm.' His voice quavered.

The young king frowned. 'But...how can you? It belongs to the peasant girl.'

'That maid is not who she seems, Malcolm.' He knocked against his head with one fist. 'Of course! It all becomes clear now! I thought there was something different about her, something bold, unusual.'

'My lord, you make no sense.'

Ferchar smiled. 'It makes perfect sense, Malcolm. You see, I have just worked out who that chit *really* is.'

The strengthening wind blew wraiths of cloud across the waxing moon, ragged strips of white that clumped together, then dissipated in a moment. In this luminous twilight of early evening, beyond the haphazard mesh of branches against the sky, the stars twinkled. The dry husks of beech nuts crackling under her feet, Tavia trudged along the path through the copse of trees to her home, her heart sinking. With Benois following her, a reluctance dragged at her steps, making her slow. She had no wish to bring him into her world, present him with the intimate details of her humble life; she had no wish to spend any more time with him. With the kiss against the wall, he had come too close, too close to the flimsy barrier that shielded her vulnerability. He'd had no right to kiss her…no right at all! She pursed her lips, frowning, annoyed as she remembered her wanton reaction to him. Her body still thrummed from the onslaught of his kiss. Nay, he didn't belong here, with her…she wanted him gone! Before…what? Before she gave herself utterly to him? She closed her eyes, shocked by the way her thoughts led her, nay, pulled her inexorably, as if she had no choice in the matter.

Although she was loathe to admit it, he had probably saved her from a nasty incident at the castle, and had helped her to secure a physician for her mother. When they had reached the doctor's house in the middle of Dunswick, Tavia had looked on in amazement as Benois handed over a pile of shining coins to the befuddled physician. The man quickly changed his manner from one of doubtful hesitation to fawning obsequiousness at the sight of all that money, promising to visit her mother as soon as he was dressed.

Following the stubborn line of her rigid back, Benois smiled softly. He knew she resented this involvement in her family life—every movement, every gesture she had made since he had dragged her out of the castle had been couched in hostility. The kiss, he admitted ruefully, had been a mistake. How could he have known the feelings such a fleeting touch would kindle within him? He had thought himself immune to such sensations, cut off a long time ago from that world of passion, of desire.

He told himself he would see her home safely, then bid her *adieu*, but he couldn't deny a growing curiosity about the girl, about her history and her home life. No doubt King Henry would be champing at the bit now, demanding to know from Langley why the Princess Ada wasn't in their hands.

Catching the toe of her shoe in her trailing sleeve once again, Tavia cursed. 'These wretched sleeves—how does the Princess manage in them all day?' Her voice reverberated oddly around the silent trunks of the wood. Somewhere, up above, an owl hooted.

Benois chuckled, a deep throaty sound. 'Because she is a lady, a royal princess. She spends her days in the women's solar, not trudging about the fields.' He lengthened his stride to overtake her, forcing her to stop. 'If I knot them up, it should make the going easier.' Hooking up the sleeve end, he tied it fast, shortening the sleeve so that it no longer skimmed the ground.

'Thank you.' Tavia's response was tight-lipped. She tilted her head up to him, meeting his eyes. 'Haven't you got anywhere else you'd rather be?' she demanded, rather rudely. Blood rose hotly in her cheeks as his sparkling eyes brushed her lips.

'I'll see you home, then I'll be on my way,' he stated firmly.

'My home is along the valley...' she gestured vaguely with her hand, the knotted sleeve swinging under her slim arm '...so you can take your leave now.'

He grinned. 'Nay, mistress. I'll see you to the door. I

wouldn't put it past you to nip back into the city and visit old Ferchar once more.'

She bristled under his words, hating him for reading her mind. 'You sound like you don't trust me.'

'I don't.' His teeth flashed white in the moonlight, the look of a rogue. 'Listen, you chided me before about not taking my leave properly, now you can't wait to be rid of me. What's changed?'

What's changed? she wanted to yell at him. You kissed me. And I want more. The thought knocked, hot and demanding, into her brain. She swiped one hand across her mouth, wanting to scrub the burn of his lips away. 'Nothing,' she mumbled, dropping her gaze. 'You're still the same arrogant, violent barbarian that I can't seem to shake off!'

The cottage, nestled under the hulking shape of the steep-sided crag, lay in darkness. Beneath the stark rising moon, the landscape around faded to a pattern of contrasting grey tones; the mountains behind appeared as bulky, looming shapes, like monsters of old; the trees were a lighter colour, the frilled grey lace of their branches touching the moonlight sky.

Blood hurtling through her veins, Tavia increased her stride, tripping and stumbling over the spongy turf to reach the door. For a moment, as the flat of her hand touched the rough wood of the door, she paused, as if wary of the conditions she would meet inside.

'Who is it?' a voice rose querulously from the corner. Relief flooded through her. Flinging the hood of her cape back, she stepped through the dimness to the pallet bed, her mind alive with questions. Where was her father? How could he have left her mother in this state? The cottage was freezing; no fire had been lit, and her mother shivered beneath a thin blanket. Fumbling with the jewelled brooch at the throat of her cape, Tavia swung her fur cloak, warm from her body, down over her mother.

'What ails her?' Benois asked bluntly. He ran a quick, assessing eye over the older woman, the pale, sweating skin, the dull eyes, and his heart snapped shut. He knew, without a doubt, that this woman would die.

'If I knew that, then we would have no need of a physician,' Tavia answered, her voice etched with worry as she knelt down in the dry earth beside the bed and seized her mother's hands, trying to warm them.

'I'll light a fire,' Benois offered, no hint of emotion, or reaction in his voice.

'Thank you,' Tavia managed to bite out. 'I'm sorry…it just—'

'No need,' he cut her apology short. 'Tend to your mother.'

She could hear him moving about the cottage, finding the woodpile, the kindling. No matter what he thought about her, about her lowly life, the only thing that mattered now was that her mother lived. Mary pawed her arm. 'Are you the priest?' her voice whispered hoarsely. 'Have you come for me?'

Sadness clutched at Tavia's chest. ''Tis I, Mother. Your daughter, Tavia.' As the newborn light of the fire flared at her back, she stared, appalled, at her mother's hands. 'Benois, for God's sake, bring a light over here,' she gasped, an edge of desperation to her voice.

Benois approached the bed, carrying a spitting rush torch. Peering close, Tavia realised in shock that the tips of her mother's fingers had turned black. Nausea scoured her innards, a rolling wave of sickness, and she swayed a little. Benois's hand touched her shoulder, the nurturing heat of his fingers offering some comfort.

'I should never have left you,' Tavia whispered, guilt descending on her like a physical burden. The flickering light only served to highlight the pitiful state her mother was in; her frame seemed to have shrunk, bones sticking prominently through her thin skin.

'I'll see if the doctor is on his way,' Benois stated tersely. 'I'll take the light to guide him; the fire is well away now.' He didn't wait for an answer, pushing out through the door and standing for a moment, inhaling the cool night air. Closing his eyes, he fought the memories from long ago: the fire, the charred bodies of his parents, his sister. Seeing that woman lying in there, that woman fighting for her life, made him think of his own mother, struggling for breath in that chamber full of fire, unable to escape, unable to even call for help as the smoke overcame her. He couldn't help then, and he couldn't help now, curse it! Where in hell's name was the physician?

As the door closed behind Benois, Mary clutched at her daughter's sleeve. 'Tavia, there's something I must tell you— something important.'

'Is it about Father?' Tavia hunched down by the bed. 'Why is he not here?'

Her mother laughed weakly. 'You didn't expect him to stay around, did you? With me like this? Nay, child, he's long gone, and good riddance, I say. He's taken all his things, all the money, and cleared off.' She clutched suddenly at Tavia's arm, seeming more lucid now. 'There's something I must tell you, Tavia. I am a fool if I think I have much longer for this world…'

'Don't say it, please.' Huge fat tears began to roll down Tavia's cheeks, plopping on to the fur cloak, shining pearls of heartache.

'Be strong, Tavia…and listen.' Her mother's voice became more insistent, demanding. 'Dunstan is not your real father.'

Tavia gaped at her, uncomprehending, unable to speak even if she had wanted to.

'After I married Dunstan,' her mother continued in a reed-like whisper, 'I secured good work up at the castle, as a seamstress. King David admired the garments that I made, and he paid well. I became acquainted with the King's younger brother, Earl Henry of Huntington and...' Her voice trailed off, weak from the effort of speaking.

'And I was the result?' Stunned by her mother's words, Tavia's voice emerged as a half-hearted croak. 'But how?'

Her mother's lips curved into a smile. 'Surely I don't need to tell you that, my love. I was two years into the marriage with your father, and resenting every moment of it. Earl Henry was kind, and attentive—'

'And took advantage of you!' Tavia snipped across her mother's speech. How typical of these nobles...sleeping with low-born wenches whenever the need arose, and casting illegitimate offspring without a care in the world!

But her mother was shaking her head, her fine hair rustling against the nubbly linen of the pillow. 'Nay,' she protested vehemently, 'he wasn't like that! We knew we could never marry; our worlds were simply too far apart. But we did love each other...and he loved you, too.'

'Why are you telling me this?' Tavia blurted out.

'Because you were special to him, you were his favourite, born out of love, as opposed to the enforced marriage that his royal position pushed upon him. Remember, you met him once.'

Tavia nodded, recalling the handsome noble astride his horse, resplendent in a vibrant royal surcoat, his red hair gleaming in the sun. He had been alone, approaching Tavia and her mother as they had walked up the secluded valley near Allandale. Her mother had wanted to see the wood anemones, a magnificent sheet of white fragile flowers deep in the wooded valley, but now, looking back on that day, Tavia suspected her mother had contrived the walk specifically so Henry of Huntington could meet his eldest daughter. Her heart raced at her mother's revelation…from excitement…or fear? A huge lump lodged in her chest; now, she would never see her real father again.

The smile slipped from her mother's face, her skin sunken, withered with illness. 'My heart broke when he died,' she mumbled. A single tear glistened on her cheek. 'He should have been king after David. He deserved that right—he was a good man.'

Tavia leaned across the bed, curving her arms around her mother's limp body, astounded, nay, perplexed by the information Mary divulged. Was her mother suffering from delusions brought on by her illness—should she believe her? The similarity of her looks with Princess Ada and the young King Malcolm could not be denied—maybe there was an element of truth in her mother's words.

'You can reclaim what was his, Tavia. You have the key to it all.'

Tavia frowned; the words made no sense. She drew her shoulders back, tracing over the familiar lines of Mary's gentle face, anxious that she had begun to step back from reality once more.

'Please believe me, Tavia.' Mary's eyes closed with the effort of talking. 'The knife, Tavia…when we met him that day…' Her mother's voice faded to a wheezing rasp.

'Nay! nay!' Tavia pulled at her shoulders, realising in horror that her mother had slipped away. A terrifying wretchedness washed over her, as she clutched the limp body to her own, desperate to inject some life back into those frail bones.

The door opened behind her.

'The physician's here,' Benois stated, ducking his head under the carved wooden lintel, preceding the elderly man into the cottage.

Tavia half-lifted herself from the body on the pallet, face wet with tears. 'You're too late.'

Hunkering down by the fire, Benois threw a couple of logs onto the dancing flames, stirring the glowing embers with an iron poker he had found propped up against the wall. Spreading his palms flat against his thighs, he eased into a standing position, narrowly missing banging his head on an iron skillet hanging from the wall. Glancing over at the lifeless body lying on the bed in the corner, he frowned slightly—surely the body must be washed and wrapped, prepared for burial. He wasn't certain of this country's customs, but no doubt they were similar to those of England—dead bodies could contaminate the living and needed to be buried as quickly as possible.

He wondered where Tavia had gone. After the doctor had officially pronounced her mother dead, she had fled from the cottage, leaving Benois to bid farewell to the physician. He had thought it best to leave her to her grief—he knew his presence would offer little consolation to her under the circumstances—but now? Now, he thought she had been away for too long. Pulling open the door, he stepped outside.

At first, he could see nothing. The bright moon that had aided their descent into this valley had been obscured by thick cloud. His pupils adjusted, allowing him to see his surroundings more clearly. Where was she? From the corner of his eye, he snared a fraction of movement in the byre, an open thatched shed used to house some of the animals in winter. He strode over the muddy yard, relishing the unhampered blood moving through his body after being cramped up in the cottage for so long.

Tavia sat in the middle of a pile of sweet-smelling hay; a pile of dry grass scented with summer. Her head was downcast, her hands covering her face. She jumped as Benois appeared at the door, hands dropping from her face and falling limply at her sides, fingers rustling against the bleached hay.

'Go away!' she murmured, her voice cracking with tension. 'Leave me alone!' Tracks of tears streaked her ravaged face.

Ignoring her rudeness, Benois shrugged off the powerful urge to drop to his knees beside her and gather her hostile, grieving body into his arms. 'Why not come in now…sleep. The hour grows late and you'll freeze out here.'

She slumped a little, amazed at the concern in his voice, hugging her arms around her drawn-up knees. 'Nay…I can't go back in there…with her.' Her eyelids flickered down for a moment; she tried to remember her mother in life, rather than the husk that remained on the pallet. Her mind seemed stuffed with straw, her thoughts incoherent; she found it hard to concentrate on even the smallest detail. 'We need to fetch the priest,' she blurted out suddenly, relieved to have found something practical to say, conscious of his unnerving regard from the doorway.

'I'll fetch one on the morrow,' he found himself announcing. Hadn't he intended to return to England tomorrow? Since when had he been so concerned for another's welfare?

She dipped her head jerkily in agreement, unable to trust her voice.

'Shall I…carry her body out of the cottage?' Benois offered. 'So that you can sleep?'

Eyes blazing, she sprung up from the straw like a vixen. 'Nay! Leave her! Let her spend her last night in her own bed!'

'She is dead, Tavia,' he reminded her brutally. His voice held a curious detachment.

Balling her fists, she thumped one into the middle of his chest, hurting her knuckles against the thick band of muscle under his tunic. 'I know, Benois. And I feel like I have died with her.' Her grief-stricken face lifted up to him.

He cupped his warm palm around the curve of her shoulder. 'Don't say that. Don't let your heart go with her.'

A peculiar inflection in his tone caused her to examine him more closely. 'What would you know, Benois? How can you even begin to understand what I am feeling? Death is a game to you, a way of life that you thrive on. Death means nothing to you.'

He sucked in his breath at her accusation, vivid images of the past crowding into his brain, too fast for him to stop, to extinguish. He gripped her shoulders, holding on to her as if she were a rock, the only rock in a churning, treacherous sea that could save him. He wanted to shake her, push her away, make love to her, he knew not what, but anything, anything, to drive these thoughts from his brain.

'Benois?' Her voice floated through to him, a bright sound in his sea of anguish.

'I lost my family in a fire,' he said thickly. The skin on his face turned a deathly white. 'I do understand.' His eyes sought hers, and instinctively she brought her hands up to frame his face, to offer some sort of solace within his despair. He shut his eyes at her touch, moving his hands from her shoulders to clasp her against his body in a tight embrace. The tears fell easily as she wept and rocked against the comforting beat of his heart, and together, they held each other tightly as if they could stay like that for ever.

Chapter Nine

At some point they must have fallen asleep in the mound of hay at the back of the byre. Tavia had a vague recollection of strong hands guiding her, turning her in her grief, and tucking her into her cloak as she lay down on the cushion of dried grass. She had dozed fitfully for a time, her mind racked with doubts until she woke with a jolt, her brain still busy with the events of the day. The viciousness of Ferchar, her mother's odd little story before she died…and Benois's kindness. Her stomach lurched. In truth, she didn't know what she would have done, how she would have coped, without his strong, steady presence at her side. Oh, aye, she had thoroughly resented his very existence when he had hauled her out of the castle, hated his domineering, arrogant manner…but now?

Lying on her back in the hay, she moved tentatively, the dry stalks prickling the back of her scalp. Despite sleeping in the shed, the wide doorway open to the elements, she felt warm. Her skin tingled as she drew comfort from the thick, heavy weight of Benois's arm across her stomach, the weight of his limb creating a delicious, secure feeling. No wonder she felt warm; her cheeks flushed hotly under his possessive touch. She listened to his breathing, even, steady, and drew a deep, shuddering breath, some of the taut emotion that had bound her in knots leaking away. She hated to think she had become reliant on this man, vowing that, once this night was over, she would fight to gain her independence once more. But just for this night, just for this one night, she would relish the feel of this man next to her, draw comfort from his big, muscular body and remember the moment for ever.

She shifted her head, studying Benois's features. He seemed much younger, the harsh lines of his aquiline face softened with sleep. Flexing her fingers, she resisted the impulse to smooth them along the tempting angle of his jawbone, focusing instead on the dark, spiky lashes fanning across his cheek. He sprawled on his front, his head angled towards her, the toes of his boots almost touching the threshold. The fine curve of his mouth tilted upwards, smiling, as if he dreamed of something wonderful. Tavia wondered at his last words, words that haunted her, hinting at some of the horrors that possessed him. His family…destroyed in a fire? How had it happened? And when…?

'What are you thinking about?' The fearsome, metallic eyes shot open, instantly demanding, his intelligent gaze searing into her.

'Er…?' Tavia grappled for an answer, dumbfounded by his unnerving ability to know what she was doing, even when he appeared to be asleep! 'I was thinking about what you said…about your family,' she replied, truthfully.

His eyes hardened, grey steel. 'Forget it,' he said, callously. 'Forget I ever said it!'

'Why?' Tavia asked gently. 'Did you make it up to offer me some comfort?'

His grip around her middle tightened fiercely. 'Do you really think I would do such a thing?'

'Nay,' she admitted.

Benois flipped over onto his back, the heavy weight of his arm lifting from her middle. He concentrated on the rough-cut cross-beams of the roof, hating her for prying, but, oddly, wanting to tell her.

'My family died in a fire,' he said eventually, his voice hollow, toneless. 'End of story.' The memories stamped back, vividly, crowding into his brain to torment him. Sweet Jesu, would this torture never end?

'Is it?' she asked quietly. Would he lash out at her, like the last time?

The silence extended between them, expectant, waiting.

Tavia held her breath, willing him to speak, willing him to lower his guard with her, to tell her more about himself. The taut lines of his stern profile appeared more prominent in the dark: the shadowed hollow of his cheek, the firm curve of his lip.

Suddenly, Benois jerked upright, pulling his knees up, resting his head in his hand. His voice, when it finally came, seemed cracked, muffled somehow. 'It was when I was just a squire, in training with Geoffrey Plantagenet. I lived with my family in a small fortified manor, but took all my meals with the other squires and knights in the great hall of the castle. My father also worked at the castle, but that day he went home earlier than me.' He ducked his head, pushed an unsteady hand through his hair. 'I should have gone with him…but I was detained.'

'What happened?' Tavia whispered, a sensation of horror building in her chest.

'My parents and younger sister slept in one of the chambers in the tower. When I got home, the whole tower was in flames.' He covered his face with his flat palms. 'I ran and ran, up those stairs, tried to open the door, but I couldn't. I couldn't save them.'

He lifted his head, turning his ravaged gaze on Tavia. She gasped at the haunted look in his eyes.

'But it's not your fault, Benois. It's not your fault.'

Guilt washed over him, an old friend that hung about him like unwanted clothing. He shrugged his shoulders. 'I know, Tavia. But it doesn't make it any easier to bear.' He glanced down at his palm, rubbing his fingers over the ridged scar.

'Is that how you hurt your hand?'

He nodded. 'Aye. 'Tis the imprint of the door latch. The fire on the other side made the metal hot.'

'Sweet Jesu!' The horror of his past clouded her brain for a moment. 'I am so sorry.' She reached out to clasp his damaged hand, her touch cool and sweet. He didn't pull away.

Through a haze of despair, of the suffocating grief that had held him captive for all these years, he clung on to her beautiful turquoise eyes, aware that the bonds of his guilt seemed to weaken somehow, to slip away. He drank in the fine details of her beautiful face; the skin like smooth cream, that in this mysterious half-light held the quality of silk. With a shudder, wrapping one powerful arm behind her back, he crushed her to him, melding his upper body to hers, feeling the soft yield of her rounded breast, the flatness of her stomach against the hard muscle of his.

The compulsion to lose himself in her beauty, to disappear in the svelte lines of her body blossomed and grew, accelerating into a rush of desire that pelted headlong through his arteries. His lips found hers, and he was lost.

Under the pressure of his lean, hard body, Tavia's head spun; as his lips crushed against hers, hungry and demanding, she felt herself pulled at breakneck speed towards a thundering maelstrom of passion. She clung to him, a small voice of sanity lurking in her head, telling herself she sought an outlet, a refuge for her grief, nothing more.

His lips flirted with hers, tantalising, demanding more. Her fingers curled into the hard muscle at his shoulders, the expensive nap of his cloak smooth and rich beneath her hands. Her breath seemed to stop in her throat, her whole being entwined with a fluidity, a weightlessness that lifted her high up into the heady realms of passion. His hands plunged upwards into her hair, sifting through the loose red strands, before he tugged impatiently at the leather bond that held the end of her plait in place. As the gold-red waterfall of hair flowed over her shoulders, he lifted his mouth from hers, devouring the sight of her unbound tresses in silent wonder, almost in disbelief. The air sifted over her scalp as the tension of her bound hair was released; at the sublime sensation, she wanted to cry out in pleasure. Throwing back her head, she jumped as Benois traced the column of her throat with his lips.

Breath jagged with desire, Benois turned her carefully in his arms, as if she were made of fragile glass, and eased them both down into the soft mound of hay. His hand smoothed down the side of her body, gently caressing her breast, the narrow indentation of her waist, the flare of her hips beneath the falling gathers of her dress. Her breath snared at the possessive touch; no man had ever been so close to her before, but she welcomed it eagerly, not wanting to push him away. Desire burst within her: a growing, shining bubble that shattered like a million tiny fragments of a star throughout her body. Blood stampeded through her veins, hurtling at such a pace she wondered whether she might lose all conscious thought with the pleasure of it.

The voice in his head commanded him to stop. He had to stop, before the maid became his. He had to do it, for his sake as well as hers. Reluctantly, he wrenched his lips away, senses gulping at the magnificent sight of the woman beneath him: golden-red hair fanning out in glorious ripples on the hay, pulse beating wildly under the delicate skin of her throat and her face set in an expression of such exquisite rapture that he had to tear his eyes away, for want of kissing her once more.

'No more,' he muttered. 'I cannot do this to you.' Benois rolled away from her, springing up into a sitting position, knees drawn up.

Tavia lay there, flat on her back, shocked and astounded, bereft of his touch. Nay! she wanted to rail at him, to shout and to tear at his clothes, nay! You can, you can do this to me! She didn't care as to the consequences of their actions, she just wanted him, wanted him hungry and passionate and demanding. Her body still screamed for him, yearned for him, every fibre of her being bawling out for release, yet now he sat apart from her, expression cold and hard, eyes devoid of emotion. Humiliation, shame, hot, blinding shame washed over her; of course, he was like all the rest, all of those suitors who had thought her too lean, too headstrong to marry. They had come and found her wanting, just as Benois had. But only he had come close to possessing her. And why? Because she found him handsome, good-looking. Foolish, foolish girl! Drawing a deep, shaking breath, Tavia rolled away from him, huddling into a tight little ball. 'Oh, well,' she muttered, endeavouring to conceal the hurt in her voice, 'at least you realised sooner rather than later. No harm done.'

He baulked at the jolting offence of her tone. Better, though, that it was like this, he told himself. Better that she hated him; it would make it easier to sever the tie, if there were one, between them. The woman placed him in a dangerous position; already he had told her things about his past that he had never spoken of before, and he resented it. That feeling, that feeling of being vulnerable, exposed, carved into him like a sharp blade, slashing through the thick, impenetrable hide that he had built over his painful memories.

'You'd better go to sleep,' he ordered her coldly. 'Tomorrow will be a long day.'

She bit her lip, tying to dampen down the bubble of tears that threatened to break from her chest. Moments before, this arrogant, powerful man had been about to bed her, and she would have given herself to him willingly. And now, now all she felt was an utter disgust at herself—he didn't want her, he didn't find her attractive. Why had she ever fooled herself into thinking otherwise?

Trying to ignore the icy tentacles wrapping around his heart, Benois's eyes traced the maid's rigid back, the ramrod set of her spine. Tension poured from her, in every slight, jerky movement, from every line of her graceful body. He wanted to blame her, to rail at her for allowing him to speak, to divulge the secrets of his past. All he wanted was to forget, but in speaking those words to her, the raw memories had been unlocked once more.

He lay back in the straw, endeavouring to control his breathing, still ragged from their love-making. To stay with her would be to destroy her, he decided. His guilt, his grief would mar what little joy they might have. He brought his arms up to pillow his head, thinking. Better to go now, to leave and return to King Henry, and tuck away the fragile memory of this bold and beautiful maid close to his heart.

The small church that served the hamlet in which Tavia lived was constructed of stone: large, unwieldy lumps of granite, the various mineral seams that streaked the rock sparkling in the afternoon sunshine. A low wooden fence surrounded the building and graveyard, again of simple construction: knobbly hazel sticks driven into the ground and joined together with thin, pliable willow branches. Her family had been coming to this chapel for as long as she could remember, Tavia thought, to hear the priest's sermon on a Sunday and to be present at weddings and funerals. Somehow, she had never envisaged walking to her own mother's burial, but here she was, following the hastily constructed coffin, hoisted up on the shoulders of their neighbouring farmers. There was no sign of her father; he had obviously decided to leave for good, never to return.

Misery clung to her heart; for her mother, aye, she grieved, but although she hated to admit it, she grieved for another as well. When she had awoken that morning, her muscles stiff and aching from sleeping in the open barn, the hay beside her had been cold. Benois had left. In her restless sleep, in her dreams, maybe, had she imagined the light kiss he had placed on her forehead before he swept away into the darkness? After he had rejected her, after she had curled away from him and desperately sought oblivion, forgetfulness in sleep, she knew he would go. In his own way, he had been kind to her; he had taken the honourable, chivalric path. He could have gone ahead, made love with her anyway, despite not being attracted to her. She had known many men who would. She should be happy that he had stopped when he did—at least her virginity was intact. So why did her heart feel like it was breaking?

A sharp stone cut up into her soft leather sole, stopping her thoughts. She still wore the fine shoes that belonged to the princess, but had changed back into her own rougher, more practical clothes for the funeral. Bodies were buried quickly here, sealed up inside the wooden coffins when the blood was scarce cold. Tavia still could not believe her own mother was carried before her; the whole event seemed tinged with a surreal, nightmarish quality. Surely her mother was back at the cottage, her capable hands kneading the dough for their bread, stirring the pottage for breakfast?

She flinched at a sudden eruption of noise behind her, someone shouting, and a sound of thundering hooves. Turning, her heart swooped, then plummeted as a group of Scottish soldiers pounded up the hill towards her, chainmail flashing in the sunlight, green and gold pennants flapping furiously with the forward motion of the horses.

'Mother of Mary!' Tavia breathed, clutching at her neck, unable to quell the panic rising in her chest, as she recognised Ferchar's cruel features under one of the helmets.

'Go on!' she ordered the men who carried the coffin. 'Take the coffin inside the church. I'll deal with this!'

The farmers, balancing the coffin on their shoulders, looked doubtful, first at her, then at the approaching horsemen.

'Do it!' Tavia begged them. 'Do it for my mother's sake!' She watched as the farmers resumed their forward pace, negotiating the coffin through the narrow, awkward gate of the church.

A *frisson* of fear laced through her as Ferchar pulled his animal to a halt beside her. His features, grim and relentless under the thick metal nose-piece of the helmet, assessed her bedraggled, forlorn state. His horse snorted in protest at the abrupt stop, pawing at the ground impatiently. What does he want with me? thought Tavia, wildly, raising her hands as she realised both Ferchar and another knight were boxing her in neatly with their horses. Soon she was surrounded by the gleaming, sweating flanks of horseflesh, unable to run.

'Tavia of Mowerby?' Ferchar challenged her, wiping a slick of sweat from his top lip. Obviously the ride from

Dunswick had been hard going; Tavia wrinkled her nose as the stench of exertion wafted down from the regent.

'You know I am,' she threw back. The booted foot of the knight on horseback behind her jabbed her in the middle of her spine.

Ferchar sighed, leaning forward on the pommel of his saddle to address her. 'I thought you'd learned your lesson with me, young chit. What goes on here?' He moved his head in the direction of the funeral procession.

'I am burying my mother today,' she retorted coldly. 'So if you'd kindly step aside, my lord, I wish to pay my last respects.'

'Good riddance to her,' Ferchar spat out. 'If it wasn't for her, we'd have none of this trouble today. Useless whore.'

Tavia trembled under the onslaught of his vicious words. 'She was a good woman. How dare you speak ill of the dead?' she shouted up at him, eyes flaring with anger. 'My mother's no whore!'

'That's not what I've heard.' Ferchar raised an eyebrow. 'What do you know of her past?'

Tavia hung her head, mind racing. Was Ferchar referring to the very same words that her mother had spoken to her before she died?

'Hmm. I thought so.' Ferchar mistook Tavia's silence for confirmation that she knew something. He pulled up on the reins with his gloved hands, digging his toe into the horse's chestnut flank to keep it steady. 'You, young lady, need to come with us.'

'Nay, I need to see my mother laid to rest.'

'You'll come with us, maid, willingly or not.'

A chaotic scene reigned at Langley Castle. Knights on horseback crammed into the inner bailey, chainmail shining like silver fish scales, bright scarlet tunics, emblazoned with the golden lions of King Henry II. Servants ducked here and there, mindful of the skitterish hooves, adjusting a stirrup here, handing up parcels of food there. And in the centre of this busy scene sat King Henry himself, a thickset, stocky man, his hair the colour of fresh carrots, his fair skin ruddy from a lifetime spent outdoors. His experienced eye ran over the preparations for the march northwards, missing not the smallest detail as he barked orders at his men to make haste. Yet his smile was wide in greeting as Benois nudged his horse alongside him.

'I'm glad you decided to join us.' Henry leaned out from his saddle and slapped Benois jovially on the back. 'What kept you anyway? Langley's been back above a day.'

'Nothing important,' Benois replied, his mind filling suddenly with the beautiful, seductive image of Tavia, sleeping in the hay, her gown flattened against her slender form, revealing her delicious contours. Hell's teeth! Why could he not tumble her from his mind?

'Hah! That's not what I heard,' Langley chortled, pushing his way through the mass of horseflesh to join them.

'Save it, Langley,' Benois growled at his friend. For some reason, he felt reluctant to divulge any more details of his encounter with Tavia of Mowerby.

Langley eyed him for a moment, startled, as the teasing smile slipped from his face. He had no wish to pry; all he knew was that Benois had finally returned at some early, godforsaken hour of the morning, whilst he still snored beneath the covers. Exhaustion clouded Langley's round, friendly features; the arrival of the English king at his castle yestereve had resulted in a flurry of non-stop activity. Two messengers had ridden ahead of the king, warning Langley of his impending arrival.

From the moment Henry had descended from his horse on to the greasy cobbles of the inner bailey, Langley felt he had been constantly running around, chasing up his stewards, making sure the chambers had been made up properly to ensure that everything would meet the King's strict high standards.

Henry sensed the unspoken tension between the two men. 'Is there something you're not telling us, Benois?' He smiled. 'Other than the fact that a peasant girl managed to dupe you?'

Benois grinned ruefully, shooting an apologetic glance at Langley. His friend didn't deserve to be the butt of his ill humour. 'My apologies, Langley,' he muttered, gruffly. 'I didn't mean to bite your head off. It's just that maid…'

'Got under your skin?' Langley ventured.

'Aye…like an irritating fly.' Benois laughed. He should never have gone after her, should have left her to fend for herself with Lord Ferchar. The brittle casing around his heart, the unbreakable shell that protected his emotions, had begun to soften, he knew that now, all because of what he had told her. He wished he had not. Benois looked around him, at the excitement in the faces of the knights, at the swords and helmets glinting in the sun. This was the life he had chosen for himself: a hard life of war and fighting, with no space or time for thought. He would do well to remember that.

'Benois…?' Henry had asked him a question.

'Sorry…?' Benois forced himself to focus on his king's words.

'I said "I need your eyes and ears on this one", I don't trust Lord Ferchar one bit.'

'Was it he who called the meeting, or the young King Malcolm?' Benois forced himself to concentrate on the situation.

'Lord Ferchar himself. He wants to discuss Cumbria and Northumbria.'

'Do you think he'll yield?'

'The fact that he's called a meeting is a start. It might put an end to all this fighting.' Henry raised one arm in the air, summoning the soldiers' attention. 'Let's ride north, to Scotland,' his voice boomed out over the expectant crowd.

'Tavia! How lovely to see you again!' Princess Ada stood at the top of the steps that led into Dunswick Castle, her fine gown of blue silk forming a startling contrast against the rough-hewn planks of wood that formed the great door behind her.

'It isn't exactly a social call,' Tavia ground out, as one of Ferchar's soldiers dragged her mutinous body up the steps. She felt hot, bedraggled and furious. Was Ada really as naïve as she appeared? She searched the princess's pale, fragile features, realising with a sickening lurch that, if her mother's words were true, then Ada was her half-sister.

'Come on!' the soldier growled at her. 'Lord Ferchar told me to take you to the great hall!' Tavia threw a look of friendly apology at Ada, as the solder bundled past her. It wouldn't hurt to have the princess on her side.

'I'll come too!' Ada announced girlishly, seizing Tavia's other arm in companionable style. Tavia clamped down on an inconceivable desire to laugh—Ada was acting as if they were about to wend their way around the market stalls!

In the great hall, the evening feasting had already begun; the peasants, tired and hungry from the day's chores in the open air, now relaxed at the trestle tables, laughing and joking as they chewed hungrily on the fare provided by the king. Ferchar was already seated in his customary position at the top table, King Malcolm at his side. The regent had thrown his cloak to a servant at the side of his chair, and now threw back his head to swallow a full cup of mead, drops of the honeyed liquid spilling from the sides of his mouth.

As the soldier tugged her along, Tavia struggled to control the panic, burgeoning and fluid, as it cantered through her body. It was not above a day since she had stood in the same place arguing with Ferchar about the money owing to her, but then, Benois had intervened, Benois had calmed the situation and pulled her away as her temper began to get the better of her. A strange pang cuffed her heart—where was Benois now? She would do well to keep a level head with Ferchar this time; it was obvious the soldiers responded more to his command than that of the pale, ineffectual Malcolm.

'Sit down,' Ferchar ordered, wiping his sleeve across his mouth. His lips gleamed fleshily in the light from the rush torches that thronged the hall.

Beside her, Ada smiled sweetly, seemingly completely unaware of the tension between Tavia and the regent. She slipped delicately on to the bench, patting a space between her slight figure and Ferchar's ornately carved chair, so that Tavia could sit down.

Despite the unnerving situation she was in, Tavia's stomach rumbled as she took her place. Unable to eat before her mother's funeral, the sides of her belly seemed to cave in at the enticing sight of all the food spread before her. How these rich nobles ate! She thought of the meagre meals her family had endured, especially during the lean winter months when snow lay on the ground: meals of plain boiled root crops, or oats softened with water. But here! Here lay a vast feast, surely more than all these people could eat; plump roast game birds—partridge, quail and pigeon—their skins still steaming from the ovens, jostled for space on the table with poached fish and floury rounds of bread.

Ferchar saw her eye the food, and smiled nastily. 'Answer my questions, maid, and then I may allow you to eat.' In her numb, befuddled state, Tavia realised he turned something between his fingers—a dagger. Her dagger?

'Where did you find that?' she asked, wanting to snatch the pretty knife out of his bulky grip.

'Aha! So you recognise it!'

'Of course, it belongs to me!' she replied carefully.

'And who gave it to you?' Ferchar said slowly, an avaricious gleam in his eye.

Tavia frowned. 'Why, my mother!' Sadness chiselled through her heart…her mother, who she would never see again. Who she had failed to see properly laid to rest because of this man dragging her away. She chewed on her lip, fighting to hold back the tears.

'And how did your mother, a destitute peasant by all accounts, come to own a knife such as this? Did she steal it?'

The sardonic curl of the regent's lip suggested he was enjoying this, like a game of cat and mouse. It was if he held some information of which she had no inkling, and pulled her towards the truth slowly, through the labyrinth of his questions.

'Nay!' she responded hotly. 'Nay, we are not thieves.'

'I'll tell you how,' he cut in across her protest. 'Your mother was given this knife by her lover. Her lover, Earl Henry of Huntington, younger brother to King David.'

At her side, Ada began to choke on a piece of bread at which she had been nibbling absentmindedly. Malcolm, using his eating dagger to try to extricate the fine bones from a piece of fish, dropped the knife with a clatter, his mouth gaping. Tavia's world swayed; the walls of the hall seemed to fall inwards, grow dim. So her mother had spoken the truth on her death-bed and Tavia had not known whether to believe her, wrongly deducing that her mother was too ill to think straight.

'This knife belonged to Earl Henry, your father—' Ferchar's venomous tones brought her back to the present '—and you, my girl, are going to tell me what this inscription means.'

Tavia frowned at him, confused. 'But I can't even read,' she replied in a shaky voice. 'I'm a peasant…remember,' she added sarcastically. 'And that—' she pointed at the knife blade '—is Latin script.'

'I know what it says,' Ferchar said slowly, hunching over the blade as if possessed by it, 'but it doesn't make any sense.'

Tavia tilted her head on one side, her mind swimming with hunger, with exhaustion. At this precise moment, she didn't really care if Ferchar decided to kill her. 'And what does it say?' she murmured disinterestedly.

'It says "Seek and thee shall find". What does it mean, girl? Did the Earl say anything to you? Or to your mother?'

Tavia lifted her shoulders, feeling the tension rip along the muscles in her back. 'I don't have a clue,' she replied, a note of resignation in her voice.

Ferchar's face darkened angrily. He didn't believe the stupid chit for a moment. Not that she was stupid. Nay, she was a clever piece, make no mistake. She knew what was meant by the inscription on the knife, and if she knew that, then she could lead them to the treasure—the gold that Earl Henry had hidden long ago as a safeguard against the invasions. It was rumoured that the Earl had told his daughter where the treasure was hidden, but no amount of questioning had resulted in any information from Ada. But it was Tavia, his other, *illegitimate*, daughter, whom the Earl had surely told, and Ferchar would make sure that Tavia would tell him.

'I think a spell in a locked chamber, without food, will loosen your tongue,' he announced grumpily, picking up a chicken leg and beginning to munch noisily. 'Guards, take her upstairs.'

Chapter Ten

As the four o'clock bell tolled sonorously, its rich voice resounding over the huddled rooftops of Dunswick, a group of English soldiers rode through the hushed, cobbled streets. It appeared as though the whole town had been alerted to their arrival; doors were banged shut hurriedly, frightened mothers called for their children as they scuttled down alleys and ducked around shadowy corners.

The guards at the castle eyed the band of knights warily as they approached, their horses' hooves clattering over the wooden drawbridge, the sound bouncing beneath into the deep inky waters of the moat. Despite appearing to remain still and in position, the grim expressions of the Scottish guard twitched slightly, acknowledging with that small movement the bold red-and-gold colours of the English tunics, fingers twitching as if to seize their swords. But Lord Ferchar had been insistent—let the English King and his men through, with no challenge. But it was difficult for them not to feel some hatred towards these men, these warmongers who had ceaselessly attacked their city, their homes and their livelihoods. Now they must sit back and watch as King

Henry pulled up his reins on his horse and dismounted before the stone steps that led up to the door of the castle.

Benois swept his eyes around the inner bailey, his steely gaze checking the area for potential dangers. Despite the open invitation from Lord Ferchar, he still suspected some sort of trap. And although the group of knights escorting King Henry numbered not above twenty, Benois had insisted on the whole battalion accompanying them, to wait on the outskirts of the city. If Lord Ferchar decided to play games, then the English retaliation would be swift. Mounting the steps, following the king, Benois remembered the last time he had been here, extricating Tavia from her increasingly risky confrontation with Lord Ferchar. How her foolish boldness had led her into danger, her determination to fight for what she was owed. He wondered if she had learned her lesson.

His chest squeezed unexpectedly, constricting with a strange fleeting sensation. He wondered what the maid was doing now, how she was faring after the death of her mother. Raising his eyes, he tracked the lazy wheel of some ravens, lifting in a croaking bunch from one of the towers, black wings shining against the luminous blue of the evening sky. A curious listlessness surged through him as he watched Henry spring up the steps in a customary burst of overpowering energy. He knew the king needed him, would pay him handsomely for his loyalty, but whereas before this nomadic, military existence had satisfied him, now he found it strangely lacking. When had everything changed? A pair of bright aquamarine eyes sparkled in his mind's eye, openly berating him.

'Benois! Make haste!' Henry bellowed from the top step, his loud voice making up for his lack of stature as he frowned at his commander's tardiness. 'What's got into you?'

She has, he thought, as he swung his leg over the saddle and dismounted, patting the animal's gleaming rump as one of the stable hands led the stallion away. He climbed the steps, his pace calm and measured, joining Henry under the ornate, recessed archway. Henry's stern hazel eyes assessed Benois briefly, before turning into the gloom beyond the open door. A servant led them through to the great hall, pushing aside a thick curtain of tanned hide, and, bowing low, indicating that they should precede him.

Another servant was already pushing himself through the crowded hall, no doubt to warn Ferchar of their arrival. But, far away on the high dais, the regent seemed heavily involved in another affair. Benois scanned the space, checking for any obvious threat or danger, absorbing the comforting sound of people eating and laughing, his eye at last gliding along the row of high-born nobles at the top table.

God in Heaven! What was she doing here?

He picked out Tavia immediately, her slender frame flanked by two burly shoulders, her face stark white with exhaustion and…fear? Ferchar lifted himself unsteadily from his chair, barking an order at the soldiers, watching as they half-carried, half-dragged her towards a low door at the side of the dais. What had the stupid chit gone and done now? Why had she not heeded his warning?

Clamping his lips together in a forbidding expression, Benois lifted his hand to pull off his steel helmet, feeling the thick, fuggy air of the great hall swirl around his scalp as he yanked it off, before following Henry's rapid pace through the trestle tables. With every step he took, anger and irritation welled within him—he wanted to strangle her! Hadn't she learned her lesson? Had none of his words sunk in? She had been fortunate the last time that he had followed her into the city, saved her skin. But now…? Now it would serve her right if she received more than she bargained for. She did not deserve his help… If she continued to defy him, then he'd be damned if he rushed to her aid once again!

Tavia rubbed furiously at either side of her arms, trying to ease the bruising in her shoulders where the soldiers had ruthlessly gripped her. After hauling her up seemingly endless flights of stairs, they had finally dumped her in this icy, dark chamber. A shaft of fading sun streaming from the narrow arrow slit provided her with a faint light, but not enough to stop her stubbing her toe on something hard as she moved across the room towards it. Gradually her eyes became accustomed to the muted tones, the angles of various pieces of furniture beginning to reveal themselves: a bed, an oak coffer and a low stool in front of a black, cavernous fireplace. In despair, she pressed her hands against the gritty stone either side of the arrow slit; no hope of escape from here, she doubted even if she could squeeze her body through the small gap, let alone work out how she could drop to the ground. Nay, she would have to think of another plan of escape.

Her mind struggled to comprehend Ferchar's demands; his questions surrounding the writing on the knife confused and confounded her. He obviously had no intention of allowing her freedom until she told him…what? Her whole world had been turned upside down, but she told herself to focus on her current predicament. All that mattered now was to escape from this place, run as far away as possible from Ferchar and his men. Searching the shadows, her eyes alighted on a large earthenware pitcher, and she stepped over to it, lifting it easily. She vowed not to be defeated…just yet.

Hiding behind the door, Tavia realised that she could be waiting all night for someone to open it, but luck was on her side. It wasn't long before she heard the steady tread of someone on the steps outside, the sound of the heavy oak bar being lifted. Raising herself from the low stool on which she sat, her heart racing, Tavia hoisted the jug above her head, feeling the ligaments in her wrist sag against the weight.

The jug landed on the unsuspecting soldier's head with a horrible cracking noise. The man slumped, sprawling heavily on to the wooden boards with a tremendous thump. Shards of pottery clattered from her hand; the pitcher had broken under the impact with the man's head. She wondered if he were dead, her guilt forcing her to crouch on to her knees beside him, to check his breathing. Thank the Lord! The soldier was alive. Shame pierced her heart as she noticed a platter of food, now dislodged from one of his hands, the contents spilled messily over the chamber floor. The soldier had had the thoughtfulness to bring her some food, and this was how she repaid him!

She moved through the doorway, pulling the wood quietly shut within the doorframe. Her right hand slid across the iron latch, sticky with wetness, but she thought nothing more of it as she began to step lightly down the spiral staircase, a block of fear lodged in her throat. Her knowledge of the castle layout was hazy, but her main aim was to avoid the great hall, easily identifiable by the noise of people talking and laughing, enjoying themselves.

At the bottom of the stairwell, she hesitated. She was obviously in a part of the castle not often used; no rush torches lined the corridor as was customary, so she made her way to the left, trailing her hand along the wall to guide her. She believed herself to be one floor higher than the great hall, on a gallery level. Up ahead, she could see a patch of light, a section of the corridor that opened up, most probably on to the great hall below. She would have to be careful; this second level was often where most of the bedchambers would be. Approaching the end of the wall, she peered around the stone, her gaze immediately drawn to the scenes of jollity below her. Tavia sank without a sound to her knees; if she crawled along this part, then the wooden half-railings that lined one side of the corridor would hopefully hide her. With shaking limbs, she inched forward, movements jerky with nerves, breath held in panicky expectation.

A shriek of laughter from below, and she froze, midway along the gallery, hairs standing up on the back of her neck. But no shout followed, no call for the guards, and she let her breath out slowly, and began creeping forwards once more. She noticed her right hand was streaked with red; in her haste to escape the chamber, she must have cut it somehow. And then, she was there, at the other side of the gallery, her whole body obscured once more by the thick stone wall. Her limbs felt wobbly, untried, as if she had sprinted for miles. Heart thumping, she clung to the wall, using the stones to pull herself up. A weakness stole through her; she must have been more frightened than she thought. Her eye travelled back along the gallery, silently congratulating herself on her efforts, and then she froze. Bursting out of the darkness, the flare of a torch. Someone was walking along the corridor!

Her head whipped around, adrenalin seizing her limbs, forcing her to move once more. Convinced the person with the torch would pursue her, she bolted down the passageway, hoping its gloomy shadows would obscure her form, her headlong pace making her arms, her legs, bump against the hewn stone. She felt, rather than looked, for somewhere to hide, her hands rasping painfully against the wall. And then her foot plummeted through the air, encountering nothing, no solid base to land on. A staircase! Tavia's heart missed a beat as she pitched forwards, tumbling down into the blackness, fingers spread out before her, scrabbling for a handhold, frantically trying to regain her balance.

Oof! She thumped heavily against a hard, unyielding frame—a man, judging from the shadowy bulk of him, who climbed up the stairs. Huge, muscular arms roped around her back, immediately steadying her, although her feet still flailed several inches from the relative safety of the steps.

'I beg you pardon, sir,' Tavia choked out, unnerved by the collision. 'I missed a step. I'll be on my way now.' She swung her feet a little, a gentle reminder that he should put her down. With luck, this man might think her just another of the castle servants, and let her on her way.

'I might have guessed,' a familiar voice drawled. Silver eyes glittered, diamonds in the shadows.

Her mind tussled for comprehension. Benois? But surely he was miles away by now? 'Wh…what are you doing here?' The steady beat of his heart thumped enticingly against her chest.

'I arrived with the king…King Henry…at Lord Ferchar's invitation.' The coldness of his explanation scoured her skin—he appeared indifferent, aloof. 'Lord Ferchar has agreed to renegotiate on the border lands.'

An awkwardness swept over her, the blood on her cut hand flowing freely to the floor, thin drops of red, spotting against the folds of her skirt. 'Oh, well, I am just looking for a way out,' she explained, her voice creased with fatigue.

All but dropping her on the step, his arms fell away from her sides abruptly. Benois shook his head, two or three chestnut strands falling over his forehead. 'I can't believe you were stupid enough to come back here.'

'Do you think I came back willingly?' How dare he chastise her when he had no knowledge of the facts?

His shoulders lifted, a dismissive shrug. 'At this moment—' his tone rasped over her '—I don't really care.'

'Ferchar locked me up in a chamber.' Her voice notched up a little.

'I saw the guards taking you away when we arrived.'

'What? You knew I was here…yet you did nothing to help me?' The moment the words were out, she regretted the speaking of them. Why in Heaven's name should he help her? He had made it perfectly clear that he wanted nothing more to do with her.

'You don't deserve my help, Tavia,' he lashed out suddenly. 'I told you not to come back here, and you did!'

'I did not!' she argued back. 'Ferchar came and dragged me away from my own mother's funeral; believe me, Benois, I had little choice in the matter.' She raised her hand, attempting to push her hair back from her face. Her hand, streaked with blood, smeared across her face.

Benois seized her arm. 'Good God, woman, what have you done to yourself?'

'It's nothing.' She tore her hand away, hiding it behind her back.

He raised his eyebrows at the bloody marks streaked across the pale skin of her face. 'I think not,' he murmuring, reaching around her to bring her hand back, to study the ragged gash across her palm. 'You've cut yourself badly.' Voices beneath them on the stair galvanised him into action. 'We'll go to my chamber.'

He bundled her along the corridor, his touch firm, assured, as he half-carried her into a room further along. Rush torches slung into iron rings fastened around the chamber wall already burned steadily, washing the whole space with their yellow, comforting glow. A charcoal brazier packed with glowing coals filled the room with a welcome heat.

Benois led her over to one of the torches, snatching her hand up to the light. The jagged gash gleamed stickily across her palm, the clotting blood still oozing. 'How did you do this?'

'I told you, Ferchar locked me in a chamber. I escaped.' Tavia willed herself to keep a note of independence in her voice; Benois must never think that she couldn't cope, couldn't look after herself. She tried to pull her hand away, wanting to dismiss the injury, but he held on fast, his lean, muscular fingers wrapping her pale, bloody hand with unexpected gentleness.

'You're fortunate you don't need stitches.' Movements quick, decisive, he allowed her hand to slip from his, enabling him to fetch a stool from the other side of the chamber. 'Sit here...I'll find something to bind it with.' Benois strode to the bed, throwing back the furs, the woollen blankets, tossing them into a heap on the floorboards until he found the sheet that he was looking for. Tavia's eyes widened as he ripped it several times, tearing the material into makeshift bandages. Bringing over the bowl of clean water from the oak coffer, he knelt down on the floor beside her, soaking one of the shredded cloths in the bowl and cleaning the gash.

'You don't need to do this,' she said hurriedly, shy under his ministrations.

'Nay, I don't.' He looked up, unsmiling. 'I should have just left you to whoever was coming up the stairs.'

'If you hadn't come up, I would be away by now.'

He sat back on his haunches, the wet clothing dripping from his fingers. 'You really think so?' His sarcastic tone vexed her.

'You don't believe I can take care of myself, do you?' Tavia stood up, hastily, irked by his punishing manner. Caught by the flick of her skirts, the stool crashed backwards, clattering on the wooden floorboards behind her. 'Why, I escaped from that room all by myself...'

'How clever of you,' he commented drily, but his tone held no praise. 'And what poor soul did you involve to help you?'

'Nobody. I hit the guard over the head with the jug. I did it by myself.' Tavia set her hands on her hips, tensing a little from the pain in her hand, vaguely aware of a dizzy feeling clouding her mind.

'Sit down.' Benois reached for the stool, set it upright.

Nausea rose in her gullet, as she plopped down hopelessly on the stool, all fight drained from her, suddenly. 'I don't feel very well.'

'I'm not surprised,' Benois replied bluntly. 'You must have lost a fair amount of blood.'

'I must have cut it on a piece of the broken jug,' she muttered, as his face loomed over her hand. His dark lashes fanned out over his steely eyes, his mouth compressed in a rigid, stern line. She flinched as his fingers touched hers, trying to pull her hand out of his grip. 'I can do this!'

'Nay, you cannot,' he replied calmly, flinging the bloodied rag back into the bowl of water, beginning to bind her hand tightly. 'Stop fighting me, Tavia, at least until I have finished this.' His brow creased as he concentrated on finishing the bandage neatly, the touch of his cool fingers sending a flicker of desire along her arm.

The moment he tied the two loose ends of the bandage together, she pulled her injured hand away from him, lacing it against her stomach, trying to work up the energy to leave, to stand up even. 'I need to go now.'

He stood, placing a hand on her shoulder. 'Ferchar knows you've escaped already…the guard has been alerted…listen.' He jerked his head towards the door.

From outside the door, a sound grew, a noise of pounding footsteps, of fists thumping purposefully on chamber doors. Harsh shouts demanded that every room reveal all occupants, answering protests stifled quickly.

Benois hunkered down, his knees in their woollen braies

almost touching hers. The leather cross-gartering over his calves creaked against the movement. 'Seems like Lord Ferchar is very reluctant to let you go,' he surmised, the heat of his breath flowing her skin. 'Any reason why?'

Tavia breathed in the scent of him, a heady masculine aroma, spiced with woodsmoke and leather. 'I'm not certain,' she hedged, not wanting to involve him in the details she had only just learned herself.

He knew she could tell him more, knew from the stubborn position of her chin, the awkward way she held her body away from him. Benois sprung to his feet, irritated. He should just throw her out into the corridor now, push her towards the guards, have nothing more to do with her!

Tavia hunched forlornly on the low stool, cradling her injured hand. Her hair glowed like rich claret in the torch-light, her thick braid slipping forwards over one shoulder, the curling end, secured with a leather lace, brushing the floor. A sense of desperation flooded through her, a raft of complete helplessness; her bottom lip wobbled. This was ridiculous, she chided herself, sternly. Surely she had escaped from worse situations than this? But at this precise moment, she had absolutely no idea what to do next. The pain from her hand, grief and exhaustion—all combined to make her weak, and the more she tried to fight it, the worse it seemed to become.

The shouts moved nearer; Benois's eyes raked her huddled stance. His gaze slipped over her injured hand; he cursed, noting the faint stain of blood beginning to seep through the makeshift bandage. He told himself that he only helped her because she had hurt herself; he would do the same for anyone, man or woman. But in his heart, he knew it was a lie. From the time he had left her at the cottage, Tavia had never been far from his thoughts.

'Come,' he announced, urging her upwards, 'you must hide before Ferchar's soldiers reach this room.'

'I…' She opened her mouth to remonstrate, the objection dying on her lips as he bent down to pick her up, looping one muscled arm behind her back, the other beneath her knees, scooping her up high against his chest. Striding over to the bed, he tipped her into the middle of the linen-covered straw mattress, her arms and legs flailing.

'Lie down,' he ordered sternly. 'Lie down, as flat as you can. And for pity's sake, keep quiet!'

Fuming, Tavia sprang up, reaching over to flick the hem of her gown back down over her calves and fine-boned ankles that had become exposed with the movement. Catching her prudish movement, Benois smiled before picking up the woollen blanket discarded earlier onto the floor.

'I said, "lie down"!' he said, moving back to the bed. Pushing one huge, bear-like hand against her shoulder, he shoved her back downwards, the force literally bouncing her slender frame against the mattress. 'Don't give me a reason to not help you!' he growled. As Tavia glared at him, he flapped the blanket wide, letting it float over her, covering her completely from head to toe. The coarse fibres of the blanket tickled her nose; she brought up one hand slowly to lift the smothering softness away from her mouth so she could breathe. A heavy fur landed thickly on top of her, followed by another.

Someone banged on the door; fear tore at her chest. She heard Benois open the door, answer the guard's questions with his deep, velvety rasp. Whatever he said seemed to satisfy them, and, holding her breath in the roasting heat of the bedclothes, she heard the door latch click back into place, the iron key turn with a satisfying clunk.

'You can come out now,' Benois said. The bedcovers were

thrown back, and Tavia emerged, blinking, into the light of the room. Pushing herself upright, she fought the haze in front of her eyes, looking over towards him.

And gaped.

Benois had removed his surcoat, his linen chemise, and now stood a few feet from the bed, clad only in his braies, naked to the waist. The honed muscles of his chest appeared as if carved from wood, the sheen of his skin a polished lustre in the torchlight.

The bunched muscles of his shoulders, his arms, flexed powerfully as he took a step towards the bed.

'Oh…!' She gulped, ducking her gaze, a wave of colour suffusing her face as she studied a loose thread on the blanket.

'What's the matter? Never seen a half-naked man before?'

Nay, she wanted to shout back, at least not one built like you! 'Of course I have,' she lied, a jolting primness strangling her voice.

'Really?' The hint of sarcasm in his voice made her wince.

'I should go,' she blurted out, hurriedly pushing back the covers on the other side of the bed.

'Where? Where will you go, Tavia?' His voice was harsh again, demanding.

Her head whipped around; she studied his face for meaning, for understanding. If she concentrated on his face then she would not have to look at his body, and maybe these strange, flipping sensations that churned in her belly, her breast, would disappear.

'You have nowhere left to run, Tavia,' Benois explained patiently. 'Ferchar will hunt you down. You must finish this now, whatever it is between you and him, otherwise you will run for ever.'

Chapter Eleven

❦

Tavia stood up, pivoting slowly on her leather soles, her frazzled nerves straining thinly under Benois's questioning perusal. Wrapping her arms across her chest, feeling the flex of the tight bandage against her hand, she knew he was right, damn him! There was nowhere she could hide from Ferchar. The man was well known for his grim tenacity; if he wanted something, then he would achieve it. Every instinct, every fibre of her being, badgered her to trust this man, to tell him of the mystery that surrounded her birth, the strange answers that Ferchar seemed to think she possessed. But how could she involve him in such personal matters? He regarded her as nothing more than a nuisance, making no effort to conceal his irritation on seeing her again at Dunswick. She must have imagined those fleeting bonds that tied them after her mother's death; he had effectively severed them by stealing away in the middle of the night.

Tavia balled her fists in frustration. The urge to sort out the problem gnawed at her, but at the moment her mind seemed washed with a blank, white exhaustion, devoid of solutions.

'Well, I can't stay here, can I?' she snapped, finally.

'Why not?' he questioned, equably. The hairs on his chest covered his smooth skin like golden down.

'This is your chamber,' she stuttered. 'Mayhap I should return to the chamber in which they locked me up.'

He frowned. 'What...so your whole escape attempt will come to nothing?'

'Well, what do you suggest?' Tavia forced her limbs to move around the bed, to walk up to him. Her mind worked uselessly, yielding no answer. 'I can think of nothing more.'

'Nay, surely not, surely the indefatigable Tavia of Mowerby can't have run out of ideas?' he mocked. 'What would you have done if you hadn't met me?'

'I would have left the castle, returned to the cottage.'

Benois raised his eyebrows. 'And Ferchar's men would have found you there the next morning, brought you back. And the whole thing would have started again.'

The energy drained from her; her body slumped, but she willed herself to remain standing, tipping her head defiantly to one side. 'So what is your suggestion?'

'That you stay in here tonight...and on the morrow I will ask King Henry to grant you protection from Ferchar. That way you'll have the English crown on your side.'

Laughter bubbled up inside her. 'But that's preposterous! Why would King Henry help me...a peasant? And you... why you're just a...' The word 'barbarian' echoed in her brain, but remained unsaid.

'A...what? A Brabanter...a mercenary fighter with nothing to lose? You're correct, Tavia, I am those things. But I am also a good friend to Henry, and that's what would count in this matter.'

Tavia picked at the fraying edge of her makeshift bandage, mute for a moment, trying to compel her sluggish brain to concentrate on his words. 'Why are you helping me?' she whispered. 'You were prepared to give me up back there on the stairwell. You've…you've made no secret of the fact that you want nothing further to do with me.' The image of their closeness in the barn at her cottage swept unbidden through her thoughts.

He touched her elbow lightly, his fingers whispering against the silk sleeve of her gown. Mesmerised by the polished beauty of his chest, she fell away, the backs of her knees bumping against the frame of the bed. How could he know that his brief touch sent of spiral of desire shooting through her body, direct to her heart?

'Despite what you think of me, I'm not completely heart-less, Tavia,' he replied slowly. Beneath her wide-eyed, luminous gaze, the last vestiges of his anger, that boiling rage he had experienced on seeing her at Dunswick Castle again, leaked away. 'I am well aware that you have nobody to protect you. Your parents have gone, you have no guardian.'

She shrugged her shoulders, toeing the ground with the soft leather of her slipper. 'I am not afraid, Benois.'

'I know, Tavia, I've seen more courage and bravery from you than most of my soldiers, but it wouldn't hurt to have someone on your side.'

A deep, shuddering breath of relief seized her body. *Someone on your side.* The words wove around her softly, permeating her skin like a balm. The hollow grief that had washed through her at her mother's death receded a little.

'Then I thank you,' she offered simply, stepping forward. Instinctively, she raised her good hand to the side of his face, a sincere gesture of gratitude, feeling the prickle of stubble against her palm. His hand came up immediately, over hers, nurturing warmth, the colour of his eyes sharpening to a deep, glittering jet. In the corner of the chamber, the loose burning coals shifted, tumbled within the charcoal brazier. Benois pressed her palm closer into his cheek, closing his eyes briefly at the delicious, floral scent of her skin, the exquisite touch of her fingertips. The steady beat of his heart lurched forwards, increasing rapidly at the maid's closeness.

'Benois…?' Tavia pulled tentatively at her hand, aware of the dangerous shift in atmosphere between them. 'Let go,' she murmured, 'please.' Her voice wavered, laced with a tremulous desire. How could she have let this happen; how could she, the ever sensible, practical Tavia of Mowerby, have allowed herself to desire this man? But she knew why; beneath that cold, war-roughened exterior she had glimpsed something else: a heart capable of kindness and compassion.

The stern lines of his face grew solid, inflexible at her plea; his body stiffened as he tried to ignore the unwanted rush of feelings coursing through his body. Guilt nipped at him; he cursed his inability to remain unresponsive around her, to remember what he was, who he was in her presence. What kind of magic did she weave, with her dark red hair and her cornflower-blue eyes? Christ in Heaven, he was a soldier, not some lackwit dog trained to follow a lady's skirts! Yet the last time he'd been with her, he'd poured out the details of his past like some blubbering child, caught in the snare of her own grief. He drank in the fine details of her face, resenting her beauty, her kindness, hating her for dredging up the long-lost memories, for making him *feel* again. There was only one way to assuage this driving need for her, to dampen these flames of yearning.

Benois dropped his hand, only to wrap his bare arms around her, welding her to his unyielding, muscular frame. Tavia's eyes widened as his chestnut head dipped, his lips lowering to meet hers. Heart pounding in her chest, she leaned backwards, away from him. 'Nay, Benois, you must not do this,' she protested faintly. But already, as his big body loomed closer, a fluidity coursed through her muscles, making a mockery of her half-hearted objection. The raw, masculine scent of him tormented her nostrils, an earthy, spicy tone that plucked at her heartstrings. Arms braced around her waist, he drew her slowly upwards, giving him greater access to her mouth, his lips slanting across hers, greedy, unremitting. A deep hankering ignited in her belly, a craving for something more, for something unknown. Her hands, hands that rested lightly on the solid panels of his chest with the thought of pushing him away, now crept upwards to the corded muscles of his neck. Her legs, her whole body, weakened under the onslaught of his mouth, the deepening demands of his kiss, and she crumpled against him, unresisting, lost.

As her slim frame sagged against him, he felt no elation at the conquest. He was using her to prove a point, to establish that he could possess her without emotion, without any depth of feeling. He would claim her with that pure cold-heartedness for which he was notorious. But as his hands roved across the sensuous lines of her body, down the graceful line of her back, the gentle curve of her hip, odd little voices began to clamour in his brain, warning him. He paid them no heed, forcing them to the darkest recesses of his mind. He prided himself on his self-control, his ability to remain detached from situations, to be uninvolved. This encounter, like all his other meaningless liaisons with women, would be just the same. Cold, indifferent, detached.

Except…it wasn't. Tavia's face, alive and sweet with passion, turned up towards him like a flower in sunlight, trusting, naïve. Her expression drew him down, down to a place he had only been when his mother, his sister, had been alive…that of love. Nay…nay…it couldn't be! His heart clenched with the knowledge, then burst into a frenzy of uncontrollable desire. The layers of hurt, of pain, peeled back; his whole world shifted, teetering on the edge of unreality. A wildness crashed into him, a grim desperation to finish what he had started seized his limbs, his brain, driving him onwards. Gripping her arms, he edged her up against the bed, tipping her back on to the furs in a puddle of skirts. He just needed to end this, to possess her, then this intense raft of feeling would disappear, and he would be in control once more.

'What are you doing?' As her spine bounced against the mattress, a coil of doubt snaked through Tavia's heart. She forced herself to steady her breathing, to slow the headlong thumping of her heart. Benois's face, lit by the flickering wall sconces, was forbidding, predatory. He flung his big body beside her, not meeting her eyes, his fingers tearing at the side-lacings of her gown, impatient with the thin leather thongs. Tavia reached over to stroke his hair, but he jerked away at her touch.

'You know what comes next, Tavia...you know where this is going?' His voice splashed over her, rough, cold. She stared at him aghast, the heated blood in her veins stilling to ice. In his frustration, Benois tore at the side-lacings, ripping the material on the side of her dress. Incensed, she slapped at his hand. His face loomed up to hers, impassive, eyes narrowed to dangerous slits. 'Do you want it...or nay?'

'Nay!' she shouted at him. 'Not like this!' Tavia sat up abruptly, hands covering her face, ashamed by her wanton behaviour, appalled at the change in him. Tears welled in her eyes, and she dashed them away, hurriedly, hoping he wouldn't notice.

He sprung up from the bed then, moving away from her with powerful strides, chestnut hair flaring in the golden light of the torches. 'What other way is there, Tavia?' he demanded, a note of despair hitching his voice.

Tavia's vision blurred with tears as she studied her hands folded into her lap. The flesh of her body still hummed, still throbbed from the ferocity of his passion. Why did it have to be him, this big man of war? She desired him with an intensity that scared her, that drove her to such extreme heights of exhilaration she wanted to scream out loud with sheer joy. But his indifference, that blank look in his eyes, frightened her more than anything.

'The way of love,' she replied, a catch to her voice. She spoke of a subject about which she possessed little knowledge, having never been intimate with a man before, yet she spoke from the heart.

His mouth curled into a sneer. 'I've no time for that. When I buried my mother and my sister, all my love was buried, too.'

'Then that's a shame,' Tavia answered slowly.

'Why?' His gaze raked her bitterly.

'Because without love, you may as well be dead.' Her huge azure eyes searched the stern lines of his face for some hint of understanding, for some softening of his earlier roughness. 'What sort of life is that, to live it without love, without emotion or feeling?'

'I seem to live all right.'

'Do you?'

He fixed his eyes on the bare boards of the floor, unwilling to deal with the emotions that seemed to churn in his chest every time he encountered this woman. His life had been so simple before he had met her, so unchallenging, so easy. Why did she force him to question the whole time, force him to think about what had gone before, and what might come after?

'Go to sleep.' He deliberately ignored her lilting questions, unwilling to admit that maybe, just maybe, the maid's words held the truth. 'Over there.' He pointed at a low pallet bed in the corner of the chamber, made up with a few blankets. 'I'll take the bed.'

The pallet in the corner of Benois's chamber had been furnished with a sturdy, horsehair mattress, before being made up with fine linen sheets and furs. Tavia curled on to the mattress, pulling the covers tightly up to her neck. A sadness clung to her heart, a sadness beset with Benois's raw, stricken expression as he stared across the chamber towards her. Yet despite his brusque, curt behaviour, she knew, she knew that deep down, there was the faint gleam of something she could hold close to her heart.

She forced herself to remain awake, resolutely holding open her aching, exhausted eyelids until she could hear the deep, even breathing from the bed. Under the suffocating mound of bedclothes, her skin prickled uncomfortably; she had climbed under the covers fully dressed. She shifted her head on the pillow, trying to make out Benois's shape in the cloying darkness; he appeared to be sleeping soundly. She slid out from beneath the bedcovers, hesitating fractionally as the straw within the mattress rustled with her furtive movement. With the wooden shutters clamped firmly over the window embrasures, and no light coming from the corridor outside, the room was lit only by the faintest glow from the charcoal brazier, on the other side of the room. Standing up, she used her fingers to finish the work that Benois had started, fumbling for her side-lacings. Feeling the fabric slacken off around her waist, she bent down and pulled the whole gown over her head, throwing the hampering fabric on to the pallet with a sigh of relief. Checking that

Benois still slept, she bent over once more and grabbed the hem of her underdress, again drawing the whole garment upwards, struggling with the tight sleeves over the bulkiness of her bandaged hand.

She had already kicked off her shoes before flinging herself on the bed, and now she rolled down her woollen stockings, bundling them up individually to tuck them neatly in her shoes. Clad only in her loose white shift, Tavia stood for a moment, savouring the soft air flowing about her freed arms and legs. She lifted her good hand, absentmindedly kneading the muscles at the back of her neck. If only she could have a bath!

Searching the darkness for some alternative, she spotted a jug and basin set on an oak coffer, next to the charcoal brazier. The temptation of cool water against her skin loomed too large to resist, and, praying ardently that Benois would not wake up, she tiptoed over to the other side of the room, relishing the feel of the polished oak floorboards beneath the bare soles of her feet.

Lifting the heavy jug awkwardly, Tavia poured the water as quietly as she could into the basin, her fingers seizing on a pristine washcloth. Dipping the cloth in the water, letting it float for a moment to absorb the cool water, she wrung it out, uncaring that she soaked the bandage around her hand.

Pressing the wet cloth to the heated skin of her face and neck, she almost cried out loud at the sweet sensation, tilting her head back so she could smooth the flannel down her neck. Rivulets of water trailed down the slender column of her throat, trickling down between her breasts. She sunk the cloth once more into the water, barely wringing it out this time, but squeezing it hurriedly to the curving hollow at the base of her neck, before sliding it along her outstretched arm.

* * *

From the bed, Benois watched her, half-shuttered eyes sparkling, keen. The tantalising whisper of clothes being removed had alerted him, but he had kept his eyes closed, curious to discover the maid's intentions. He had not slept, Tavia's words churning in his brain, challenging him. His thuggish behaviour had been appalling, threatening even, throwing her down on the bed as if she were nothing better than a low-born camp whore. Guilt churned in his gut, lacerating his conscience. He let his breath out, slowly, regretfully, opening his eyes at the slap of water in the earthenware basin.

His traitorous senses leapt at the sight of Tavia clad only in her diaphanous chemise; he held his breath, following her sensual movements. Dipping her head forwards, looping her braid over her shoulder to expose the delicate bone structure of her neck, Tavia applied the saturated cloth to the back of her neck. He imagined the droplets spilling over the fine skin of her back, her delicate shoulder blades, beneath the gauzy shift. With her arm raised, bent at the elbow, the light from the charcoal brazier highlighted the translucent quality of her skin, the fragile hairs on her arm creating a spangled aura about her bare skin. Like an angel.

He drew a deep, stumbling breath. What was happening to him? His attempt to possess her had failed, and he knew why—despite what he thought he would achieve, he had no wish to treat her like all those other faceless women he had lain with. She was so unlike anyone he had ever met before, so kind and good and forgiving. Every moment he spent with her, he felt his own emotional coldness begin to melt, the numbness that had beset him for years starting to recede, his body and mind beginning to come alive once more.

Tavia whirled around at the slight sound from the bed, eyes

seeking Benois in the darkness, the soaking washcloth scrunched to a ball in one hand, scattering pearls of water to the floor.

His gaze flared at the breathtaking sight of her: the dampened bodice of her chemise revealed the soft, shadowy curves of her breast, the seductive indentation of her waist...

'I thought you were asleep!' she spluttered, crossing her arms defensively in front of her. He grimaced, sitting up abruptly in the bed, his eyes averted. The sheet slipped down about his waist, exposing the rugged musculature of his chest.

Turning her back, Tavia flung the washcloth back into the bowl. The material made a soft, plashing sound, slopping the water over the sides of the reddish earthenware bowl and on to the light oak wood of the coffer. Benois reached down and grabbed his linen shirt, discarded at the foot of the bed. He pulled it over his head, leaning back against the pillow.

'I'm sorry,' he said abruptly. His words, unexpected, were clipped, toneless.

Tavia moved back to the pallet bed, pulling a blanket over her thin chemise. 'Why? You weren't to know that I wanted to wash.' Her face shone out of the darkness, pale and exhausted.

Benois flinched at the softness of her tone. 'Nay, not because of that.' The halting regret in his voice caught her attention, forced her to look at him. 'Because of the way I treated you. I...I'm sorry.'

Her breath twisted, snared in her chest. Without thinking, she stepped towards the side of the bed, her limbs shaky from the impact of his apology. 'You scared me,' she whispered, the fingers of her left hand trailing across the fine pelt of the bed fur.

'I know.' He reached up, touching the sweet curve of her

chin, his fingers skimming the loose, lustrous tendrils of her hair. 'I thought it was the only way I could...' He stopped, his hands falling back on to the bedcovers, fists clenching. A muscle jumped in the corded hollow of his neck. How could he tell her that he believed that by bedding her, his ravaging desire would be sated, satisfied and he would be free again, free from the lurching emotions that this maid engendered within him? 'I thought it was the only way...I could be free of you,' he explained hollowly.

Chapter Twelve

The morning light filtered through the uneven gaps in the wooden shutters, creating fragments of light on the floor of the chamber allocated to King Henry. Yet despite the earliness of the hour, the energetic king had risen already and now paced the room in consternation.

'What in God's name has got into you, Benois?' Henry turned to his most trusted commander-in-chief, who lounged nonchalantly against the side of the window embrasure. 'I've never heard anything so preposterous in my whole life!' Half-dressed in his linen shirt and braies, the king began to stride across his chamber again, a frustrated edge to his dynamic gait, pursued by his squire who, clutching the king's surcoat, scampered after him.

Benois sighed, reaching up one hand to undo the wrought-iron catch that held the shutters closed, folding one back against the stone wall. The wide sleeve of his dark green surcoat fell back slightly, revealing the gathered cuff of his shirt, stark white against the tanned skin of his wrist. Columns of light shafted into the chamber, and he peered out, his gaze drifting over the pattern of rolling fields that stretched beyond the city outskirts to the craggy hills beyond. Had the chit really changed him that much? He knew what he requested of the king was unusual, went against his normal character, whatever that was, but preposterous? Never that, where she was involved.

'Who is the maid, anyway? Is she of noble birth?' Henry turned his sparkling, gimlet eyes towards Benois.

'Nay, she's a peasant….with the makings of a fine cross-bowman, though.' Benois leaned his palms flat on the window ledge, peering right over the edge of the high window down to the inner bailey. For some unknown reason, the image of Tavia, thrown back against the bed furs, her pulse beating frantically at the base of her slender neck, burst into his brain. He dug his fingers into the gritty stone.

Henry threw his arms into the air, hands outstretched in a dramatic gesture of disbelief, before resuming his furious pacing. 'This is the first time, the first time, Benois, since we were knights in training together in Anjou, that I have ever doubted your impeccable judgement…why, it's the first time you've ever shown any concern towards a woman since… since…' Henry stuttered to an uncomfortable halt, reddening at the words he had been about to say.

Benois surveyed his king coolly; he was used to the customary rages, the tirades and outbursts, but at the moment he did not feel inclined to help Henry out of the embarrassing silence.

'It's what makes you my best knight, Benois,' Henry's voice boomed out over the stilted pause, 'the fact that you're so emotionally hard-headed. Even in the heat of battle you never lose your direction, your focus—and I have no intention of losing that. If you've lost your heart to some low-born Scottish peasant girl, then you need to end it…quickly.'

'The girl means nothing to me,' Benois heard himself

saying, 'other than Lord Ferchar seems to be showing an unusual interest in her. I think it would be to our advantage if we offered her protection. She obviously has something Ferchar wants; with it, we may gain some political advantage over him.'

'Then he'll be loathe to give her up without a fight, Benois. And at this delicate stage of negotiation over the border lands, I'm reluctant to add any other conditions to the deal.'

Benois pushed himself upwards and back from the stone window, coming back into the chamber. 'So you'll not help her.'

'Nay, Benois, I will not.' Henry's eyes gleamed. 'Nay, the only way that girl can gain our protection is if you bed her and marry her yourself.' He cackled with laughter, raising a surprisingly white hand to his lips. 'And I can't see that happening in a million years, can you? Everyone knows how you feel about marriage, about the humdrum nature of domestic life. Besides, I would never give my blessing to such a liaison: a high-born noble tied to a peasant chit…it doesn't bear thinking about. And…' he wagged a finger in the air '…I don't want to lose my best soldier…or my friend.'

'It would change nothing,' Benois replied slowly. 'I would still be the same man.'

'Don't you believe it.' Henry waggled his fingers. 'I've seen men, great knights, brought to their knees by mewling women. Don't go that way, Benois. Never that way. Remember the coin you can earn with me—you don't want to forgo that.'

The fire in the great hall, unhelpfully lit with wet wood, belched out huge gasps of ashy smoke, making the few people in the hall cough and splutter while they attempted to break their fast. Peasants rubbed at their eyes, smarting from the acrid nature of the smoke, whilst digging into their bowls of warm gruel, or broke into fresh rounds of bread.

'Good God!' bellowed Ferchar furiously, as he entered the hall, the impressive length of his fur-lined cloak sweeping through the wisps of straw that lay scattered about the floor. 'What have those lackwit servants gone and done now?' He coughed at length as he climbed the steps to the top table, before plonking himself down into his seat next to Malcolm. 'Mother of Mary, you think we pay them enough, with all the meals and lodging on top, and yet they still can't do a job properly!'

'The wood was wet.' Malcolm explained, chewing dully on his bread roll. His red hair hung down limply around his rounded features, making him look far younger than his nearly sixteen years.

'I can see that!' Ferchar said irritably. 'The fact is…oh! I don't even know why I'm discussing such trivial domestic matters!' He thumped the wooden planks of the table, causing the pewter platters to jump. 'Have you sorted out the plan for today's hunting? We need something to keep King Henry sweet.'

Malcolm wondered when he had become Ferchar's servant. Surely it was supposed to be the other way around? Ferchar was supposed to be helping him—he was the king, wasn't he? But it did seem easier this way, especially as Ferchar seemed to have the authority and experience when dealing with the English king. Somehow he felt happier deferring that responsibility. 'Aye, the stables are saddling extra horses, and a picnic is being prepared for us to take out.'

'Excellent.' Ferchar rubbed his hands, before frowning, suddenly. 'And any news on our…er…other problem?'

'The soldiers can't find her anywhere. Young Wulfric has a lump on his head the size of an egg.'

'Bloodthirsty wench! Just wait till I get my hands on her. She can't have gone far. Make sure the soldiers cover every inch of the city. All the gatehouses were alerted last night. We'll hunt her down.'

'I hope you do. I'd like to know my "new" older sister.'

Ferchar laughed. 'Probably a bit uncouth for your refined tastes, Malcolm. Remember, the girl's been brought up as a peasant. Anyway, there's plenty of time for all that after she's found the fortune that her father, Earl Henry, has hidden away somewhere.' He stuffed a spoonful of porridge into his mouth, loose globules of white sticky oats spilling over his chin. He wiped them away with the sleeve of his surcoat. 'And none of this to the English king; I don't want him knowing of this gold, or he'll want...well, well, well.'

Ferchar stopped mid-sentence as his gaze riveted to the door at the back of the great hall. Through the wreaths of grey smoke, the diminutive figure of Tavia appeared, flanked by the heftier bulk of an English soldier, immediately recognisable as one of the nobles who had accompanied King Henry the previous night.

'Ah! My good man!' Standing up, Ferchar raised his right arm to gain Benois's attention. 'Thank the Lord you've found her; we were beginning to worry. Both of you, do come and join us to break your fast.' He motioned to the bench beside him.

Tavia grimaced at the patronising note in Ferchar's tone— surely he didn't expect Benois to believe in this thin veneer of benevolence? No doubt this obsequious behaviour from Ferchar was entirely due to the forbidding figure at her side. She noticed how the peasants looked up to him as they walked beside the trestle tables, heard the muted whispers of awe as they exchanged their scant knowledge on the infamous English commander.

'It seems your fame precedes you.' Tavia glanced up at him as he took her elbow to help her up the steps to the dais.

'And not all of it good, I suspect,' he replied, a terse smile about his mouth.

One foot on the first step, Tavia gaped at him, incredulous. Was he actually apologising for some of his past deeds? Was he beginning to regret all the fighting and the bloodshed?

'Close your mouth,' he murmured, one hand moving to the side of her hip to give her a little push. 'And get a move on.'

'You are in no position to order me about,' she hissed down at him. 'Especially after what happened last night.'

He flushed, the colour washing over his high cheekbones. 'For which I have apologised,' he reminded her swiftly. She scampered up the last steps, lest he should be tempted to boost her on again. Knowing the regent's unpredictable moods, she approached Ferchar with trepidation; Benois had already told her that King Henry was not prepared to grant her any protection against this man. Loathe to admit it, she was glad of Benois's burly frame at her side.

'So, have you come to your senses, my lady?' Ferchar flicked his watery, fish-like eyes over her.

Tavia lifted her chin. 'What do you want of me, Lord Ferchar?' Her tones, quiet and modulated, sang out over the noisy chattering that filled the hall.

Ferchar narrowed his eyes. 'You know what I want, Tavia,' he hissed. 'The knife. I want you to tell me the meaning on the knife.' He glanced at Benois, unwilling to involve the English knight in the affair; no doubt he would run to King Henry at the earliest opportunity. 'Rumour has it that Earl Henry told his daughter of the place where he had hidden the…' He wavered for a moment, looking at Benois once more. 'Well, you know, the subject that we talked of last night. His youngest daughter, Ada, knows nothing. You're his eldest, therefore he must have told you. If he gave you the knife, then he must have given you some hint, some clue…?'

Benois, intent on the interplay between Ferchar and Tavia, but content to keep quiet and study the calm beauty of Tavia's face, frowned suddenly, jolted out of his calm reverie. 'Is this true?' He snared Tavia's arm in a firm grip, the movement insisting that she look up to him. 'That you're the daughter of the late Earl Henry?' The warmth of his fingers seared through the coarse wool of her sleeve.

Her azure eyes lifted, a breathtaking clarity in their depths. 'I suppose it must be,' she replied gloomily. 'My mother, God rest her soul, tried to tell me as she was dying, but I refused to believe her.'

'Of course she is!' snapped Ferchar, annoyed that Benois had interrupted him. 'Why, if you saw her and Ada together, why, they're the spit of each other. Aye, she's one of Earl Henry's byblows, make no mistake.'

Tavia bristled under Ferchar's sneering tone. 'It wasn't like that between him and my mother—they loved each other!'

'Hah! So you'd like to think!' Ferchar smiled contemptuously. 'Don't kid yourself that your father was a saint when it came to finding suitable bedmates!' Leaning forward, Ferchar curled his fingers around the jewelled knife that lay on the table, handing it to her. 'Here, take this. Study it while you eat; you may come up with some ideas.'

Taking the knife by the hilt, Tavia sensed Benois's eyes on her as she stepped forwards over the bench and sat down, leaving a space between herself and Ferchar for Benois. The comforting curve of his upper arm pressed into her shoulder as he took his place next to her.

'How long have you known?' Benois murmured to her, beginning to heap her pewter platter with food. Setting the knife down before her, Tavia watched as the pile of food grew higher and higher: three rolls of bread, several slices of cheese and cold meat, three apples...

She clutched at his sleeve. 'Benois, stop! I'll never eat this much!'

'How long have you known?' he asked again, calmly swapping her plate for his empty one, and placing one bread roll and one slice of cheese on her plate.

The knife glinted on the oak boards next to her plate; she picked it up, turning it between her fingers, wondering at the slight accusation in Benois's tone.

'As I said, my mother talked of Earl Henry as she lay dying; I thought she was rambling so I didn't know what to believe.'

'She never said anything before that time?'

Tavia lifted her gaze to him. 'Nay, she never spoke of it.' The delicate tracery of flowers caught in the gleam of the candles; they were small, but distinctive, five petals enhanced by trailing filigreed foliage. Leaning into Benois's comforting side, so that only he could hear the murmur of her words, she said, 'I could be here for ever unless I find this gold for him.'

'Is that what he thinks this knife holds the key to? Gold?'

'Aye, and he's never going to let me go unless I find it.'

Benois glanced up and caught Ferchar's jealous, possessive look riveted on Tavia's neat head as she bent over the knife. And he might not let you go even if you do, he thought.

The distinctive sound of bits jangling between the teeth of horses, and grooms calling to each other across the bailey, dragged Tavia reluctantly from sleep the following morning.

Ferchar, his behaviour no doubt modified to leniency by
Benois's overbearing presence, had graciously allowed Tavia
to sleep in a comfortable, unlocked chamber. The regent's
meaningful expression, however, as he had instructed a
servant to prepare a better room for her, indicated that he still
expected her to come up with a location for Earl Henry's
treasure. Thankfully, she had seen no more of Ferchar that
day, nor Benois either. The men had spent the day hunting
in the forests, with the intention of discussing the border
issues as they rode.

Tavia had spent most of the previous day in Ada's child-
like company, listening to the younger girl chatter on about
her life at court. At times, the princess seemed much younger
than her eighteen years, a legacy of having spent her whole
life closeted by the rarefied upbringing of a noblewoman.
From time to time, Tavia would glance at the maid, still astounded that they should share the same father, that royal
blood ran in her veins. Her muscles had ached from following Ada around the castle, the stables and the grounds; she
was glad to sit down for the evening meal which they ate in
the comfortable surroundings of the women's solar.

The shouts from below echoed more loudly, more insis-
tently. Tavia sprung from the bed, bolting to the window embrasure to push aside the tanned hide that covered the opening
in the thick stone wall. Balancing her palms on the ledge, she
leaned forwards, trying to glimpse what was happening down
below. A cool breeze brushed her heated face, sifted through
the looping tendrils of her hair as it spilled over the stone ledge
like a magnificent red banner of glory. From this high vantage
point, she watched the tall, commanding figure of Benois
pulling on his thick, leather gauntlets as he strode out over the
cobbles to his horse, already saddled and pawing the ground
impatiently at the sight of his master. King Henry walked

alongside Benois, talking animatedly, his arms flicking emphatically into the air with decisive gestures. Benois, his face impassive, listened attentively, nodding in agreement now and again.

Her heart deflated with a jolt. Where was he going? Without thinking, her brain befuddled from sleep, she grabbed a fur from the bed to throw around her shoulders, to cover her thin nightgown, before wrenching open the chamber door. She plunged down the shadowed stairs, unmindful of the freezing stone against her bare feet, hoping that the door at the bottom would lead out on to the inner bailey. As she reached the lowest step, trying to gain her bearings in the sepulchral gloom, the door leading to the outside suddenly opened inwards, flooding the small space with clear, blinding light.

'Oh!' Tavia blinked in surprise. 'It's you!'

Benois, the dark grey of his eyes streaked with silver, stood on the threshold, dressed in chainmail. The fine links of his hauberk fitted his upper body like a second skin, shimmering like the scales of a fish with the tiniest movement. The hauberk fell to his knees, where he had dispensed with the usual chainmail leggings in favour of braies cut from a supple leather. His boots, expertly constructed from a thicker hide, were closed with leather laces that extended from the top of his foot before criss-crossing over solid calf muscles to his knees. Over the top of his hauberk, he wore a surcoat of red, emblazoned with the two golden lions of King Henry. The lions glittered in the half-light as he bowed formally. 'Good morning, Princess.'

Was it her imagination, or did his tone contain the faint hint of mockery? No doubt he wanted to chastise her for not revealing her secrets earlier. 'Nay, don't address me so.' Tavia frowned at him.

'But it's what you are, my lady.' He folded his arms across his chest, assessing her languidly.

'Nay,' she explained. 'I may be Earl Henry's daughter, but because of my illegitimacy, the title is not recognised.'

'Even so, royal blood flows in your veins, which gives you certain rights and privileges; there's no denying that.'

The cold from the flagstones seeped through the skin on the soles of her feet; she shivered slightly, chewing on her bottom lip. 'I should have told you sooner...I...I should have trusted you.'

Benois laughed, the sound immediately dissipating the strained atmosphere between them. 'Nay, no matter, maid. I can understand why you chose not to...trusting someone else is something we both find difficult.'

He jerked his head around suddenly as someone shouted his name from the yard, then turned back to her, speaking with low urgency. 'Tavia...I have to go...King Henry wants me to go with young Malcolm, visit a couple of the more intractable Scottish barons who might prove difficult along the border. I was coming to see you...to tell you.'

'Will it be dangerous?' she uttered, eyeing his chainmail, fighting to hold back the crestfallen note in her voice.

'I doubt it,' he murmured. 'Why? Are you concerned for my safety? I thought you'd be glad to see the back of me.'

'I am,' she responded dubiously.

'And don't worry about Ferchar. Henry will stay here—he has promised to keep you safe...now he knows you're of royal blood.' He uttered a short bark of laughter. 'I trust my King with my life, and so should you.'

'I will.'

'It was kind of you to come down and see me off.' Benois swept an amused, wary look over her tousled hair, the cumbersome fur around her shoulders that highlighted the delicacy of her face to sweet perfection, her naked toes peeking out from under the long hem of her nightgown. 'Even if you did forget to put your shoes on.' The corners of his mouth crinkled up into a smile. Against the dull grey of the flagstones, her feet glowed pale pink, a pearly pink like the luminous innards of a shell. He longed to touch them, to kiss them. His fingers curled within the stiff leather of his gauntlets. After his last disastrous encounter with Tavia, he had made a promise to himself that he would never touch her again.

'Well, I must take my leave.' His voice held a throaty edge. Tavia made a movement, as if she intended following him into the bailey, but he stayed her, one gloved hand pressed against the soft rounded edge of her shoulder. 'Nay, don't come out, the cobbles are filthy...besides...' he leaned closer '...dressed like that, you'll attract too much attention.' He swept one last lingering glance over her glorious *déshabillé*: the auburn tresses of hair tumbling with wild abandonment over her shoulders, the gauziness of her linen nightgown revealing more than concealing the shapely length of her legs.

Trembling beneath the seductive possessiveness of his voice, she watched him power across the slick, greasy cobbles, leaning weakly against the door jamb. Her position shielded her from most of the soldiers, and she kept herself within the shadowed recess of the door. Benois reached his destrier, nodding to Henry before throwing himself up into the saddle, snatching up the reins to wheel the animal about. Beside him, Malcolm had already mounted up, and now was fiddling nervously with his stirrup.

His eyes sought out Tavia's small figure in the doorway, made more fragile in appearance by the thick oak arch that framed her. Her candid expression shone out, her skin luminous in the shadows, following his every movement. Benois swallowed, trying to fight back the desire that boiled within him. Just one kiss, he thought, the ironclad bonds of his promise slipping apart at the sight of her. Just one kiss and then I will be gone.

He tapped his heels gently against the horse's flank, urging the animal around to the open doorway where she stood, and swept his whole upper body down from the saddle to seize her up, one powerful arm manacled against the curve of her spine. He brought his mouth over hers in a brief, passionate kiss, his firm lips plundering her softness, her vulnerability. In a flash, he had placed her carefully down on the step again, running one unsteady hand through his hair, his eyes the colour of a knife-edge.

'I needed something to remember you by,' he explained roughly, his voice laced with the jagged edge of longing, 'but I find it is not enough.' He reached out his leather-covered fingers, catching at a stray silken loop of her hair to tuck it behind her ear.

'Stay safe, Tavia.'

She stared at him. Memories came flooding back at his gruff utterance.

'Don't look so shocked, Tavia. It was just a kiss.' He grinned, attempting to negate his own strong surge of desire.

'Nay, it's not the kiss,' she replied shakily, 'it was how you tucked my hair behind my ear. Like that, leaning down from your horse.'

He shrugged his shoulders. 'What of it?'

'I know where Earl Henry hid his treasure, Benois. I know what the message on the knife means.' Her mind flooded with strong, vivid memories.

Benois cursed. 'God in Heaven, woman. You do pick your moments!' He glanced over at Henry, who beckoned impatiently, wanting them to move off. 'Listen to me, Tavia, do nothing until I return. I'll not be gone above two nights. Do nothing. Promise?'

The steel grey of his eyes held hers.

'I promise.'

'Good girl.'

Tavia watched the proud, broad line of his back as he led the small party of Scottish and English soldiers out through the main gate. Then he was gone.

Chapter Thirteen

Mindful of the injury across her palm, Tavia used her right hand to support the heavy yew crossbow as she lifted the end of the stock to her eye, sighting the target. Her muscles ached a little, as if complaining against the unwieldy weight of the bow. She had begged the weapon from the castle armoury, in an attempt to make the hours pass more quickly while Benois was away. The strengthening sun warmed the back of her neck as she viewed the large disc of compacted straw, the centre daubed with animal blood to make a target. Drifts of pink and white blossom blew sporadically across the archery practice area, sailing over the orchard wall to settle on the grass like circles of white lace.

Tavia sighed, lowering the crossbow as she spotted the sylph-like figure of Ada slip through the wooden gate that connected the orchard to the archery area. Caught up in her own thoughts, she had hoped to escape Ada's constant prattle, at least until the noon bell, yet it seemed her younger sibling was relentless in her pursuit.

'I've been looking everywhere for you!' gasped Ada, reaching over to clutch at Tavia's sleeve. 'Of course I'd forgotten how skilful you are with a crossbow; I should have looked here first.' A gown of light blue complemented Ada's auburn hair, matching the ribbons that had been carefully braided into her long swinging plait.

'It helps to keep in practice,' Tavia explained defensively.

Ada nodded disinterestedly, instead casting a doubtful look over Tavia's coarse *bliaut*, woven loosely from a serviceable grey wool, over the frayed cuffs of her underdress of brown linen. 'Ferchar asked me to find you some decent clothes.'

'How kind of him,' murmured Tavia.

Ada's eyes lit up, a beatific expression crossing her face at the mention of Ferchar. 'He is always kind,' she intoned. 'He was quite right when he said you can't go around dressed like this any more, not if you're Earl Henry's daughter…and my sister!' Ada seized Tavia's hand eagerly, her manner animated. 'I can't believe we're related; I've always wanted a sister, and now I have one!'

Tavia watched Ada's intense, vivacious expression as she chatted away, and was surprised that she didn't feel a stronger bond with the girl. A vague feeling nagged away at the base of her consciousness: a feeling that something was not quite right with Ada. She appeared as someone out of kilter with the rest of the world, possessed by a manic desperation that coloured every gesture, every nuance of tone.

'Have you thought any further about the knife? What it means?' Ada asked abruptly, in a sing-song voice. She's been sent by Ferchar, thought Tavia immediately, detecting the false note in Ada's speech.

'Nay, nothing,' she replied blandly, hugging the secret close. When Benois had leaned down from his horse yesterday morning, tucking the wisp of hair behind her ear, she had been carried back to an earlier time, to a spring day when she had walked with her mother up over the moors behind their cottage. They were going to meet someone, her mother had said, someone important to them. They had walked across the craggy, windswept moor for more than an hour, before dropping down into a narrow, sunlit valley, bisected by a tumbling stream. Densely wooded with the ghostly white stems of birch and the thick, sinewy structures of oak, the valley appeared as a secret place, undiscovered and untouched by man. Stepping along the bare, dry earth of a sheep path, Tavia had looked up and almost gasped out loud in wonder. Ahead, a magnificent oak spread long, muscular branches wide, incandescent with new shining leaves in the early sun. Beneath this sentinel of the woods lay a carpet of flowers: stunning pale wood anemones, five white petals around orange stamens, spangled over the mossy ground.

'What a beautiful place.' Tavia had reached forward to touch her mother's back with her fingers.

'I know,' her mother had answered. 'It's why we chose it.'

A man on horseback had been waiting for them, dressed in the royal colours of his brother, King David. At their approach, he had dismounted, smiling at the daughter he had never seen. She had been too young to realise the full implications of the meeting, but now, now in the light of what had occurred in the past few days, these events had moved sharply into focus—this handsome man had been her father. He had brought some food and they shared it under the oak tree together. And when he had kissed them both, and bid them *adieu*, he had climbed on his horse. At the last moment, he had leant his big frame down from the horse, and, tucking Tavia's hair behind her ear, had spoken those words: 'Stay safe, my sweet.' The flowers in that valley, those pale windflowers that fluttered against the breeze, were the same flowers etched into the knife slung into the leather scabbard around her hips.

'Haven't you had any ideas?' Ada's plaintive cry interrupted her reverie.

'Nay, I said not,' Tavia responded reluctantly. 'Come, why not show me these clothes you've found?'

Ada's eyes widened with pleasure, keen to forget the request that Ferchar had asked of her. She wound Tavia's arm through her own, and they walked together out of the archery area, passing through the courtyard at the back of the kitchens where the low bushes had been draped with laundry to dry, and through into the inner bailey. Tavia's heart sunk as she saw Ferchar and King Henry locked in conversation by the main door of the castle. Ada's arm tensed against her own as they approached; Tavia sensed her fear. Both women made a low curtsy.

'Ah! The two sisters together! How charming!' Ferchar exclaimed, his gaze slithering lustfully over Tavia's neat figure.

'Hello, my darling!' Tavia looked on in surprise as Ada coiled her arms about Ferchar's neck. There was obviously far more between these two than first appeared. Ferchar pushed Ada away, irritated. 'Good God, woman!' he blustered. 'How many times have I told you about displays of affection in public? It lowers my standing among the people!'

'I'm sorry.' Ada stepped away, ducking her head. 'It won't happen again.'

'Just make sure it doesn't,' Ferchar snapped. He cast a disparaging glance at Tavia. 'I thought I told you to find some clothes for…er…her.'

'We were just on our way, my lord,' Tavia spoke gently, hoping to alleviate Ada's mistake. 'She had a little trouble finding me, that's all.'

'Just make sure we can find you, my lady. King Henry has persuaded me to give you more freedom than I would like.'

'But it does no harm to rein these women in now and again,' said Henry. He stared down his nose at Tavia, running his eye contemptuously over her neat figure.

He disapproves of me, she thought, in shock. I wonder why? Benois obviously held his king in high esteem; for his sake, she wanted to as well, at least till Benois returned.

'May I borrow the lady for a few moments?' Henry turned to Ferchar, who inclined his head in agreement. Panic slid through her veins as Henry patted her arm in an avuncular fashion, despite being almost the same age as Benois, and began to steer her in the direction of the gardens. 'Now, you think I am displeased with you, but I assure you, that is not the case.' They walked past the southern end of the castle, the grey stone walls towering high on their left-hand side, until they reached the wide spread of the vegetable garden set between coarse stone walls. The garden had been laid out into a series of rectangular beds, uneven cobbled paths in between. Neat rows of vegetables sprang up from the rich, brown earth, not fully formed yet, pale green in their infancy. The spring sun had been unusually warm, encouraging the seeds to germinate earlier than expected. The fluttering green shoots of peas had already begun to twine up the hazel supports, bordered by the fleshy, rounded leaves of broad-bean plants. Tavia's heart twisted suddenly, a pang of longing for the small vegetable patch at the cottage, a pang of longing at the image of her mother kneeling in the earth, planting.

'I'm sorry, I didn't hear you,' she said suddenly, realising King Henry was talking to her.

'I said, "I don't want you to get hurt",' Henry replied patiently, stopping for a moment. The white ermine of his short cloak ruffled in the breeze.

She laughed. 'I doubt Ferchar could do any more to me than he's done already. Besides, it will all be over soon.'

'I wasn't talking about Lord Ferchar,' Henry cut in, a little tetchily, taking her arm and resuming his brisk pace. 'I was talking about Lord Benois.'

'Benois?' Her voice curled over the sound of his name.

'Aye. It appears there is something between the two of you. Yesterday morning, I saw you…in the bailey.'

'A kiss. It was nothing.' A blackbird, startled by their quiet approach, flew off, squawking, seeking refuge in some nearby bushes.

'Just so long as it is nothing. I hope you don't expect him to commit to…well, marriage, for example.'

'I don't expect him to commit to anything!' she protested. 'Least of all, me! I am nothing to him!'

It seemed as though Henry didn't hear her words. 'Because Benois would rather fall on his own sword than be trapped into anything so dull as the domestic apathy of marriage.'

'Then it's just as well I'm not planning on asking him,' she quipped back, a peculiar constriction binding her chest.

'He'd never marry, not after what happened to him…his family.' Oblivious to her light-hearted reply, Henry made the pronouncement dramatically, as if she had no knowledge of Benois's past.

'I know what happened to him, sire, and I'm sorry for it.'

'He told you?' Henry's keen hazel eyes narrowed, at once demanding more information. 'He told you what happened to his family?'

She nodded, amused by the look of puzzlement that crossed Henry's face, before he recovered enough to begin speaking once more. 'It was a horrible time, but because of it, he has become the greatest fighting man, the finest soldier I have ever seen.'

'Are you suggesting that's a good thing?' she blurted out, astonished.

'For me, aye, it is. And I don't want that to change.' Henry glared at her, his eyes piercing and intent. He's warning me off, she thought in a flash; he wants me away from Benois. She took a step back, hesitantly, a sense of disbelief washing over her. Henry's words held power and authority; he had known Benois for a long time, whereas she had known him…how long? Not above a handful of days. But since that kiss on the threshold, some brief, indefinable hope had flared within her, had grown, fed by the tiny crumbs Benois had thrown to her as he bade her farewell. He had apologised for the way he had treated her when she had slept in his chamber; aye, he had scared her, but he had also awoken in her a craving, a need that would not disappear.

She sighed, a long tremulous breath. The fragile idea, the dream she had begun to nurture, shattered into a million tiny pieces, dust in the wind. In truth, he had given her little, yet unwisely she had taken his small gestures of kindness and assembled them into something more meaningful, something greater! How could she ever hope to turn Benois away from a world of soldiering? It was his life. By heeding King Henry's words, she could leave now, before she made an even greater fool of herself, before Benois returned. And in order to leave, she would have to tell Ferchar the location of Earl Henry's gold.

Benois tightened the muscles of his honed inner thighs to squeeze his horse into a quick trot towards Dunswick Castle. Inside his steel helmet, his scalp felt sticky and hot; he longed to remove it and immerse himself in a cool bath. The ride back from the western border lands had been more than a day, over difficult, hostile terrain, yet all through that long journey, Benois couldn't work out why Henry had sent him on such a fruitless mission. Malcolm hadn't needed him—the young man's powers of communication were perfectly adequate for the task; in fact, dressed in English colours, Benois's presence had been more of a hindrance than a help, scaring people witless before Malcolm had had a chance to talk to them. After two days of marching from border castle to border castle, watching King Malcolm inform his people that King Henry now had control of the border lands, Benois made the decision to return to Dunswick to be with his king. And her.

The early afternoon sun beat down on his back, and, all about him, people were bustling about the town, faces happy and smiling as they went about their daily chores. Without openly acknowledging Benois's formidable presence, high on his black destrier, they made a path for him through the crowds, so he could reach the castle easily. He pulled lightly on the reins, slowing the horse to a walk as he approached the drawbridge to the castle, wincing at the pain in his right shoulder. Damn! He had thought the wound would have begun to hurt him less by now. The bundle of linens, wrapped over his shoulder and under his armpit to make a tight bandage underneath his hauberk, felt loose: it had come undone. His mouth tensed ruefully—only an amateur would have failed to notice the over-zealous guard at one of the border castles! Yet his mind had been elsewhere, and he had caught the sword point at the top of his arm, as the weapon had dug up along the loose sleeve of his chainmail.

The hooves of his horse clattering over the wooden draw-bridge, his heart lifted at the thought of seeing Tavia again. The memory of how she had looked on the day he left remained vivid in his mind's eye: her skin rosy and flushed from sleep, the sweep of lustrous fur around her shoulders emphasising the delicate bone structure of her neck. His heart quickened at the vision; he had wanted to seize her right then, sweep her up into his arms, and race upstairs with her, back to the downy, sweet-smelling warmth of her bed. He frowned, trying to dispel the tantalising thought, the voices in his head warning him, forcing him to remember what happened the last time with the maid! Pulling the horse to a stop in the inner bailey, he dismounted carefully, handing the reins to a groom. Lifting off his helmet, he pushed back the mail hood that formed part of his hauberk, shoving his hand through his hair, relishing the coolness of the breeze against his heated scalp. The inner bailey seemed quiet—where was she? He needed to see her, hear her kind voice, touch her…nay, not that. But the least he could do was make sure she was safe. Striding up the steps two at a time, he swept into the great hall. At this hour, the massive, high-ceilinged chamber was empty, apart from two figures seated at the top table: King Henry…and Langley!

'Langley!' Benois hailed his friend, covering the length of the hall in just a few quick strides. He sprang up the wooden steps and on to the high dais, to clap his friend on the back. Langley glanced up, gave a sheepish smile. 'I didn't expect to see you!'

'And I certainly didn't expect to see you…so soon!' Henry frowned, his expression stern. 'Surely you haven't managed to visit all the border castles?'

'Nay, I haven't.' Benois threw himself into the chair next to Langley. 'But Malcolm is still hard at it.'

'Explain.' Henry's lips settled into a terse line.

'Malcolm is doing a fine job on his own, Henry.' Benois sensed his King's irritation. He drank water thirstily from a pewter goblet in front of him.

'I gave you an order, Benois,' Henry replied slowly, 'and I expect you to follow that order.'

Benois set the goblet down, placing it back on the table

with deliberate slowness. His eyes glittered like chips of honed granite. Henry recoiled, flinching back into his seat under Benois's crushing regard. Caught in the middle of the two men, Langley cleared his throat.

'I realise, of course,' Henry's voice faltered, 'that I am in no position to insist that you follow my orders.'

'My thoughts exactly.' Benois's response was clipped. 'I have no wish to fall foul of you, sire,' he continued respectfully, 'but there was no need for you to send me on such a mission.'

'Maybe there was,' murmured Henry.

'Tell me.'

'That woman will make a fool of you, Benois. You came back because of her, didn't you?'

Benois leaned back slowly in his chair, his eyes sweeping Henry's face. 'So that's it.' He smiled briefly, shaking his head. 'I never suspected you to be the jealous type, my lord.'

'*Sacré bleu!*' Henry swore. 'Benois, this is no laughing matter—she will ruin you, make no mistake of it! Once your mind becomes distracted with a woman, you will lose your skill, your prowess on the battlefield!'

'And what makes you think I want to carry on with a life like that?' Benois said slowly. 'I've spent all my years fighting your battles for you; maybe it's time for a change.'

Henry's eyes darkened. 'I knew it! I knew she'd crawled under your skin!'

'Where is she?'

Langley began to rip a bread roll into small pieces, white crumbs scattering over the dark oak of the table.

'Look at you, man, you've gone soft in the head over that girl already.'

'Where is she?' Benois repeated, standing bolt upright from his seat. 'Henry, tell me, where is she?'

Chapter Fourteen

The sunshine percolated through the fresh young growth
burgeoning on the spreading oaks and spindled birch,
reaching down to the arching fronds of the ferns on the
woodland floor. The trees were alive with birds, calling and
whistling over the frilling tops of the branches, whilst in the
undergrowth, they foraged in the deep piles of decaying
leaves. Through the dappled shadows of the wood, Tavia
steered the grey palfrey with confidence, trying to ignore her
restive heart, trying to prevent her thoughts from straying
from their current purpose. She had found the wooded valley
easily, following the route she had oft taken with her mother
in her mind's eye. It had been only when Tavia had discovered the true identity of her father that the significance of her
mother's destination had become clear.

Behind her, Ferchar snorted with laughter at some jest, no
doubt ribald, that his soldier related to him. He had been delighted when Tavia had told him she knew of the location of
her father's treasure, and had begun making preparations
immediately for the short trip. Tavia tried to keep her balance
as the mare began to descend on the narrow path, hooves

slipping a little on the loose stones over the dried earth. This track would eventually lead to the valley floor. Tavia's thigh muscles protested painfully as she gripped the saddle under her, the weight of her body thrown back awkwardly. Would she never become accustomed to this accursed riding? An image of Benois thundering into the bailey on his midnight black destrier flew into her mind—an image of man and animal working in perfect harmony together, a symbol of power and grace. She hoped, wherever he was, that he was safe. Her heart flipped lopsidedly; she chewed her lip, hoping she had made the right decision in breaking her promise to him, by going to Ferchar before he returned. She hunched her shoulders forwards, but, nay, she had done him a favour—in truth, would he really care? More like he would be glad to see the back of her.

'How much longer, my lady?' Ferchar's shout took on the petulant whine of a child.

'Not much further, my lord,' Tavia replied, keeping her eyes firmly ahead so she would not fall off the horse. 'If I remember rightly, the place lies at the bottom of the valley.'

'You'd better remember rightly, my lady,' Ferchar blustered, 'or I'll clap you in irons for leading us all on a wild goose chase.'

Tavia began to feel more stable as the horse levelled out onto the path along the bottom of the valley. All around her, the fluttering wood anemones spangled across the valley floor, scattered like white stars on a green background. Tavia swept her gaze around in awe at the beautiful sight: the filtering light, the delicate petals…

'Is it here?' Ferchar rapped at her. She hadn't been aware of her horse stopping.

'A little further.' Tavia tapped her heels lightly against the horse's flanks to urge the animal forwards. To her right, the

rushing, warbling notes of a stream drifted into the air…
There! The spreading oak, ancient in form, the breadth of its
trunk patched with the pale blue-green florets of lichen rose
before her: the key to her freedom. Her eye darted to a
curious outcrop of rock, shafting upwards on a slant from the
ground, its riven surface decorated with the softer shapes of
ferns and mosses. Reining in the horse, Tavia swung her leg
forwards over the horse's neck, jumping down neatly to the
spongy ground. Without waiting for Ferchar, she forged her
way through the undergrowth, the low plants catching at her
hem, the pungent scent of wild garlic filling the air. Reaching
the rock, she worked her way around until arriving at a
jagged crevice just big enough for her to crawl into. Tavia
hesitated, unsure, as Ferchar, flanked by two burly soldiers,
crashed to her side. Wiping the sweat from his face with the
sleeve of his surcoat, he stared expectantly at her, pale eyes
brimming with excitement.

'Go on!' He choked the words out. 'This is it, is it not?'

Dryness invaded her throat, as she ducked her head, using
both hands on the rock either side to ease herself into the
narrow space. Under her fingers, the rock felt cold, gritty, un-
inviting. A smell of dank, rotting vegetation pervaded the air,
as she felt her way along the rock. She was certain this was
the place, so certain that she could almost feel her mother's
presence in this tiny cave—was this where the lovers had
met? She smiled to think of them together.

'Have you found it?' called Ferchar, his voice muffled
from outside the cave. Tavia, running her fingers along the
wet shale, chose not to reply. At her level, the rock was
smooth-faced, but, raising her arms upwards, she realised the
crevice was deceptive, for the sides of the cave stretched high
above her head. Lifting her eyes in the gloom, she peered
upwards into the darkness. And there it was.

On a narrow ledge, just above the top of her head, sat an iron strongbox, rectangular, with a heavy metal hasp sealing the lid, flecked with orange rust.

'I've found it!' she squeaked, squeezing her way out of the entrance, blinking in the daylight. 'But it's too heavy for me to lift down.'

'Get in there!' Ferchar growled to the stronger-looking of the two soldiers. The man looked doubtfully at the size of the cave entrance before managing to wiggle himself inside and extract the strongbox. Bending at the knees, he placed the box before Ferchar. The other soldier fetched his mace from the horse, and smashed down on the lock. The sound reverberated about the woods, bouncing back from the solid trunk in a cacophony of noise. After a few minutes of heavy bashing, the lock disintegrated in a shower of iron flakes.

Ferchar sprung down, his bony fingers throwing back the lid. Tavia gasped. The two soldiers took a step back in awe at the sight. Ferchar just smiled and plunged his hands into the pile of glittering jewels, crowns, rings, necklaces, all wrought from the finest gold and silver. 'My God!' he breathed, 'I've actually found it.' His hands moved reverently over the strings of pearls, the filigreed brooches studded with rubies, with sapphires, his fingers encountering a single piece of parchment, folded, nestling amongst the jewels.

'Tavia.' Ferchar read the words written on the outside of the paper, handing it to her with scarcely a glance, unable to wrench his eyes from the glittering tumble of gemstones.

Tavia broke open the red seal of wax, stamped with Earl Henry's coat of arms, and unfolded the parchment, a nervous shake to her fingers. Powerful black marks rose up from the paper… 'I can't read it.' She looked up, disappointed.

With an impatient snort, Ferchar snatched it back, scanning the contents. '"To my darling daughter, Tavia,"' he intoned derisively. "'If you have found this box, then I must be dead, and I'm sorry that I couldn't have known you better. Unfortunately, my circumstances dictated that the situation between your mother and me could not have been different. I have always loved your mother and you, and whatever path you choose in life, the contents of this box belong to you…" Pah!' In disgust, Ferchar threw the note to the ground. Tavia bent and picked it up, folding it so she could tuck it into the pouch hanging from her girdle. A warm glow surrounded her heart— Earl Henry had loved her mother, deeply, of that she was certain.

'And as I am now your guardian, my dear,' Ferchar leered obsequiously, 'anything that belongs to you, belongs to me.' His head whipped towards the two soldiers. 'Shut your mouths and stuff that lot into the saddle bags…and you—' he glared at Tavia as if expecting a protest '—mount up. If you behave yourself, I might let you have a small trinket… for now. Something to remember your parents by.' He spoke of her parents as if they disgusted him, as if what they had done was beneath the bounds of propriety. Tavia clenched her fists at her sides; she would not allow Ferchar to sully the beauty of her parents' relationship with his derisive speech.

'I don't want any of it, just this.' She patted the embroidered pouch containing the parchment.

'As you wish,' Ferchar replied, tilting his head to one side in puzzlement. How could the stupid chit not want any of this fortune? She clearly was addled in the head! 'Then mount up, girl, and we'll head back to Dunswick.'

Tavia lifted her head. 'I wish to stay here a while; I'll follow on.' The yearning to spend some time in that special place, without the distractions of Ferchar and his men, flowered in her breast. This was the place where her parents had met, talked, made love, the place where their energy had been concentrated. She wanted to be a part of that.

Ferchar's brow furrowed. 'I can't leave you here without an escort, and I need these solders with me, considering the amount of gold I'm carrying.'

'I know my way back. I'll be quite safe.'

'I'll stay with her.' A familiar, resonant voice cut across their deliberations. Tavia's head bounced up, her heart pounding immediately, the beats tripping over one another in rapid succession.

The gold lions emblazoned across Benois's scarlet surcoat glimmered in the sun as he strode into the clearing, the embodiment of overpowering masculinity, leading his snorting, sweating horse. His piercing, contemptuous glance perused Tavia's pale, exhausted face; she quailed under his stern regard, at once sensing his anger.

'So be it,' announced Ferchar hastily, in a hurry to return home and assess the true worth of their discovery. 'And I trust you, my lord Benois, to act in a fitting manner around the sister of the king.'

Benois bowed jerkily, watching as the small party climbed on their horses and made their way out of the clearing, saddle bags bulging lumpily with the jewels. His disdainful glance flew to the strongbox, now forlorn and empty, nestled amongst a clump of white wood anemones.

'So you found it after all,' he murmured, almost to himself, leading his horse over to a nearby branch. 'You promised that you would wait until I returned.' His voice slid over her, gritty, condemning.

'It wasn't like that!' she protested sharply. A cold, isolating feeling slipped through her veins. 'King Henry implied that you would be gone for a long time, and I...I...' She toed the damp ground with the soft leather of her shoe.

'You...what?' Benois loomed up close, towering over her. 'You thought that you could do it without me? Is that it?' He wore no helmet, the sable strands of his hair gleaming silkily in this shifting light under the trees. The chainmail coif of his hauberk had been pushed back from his head to gather in metallic folds emphasising the ruggedness of his features, the corded muscles of his neck.

'You didn't need to come after me, Benois. I thought...' She twisted her fingers into a painful knot. How could she tell him that he was better off without her? That King Henry thought he was better off without her?

'Thought what? Go on, tell me, I'd be interested to know what goes on in that head of yours.'

'I thought you would prefer it if I wasn't at the castle when you returned,' she blurted out in a rush, the blueness of her eyes seeking his, asking for his understanding.

'You...what? Whatever gave you that impression?'

'Your king suggested it would be a good idea,' she replied, twisting her slender fingers into an agitated knot about her girdle.

The grey turbulence of his gaze flicked over her, his mind recalling their last kiss, the warm, pliable feel of her body as he swept her up against him, the soft touch of her lips. An overwhelming sense of protectiveness swept through him— what had Henry been thinking? 'My God, woman, when I think of you, on your own, with Ferchar...who knows what could have happened?' Without thinking, he stuck one hand furiously into his hair. A fleeting look of pain traced over his stern features; he paled visibly. He bit his lip, trying to recover from the raft of agony that swept across his body from his injured shoulder.

Tavia grabbed his elbow. 'What's the matter? What have you done to yourself?'

He shook her hand away. 'It's nothing,' he snapped. 'Just a scratch.'

'Nay.' Tavia spoke slowly, touching a finger gently to the patch of blood blossoming at his shoulder through the metallic links of his chainmail. 'It's more than a scratch.'

'Leave it,' he growled, resisting the urge to knock her hand away. How typical of a woman to avoid the argument in hand by homing in on insignificant details, trying to distract him.

Tavia planted both hands on her hips. 'Nay, Benois, I will not leave it. That needs to be looked at before it develops into something more serious.'

He set his mouth in a mutinous line, impassive before her. 'Stop nagging at me, woman!'

She shoved at him then, annoyed at his stubbornness, placing two hands flat on his chest. He swayed from the force of her attack, amazed at the power in that small, lithe body.

'Sit down,' she ordered, 'before you fall down. Otherwise I might have to get cross with you.'

He smiled weakly at her words. 'You talk to me like a child.'

'That's because you're behaving like one,' she replied archly.

'It was only a nick,' he began to explain. Tavia reached her hands up, placing both palms on his shoulders in a vain attempt to pull him down. The urge to loop his arms about her slim waist, to swing her around, loomed temptingly, but a further glance at her determined expression made him realise the foolishness of that decision.

'I'm all yours,' he acquiesced finally, subsiding to his knees before her. The fragile scent of the windflowers lifted on the breeze as he knelt on the ground, crushing a few of the delicate heads beneath his powerful calves.

'We need to take this off.' Tavia tugged at the hem of his surcoat, his hauberk. As she reached down, the wide neckline of her dress gaped forwards, offering a tempting glimpse of her rounded bosom.

'Let me.' He pushed her fingers away, pulling off the surcoat, then his hauberk, followed by his white linen shirt, covered with a soaking patch of blood on one side. Removing his garments made him almost gasp out loud at the ripping pain in his shoulder, but he managed a shaky smile when he finally knelt before her, naked from the waist up.

'Oh!' Tavia gawked at him, the tapered muscles at his waist, the honed plates of muscle across his chest. Her determination to tend his wound had driven her on; now, faced with a broad, naked torso, her sense of purpose shrivelled in a moment.

'What's the matter, Tavia?' he teased, wide mouth breaking into a grin. 'Is it worse than you thought?'

Aye, she thought, much worse. But it wasn't the wound she was referring to. It was her own reaction to this powerful body just inches from her own. With trembling fingers she plucked at the loose, ineffectual dressing, almost throwing it to the ground in disgust.

'When did this happen?' she asked, studying the puckered skin around the wound. 'You stupid fool!' She must, must force herself to ignore the physical beauty of this man.

Benois raised an eyebrow. 'I didn't do it deliberately. And if you're going to give me a tongue-lashing, then I'll take my chances elsewhere, thank you.'

She caught the amused flare in his eye, and chewed on her bottom lip. Being angry with him was the only way she could handle this situation, and it would make it all the more difficult if he were kind to her.

'Sorry,' she mumbled. 'It's just that, well, it's worse than

I thought.' She met his silvered eyes. 'Did nobody think to clean it?'

Her hand felt warm against his shoulder. God, but she was breathtaking up close. How could he have ever left with Malcolm that day? 'One of the men had a go,' he answered, a guttural thread to his tone.

'I need to clean it. Where's your water bottle?'

He jerked his head in the direction of his horse, and watched the enticing sway of her hips beneath her gown as she fetched it.

'Ouch!' He sucked in his breath as she splashed the water over his wound, and began dabbing it with a clean piece of his linen shirt. She frowned. 'I don't think it needs stitches, the cut doesn't seem too deep. I'll bind it with my veil.'

He tracked the graceful movement of her slender arm arching over her head, plucking the gossamer veil from her rich, glorious hair, sweeping the material down so she could fold it into a serviceable bandage. Fronds of wine-dark hair curled tantalisingly around the creamy oval of her face, gleefully escaping from the practical braid that swung down her back. The faded gown in which he had last seen her had been replaced by a fashionable *bliaut* of sage green, with an underdress of cream linen. The ladies of the castle had obviously been ordered to dress this new-found royal daughter in clothes more befitting to her rank. He doubted it would change her.

'Stick your arm out so I can wrap this underneath your armpit,' Tavia ordered, her tone brisk and efficient.

'Whatever you say, my lady,' he replied in a mocking chant, extending his right arm outwards.

She looked at him sharply, disapproving. 'Do you want me to help you, or nay?'

The pain in his shoulder had subsided to a dull ache after

her vigorous cleaning, but the movement sent another sear of agony through the limb. He tipped his head to one side. 'It's a long time since someone has tended me so,' he replied through gritted teeth.

'That's still no excuse for bad manners,' she chided softly, starting to bind his shoulder. He nodded, mindful of the delicate scent of lavender lifting from the veil to his nostrils and drew a deep shuddering breath, willing her to finish.

'There, now,' Tavia said, after what seemed like a lifetime, ripping the trailing end of her veil so as to fashion an effective knot. She took a step back, admiring her work, her heart jolting as the lowering sun highlighted the ridged and furrowed muscle of his torso. 'Maybe I could help you back on with your shirt?' Doubt clouded her voice.

He smiled ruefully. 'I stink to high heaven, woman. Surely you must have noticed? Is there no place around here to wash?' He cast his eyes across the budding green foliage of the glade. Above him, a branch sidled in the breeze; the lean planes of his face leapt from mysterious shadow into brilliant light.

'Come,' Tavia said, glad of the distraction from his magnificent body. 'I know a place.' She moved to the edge of the clearing, a wood nymph against the backdrop of swaying branches, of arching, staggered ferns, and stretched her arm towards him, a gesture of innocent friendship.

Benois pushed himself up awkwardly from the forest floor, a strange clumsiness invading his movements. Heart thumping, he stepped toward her, instinctively clasping her cool, strong fingers. Her long hem swished through the undergrowth, the pale anemones backed by dark green foliage; she stepped carefully as if wading through shallow water. He followed her silently, appreciating the elegant line of her spine flowing beneath the well-fitting gown, the determined set of her shoulders. It was a mystery to him, how this maid had managed to constantly dominate his thoughts, his every waking moment. This girl appeared so completely at odds with his own jaded perception of a woman, a perception moulded and tarnished by years of watching the emotional shenanigans of the ladies at court, by years of ruthless soldiering. Once, he had thought being a soldier was the only thing that kept him alive, able to live with the memory of losing his family; now, he was not so sure. Tavia was so different, so incomparable: her quick wit, her indomitable spirit, and that fierce beauty that drew him again and again, like a fish to a lure.

The breeze sifted through the canopy of trees above their heads, a gentle sighing through the branches with their new, bright-green growth. And then, a more persistent noise to their right; the incessant bubbling of a brook, growing louder and louder until it managed to drown out the wind in the trees. Tavia stopped so suddenly, Benois almost ran into the back of her. He thought his chest might explode with the effort of holding his body rigidly away from her, of resisting the temptation to move up close behind her, to wrap her in his sinewy arms.

'There!' Tavia announced proudly, twisting sideways, a soft smile curving her lips. He stepped forward. The sound of rushing water swelled and spread. Below him, some six feet or so, lay a pool, cool and green in its depths, sunlit. To his right, a stream cascaded down over a series of serrated rocks before dropping in separate strings of moving water to break the surface of the pool in widening, circular ripples.

'How did you know…?' he breathed, all gruffness erased from his voice.

'That this was here?' She laughed, finishing his question

for him. The limpid blue of her eyes reached his. 'My mother met Earl Henry in these woods; this was their special place.'

'My God,' he murmured. 'It's beautiful.' He stood, motionless, at the side of the pool, entranced by the dancing water, the brilliant green of the leaves. The air thickened, sultry, fragrant with the heady scent of flowers.

'Go on,' Tavia urged, panicking at his hesitation, 'go and bathe! You're right, you do stink!' The midnight fringes of his eyes met hers as he began to undo his belt. She averted her eyes hastily at the slither of leather in the loops. 'I'd better go,' she mumbled.

'I have no intention of offending your maidenly modesty,' Benois assured her quickly. Now he'd found her again, safe, unharmed, he was reluctant to let her out of his sight once more. He pulled off his braies, then his leather boots in quick succession, suddenly standing before her in his bleached linen loincloth. He turned, executing a neat, perfect dive. Quivering under the impact of his near-nakedness, Tavia watched his muscular beauty plunge into the water, chewing at the inside of her cheek.

Benois floated to the surface, clearly relishing the cool silk of the water against his naked skin. She moved tentatively to the edge of the pool, wondering whether to stay…or go. To stay was to enter the unknown, to flirt with danger. Leaving Benois to his bath would be the safer option. She could see the white glow of his corded limbs moving beneath the glassy surface, the strength in his shoulders as he broke upwards, tossing his head to flick the water from his eyes.

'What's it like?' she called down, watching him with envy as the water spilled over his burly shoulders.

'Like Heaven,' he responded, grinning, his teeth white and even in his tanned face.

Beneath the heavy folds of her gown, her skin began to

prickle and itch; the water sparkled enticingly below her. Wrenching her eyes from Benois, she prowled along the side of the bank, leather soles slipping on the mossy grass, trying to suppress the urge to dive into the water beside him.

'Why not come in when I come out?' Benois suggested, noticing the way she tugged irritably at the folds of her skirt. His melodious tone was careful, guarded.

'Could I?' Tavia's head shot around, questioning with such child-like glee that he wanted to laugh out loud.

He shifted his shoulders under the water, a gesture of indifference. 'Why not? Ferchar gave no indication of when we should return.' At his words, Tavia ducked her head, fumbling with, then loosening the fastenings of her gown, her eagerness to enter the water evident in her nimble fingers.

'Wait till I climb out, Tavia!' Benois eyed her warily. 'Let me dress so you can disrobe in private!' He groaned inwardly as she yanked the voluminous folds over her head. Through the churning rush of water, she hadn't heard him. Reluctant to leave the water, but realising he must for the sake of his own sanity, Benois swam to the edge of the pool, to a place where he could regain his footing, to a place where the stones on the stream bed moved loosely under his feet. Fixing his gaze on the muddy, crumbling earth of the bank, he levered himself up on strong forearms, the water spilling down, running over his honed skin in a shower of sparkling droplets. In the corner of his vision, he caught a flicker of white, and knew, without looking, that Tavia wore only her shift. Christ in Heaven! Would she never cease in placing temptation in his path?

'You had better get in,' he muttered roughly, striding towards his discarded clothes.

With a small whisper of delight, Tavia sank into the delicious water. Unthinking, Benois lifted his eyes, checking the source of the sound. Desire smacked into him like an arrow in the chest. Tavia floated on her back, her face set in an expression of intense rapture, the white folds of her chemise fanning out around her, revealing the shapely curves of her slim frame.

He was lost.

Tavia's eyes sprang open at the sight of Benois, still wearing his loincloth, splashing towards her. 'I thought you were dressing.' She frowned, arching at the waist so that she could tread water, her slender arms making wide circles on top of the pool.

His expression was raw, intense. 'I changed my mind.' Standing chest deep in the pool, he seized her hands. 'I cannot resist you, Tavia. God knows, I've tried, but I cannot.' His words emerged starkly, roughened by the emotion in his voice. 'I'm sorry.' He wanted to be with her, to make love to her and to experience those intense emotions he had spent his whole life running away from.

Tavia clung to his forearms, steadying herself, though her heart raced at breakneck speed. 'Nay,' she whispered, wondering if her chest would burst. 'Don't be sorry.'

The jewelled granite of his eyes glittered; he lifted her hand, pressing his lips to the soft skin of her inner palm. 'Christ, woman,' he murmured, 'this is the moment when you must push me away. I'm giving you that chance.'

'I cannot,' she replied, truthfully, a glorious feeling of joy suffusing her body.

His mouth, warm, questing, descended on hers. For a moment, shocked, her feet flailed beneath her, trying to find some sort of foothold, to gain balance in those crystalline depths, before his strong arm swept around her, pulling her securely into his hard body. His lips roamed over hers; her limbs melted under the assured skilfulness of his kiss, softening to a point where solidity fled, flowing into the rough outlines of the man before her. Her hands wound tentatively to the back of his neck, the silken fronds of his hair brushing seductively against her fingers.

Snared by the fervency of his passion, she had been unable to lie to him, in truth wanting this time to go on…for ever and ever. His hands moved from her shoulders to cup her face, to deepen the kiss, his tongue playing along the seam of her mouth, seductive, inquisitive. She inhaled sharply; her blood thickened, stilling momentarily under his seeking touch, before pelting through her body with increasing speed. They clung to each other, his broad torso breaking the smooth, pebble-like skin of the pool, his head dipping to hers, the sable strands of his hair meshed with rich red tendrils. The accelerated bumping of her heart picked up a notch, thrilling her, scaring her. Under his touch, Benois urged her towards a land hitherto unknown to her, a land of dark, secret desires, of unbridled passion. A land she yearned to discover.

Her fragile touch at the back of his neck sent spirals of desire coursing through Benois's lean frame. Through her curious fingers, he sensed her acquiescence, her acceptance of the unbelievable fire that burned between the two of them. He crushed her to him, hip to hip, belly to belly, and under his searching mouth she gasped in shock at the rigid evidence of his desire against her.

'Not here!' he growled, ripping his mouth away. Her lips burned, seared by the intensity of his kiss. He carried her from the water easily and strode through the pool to where the stream ran shallow again. Climbing steadily up the gentle slope of the bank, he shifted her weight slightly so that she rolled against him, her right flank high against the rippling muscle of his chest. Sodden with water, the delicate folds of her chemise clung to her, emphasising the rounded curve of her breast, the soft flare of her hip. Tavia buried her head in the powerful shadows of his neck, unable to meet the diamond intensity of his gaze.

He laid her down on a cushiony bed of anemones, the delicate scent rising into the air as she lay back, the spreading canopy of an oak tree above her head. He settled his long, lean length beside her. In shock, she realised he was naked.

'Someone might see us,' she whispered, sealing her fate with those words, knowing what was about to happen, wanting it to happen with all her heart.

'Do you really care?' he breathed into her ear, the warmth of his breath sending paroxysms of spiralling desire through the very core of her.

'Nay.' She shivered.

He smiled, his strong fingers trailing a silky path across her cheek, down her neck, down further. She jerked violently, releasing the smallest sigh at the thrilling sensations bubbling into life under his touch.

He pushed at the wet fabric covering her shoulders, in a moment exposing one creamy shoulder, gleaming like a pearl in the dappled green light of the forest. Her breath hitched; a slow coil of emotion gathering tightly in the pit of her stomach. His lips dropped to her shoulder, running a line of delicate kisses along the taut line of her collarbone…

'Sweet Jesu!' Benois sat up suddenly, pushing a trembling hand through his hair, fighting to temper his own passion, to slow himself. The white makeshift bandage at his shoulder strained against the bunched muscle in his shoulder. Tavia's heart skipped—this was it, this was the moment when he told her he couldn't carry on, that he'd made a mistake. She felt a fool, lying there, vulnerable and exposed in just her shift, and sat up, abruptly, seeking to control her own breathing, her own disappointment.

'It doesn't matter,' she said tentatively, her top teeth nibbling doubtfully at her bottom lip. 'I'll go if you like. My body's too lean for most men's tastes.'

He glared at her, uncomprehending, his eyes embracing hers in a sparkling silver net of desire. 'Are you completely mad? Who on earth told you such utter rubbish?'

Her lungs filled with a deep quivering breath. 'I…'

He reached over, gliding his fingertips over the smooth skin of her face, her neck. 'You are the most beautiful creature I have ever met,' he said, his voice low and resonant. 'And you'd better believe that!' Benois looked so stern that a bubble of laughter rose in her chest, quickly quashed as he folded her into him, pushing her back into the carpet of undergrowth. Her diaphragm flexed, then tightened with sweet awareness, excitement liquefying within her. Benois twined his fingers into the lustrous strands of her hair, the wide pads of his thumbs gently kneading into her scalp. His hands trailed down the smooth column of her neck, before playing along the wide neckline of her damp chemise.

'Benois…I…!' She thought she would explode under his touch, the pulsating maelstrom of need burning, amassing forcefully within her.

'Hush now…trust me,' he whispered, nibbling a the damp shell-like curve of her ear. He stretched his hard, sinewy length alongside her; rivers of shock pulsated through her at the proximity of his naked flesh, the scorching brand of his need hard against her thigh. Before Tavia could recover, his lips roved over hers once more, teasing and tantalising as his hand moved under the flowing hem of her chemise, up, up along the soft, satiny length of her thigh to the very core of her womanhood.

'Benois…!' she gasped, as his fingers touched her where no man had ever ventured before. All sense of reason deserted her, as her mind descended into the heady waters of passion, dancing on the intoxicating edge of the whirlpool of desire. Her body went taut, rigid with thrilling shock, as he pushed slowly into her, easing his way through tender folds. Her hands clung to his face, holding the glitter of his knowing eyes, as she relished the savage, boiling frenzy that invaded her heart, her blood. Her hands moved to his shoulders, then to the muscular line of Benois's spine as his lips seized hers once more.

He surged into her then, his own body overtaken by a passion that took him by surprise. The fleeting resistance of her virginity checked him for a moment, before he filled her completely, utterly. Consumed by him, the mild ache Tavia experienced on losing her innocence was quickly replaced by a swelling, eddying fullness as Benois continued to move within her, measured and slow at first, before gathering momentum, faster and faster. She began to move with him, dancing eagerly to his rhythm, matching the increasing speed of his powerful thrusts with a delighted eagerness of her own. She closed her eyes, the conscious part of her mind receding suddenly as the desire rippling through her body threatened to overtake—nay, to overcome her! She clung to the man above her, her security in this storm of passion, as white-hot needles of light shot through her brain, a magnificent whirlpool of scattering stars.

She cried out then, as Benois drove into her and the flimsy straining skin of the bubble burst with a blistering violence within her and glorious waves of desire flooded again and again through her body. Benois threw his head back, reaching his own peak as he shuddered in tandem with the woman beneath him.

'Sweet Mother of God!' he cried out loud, as Tavia's fingers snagged into his dripping hair and he collapsed on top of her, his body heavy, sated and alive.

Chapter Fifteen

For a long time Benois and Tavia lay there, under the oak's swaying branches, the hot slivers of the sun caressing their faces as the afternoon light pierced the verdant canopy above. The rapid beat of their hearts slackened, the tumultuous climax of their lovemaking replaced by a stillness, a delicious languor that stole through their bodies, drifting, soporific.

Lying on his back, Tavia's soft limbs entwined against him, her silken legs tangled with his rough-haired thighs, Benois studied the delicate interlacing of branches above his head, a brown net against the cerulean blue of the sky. A glorious feeling of serenity filled his body, his mind. The man that he had been, the man hardened by war and death, beset with haunting memories, had temporarily disappeared. For the first time in a long time, he knew peace, a real contentment, a fledgling joy flowing in his veins. The barbed edges of his character seemed smoothed out, caressed by her gentle touch, the alluring curves of her body. Had Tavia done this? Had this small, slim, beautiful girl filled up the hollow space in his heart with her own kindness, her own generosity of spirit, her passion? The beauty, the wholeness of the experience they had just shared, had been overwhelming. He had never known that being with a woman could be so utterly and completely fulfilling, not just physically but emotionally as well.

He sighed deeply, relishing the sweet, exhausted feeling in his muscles, following a wren's bobbing flight weave between the trees. Holding Tavia tight in his arms, he allowed his thoughts to idle, to soar with the graceful movement of the bird, a tight bud of hope flaring cautiously in his chest. The thought of sharing his life with another had never entered his head before; the idea was so foreign to him that he almost dismissed it immediately. But the image of him taking Tavia, pregnant with their child, back to his homeland, back to lay the ghosts of his family to rest once and for all, burned vividly in his mind's eye. Could it be possible?

Against his flank, Tavia shifted, murmuring in her sleep. Her flushed cheek pushed up against his shoulder, her fingers fanning out lightly across the middle of his chest, over his heart: a butterfly's touch. Emotion rippled through him, caught him by surprise. When they had been together, he had become utterly, completely lost, sinking into her smooth caress with a raw abandonment. What a hot-headed, arrogant fool he'd been at Dunswick to believe that possessing her would suppress his desire for her; he couldn't have been further from the truth.

'What are you thinking about?' Tavia mumbled against his shoulder, her voice warm and befuddled with sleep. The folds of her chemise, damp, grass-stained, bunched about her thighs as she snuggled into his muscled flank. The present moment dominated her thoughts; she luxuriated in the feel of the man beside her, in the pleasure they had shared.

'I was thinking of how badly I treated you at Dunswick.' He grimaced at the memory. The glistening bubble of his dream, his dream of their future together, began to disintegrate.

'Nay, don't speak of it,' she hushed him, raising a finger to the well-defined curve of his lips. Her sleeve hung down from her delicate wrist; he could see the tracery of blue veins on her pale forearm.

'I was a brute,' he admitted, turning his face into the scented pillow of her hair, the perfumed strands tickling his cheek. A tiny voice niggled at him, telling him he was still a brute, that he would never change. How could he ever hope to give Tavia a semblance of normal life with his scarred history? He shifted his head away from her, searching for the gleam of his sword in the long grass, his gaze drawn instinctively to the weapon that had fought in so many battles, had ended so many lives. 'I am a brute,' he corrected blandly, the light leaving his eyes.

She laughed, moving her hand to cup the side of her face. 'If I thought that, then I would never have lain with you.'

'Then you thought wrong, Tavia.' The taut muscles in his arm flexed against her back, her shoulder.

They both jumped as a crack of thunder split the air. Storm clouds had begun to billow up from the west, puffy grey mushrooms of rounded air that began to encompass the blue sky with surprising speed. The forest darkened, the storm clouds moving over the setting sun, blocking out the light.

She twisted around in his hold, the laughter drying up in her throat. Pushing herself up against his chest to see his face, the blank, indifferent look in his eyes horrified her, the mask of a soldier slipping back into place. Her heart lurched oddly, then filled with anger. She wanted to thump him, pull at his hair, anything to squeeze the emotion back into him. A wave of fury gushed through her. 'Why are you being like this?'

'Like what?' His big hands cupped her shoulders, supporting her, setting her gently away from him as he sat up, leaning over to extract his tunic from the pile of discarded clothes beside them.

'Like you don't care any more,' she ground out, her blue eyes spitting fire as she sprang to her feet, arms folded tightly across her chest. Her hair, loosened at some point during their lovemaking, fell forward over her shoulders in glorious, glossy loops, the curling ends reaching past her hips.

'I've never "cared", Tavia. That's just who I am.' He wrenched the tunic over his head.

Her fury made her bold, stoking her courage. 'Nay! You're not like that!' She poked him smartly in the chest. 'That's where you are wrong. You do care. You cared enough to follow me into the city of Dunswick, you cared enough to take me away from Ferchar when I was about to make a fool of myself, you cared when my mother was dying. Don't try to pretend you don't!'

He glared at her, stunned by her outburst.

'You like to make out how little you care for people, but it's all a lie. I've seen you, Benois. I know you.'

A muscle jumped in the hollow of his cheek. He began to pull on his braies with short decisive movements, sitting down to lace up his boots. 'If you knew the real me, Tavia, you wouldn't be standing there now.' One lock of chestnut hair fell forwards over his tense, strained expression.

'I know you,' she repeated, laying one soft hand on his arm. Her fingers burned through the fabric of his tunic.

He knocked her hand away, his face dark, intimidating. 'You don't know what I'm capable of.' It's better this way, he thought. The maid was too good for him, too tender in her nature, too generous with her love. In contrast, he was flawed, hard and bitter with memories—he would only succeed in making her miserable. Now she was wealthy, with royal relations, she would be well looked after. A more suitable husband would be found, one who was as kind and generous as she was.

'Fine.' Tavia turned away, tears threatening, crestfallen after her outburst. Her shoulders slumped forwards in defeat as she picked her crumpled dress up from the undergrowth and yanked it over her head. She wanted to push her fists against his chest, to cry, to scream against him. But what purpose would it serve? She had tried, tried to reach him, but to no avail. Why did she even bother to fight? But in her heart she knew, she knew in that brief, wretched moment that she fought for his love, for a return of the love she held for him. She loved this man, this infuriating, impossible man who had terrified and teased her, who had stolen kisses and…had bedded her. Aye, she loved him, but he would surely break her heart.

'Take me back to Dunswick.' Tavia stalked off, back rigid and unyielding, wretched humiliation swimming chaotically through her body, in the direction of Benois's horse, which waited patiently beneath a stand of trees. At the same moment, the brooding mass of cloud released the first raindrops, fat and heavy, spattering on to the ground. Thunder clashed above them, echoing around the forest, followed swiftly by lightning, a stark white flash of ghostly illumination.

'Too late!' Benois charged over to her, his hand landing heavily on her shoulder to stop her agitated steps. She ducked, wriggled, attempting to wrench herself away, but his fingers tightened, holding her fast.

'Let go of me!' she snarled back to him through the stinging raindrops, trying to hook her fingers into the reins of his horse. Rain sluiced over her face, making her blink to clear her vision.

He pulled the leather straps from her hands. 'Tavia, stop, we can't travel in this! It's not safe!'

She peered up at him through the slashing rain. 'Is this your idea of a joke?'

'I'm deadly serious...we need to find shelter.'

She bridled beneath his words, knowing he was right, resenting the circumstances that meant she had to spend more time alone with him. Right now, she needed time on her own, time to lick her wounds, to recover her equilibrium, to tuck away the memory of their joining close to her heart. But the change in the weather made that impossible.

'Follow me,' she said quietly.

Benois watched Tavia as she leaned one shoulder against the craggy outline of the entrance to the cave, staring out bleakly at the torrential rain. Against the cracked grey stone, he traced the fine curves of her profile, her damp pale face imbued with a luminous quality, her slim frame strong and capable, despite her diminutive proportions. Astonishment had crossed his features as Tavia squeezed through the narrow fissure into the cave, shaking his head in disbelief as she had turned, beckoning him in. He had settled himself comfortably, leaning back against the rock and stretching his legs out over the rug he had snatched from his horse, while she, Tavia, had ignored him, standing by the exit to the cave as if she couldn't wait to leave. He didn't blame her; he had hurt her with his indifference, his coldness. But he had to be like this; it seemed the only way to make her understand that he was not the man she believed him to be. She had to realise what kind of man he was, for her own sake, otherwise his black-hearted soul would destroy her.

Thunder ruptured the air above: swift, violent, guttural. Tavia jumped back as the interior of the cave lit with the stark white of a lightning strike.

'I'd sit down if I were you,' Benois advised mildly, starting to unpack the contents of his leather satchel. 'The storm will not pass any quicker with you watching it, much as you wish it to.'

Tavia prised her gaze away from the opening, sought his shadowed form in the recessed confines of the cave. 'Do you really think I want to sit with the likes of you, Benois? After the way you spoke to me after…after…'

'I bedded you?' He supplied the words for her, raising the dark slash of his eyebrows. 'Try not to attach too much importance to the whole affair, Tavia. I realise it isn't every day you lose your virginity, but—'

'Stop!' She held up her hand, incensed. 'Mother of God, Benois, you talk about my…me…as if I were a commodity, or something ugly to be dealt with. How can you be so coarse…so crude?'

His eyes glittered in the darkness, spiked chips of ice. 'Because that is what I am, Tavia, a rough, crude soldier. You seem to have trouble accepting that idea.'

She thumped her hand against the rock, grazing it, ducking her head so he wouldn't see the frustrated tears flood her eyes. Shame washed over her, blinding, hot. 'So you just wanted me for my body, then?' Her voice, when it eventually emerged, was thin, jerky with hostility.

'You're an extremely desirable woman, Tavia. What were you expecting? An offer of marriage?' The neutrality of his tone infuriated her.

'Nay,' she blasted back, 'but maybe something a little kinder than outright rejection!'

He winced at her words, covering the movement with a shrug. It was better this way, he kept telling himself. It was better she knew what kind of man he was before it was too late.

Tavia balled her fists by her sides, flouncing across the

cave to stand over him. 'My God, Benois, you really had me fooled, didn't you? There I was, thinking we were sharing one of the most incredible experiences of my life and you squash it with your foul words, take all the beauty from it, and distort it into something ugly and disgusting. Thank you very much.' There! She'd said it. She'd told him the truth. It wouldn't matter anyway, as he seemed so keen on shoving her away, he may as well know how she felt.

Mouth slack with astonishment at her words, Benois jumped to his feet, towering over her once more. He had never heard a woman speak like this, ever, with such energy, such naked truth, such passion. Her face, flushed with agitation, lifted up to his, searching for answers.

'Stop trying to change me into someone that I'm not,' he whispered. 'I'm not some court dandy who'll shower you with flowery verse and tender phrases.'

'I'm not asking you for that,' she replied simply.

A peculiar sensation gripped his innards. He seized the top of her arms, almost lifting her bodily from the ground, hauling her slight frame up against him. 'Then what is it that you want from me?' His voice boomed about the cave, probing, questioning. 'What is it you want from me?'

Her eyes, fringed with long wet lashes, widened, locked with his. In the ringing silence, her clear, bell-like tones sang through the high recesses of the cave. 'You know, Benois. You know.' *I want your love.* The words echoed, bounced in her mind, but remained unspoken.

But he knew what she asked of him, knew what she wanted. 'You ask what I cannot give, Tavia,' he replied bitterly. 'You ask too much of me.' His eyes slid beyond her to the cave entrance. 'The storm has passed,' he announced coldly. 'We must return to Dunswick.'

Her heart closed up with sadness.

* * *

Tavia sunk deep into the wooden bath tub, allowing the hot, steaming water to engulf her shoulders, her neck. The tightness of her muscles began to slacken and stretch, languishing in the delicious sensation. She curled her toes, feeling the soft linen at the end of the bath, linen that had been placed over the rough wood of the tub before the water had been poured in. Rose petals floated on the water's surface, the heat allowing the flowers to release their heady scent. Exhaustion dragged at her eyes, her limbs, a bleak wretchedness that she couldn't wholly attribute to physical activity. A raft of sadness welled up, unexpectedly, and she sank deeper, willing the water to wash away the pain, the heartache, just for a moment.

They had ridden back to Dunswick in a stony, unbroken silence, her borrowed mare plodding docilely behind Benois's restless stallion. They had only spoken when it was necessary and then each word was beset with a polite, guarded formality. With each passing moment, Tavia regretted her blatant outspokenness towards him, her careless lack of thought as she blurted the truth out. She had shamed herself before him, lost her dignity, not once, but twice, and now…now there was nothing. The horses had walked through the woods lit once more by filtered evening sunlight, branches drooping heavy with rainwater, each catching the light to create a sparkling net. As the horses brushed through on the narrow path, some branches sprang up, let free of their weight of water, releasing their load into an arc of shimmering droplets.

As soon as they had ridden into the inner bailey, Benois had dismounted, stalking off without so much as a backwards glance. She had wanted to shout, to yell after him, to accuse him of running away, but she knew it was too late; she had declared her feelings for him, and he had shoved them back in her face. Better to cherish the memory of that time in the woods together, to keep it safe within the sanctity of her heart, and hold it there for ever.

'Where have you been?' Tavia jumped as Ada burst into the chamber without knocking. So much for having time to lick her wounds. Ada plonked herself on the bed, eyes gleaming with an avid curiosity. She ran her hands experimentally over the bed furs, glossy in the candlelight, a sly look entering her eye. 'Ferchar's been going mad.'

Tavia squeezed the flannel, watching the drops fall back into the water. 'There was a storm,' she intoned dully. 'We couldn't return until it had passed.'

'Ferchar was most put out when you didn't come back.' Ada leaned forward conspiratorially.

Tavia pinned Ada with a fierce stare. 'But why…? He knew I wanted to spend some time in the woods.'

'Tavia, you were gone for *hours*…' Ada widened her eyes dramatically '…and you were on your own, with Lord Benois.'

Despair seeped through her. She shrugged her shoulders. 'What of it? Ferchar agreed that Benois should stay with me, for protection.' She lowered her head, grimacing at the irony of the word. She couldn't have been more vulnerable if she had tried—a veritable lamb to the slaughter.

'Something happened while you were away.' Ada slid off the bed, padded forwards to the side of the tub in her soft, leather shoes. Tavia brought the flannel along her arm slowly, alert to the sharpness of Ada's tone.

'King Henry has told Ferchar that he has no claim on your fortune, despite the fact that he is now, by rights, your guardian. Those jewels belong to you, Tavia. Just you.'

Benois ate hungrily, loading his plate with floury bread rolls, thin slices of ham, trying to concentrate on the conversation that wrangled good-naturedly between Ferchar and King Henry alongside him. He failed completely, his mind continually walking the same path, returning to an idyllic scene in a magical forest with a beautiful maid. His mind and body seemed utterly bewitched, despite his determined efforts to push her from his thoughts. The bread roll broke into bits beneath his tanned fingers.

'So you'll make sure the soldiers are ready leave on the morrow, Benois?' At his side, Henry slapped him genially on the back.

'Leave?' Benois frowned at his king, uncomprehending.

'Aye.' Henry laughed. 'Have you heard a word that I said, Benois? Our job here is done; Ferchar and I have agreed the new border lines between Scotland and England, so there is no reason for us to stay.'

Maybe I have a reason, thought Benois suddenly. A reason that lights up my world with her incisive blue eyes, her quick intelligence, brings a warmth and softness to my rough, hard existence. Her words from the previous day echoed in his brain; she thought him capable of love…could it be possible?

'Besides, we must allow Ferchar to sort out…er…more domestic issues.' Henry frowned slightly at Benois's disinterest.

'Tavia of Mowerby, to be precise,' Ferchar grunted through a mouthful of smoked trout, small slivers of pink fish falling down on to his chin. He wiped the debris away with the back of his hand, leaving a faint smear of grease.

'Does she need to be…sorted out?' Benois asked lightly.

'Your king here…' Ferchar gestured with his knife '…has decreed that the contents of the dead earl's coffer belong entirely to her. Although I can't see why.' He stuffed another piece of fish into his mouth, hurriedly, as if he were trying to hide it away. 'The chit could easily lead a comfortable life on a quarter of the amount in the coffer.'

Henry sighed, leaning back against the carved oak of his chair. 'I've told you, Ferchar, it's not my decision, it's the law. Although as her guardian you are in a position to offer any advice, remember. But the only person who has any claim on that money is Tavia and…her husband, should she choose to marry.'

'Aha!' Ferchar's eyes lit up, and he all but bounced in the chair with excitement. 'Should she choose to marry', he repeated Henry's words, rolling them around his mouth as if testing them.

In a corner of the great hall, a motley collection of musicians began to play a melody. The delicate sound of the lyre, mingling with the lighter warbling notes of the flute, lifted into the air, and the knights and ladies looked at each other and smiled, beginning to push back the trestle tables against the stone walls of the hall in anticipation of an evening of dancing.

'Guard your tongue, Ferchar,' Henry warned. 'The women approach.'

A burst of colour at a side door to the great hall heralded Ada and Tavia's entrance. Ada hung from Tavia's arm, dragged at it even, laughing and chattering as they moved forwards through the throng of people towards the high dais where the nobility sat. Tavia's face remained unresponsive, despite Ada's attentions. Her face, white and drawn, was set with tension.

I've done this to her, thought Benois, following her graceful approach, shocked by the weary nature of her steps. A surge of guilt rushed over him. I'm the one who's pushed her away, torn apart the beauty of all that we've shared. How her appearance differed from how she had been in the woods—there, she had smiled, laughed with him, dressed only in her threadbare shift, the skin of her feet a pearled nakedness against the forest floor. Now, her beautiful hair had been secured into a great number of braids, looped into a complicated pattern about her crown, whereas before the tresses had spilled out over her shoulders in complete abandon. Her gown, fashioned from expensive cloth, trailed along the floor behind her, slowing her movements. She looked trapped, beaten down by circumstances. The sooner he was out of her life, the better.

'Come, sit and eat.' Ferchar raised himself laboriously from his seat, indicating that the ladies should join them at the table. Tavia hung back slightly, so that Ada would take the empty seat next to Benois. She didn't feel strong enough to withstand his hostility this evening; she felt wrung out, crushed. If she avoided him completely, then he wouldn't be able to make her cry.

Slipping on to the bench beside Ada, she kept her head lowered, staring forlornly at her pewter plate, looking on doubtfully as Ada placed various items of food before her. To her eyes, the fare appeared limp, unappetising; in the flickering light of the hall, the fish gleamed with a slick film of grease, the bread appeared dry, stale. Her stomach churned. Ada's shoulder jogged constantly against her own as she talked animatedly to Benois, who replied every now and again with a series of detached grunts. God in Heaven, thought Tavia, as she chewed and chewed on the brittle lump of bread, how much longer would she have to endure his presence? Every glance, however fleeting, every nuance of his voice, sent her heart springing hopelessly with joy, only to be withered a moment later by the grim reality of her situation. She loved him, but he didn't love her. She had to face up to practicalities, and admit that she had allowed her head to be carried away by her heart.

'I suppose Ada's told you the good news, my lady?' Tavia jumped as Ferchar's voice boomed along the table towards her. She grabbed at her tankard, the dull metal of the pewter winking in the candlelight as she lifted the vessel to her lips, gulping down the unpalatable crumbs of bread, before turning in the regent's direction. 'You're a very rich young woman, now.' Ferchar's smile stretched wide across his yellow teeth.

Tavia inclined her head in acknowledgement at Ferchar's revelation, endeavouring to avoid her eyes alighting on Benois's brooding presence. The fortune meant nothing to her, nothing at all. All value, all purpose, had been deleted from her life, as if brilliant sunshine had disappeared suddenly behind a cloud, to leave everything grey and subdued. Without warning, the kindled ash of Benois's eyes fastened to hers. Her breath hitched, snagged by the intense beauty of his face, so familiar to her now that it should not have caught her unawares. How unfair it was! Why could she not will her foolish body to remain indifferent to him, instead of flowering traitorously under every storm-wrecked glance. She twisted her eyes away from his powerful perusal, biting her lip as she fought to concentrate on the colourful ebb and flow of the dancers below.

A hand, warm and strong, curled around her shoulder. His hand!

'Come and dance with me,' Benois said from a point high above her head. The words rapped out as a command, not a request.

'Oh, but she's barely touched her…' Ada started to protest, her words fading to a whisper as she noticed Benois's expression. 'You'd better go with him, Tavia.' Ada leaned into her, whispering, 'He looks really angry.'

'My lady?' Benois held out his hand, his fingers tanned

and calloused from years of handling horses. Tavia took a deep breath, knowing that to refuse him here would be to draw attention to herself, and slid her small hand into his, feeling the ridged edges of his scar press into her skin as he helped her up from the bench.

'You'd better have a good explanation for this,' she hissed as he pulled her down the wooden steps and into the body of the great hall.

'Wait.' He frowned at her to be silent as he led her into the dancing. All about them, smiling people twirled and bounced energetically, their faces flushed with the challenge of the steps and the uplifting chords of the music. Tavia knew the dance, and so, it seemed, did Benois. For a large man, he was surprisingly light on his feet, as they began to weave in and out of a chain of people. Then the demands of the dance meant people broke into couples and he caught her up into a slower circular movement.

'Why are you doing this?' Tavia managed to squeeze out, puffing a little with the exertion of the steps.

'Because I want to talk to you, without them listening.' His rapier glance sought out Ferchar and Henry on the dais. His hand moved from her waist and they clasped each other's hands, taking one step away from each other.

'It must be serious,' she mocked him, still smarting from his cold behaviour towards her. 'I would have thought dancing was the last thing you would want to do with me. Wouldn't you prefer to be killing someone?'

He frowned at her scathing tone, taking one step forwards, so that they came together once more. 'I realise you have every right to hate me.' Her eyes flashed agreement at his words before his arm clamped around her waist to spin her around. For a moment, she lost all sense of time and space, knowing only the strong, muscular feel of his arm in the small of her back and the brawny smell of him emanating from the woollen tunic that he wore. 'But you must listen, Tavia. You need to watch your back,' he whispered in her ear as he began to lower her feet to the ground.

She pushed at his forearms, trying to unlock the steel manacle of his hold about her body, raising her eyebrows in mock surprise. 'Tell me something I don't know,' she shot back, her voice sharp with a sarcastic lilt.

He pulled her forcefully towards him. 'Ferchar is planning to marry you for your money.'

'You…what?' she gasped, shocked by his revelation.

'Keep dancing,' Benois ordered. 'They watch us the whole time.'

'How can you know this?' Tavia moved away from him, linking arms and turning with several partners before coming back to Benois.

'Something I overheard. Ferchar will not give up your father's money without a fight.'

Tavia crossed her arms behind her back, mimicking Benois's movement. Their fingers connected, held, as they followed the line of dancing couples. 'He can't marry me if I refuse. No one can force someone to marry them.'

'Don't bet on it.' Benois drew his thick eyebrows together. 'You need to take your money, Tavia, and get away from this place.'

'I *can* think for myself,' she chanted back at him, defensively. An icy knowledge soaked through her bones—he wouldn't be there to help her. She sighed; she had relied on him too much—now, she was on her own. 'But thank you for the warning,' she added, more formally this time.

'Shh. Keep your voice down.'

The musicians in the corner finished the dance with a magnificent crescendo. Everyone bowed formally to their partners, faces flushed and excited from the exacting demands, both physical and mental, of the dance. Benois grabbed Tavia's hand instinctively, aware that they had more to say to each other, but one glance over to the corner of the hall told him the musicians were taking a break, fetching their drinks and finding a seat. They had no choice but to wend their way back to the high dais, a slow process through the crowd of people.

Watching Benois's handsome figure walk alongside Tavia's fresh beauty, Ferchar experienced the sting of jealousy flaring in his heart. He leaned towards Henry. 'This isn't the first time your man Benois has been at Dunswick.'

'Really?' Henry gulped back the contents of his goblet, grimacing as the dregs of wine hit the back of his throat. 'I'm surprised.'

'Aye, it was before…' Ferchar waved his hand lazily as if to indicate some time in the past. 'Tavia came here demanding money. Benois pretended to be her husband, apologising for her brash behaviour. I saw right through it, of course.'

'I see.' Henry waved his arm at one of the serving girls, a signal for his goblet to be filled with wine.

'There's more than first meets the eye between those two.'

'Aye, you'd be right there,' Henry agreed, remembering the passionate parting kiss he had witnessed some days earlier in the courtyard. 'I'd make haste with your wedding plans, Ferchar, if you're not to lose a wife, and I'm not to lose a good soldier.'

Ada, listening idly to the men's conversation, froze, realising in a moment the significance of Ferchar's words.

Chapter Sixteen

Ada tore at one of the ivory combs securing her hair, wrenching furiously at the wine-dark strands as she tried to extricate it. A prong snapped under the ferocity of her action, falling to the wooden floorboards of the chamber, as her loosened braids tumbled down her back. Outrage seethed through her veins; pure, undiluted rage towards the half-sister who had catapulted so unexpectedly into her life. Her head pounded with the unfairness of the situation; she would never have welcomed Tavia with such friendliness, such compassion if she had possessed some inkling of that scheming whore's intentions. How dare Tavia steal Lord Ferchar from under her nose! Only she, Ada of Huntington, was destined to marry Lord Ferchar, not some low-born peasant chit!

Her maid, Beatrice, continued to fold garments carefully and calmly into an oak coffer at the side of the bedchamber, in spite of her mistress's agitation. Over the years she had become accustomed to her Ada's unpredictable rages and tirades, her erratic moods, her weeping, although of late her behaviour had worsened, becoming more frequent and uncontrollable. When Beatrice had finished her task, she closed the lid of the coffer. 'Shall I help you prepare for bed, my lady?' The servant moved quietly across the room, following Ada's awkward, disturbed pacing with knowing eyes. She did well out of Ada, gaining a good deal more in the way of perks and gifts than the other servants in this castle. Ada was easy to steal from as well; as a princess she had so much, she never really noticed when items went missing, and if she did, Beatrice would explain, calmly and carefully, that Ada had probably displaced it during one of her 'moods.'

Ada halted abruptly at Beatrice's question, head snapping around, the puffy lines of her face set into a snarl. 'It's so unfair,' she whined, her face chalk-white and strained in the candlelight. 'Ferchar is to be my husband, not hers!'

'And so he shall be, my lady.' Beatrice began to remove the pearl-studded gold pins that secured a few remaining braids to Ada's head.

'Nay! I heard them!' Ada whirled away from her maid's busy fingers, seeming not to notice as her hair dragged and caught on the pins. She turned, crouching like a caged animal, wagging one finger up at the other woman. 'I heard them talking, Ferchar and King Henry. About how Ferchar wants Tavia's money, and the only way to do that is to marry her! How could he want her, when he can have me?'

'How could he, indeed?' murmured Beatrice, keeping her response bland, non-committal.

'Am I not more beautiful than she?' Ada pouted her lips, a little greasy still from the meal she had consumed earlier that evening, and smoothed her hands over the magnificent spun silk of her gown, drawing attention to her slender curves. Her blue eyes hardened when Beatrice, picking up a hairpin from the floor, did not respond immediately. 'Answer me, damn you!' Ada's voice lowered to a dangerous, sibilant hiss. 'Am I not more beautiful?'

'Oh, my lady, aye, of course you are!' chimed Beatrice dutifully.

Ada lifted her hand, striking the maid's cheek with brutal force. 'You lie, damn you! You just tell me the words you think I want to hear! How shallow you are!' Her voice changed, becoming lilting, sing-song. She sank to her knees, clasping her hands together over her chest, as if praying. Tears coursed down her cheeks, dripping dark blotches onto the floorboards. 'Oh, Beatrice, forgive me!' Ada clutched at the older woman's skirts, her fingers nervous and fumbling over the coarse spun cloth. 'I don't know what ails me!'

'You've just got yourself in another state, my lady.' Beatrice patted her on the head. 'I think nothing of it, remember. Don't upset yourself.'

Ada raised her tear-stained face. 'I don't deserve you, Beatrice. You're so good to me.' And I make sure I'm amply rewarded for my pains, thought the maid smugly. She lifted one hand to her smarting cheek, touching it gingerly.

Head bowed, Ada shook her dishevelled locks, the curling ends moving across the oak floorboards with a swishing sound. 'If only she hadn't come,' she mumbled into her chest, 'if only she hadn't come and upset everything, then Ferchar would still want to marry me.' Ada clawed desperately for Beatrice's gnarled, work-roughened hands. 'We have to get rid of her, Beatrice. Tavia has to go.'

'Hush, my lady, you're exhausted, that's all. It will all seem a lot better in the morning.'

Ada's fingers snaked around Beatrice's wrist in a punishing grip, her nails digging into the servant's soft flesh. 'Nay, Beatrice! It will not be better in the morning!' Ada was almost shouting now. 'Because she will still be here!'

Someone rapped sharply at the door; both women jumped. Then came Tavia's voice, low and insistent. 'Ada, are you there? I must speak with you.'

Ada's head jolted up, her eyes wild, unfocused. 'Tell her to go away. Tell her that I cannot see her at the moment.'

Beatrice placed heavy hands on her mistress's shoulders, steady, reassuring. 'Let's see what she wants, my lady.' She leaned over, whispering into Ada's ear, 'You never know, it may be to your advantage.' Ada smiled, her eyes adopting a positive gleam. Taking charge, Beatrice pulled on Ada's hands, helping her up from the floor, leading her over to sit on the edge of the bed, on top of a pile of glossy furs. Moving over to the sturdy iron-riveted oak door, the maid clicked the latch upwards, allowing Tavia to slip in.

'Thank you,' Tavia said, recognising Ada's servant. Her eyes sought her half-sister in the gloom, trying not to betray her shock when she spotted Ada, sitting at the end of the bed. Her face was covered in red patches, almost as if she'd been crying; her hair was dishevelled, hanging over her shoulders in unruly curls. 'Why, Ada, what's the matter?'

'You tell me, Tavia,' Ada responded, her tone laden with annoyance. 'I thought you, of all people, should know.'

'Nay, I do not know,' Tavia replied carefully, wondering whether she had made the right decision in coming to Ada. But her half-sister, however fragile in character, was her last hope in escaping this place, and Ferchar; she had to try.

'You've stolen Ferchar from me!' Ada's voice rose petulantly, like that of a small, spoiled child.

'Now, now, mistress, don't you go getting yourself upset again.' Beatrice moved comfortingly to Ada's side. 'Best you just declare your business, my lady, and then be off. My mistress has worked herself up into a real state over this whole thing.' Her beady eyes glowered at Tavia.

'But, Ada,' Tavia choked out, astounded, 'I have no intention of marrying Lord Ferchar! That's what I've come to see you about! I need your help!'

'What about asking Lord Benois?' Ada replied. 'It hasn't escaped anyone's notice that you seem to spend a lot of time with him.'

Tavia picked at a loose thread on her bodice, desperately trying to ignore the hurt, the rejection that flooded through her slim frame. 'He's helped me on a couple of occasions. But he has other business to attend to now, for King Henry.' Her own pride prevented her from asking him for help; the less he knew about her plans now, the better.

'So he's abandoned you to your fate,' Ada responded, a cruel lilt to her voice.

Tavia grimaced. 'A fate that I have no plans to be a part of. Ferchar can keep the fortune for all I care. I just want to be away from this place.'

'Ferchar always gets what he wants,' Ada said, smiling slowly. 'He'll find you in the end.'

'That's why I need to get as far away as possible,' Tavia explained. 'Somewhere that he'll never think of looking.'

'Then I think I can help you, Tavia.' Ada spoke slowly, as if the idea was forming at that moment in her mind. 'I have an idea that will suit both of us—you will disappear and I will marry Ferchar. Just as it should be.'

The royal forest, which for decades had provided the kings of Scotland with rich, prolific hunting, expanded out to the west of Dunswick: vast, undulating slopes of woodland teeming with deer and wild boar. No one was allowed to hunt here except with the king's permission; anyone caught poaching would be punished severely. As Ferchar rode, following his master huntsman to the entrance of the forest, he silently congratulated himself on being able to offer the English king a proper finale to all their negotiations. King Henry was known for his passion for the hunt; the excitement on his face had been palpable when Ferchar had made the suggestion the evening before.

From the early hours of this morning, when the dew lay heavy on the grass before steaming gently in the strong rays of the rising sun, the master of the hunt had been striding through these forests. Watching and working with his two most trusted bloodhounds, he found the scent of the quarry, noting the location and direction of the fresh tracks. Without this man's skill and forethought, Ferchar and his noble assembly could be riding for hours with no hint of a quarry. The master had returned during breakfast, nodding and smiling, indicating the promise of a good chase ahead. Now, up ahead of the horses, the hounds strained and pulled on their horse-hair leads, eager to be off, to pick up the scent, to sprint through the woodlands with their powerful, honed bodies.

'Your man knows his job well,' Henry commented, naturally addressing the compliment towards Ferchar although the pale-faced Malcolm rode on the other side of the regent. All three men had dispensed with their destriers, the horses they normally rode in battle, and instead rode the smaller coursers, their muscled, agile frames ideally suited for the quick turns and fast gallops through the trees.

'Aye, he's been in the royal employ since he was a boy,' Ferchar explained, shifting irritably. He was certain his groom had not fastened the saddle correctly underneath the horse; he seemed to lean too much on to one side, and his right hip ached with the effort of keeping his balance central.

Henry edged his horse closer. 'And have you told Mistress Mowerby the good news yet?'

Ferchar shot a covert glance behind him, making certain that the ladies followed at a discreet distance. He smiled, reassured that Ada rode close by his future wife's side. He had given Ada the task of making sure she didn't let Tavia out of her sight, and, as usual, Ada had been pathetically grateful to him for giving her such an important job. He knew he could trust Ada; after all, he had schooled her to do his bidding ever since their father had died. His gaze narrowed suddenly at the sight of Benois riding just behind the ladies, the sunlight bouncing off the jewelled hilt of his sword.

'Nay,' Ferchar answered finally, 'I thought I would save that piece of information until you, my lord, journeyed south. It would be best if she had no allies in the castle, no one to help her should she choose to flee.'

'You mean Benois le Vallieres.'

'Precisely.'

Henry adjusted his position in his saddle, patting Ferchar on the back. 'Have no fear, my friend. I will ride south on the morrow, and Benois will accompany me.'

'Just make sure he does,' Ferchar muttered.

Bouncing clumsily alongside Ada, Tavia gripped the reins of her courser with tense fingers, wondering if she could trust her new-found sister. All morning, Ada had been nothing but helpfulness, helping her dress in clothes that would carry her through a long journey, packing her saddle bags with food and water as well as some of the precious gemstones that Ferchar had grudgingly handed back to her. In her chamber the previous night, Ada and Beatrice had outlined their plan of how Tavia was to escape. Under the ruse of going hunting, Ada and Tavia would 'become lost' and Ada, who knew the layout of the woods well, would lead Tavia to a trusted man-servant who would ride south with her, and to freedom. Tavia's mind scrambled with all the fine details of the plan, trying to ignore the enormity of the decision she was about to make. But Benois's rejection of her had effectively made up her mind. She had tried, and failed, to fight for his love; she was not about to humble herself any more.

'I didn't think hunting would be your favourite pastime.' Benois rode up alongside her, his lean figure relaxed, graceful in the saddle. He wore no hat, nor helmet, chestnut hair flaring in the strong light, and, as he lifted his hand to shield his eyes, she traced the powerful sinew in his wrist, remembering the gentleness of his fingers.

Her hands clenched around the reins; refusing to look at him, she studied the nodding mane of her horse. 'And I thought you'd be gone by now.'

'I suppose I deserve that,' he murmured under his breath.

'What do you expect, Benois?' she retaliated, not wanting Ada to overhear. 'That I'm going to speak to you with a civil tongue after…after…' She stopped, the words clawing at her throat. Tears prickled at the bottom of her eyes.

'I suppose I just wanted to make sure that you were all right.' In truth, he wasn't certain how to broach the subject that he had tossed and turned with all night; he knew he had to tread carefully, an approach with which he was not familiar.

Tavia's head shot up, faint blue circles sketched below her eyes. Yet he couldn't stop thinking how beautiful she looked, her eyes burning like sapphires in the white marble of her face as she addressed him in a chanting, caustic tone. 'Oh, aye, I'm just fine,' she replied. 'Apart from the fact that I'm about to be tied into some dreadful marriage with…him!' She nodded brusquely up ahead towards Ferchar, identifying the object of her sentence.

'Hmm.' Benois rubbed his chin, as if considering her words. 'I see your point.' He yearned to tell her that she was safe, that his night of wakefulness had forced him to come to a decision, but he had to wait until she was alone to tell her.

Her brows drew together, a fierce condemning line. She pulled at his sleeve, fingers digging into the hard muscle under the fabric of his tunic. 'Do you dare to jest, Benois? It's no laughing matter, I can assure you!' Guilt licked her heart, but she quashed the sentiment promptly. It was better that Benois had no idea of her escape plan; indeed, what would be the point in telling him? He didn't care about her anyway.

'Nay, you're right, it is no laughing matter. But there may be a way out.' His deep-set, hawk eyes searched her face with a knowing intensity.

She swiped at a small blackfly buzzing irritatingly around her head. 'Name it. I've racked my brains. There's no way out of this situation.' Her face felt set and hard, like a mask, the brilliance of her eyes glowing like aquamarines in the pale marble of her skin.

'There is if you had a husband already.' But Tavia didn't hear him; his last words were drowned out by three distinctive blasts on the huntsman's horn, as he called the pack of hounds together.

'What did you say?' Tavia glanced up.

'Later.' He threw her the briefest of smiles, before altering his hold on the reins to wheel his courser around, urging his horse to join the main group of the hunting party. The short hem of his cloak flicked upwards with the movement, revealing a bright green lining of closely woven silk.

Puzzled by his attentive behaviour, Tavia followed the supple poise of his body as he trotted towards the brightly garmented group of nobles. Everyone appeared to have dressed with great care that morning, aware of the significance of this hunting party. The vivid colours of the garments, the scarlet and purple, blues and golds, contrasted starkly with the dull green tunics of the huntsmen moving amongst the hounds. She tracked Benois's strong profile, easy to spot despite the chaos of the group, as he leaned over to speak to Henry. Benois's manner seemed different towards her today. The hostility of yesterday had disappeared to be replaced by…what? A tentative friendliness? As she closed her eyes, the sparkling granite of his eyes still glowed vividly in her mind.

'Come on, Tavia!' Frustrated by her lack of movement, Ada clutched agitatedly at her sleeve. 'What's the matter with you?' she demanded bossily. Her eyes raked the exhausted lines of Tavia's face. 'Oh, no, you've not been taken in by that one, have you?' She nodded in Benois's direction, her tone mocking and derisive. 'What did he say to you?'

'He said he might be able to help me!'

'Hah!' Ada snorted, her eyes tapering with determination. Her hair seemed to have been yanked back too forcibly today, the thin braids pulling severely at the sides of her face. 'Don't believe a word of it. It will be another trick from those English pigs! Don't dally with the enemy, because they still are, whatever discussion they've been having up at the castle.'

'But…?' Tavia protested faintly.

'Trust who you know, Tavia, and that means me, your kith and kin.' Tavia's mind reeled. At this precise moment, she didn't know whom to trust. Ada's voice ebbed to a conspiring whisper. 'You haven't changed your mind, have you?' Desperation gnawed at her voice.

'Nay, of course not,' Tavia replied hurriedly. God in Heaven! He made it so she didn't know her own mind! 'Nay,' she repeated, with more purpose this time. 'I need to be away from here…and him,' she added, her voice muted.

'Good,' said Ada, patting her arm. Her fingers dug painfully into Tavia's soft flesh, the blue of her eyes deepening with a sense of purpose. 'Look, the hounds have picked up the scent. We should have our chance soon.'

The middle of the forest seemed dense, impenetrable, the thick brown trunks crowding on to the barely perceptible track, brambles sprawling upwards, higher than a man's chest. Without Ada, who had known the forest from childhood, at her side, Tavia knew she would soon be lost. Behind them, the haunting sound of the huntsman's horn grew fainter and fainter as they drew away, their agile horses weaving through the difficult undergrowth. Ada clung to her like a leech, her left knee bumping constantly against Tavia's as if she were afraid to lose her, her expression keen and alert, darting this way and that, looking for something. Tavia smiled, trying to hide the nervous runnels of tension slipping through her veins, and caught Ada's eye. 'You don't have to ride quite so close to me, Ada,' she chided softly. 'I'm not going to run away!'

A sly look slipped over Ada's face. 'Just make sure you don't,' she replied, smiling, but her smile was tense and strained. Then she caught Tavia's surprised glance, and rubbed one hand over her face, as if trying to clear her mind. 'Sorry, I'm just a bit nervous. I'm worried that Ferchar might have noticed we've disappeared.'

A low branch snatched at Tavia's veil, and she winced slightly as she disengaged it from the silk. 'I doubt it. He seemed to be completely immersed in the hunt.'

'Ferchar asked me to keep an eye on you, make sure you didn't run away. He trusts me, you see.' Pride blossomed in Ada's voice. She drew herself up in the saddle, elegant, poised, every inch of her a princess.

'I doubt he'll trust you after this,' Tavia replied. 'Will you be in trouble?' In comparison to Ada, she felt unwieldy and cumbersome, still unused to the rolling gait of the horse.

'Nay.' Ada frowned at Tavia as if she were mad. 'He will always trust me…he loves me, you see.'

Something in Ada's voice warned Tavia not to argue with her, although she certainly didn't believe that Ferchar cared anything for Ada. A beatific smile lightened Ada's features when she talked of Ferchar, almost as if she worshipped the regent, and would do anything for him. A thread of fear coiled slowly in Tavia's heart. Had she made a foolish mistake, relying on Ada to help her flee a potential marriage with Ferchar?

The narrowness of the track forced the horses into single file, Tavia trailing the dappled grey rump of Ada's courser, glad that she had taken Ada's advice and worn dull, sombre colours so she couldn't be easily spotted through the trees. Her garments, borrowed from Ada, were comprised of a dark-blue underdress topped with a pale-green *bliaut*, edged with dark green embroidery. It would make her more difficult to discern beneath the gloom of the trees.

The undergrowth became thicker and more impenetrable. Up ahead, Ada dismounted, waving at Tavia to do the same. She slid down haphazardly, bringing the reins high over the horse's head. The courser snorted suddenly, warm air steaming against her hands from the horse's nostrils. Tavia grabbed the bridle under the animal's mouth, pulling the horse along beside her as the brambles snagged at her sweeping skirts.

'Tavia, I'm completely stuck in these brambles,' Ada called out from the other side of her horse. 'Leave your horse with me, and go up ahead. See if Dougal is there waiting.'

All Tavia could see was the top of Ada's head bobbing up

and down on the other side of her horse, no doubt wrestling painfully with a bramble. 'Can I not help you?' she asked, pulling her horse level, before squeezing in front of both animals.

'Nay!' Ada's voice took on a fervent urgency. 'He'll go if we're not there soon! Keep on going that way!' She pointed with one white finger towards what appeared to be a chaotic bundle of brambles, flanked by two large oaks. 'Just push through,' Ada hissed, as Tavia hesitated.

Tavia took one step forwards…and fell. Beneath her unsuspecting feet, the flimsy criss-crossing of branches that disguised the animal trap gave way easily beneath her slight weight, and she crashed through, the twigs snarling her clothes, catching at her neat braid. She shrieked with fright, a long drawn-out wail as her arms instinctively flew out, trying to halt her hurtling drop, clutching at the smooth earth sides. Her fingernails scraped the damp soil, filling with earth. She thumped down at the bottom of the hole, her head whipping forwards with force to hit one of the large stones that jutted out from the bottom. For a moment, Tavia lay there, winded and bruised, the air in her lungs brutally emptied out by the violence of the fall. Her body crumpled against the curving side of the pit, her mind barely conscious, as she half-lay, half-sat, hot, sticky blood washing down her face.

She willed herself to shout, 'Ada! Help me!' Her voice sounded thin and weak, rippling with pain. With difficulty, she slanted her head up towards the source of light, a circle that seemed so far away, a circle mottled green by the trees surrounding it. She squinted as Ada's face appeared, hanging over the edge of the hole; it was difficult to decipher her features, all she could make out was a dark blob against the light.

'Nay, I'll not help you, sister dear!' Ada's voice, when it came, seemed oddly distorted; Tavia thought she had misheard.

'Ada, you must help me!' she called again, her voice weakening. Her limbs held no strength, collapsed against the ground; it was as if the life-force flowed out from her.

'And I said "nay"!' A wildness entered Ada's tone. 'Think you to replace me as Ferchar's wife, you cunning, crafty wench? Well, it's not to be, do you hear me! It's not to be!'

Panic wrenched Tavia's innards—had Ada truly gone mad? 'I have no intention of marrying Ferchar,' she called up faintly. 'You know that. Just help me up, and I will disappear, Ada, please!'

'But he has every intention of marrying you, doesn't he!' cackled Ada. 'But he can't marry you if he can't find you!' Her head lifted back from the hole above and disappeared. 'And he'll never find you, Tavia, never!' Ada's voice floated away, growing fainter.

Tavia slumped back against the side of the hole, all fight drained from her. Her head ached from the impact with the stone; her whole body felt crushed and bruised from the fall. Who would find her here? Racked with pain and shock, she buried her head in her hands and cried.

Chapter Seventeen

Jamming his heels down against the metal bar of the stirrup, Benois lifted himself up in the saddle, scanning the forest for a glimpse of Tavia. Avidly he sought for that wine-dark hair, that quick, bright smile and intelligent blue eyes. He found them not. He cursed. For a long time, he had supposed her to be bound up in the colourful mêlée of lords and ladies that made up the hunting party; indeed, on a few occasions he had picked out Ada, and assumed the two sisters were together.

Since yestereve, since he had danced with Tavia in his arms with the prospect of riding south with King Henry hanging over him like a threat, a curious sense of loss had invaded his heart and a fierce sense of protectiveness had grown. He couldn't abandon her, leaving her here to the spurious guardianship of Lord Ferchar, to the possibility of marrying such a man. Surely he could take care of her in a platonic way, as a brother took care of a sister? But even as his inspection skimmed the jostling group of hunters, the chaotic jumbling of bloodhounds, he knew he was lying to himself.

Now, as he twisted his neck this way and that, searching

for her familiar figure, he realised with an icy certainty that she was not among the milling crowd. With increasing apprehension, he looked for Ada, searching out her auburn hair, identical to Tavia's. Henry rode up alongside, his rotund face flushed and elated from the successful pursuit of the stag.

'If I'd known how good the hunting was here, I would have asked Ferchar for Dunswick also!' he joked, slapping Benois on the back. 'What an excellent day!' He darted another satisfied glance at the fine stag lying in the back of the ox-cart.

'Aye,' agreed Benois vaguely. 'Have you seen Tavia anywhere?'

Henry frowned. 'Sweet Jesu, Benois! Is your mind on nothing else these days? How can you be bothered with the ladies on such a hunting day as this?'

Benois quirked one eyebrow upwards. 'I feel responsible for her.'

Henry threw back his head and roared, the red hairs of his beard glinting golden in the sunlight. 'That's rich, Benois, coming from you. Since when have you felt responsible for anything…or anyone for that matter?'

Benois's grey eyes hardened to iron. 'Since I met her.'

'God's teeth, Benois! Why not bed the wench, then you'll forget her easily enough?'

'It didn't work,' Benois replied blandly, his eyes still running over the crowd.

Henry looked stunned for a moment. 'For Christ's sake, don't tell Ferchar. He thinks she's a virgin. Hah! What a jest when he marries her! Then she'll be his responsibility and not yours!'

But Benois failed to hear his last words, having sighted Ada on the fringes of the clearing. He had already kicked his heels into his horse's flanks, steering the animal through the crowd towards her. The rest of the hunting party was starting to turn their horses, to follow the laden ox-cart back to Dunswick, and the celebratory feast that awaited them.

'Where's Tavia?' Benois rapped out as he approached the princess, his tone severe, demanding.

Ada held herself rigidly on her horse, her expression one of contempt as Benois nudged his horse alongside. 'And good day to you, too, sir,' she mocked him slightly, indicating that he should address her properly, as a princess.

'My lady…' he bowed deeply, from the saddle '…forgive me, I forget my manners. I was wondering where Tavia was.' Studying Ada, he was struck by the differences between the two sisters. Although their hair colour was identical, Tavia's physique was leaner, more athletic, in comparison to Ada's slender, curvier figure. Tavia's face glowed, flushed with health and vitality, whereas Ada's skin seemed pasty and uneven by comparison.

'She went back to the castle,' Ada explained, but her eyes wouldn't meet Benois's, instead sliding curiously away.

She's lying, Benois thought immediately. 'Why?' he rasped.

'She had a bad headache; she thought it would be better if she lay down for a bit.' Although Ada outwardly appeared calm and controlled, she could not prevent her fingers from working nervously along the reins.

Benois glared at her, his lips set in a stern line, his eyes flinty steel. 'Don't tell me she went alone?'

'Nay.' Ada leaned over and touched his arm as if to reassure him, then whipped them away quickly as he regarded her fingers with disdain. 'I sent one of the grooms back with her.'

A swelling feeling of unease settled across Benois's chest.

'I don't believe you, my lady.' He kept his voice low, not wanting Ferchar or Henry to overhear the conversation. He noted the way Ada's eyes darted continually over to the crowd behind him. Was she thinking of calling for help…or did she not want them to hear either?

Dropping her hold on her reins, Ada stroked the blond mane of her horse. 'Why wouldn't you believe me? It's the truth, my lord.' She smiled at him, her expression purposely simpering, docile.

His eyes sparked dangerously. 'Let me tell you why I don't believe you! Because everything about this morning has been strange. Strange that Tavia would hunt, and you, when Ferchar tells me you've never shown the least bit of interest in it before. Strange that you were asked to look after Tavia, yet you failed to ride back to the castle with her, as any other companion would.' Anger rippled through his tone, harsh, threatening.

'Leave me alone, stop bullying me!' Her nostrils flared with panic as she attempted to turn her horse, to squeeze past him, but he blocked her path with his bigger horse. 'I'll scream!' She scowled pointedly at his hands on her reins.

'Nay, you will not scream,' he stated, deliberately taunting. 'You don't want to attract attention to yourself, especially Ferchar's attention. And why not, I ask myself? Why not? Because Tavia is still in these forests somewhere, and you don't want Ferchar to find her.'

As her whole body recoiled backwards, her face a stretched mask of terror, Benois knew he had the truth. A savage rage welled inside him, and he rocked forward, his expression thunderous. 'By the rood, Princess, I will strangle you with my bare hands if you don't tell me where she is!'

'You'll never find her,' Ada whispered up to him, her lips curving into a lopsided smile.

Gripped by an unfathomable fury, Benois seized her bird-like shoulders, the light bones giving way slightly under his punishing fingers. 'Where…is…she?' he ground out.

'She's not going to marry him, you know,' Ada chanted out, trying to wriggle her shoulders out from under his grip. 'It's me he wants, you see, me.'

Ferchar and Henry rode up. 'Everything all right here?' Ferchar asked suspiciously.

Benois dropped his hands. 'Aye, the princess was explaining that Tavia has returned to the castle with a groom.'

Ferchar rolled his eyes. 'Then let's hope the groom had the good sense to keep an eye on her.' He glowered at Ada. 'I told you to stay with her…at all times. Why didn't you go with her?'

'I wanted to stay here…with you,' Ada tittered, her hand waggling coquettishly in front of her mouth.

'God's teeth,' Ferchar cursed. 'Well, you best come on, and pray, for your sake, that she's there.'

Benois watched the horses' rumps disappear up the track, remaining in the clearing with the grooms who were fastening the leads back on to the hounds. He knew Tavia was still in the forest; he felt her presence there as if she stood at his side. He had to find her before Ferchar discovered she had not returned; he had to find her and take her away from this place, far away where no one could ever hurt her again. Studying the hounds, watching them still eagerly sniffing the ground for scent trails, he realised suddenly how he would find her.

Scrunched woodenly against the damp earth of the pit wall, Tavia knew she must rise, attempt to climb out…somehow. Even lifting her head had become an effort, as she hoisted her eyes to the circle of light, judging it to be about the height of two men above the top of her head. Climbing the sheer walls of the pit would be an impossibility…or would it? She had to try.

A raft of dizziness threatened to unbalance her as she clambered to her feet, gasping as the pain shot through her head, clutching at the wall for support. With trembling fingers she began to gouge out the earth from the wall, intending to form some sort of foot- and hand-holds, so she could pull herself up. Tremors shook her slim frame; she still couldn't believe that Ada—Ada, who had shown her the most kindness within this new life of hers—had left her here to die! How could she have not seen it?

Nails raw and painful, Tavia tucked one toe into the first hole that she had made. Now all she needed to do was push herself up, and lean into the wall so she could create another hand-hold further up. Every muscle straining, she willed her body to force itself up the wall, trying to stretch her hand up, to heave herself up. But instead she slipped back down, knees and elbows banging against the hard earth, crumpling to the ground in a desolate, forlorn heap. She banged her fists against the earth, tears of frustration coursing down her cheeks. The hopelessness of the situation crushed down on her, pummelled at her slight strength, her sapping energy, to leave her beaten, defeated. Fear and panic surged in her chest—was she really going to die? She opened her mouth and screamed, screamed at the injustice, screamed with the bellowing sound echoing and bouncing off the sides of the pit until her throat was hoarse. At last, sobbing, she curled into a hopeless ball in the debris of twigs and leaves at the bottom of the animal trap, exhausted and utterly wretched.

She wondered if she had been asleep when the small sound crept through her consciousness. In fact, was she dreaming?

But, nay, there it was again: the sound of something snuffling excitedly at the mouth of the pit, then a yelp, an excited bark. Her heart jumped, and she hauled her upper body up from the floor, craning her neck and trying to focus on what was happening above her. A dog's head appeared in the light, a hound, with its ears hanging forward as it whined, pawing the ground, looking almost as if it wanted to jump into the pit with her.

And then…his voice. Benois. She nearly collapsed with relief. He had found her!

'Help!' she called out. 'Benois, I'm down here, help me!'

'Tavia, is that you?' She almost smiled at the incredulity in his voice. He knelt down at the edge of the trap, searching for her in the gloom.

'Here I am, I'm here!' Tavia twisted around, stumbling on to her feet, reaching her hands above her, fingers splayed, wanting the comfort of his touch. He seemed too far away! 'Benois, please, please get me out of here!' Panic flecked her voice, an edge of teetering wildness.

'Tavia, rest easy. I will get you out.' His voice, strong and vibrant, soothed her. He moved away from the hole, and she heard the deep resonance of his voice, talking to someone. She closed her eyes as another black swirl of dizziness caused her to sway violently, a boiling sickness clogging her stomach. It was as if she floated above the scene, as if she were part of it no longer; all she wanted to do was lie down and sleep, just sleep. She sagged against the wall, barely managing to hold herself up in the fog of pain and tiredness, and touched one finger tentatively to the cut on her head.

'Tavia? Tavia? Can you hear me?' Benois's voice lacerated the mists that obscured her thinking. Something dropped before her line of vision: the frayed end of a dog's lead. 'Tie the rope around your waist, Tavia,' Benois shouted down, 'and we'll pull you up.'

All she had to do was lift her fingers, grab the dangling end and tie it. 'Impossible,' she whispered weakly, and had an incredible urge to laugh. She couldn't help herself even when help jiggled in front of her nose.

High above, Benois swore.

She pitched back on unsteady feet, startled from her reverie, as he landed neatly on his feet, right in front of her.

'Sweet Jesu!' Benois took in her bloodied face, her stark white skin, her barely upright body, in one swift, penetrating glance. 'Come on, we need to get you out of here!' His eyes glittered in the half-light, fierce, protective.

Mesmerised by the wonderful sight of this living, breathing ball of energy, she stood transfixed. 'Is it you?' she whispered waveringly, stroking his face as if he were not real, but some sort of dream, or vision. The stubble on his chin rasped lightly against her fingers. He captured her hand, his own fingers warming her icy skin.

'Aye, it's me, Tavia, and we're going to get you out of here.' He grinned briefly. 'You can thank me later.'

Gently, he turned her around, pulling her drooping body back against the muscled hardness of his limbs so he could tie the rope around both of them. Her chilled limbs soaked up the warmth from his body. He called up, the sound in his chest vibrating comfortingly against her spine, and then the horse-hair rope tightened, creaking and flexing with their combined weight. Supported by the rope, Benois planted the soles of his feet against the wall of the trap, and began to climb upwards, Tavia cradled in his lap. Slowly, steadily, the circle of light came closer and closer, until at last, they broke up and outwards into the haven of green.

Tavia burst suddenly into the light, tumbling forwards on

to her hands and knees, disoriented. Collapsing back, she sat for a moment, blinking, breathing in the cool, fresh air of the forest. Benois pulled himself easily out from the hole, every movement precise, economical. Springing to his feet, he eyed her briefly, frowning, before striding to his horse held by a young boy.

'Thank you.' Benois clapped a hand on the boy's shoulders. 'I should never have found her if it hadn't been for your help.' The boy smiled, especially when Benois placed several gold coins in his hand. 'Now, begone. I don't want Lord Ferchar to notice that you, or your horse, are missing. And remember, you haven't seen us.'

The boy nodded, untying the dog's lead, the lead that had pulled them to safety, from the bridle of Benois's horse, and securing the hound before walking off into the forest. Without bothering to raise her head, Tavia guessed that it had been the strength of the horse which had dragged them out of the hole. Benois marched back to the place where Tavia huddled on the ground, his face drawn into lines of concern at her pallor, and the ugly gash on her head. His gimlet eyes, smouldering charcoal in the long shadows of the afternoon, scoured her.

With some effort, she managed to lift her head at his approach. 'How did you find me?' She stared up at him, still astounded that he should be here at all. Benois pulled out a piece of white cloth from his wide leather belt. 'I had this,' he explained gently, the breeze sifting his hair, ruffling it, making him seem younger somehow. 'It's your veil…you used it to bind my shoulder. The fabric carried your scent,' he added, noting her puzzled expression, 'so the hound followed your track with no difficulty.'

'I'm surprised you still had it,' she uttered, studying the creased and bloodied cloth that hung between his fingers.

He smiled enigmatically, tucking the material down the

front of his tunic, unwilling to confess that he had been reluctant to dispose of it; the material carried her perfume, a unique fragrance that he held dear to his heart.

'And now,' he said, bending down to swoop his arm beneath her hips, around her back, hoisting her high up against his chest, the hem of her *bliaut* falling back to reveal her small leather slippers swinging in the air, 'you come with me.'

Tavia didn't protest as he set her up on to his saddle, clutching uselessly at the pommel as the horse dipped sideways under her slight weight. But Benois kept one hand protectively at her waist, suspecting from her pale colour that she might fall, as he stuck his toe into the shining metal stirrup and swung his athletic frame on to the horse behind her. Too weary to object as his muscled thighs cupped close around her hips, or to even wriggle forwards to create some space between them, she merely subsided gratefully into the rugged haven of his chest. His arms came about her, expertly controlling the reins to manoeuvre the animal out from the hostile undergrowth.

The sunlight, dappled under the trees, fired coppery sparks over Benois's chestnut hair, stippling the bouncing motion of the horse's mane with light. The damp earth on Tavia's fingers began to dry out, and itch. She brushed at the loose soil, suddenly aware of the state of her nails, her hands, streaked with grime and blood. Pain pulsed through her temples with the steady jolt of the horse, and, without thinking, she raised her right hand to probe the wound tentatively.

'Don't touch it!' Benois seized her fingers, drawing them down again. His large, steady fingers remained over hers. 'Your fingers are so dirty, they might infect the cut. Don't worry, I'll clean it up later.'

'I tried to climb out,' she ventured, by way of explanation.

'I don't doubt it,' he murmured. 'You're not the sort of maid who would accept such a fate so easily.'

'The walls were so steep.' A shudder squeezed her chest as she remembered. 'I did give up in the end.'

Anger seized him as he thought of her, alone and frightened, at the bottom of the animal trap. 'You kept your head, Tavia.' He struggled to keep the emotion from his voice.

A thought gripped her; she half-twisted in the saddle. 'You're not taking me back, are you? You're not taking me back to Dunswick?'

'Not a chance,' he promised, grimacing at the trembling in her body. 'We ride to Langley's castle, over the border. He'll give us shelter, food.'

Reassured, Tavia shifted against him, vaguely aware of the panic that bubbled furiously at the edges of her sanity. 'I thought no one would come for me,' she blurted out suddenly. 'I thought I would be left there…to die.' Her voice rang with such a hollow, bereft note that he relinquished her hand, and brought his arm around, across her chest, hugging her close to him.

'I would have found you, Tavia. I would have razed those woods to the ground to find you.' A flare of passion furrowed the melodious timbre of his speech.

Tavia closed her eyes, savouring the feel of the man at her back, his strong arm around her, the warm play of sunlight on her face.

'Why?' she ventured, suddenly.

'Why?' he shot back, his tone unguarded, raw. 'Because—' Benois stopped. *Because I love you. I need you.* The words, shocking, vivid, burst into his brain. The silence shivered in the air between them. He knew he had to give her some explanation. 'Because I do not wish to see you married to Ferchar,' he supplied finally, knowing that now was not the time to tell her of his plan, not now, when she was tired and hurt.

The breeze washed through the woodland canopy above them, sending a gentle sighing through the leaves. The shadows from the trees danced over their faces, the strong light throwing the bark on the wide trunks into an intense pattern of tiny creases and whorls. A sparrowhawk, body motionless, head turning in rapid succession of movement, yellow eyes hunting prey for his fledgling chicks, only heard the horse's approach at the last moment. The white patches on his neck flashed as the large bird lifted off silently from the high branch, the dark bars of colour across his chest distinctive against the green of the forest.

Tavia followed the sparrowhawk's dipping, swerving flight through the trees, its odd guttural chattering warning its mate of the humans' presence. Even through the foggy layers of her exhausted mind, she knew Benois hadn't answered her properly. A tiny part of her brain pleaded to go no further, to stop questioning him, and relish that sheer joy of just being within the circle of his arms. He had made it perfectly clear at Dunswick that he desired her, but was unable to give her anything more, preferring to resume his duties with King Henry and ride south.

'Then I suppose I should say thank you,' she mumbled. 'Because if you hadn't come to look for me…well, then…' The sentence, unfinished, faded into a half-gasp, as she realised that if he hadn't cared enough to look for her, then she would have died. 'You saved my life,' she said, finally, picking nervously at the thick soil under one of her nails. 'Ada really wanted me to die.'

'She wanted Ferchar for herself,' Benois replied crisply, 'and nothing, nobody, was to come between her and her

marriage, not even the discovery of a long-lost half-sister.'
He ducked his head to avoid a low overhanging branch,
inhaling the sweet scent of Tavia's hair as his chin brushed
the crown of her head. They fell silent, listening to the
rhythmic sound of the horse's hoofbeats as he carried them
south through the trees. The track had become easier to ne-
gotiate, running wide, clear through the forest, the earth
hard-packed and dry.

As they emerged from the woodland, the land opened out
before them, a wide river valley stretching horizontally
before their eyes, with steep, rounded hills rising high into
the bright, blue sky beyond.

'The border,' Benois announced, his eyes combing the
range of hills before them, seeking the best possible route
forwards. 'We need to go up there, Tavia. Can you make it?'

'Aye, I can,' she said, with more fortitude than she felt. She
could crawl up on her hands and knees if that's what it took
to escape Ferchar's clutches.

In the slanting shadows of the late afternoon light, a warm
hush fell across the land, broken only by the plaintive call of
the curlews. The tops of the hills were flushed with a pinkish
hue, an indicator of the indestructible granite stone that had
formed the smooth curves.

'We should reach Langley by nightfall,' Benois announced. 'We can move faster over this open ground.' Tightening his arm more securely about her waist, he kicked the
horse into a trot. Tavia blanched at the sudden pain searing
through her temple, the unexpected, jolting pace sending
spirals of agony through her skull. She gripped desperately
on to Benois's forearm, the honed, interlacing muscles hard
against her sweating palms as she tried to control her breathing. Her skirts, snatched by the wind, whipped out and back
along the animal's flanks, the hem flapping wildly against

Benois's braies. Nausea scratched at the parched lining of her gullet; she swallowed frantically, hoping she wasn't going to be sick.

'Tavia?' Benois, shouting above the air rushing noisily past them, felt her body weaken against him. He yanked on the reins, hard, slowing the animal to a walk, before leaping off, moving round so he could see her face. A grey pallor cloaked Tavia's skin as she looked towards him. 'I don't feel very well,' she mumbled, her muscles screaming at her as she fought desperately to remain upright in the saddle.

'I can see that.' Benois cursed. 'Come, you need to rest for a while.'

'I'm sorry,' she mumbled, as he reached up to lift her swaying figure down from the saddle, folding her into his lean frame as soon as her feet touched the ground. 'I don't know what's wrong with me. I'm not normally like this.'

He smiled at her forced, practical tone as he half-carried her over to a large granite outcrop. 'I don't suppose you're normally thrown down a hole and left to die,' he said, settling her down on a cushiony mound of grass, so she could lean her head back against the craggy stone. Fetching his leather flagon from the horse, he held it up to her mouth, urging her to drink. The cool, refreshing water trickled down her throat, going some way towards restoring her equilibrium. Benois drew the flagon away, securing the vessel with a wide, circular cork.

Tavia laughed, some of her colour returning as the pounding in her head began to recede. 'Nay, I suppose you're right.'

His rapier eyes were on her, checking, assessing. Her face, marred by the dried-up rivulets of blood from the wound on her head, seemed to be returning to its usual colour, a faint pink beginning to seep across her cheeks. 'I'll clean your wound when we reach Langley's castle.' He leaned forwards to push a strand of hair, rigid with blood, away from her face, concern shadowing his features.

'I can do it myself,' she announced, trying to inject a thread of strength into her voice. 'You don't need to bother with me once I'm there.' Her voice sounded detached, wary.

'Aye, I do.' His voice, a liquid balm, played with her senses like sweet music.

She angled her head to one side, a puzzled smile on her lips. 'I can't understand it, Benois, why you're doing this for me. You couldn't wait to be rid of me since…since…' She pursed her full lips together, cheeks flaming at the vivid memory of their limbs entwined in the lush green vegetation of the woodland floor.

'Since we lay together,' he finished for her, impassively, watching her closely. His eyes sparked with desire, silver threads shot through granite. 'I thought it would make things easier for you if I was gone from your life. Mayhaps I was wrong.'

Tavia studied the ground, shoulders hunching beneath the linen cloth of her *bliaut*, endeavouring to attach some meaning to his words. The rounded neck, slashed to a midpoint between her collarbone and her chest, sagged forward with the movement, hinting at the shadowed depth between her breasts.

'Wrong? Are you saying that you made a mistake?' She pressed her palm against the damp ground, the tough grass prickling against her skin.

'I'm a soldier, Tavia. I have lived my life by the sword since the age of nine. I never thought I would live any differently.'

'It takes courage to change,' she replied slowly, warily, thinking she was probably misinterpreting his meaning.

'Aye, it does,' he agreed. 'And you have more of that than anyone I know.' He wound his strong fingers around her own to assist her upwards. 'Come, we need to keep going.'

'Do you think Ferchar will come?' Tavia asked hesitantly. Hand sliding from his, she rubbed it against her cheek, self-consciously, leaving a smear of dirt.

'Without a doubt,' Benois confirmed, starting to turn away in the direction of the tethered horse.

'Then what's the point?' Tavia flung her hands out towards him, persuading him to turn back, to look at her. 'What is the point in me running and running? I'm in the same situation in England as I am in Scotland.'

'Not exactly. In England, the Scottish king and his regent have little power.'

'So he'll just take me back again.'

'Not if you belong to another.'

'Oh, Benois! Stop it! Stop talking in riddles!' Frustration coursing through her bones, Tavia stamped her slippered foot against the short, tufted grass. 'What do you mean "belong to another"? I belong to no one!'

'I mean,' he enunciated patiently, 'that he can't take you back to Scotland if you are married.'

Her eyes widened, doubtful. 'But, Benois, who on earth would marry me?'

The wind, gaining strength as the sun began to set, grazed a ruddy colour across his high, sculpted cheekbones. The glowing light reinforced the shadowed indent beneath the sensuous arc of his bottom lip; she longed to touch it. Against the brilliant blue of the sky, he loomed above her, his hard, powerful frame impassive, formidable. 'I would,' he said simply.

Chapter Eighteen

Palms scrabbling the rock behind her, seeking balance, Tavia's mind tilted crazily with the full implication of Benois's words. The sunlight burned brightly behind him, throwing the front of his broad frame into shadow, but she screwed up her eyes anyway, attempting to read his expression. Unsure how to react, she laughed unsteadily. 'Nay, don't jest, Benois.' Her voice rushed out, quavering with feeble surprise.

He took a step forward, turning slightly so his sculpted features moved into the light. His eyes narrowed, darts of quicksilver energy. 'No jest, maid.' His heady, masculine aroma flared over her as he reached around her to clasp her hand, almost peeling her rigid fingers away from the granite slope. 'Come, let's talk as we ride.'

Allowing him to lead her, Tavia stepped unsteadily over the ground, uneven in places, the hem of her *bliaut* scratching against the stiff, bleached grass. Hands firm around her waist, he boosted her up into the saddle once more, springing up behind her in one effortless motion. 'Don't worry,' he said, twining the reins around his hands, the thin strips of leather threading through his tanned fingers, 'we'll only go at a walking pace, but it will make us slower.'

Tavia scarcely heard his explanation. How could he talk so easily about the speed of the horse, when they had been talking of marriage just moments earlier? Her mind still reeled, hopelessly trying to clutch at some constant, some strand of reality that she could hold on to, be safe.

'You must be completely mad,' she uttered, suddenly.

'I beg your pardon?'

She plucked at a loose thread on her girdle. 'You must be completely mad to want to marry me.'

His laughter rumbled against her spine. 'Probably. But as far as I can see, I'm the only solution to your problem right now.'

Heart plummeting, she chewed her bottom lip as reality sloshed over her. He made the whole thing sound like a business transaction. How could she have ever considered that it would be anything else between them? The fledgling hope in her chest, hope that had known life for a few brief moments, faded away. He spoke of marriage as a solution, as a way out for her, and not what it could have been, a binding contract between two people who loved each other. He certainly didn't love her, he never had, and he never would.

She hitched her shoulders up, deliberately keeping her tone level, offhand. 'And what if I refuse?'

He gave a short bark of laughter. 'I credited you with more wit than that, Tavia. You need to find a husband, and you'll need to find one quickly before Ferchar shows up.' His chest pressed against her back, heating the tense muscles that pulled at her backbone, as the destrier began to climb the steep incline at the base of the border ridge. His breath grazed the sensitive lobe of her ear as he leaned into her. 'And I haven't exactly noticed a queue of suitors to your door,' he whispered pointedly. She wrenched her head away, annoyed, as he chuckled.

'I don't want your pity!' She drew herself up, erect, proud, a position difficult to maintain as the horse's broad back sloped away alarmingly beneath her.

'I don't pity you, Tavia,' Benois replied, trying not to laugh out loud at Tavia's attempts to keep her body away from touching him. 'But I do want to help you.' Besides, he thought, I don't want anyone else to have you.

'Help? Have you so little belief in me that you think I can't survive on my own?'

He gazed down at her soft hair, itching to caress it. Over the past few days, this woman had proved her inner strength to him time and time again. 'You are a survivor, Tavia, there's no doubt about that. You're a brave, courageous woman—' his praise flowed over her '—but this time, you need my help. I can protect you.'

Tavia shifted uncomfortably at the possession in his words. 'What will King Henry say?' she said, trying another tack.

He frowned. 'Why should he say anything? 'Tis my business, not his.'

'But he is your king.'

'Aye, but he is not my master; I am beholden to none, Tavia. I soldier for Henry because I choose to, not because of any need.'

Beholden to none, she thought bleakly, recalling the time when she had first seen him, when he had strode up the aisle of the church, eyes shimmering with ire, to scatter his men like nine pins with the power of his presence. That was his life, no strings tying him to a home life, no commitments: a free spirit.

'Why would you choose to fight as a soldier when you don't have to?' Her voice, low and melodious, crept in under his defences, issuing a challenge. The simple words shocked him, forced him to search deep for the true answer.

'Because it helped me forget.' His speech hung in the air, accompanied only by the haunting wail of a curlew. 'But now, I am not so sure.'

The horse, the muscles in its neck straining under the combined weight of two people, eventually gained the top of the ridge. Tavia's eyes widened in admiration. Spread out below them, disappearing into a haze in the distance, lay England. The wind gathered strength up here on the ridge; Tavia shivered in her thin dress and cloak, Benois's proposal repeating in her mind. Marriage to Benois would mean security, and protection from Ferchar, but, she realised with a bleak sadness, nothing more. Could she really enter a marriage without love?

Benois brought both edges of his cloak around to the front of her, shielding her from the worst of the wind.

'So,' he said, 'what do you say?'

The wind almost whipped her answer away, but he managed to catch the words. 'Aye, I'll marry you, Benois. As you say, it is the only solution.'

The square silhouette of Langley Castle towered impressively against a pinkish sky shot through with a brilliant succession of blues. As the day drew to a close, the full moon began to rise, a huge white orb above rolling bands of puffy, purplish cloud, luminous in the translucent blue of the evening light. Below the castle, on a wide, level field used for fairs and tournaments alike, the first bonfire was lit: the signal for the celebrations of midsummer to begin. A great roar rose up from the waiting crowd; whereas before their expressions, in shadow, had been expectant, waiting, now their faces broke into wide grins and laughter in anticipation of the festivities to follow that evening.

Lord Langley, hands clasped over his rounded stomach, replete from his evening meal, surveyed the scene from the top step at the main castle entrance. He gained great pleasure from watching his people enjoy themselves, knights and servants alike, all mingling together with the prime objective of having fun on this longest day. The sinking, golden light bathed the tanned, weathered skin of the peasants, gilding their rough clothes. In the corner of the field, a band of travelling musicians struck up a lively tune, and soon hands were joined in dancing. Langley smiled. These people worked hard for him all year, fighting his battles, tending his fields, as they had for his father before him; in his opinion, a few nights of celebration such as this were the least they deserved.

'And so it begins.' Langley adjusted his gaze to the owner of the soft voice at his side, skimming his eyes protectively over his wife, Sabine. Dressed in a flowing *bliaut* of rust-coloured wool that complemented her smooth black hair and ivory skin, Sabine was a true beauty. What a surprise it had been for everyone when the easy-going, slightly overweight Langley had made a match with the young French countess, Sabine de Brouillard. Many commented that such a union would not last. But in the two years of their marriage, Sabine's loyalty and support to her husband could not be faulted. She tolerated his occasional buffoonery when others would have become irritated, and laughed at his gentle teasing.

Langley's eyes moved downwards to the point of his wife's waist where her girdle had been slackened off, to hang below her burgeoning stomach. Her hands clasped the growing bump with care, and his heart swelled with pride; his first child would be born some time in the autumn, and he couldn't wait, excited as a puppy.

'Do you want to go down?' He eyed the chaos on the field doubtfully, darting a protective glance back to his wife's curving belly. The jubilant crowd seemed to have gained more energy now, the dances conducted with more elaborate leaps and twirls, the noise level rising to match the effervescent mood. The wooden kegs of mead had been opened, and pewter tankards glinted in the sunlight as the honeyed nectar slipped down thirsty necks.

'Let's just watch from here a while,' Sabine suggested, tucking her hands around her husband's arm.

Langley nodded in agreement, casting his gaze up to the battlements to make certain his soldiers still patrolled. Despite the celebrations going ahead, he still felt uneasy. King Henry had left this castle several days earlier; he had received only one message to say that a deal had been struck with the Scots and the King still had not returned. His eye traced the huge blocks of stone downwards, past the battlements, past the narrow, arrow-slit windows of the gatehouse to a lone horseman entering under the criss-crossed metal of the portcullis.

'God in Heaven!' He clutched at Sabine's hands. 'Benois!'

Detaching himself from his wife, he bounded down the stone steps, landing with an ungainly thud on the greasy cobbles of the inner bailey.

'Benois!' he shouted, marching over to the steaming, sweating horse. Appalled, he realised the animal carried not one, but two people. A woman, set in front of Benois, drooped forward alarmingly.

'Benois! What in Heaven's name…?' Langley caught the bridle, halting the horse in a jangle of metal. With a jolt, he recognised the woman: it was the maid who duped them, the maid whom Benois had promised to escort back to Dunswick!

'Fetch me a priest…now!' Benois, his voice deep with controlled urgency, sprang down to the cobbles.

'What's the matter with her?' screeched Langley, peering at Tavia's pale face, her eyes closed. 'Is she dying?'

Benois grinned, suddenly, unexpectedly. 'Of course not, Langley. I'm going to marry her!'

'Forgive me,' Langley gasped, relieved. 'I did not realise.' He stared uncertainly at Tavia's chalk-white skin, her face streaked with blood, her wide skirts creased and stained with soil. From beneath her hemline, hanging forlornly against the horse's flank, her leather shoes peeped out, the pointed toes sodden with water and mud. He noticed that Benois kept one hand on her, preventing the exhausted girl from pitching forwards on to the ground.

'Er…maybe we could clean her up a bit,' Langley ventured, tentatively. 'Maybe…a bath, and a bed for the night? My priest can marry you tomorrow.'

'Nay,' Benois bit out. 'It must be this night.' On the periphery of his vision, Benois noticed Sabine's distinctive figure start to descend the steps. Inwardly he groaned. Sabine was well known for her fussy, interfering ways—the less she was involved in this the better.

'Tell me what's going on!' Langley demanded.

Benois nodded, explaining the events that had led up to this night.

'So she was a princess all along!' Langley's eyes widened as Benois told him of Tavia's real identity.

'Greetings, Lord Benois.' Sabine had crossed the courtyard, coming to stand next to her husband. 'I trust we find you in good health?'

Benois bowed a little awkwardly, as one arm still clasped protectively around Tavia.

'Our friend is to be married,' Langley explained.

'To her?' Sabine raised one dark eyebrow, peering at Tavia's crumpled form. 'She looks half-dead. She can't marry looking like that!'

Vaguely aware of the conversation bubbling around her, it took a supreme effort of will for Tavia to raise her head, to study the people around her. 'Looking like what?' she managed to blurt out.

Sabine stepped over to the side of the horse, assessing her with dark, oval eyes. 'We need to get you cleaned up, my dear,' she said in a friendly tone. 'You need a dress, some flowers…'

'And I tell you, Sabine, there's no time for such fripperies,' interrupted Benois. He gathered Tavia up, lifting her off the horse, setting her down gently on the cobbles. 'Langley, fetch that priest of yours, and I'll clean her up.'

'In that case, I'll show you the way,' Sabine suggested, although in her mind she had already chosen the very dress that Tavia should wear.

With Benois's arm about her, Tavia negotiated the castle steps, scrabbling to bring some clarity to her befuddled brain. She felt completely at odds with the merry festivities happening around her, events progressing at breakneck speed with which she struggled to keep up. Maybe the cut on her head had addled her brain, she thought, stumbling over the threshold and into the great hall of the castle, grateful for the constant support of Benois's hard frame as he hoisted her against him. The toned muscles of his arm flexed and strained against her slim back.

In contrast to the Scottish castle at Dunswick, the interior of Langley Castle appeared bright and welcoming. Light flared out everywhere, from huge rush torches flung into iron loops along the length of the hall, from a wealth of candles stuck into elaborate candelabra positioned around the top table to the warming comfort of a well-stoked fire in the fireplace. Gigantic tapestries hung on the walls, stretching from ceiling to floor, their vivid, intricate colours woven over many years by the noble ladies of the castle. It gave the whole hall a soft, embracing ambience, an ambience that Dunswick Castle had lacked. Glancing about her with pleasure, Tavia suspected the strong influence of Sabine in the design of this room.

They followed Sabine's sweeping skirts, her expression decisive and efficient as she led the way to the bedchambers on the upper floor, accessed by a spiral staircase in one of four turrets. Lifting her heavily ringed hand and pushing against the first door she encountered in the upper corridor, Sabine paused for a moment, facing Benois, her manner brisk. In the half-light, her skin appeared exotic, slightly bewitching, her large oval eyes contemplating the man before her.

'Let me tend to her,' Sabine offered, her eyes still on Benois, while she held her hands out to Tavia. 'I have asked the kitchens to send up hot water for a bath.'

'There's no time,' Benois replied, his tone curt, his eyes sharp as flints. 'Tavia can have a bath afterwards.'

'But, my lord, it's not right, she can't marry looking like that!' Sabine protested. 'I'd certainly have something to say about it, if I were marrying you!'

'Then it's a good thing that you are not,' Benois replied incisively. 'Now, please step aside, my lady, so I can tend to her wound as well.'

'As you wish.' Sabine edged back from the doorway, acknowledging defeat, peering dubiously at Tavia's drooping form. 'There's enough water and linen in the chamber to do that, at least.'

'Thank you.' Benois half-carried Tavia through the oak doorway. Sabine clutched Tavia's sleeve as they brushed past her. 'My lady, do you wish me to stay?' Her liquid brown eyes met Tavia's.

Tavia shook her head. 'Nay,' she replied faintly. 'I'm quite safe with him.' As soon as the words had left her lips, she wondered at the truth of them. Was she safe? Was she safe when every time Benois came near her, her heart cascaded into a whirlpool of excitement? As Sabine nodded, pivoting on her heel and disappearing down the corridor, Tavia almost wanted to reach out her hands and beg her to stay.

Benois led her over to a low stool, next to an oak coffer on which a bowl and an earthenware jug had been placed. Beside these items, a pile of fresh linen towels were stacked high, the scent of them reminiscent of windy, sunlit days when the servants would drape the laundry over the large bushes in the garden in order to dry it.

'Sabine doesn't like you very much,' Tavia commented, starting back slightly as Benois applied his fingers gently to the blood-encrusted hair on her forehead.

He chuckled, a rich, throaty sound bubbling in his chest. 'Sabine likes to do everything properly, even someone else's marriage. I seem to remember days, months of preparation for her marriage to Langley; the poor man was beside himself! She thinks I'm rushing you.'

Tavia laughed, her face lifting up to his, searching the tanned, angular features that had become so familiar to her over the last few days. 'Well, you are, aren't you?'

Benois gazed down at her, this beautiful angel who had

sprung so unexpectedly into his life. 'With good reason, Tavia. You know this is the only way I can protect you. Once we are married there's nothing Ferchar can do.' He dipped one bleached linen square into the bowl of water, watching the open weave of the fabric darken and sink as it absorbed the water. Wringing the cloth out, he bent over her, pressing the wet material to her forehead. 'I'm sorry if this hurts, I'll try to be as careful as I can,' he murmured. The dripping water ran down her face, under the round collar of her gown to prickle uncomfortably against her bare skin, as he slowly cleaned around the wound.

'Are you sure about this?' Tavia blurted out suddenly. 'I mean…marrying me?' she added in a small voice, trying to clarify her words. 'I suppose…I suppose I'm not exactly the sort of woman you'd choose to marry.'

The hand dabbing at her forehead ceased, suddenly. 'So tell me, Tavia, what sort of woman should I marry?'

She struggled to find the right words to try and explain her feelings. 'Well, taller than me I suppose, more curvaceous…probably less opinionated…' She trailed off as the corners of his mouth began to twitch. 'Am I right?' she finished tentatively amidst his roar of laughter.

'You couldn't be more wrong.' The grey of his eyes softened to ash, sparkling with diamond light.

'Even so, have you thought of the consequences of your actions—for example, what's going to happen afterwards?' Her voice emerged awkwardly, spiky with reserve.

He shrugged his shoulders. 'We'll be man and wife. I wouldn't question the situation too much, maid, I might change my mind.' Why couldn't he just tell her, be direct with her, that he couldn't bear to see her married to Ferchar…or anyone else for that matter?

'Just as long as you're not marrying me for my unexpected

wealth and position,' she continued huskily, trying to alleviate the odd tension that had fallen between them.

Benois smiled, rinsing the bloodied cloth out in the bowl. 'Nay, maid, I'm certainly not marrying you for your money.' *I'm marrying you for your beauty, your kind soul, your quick wit and generosity and numerous other curiosities about you that are impossible to describe,* he thought suddenly.

Tavia's eyes watered as the linen towel snagged once again on her hair.

'Ah, this hair, it's impossible!' Benois cursed.

'Leave it,' Tavia suggested, her hand curving upwards to stop him dabbing at her forehead. The skin of his right forearm felt smooth, like hard burnished wood beneath her fingers. Her hand fell away, reluctantly, as he threw the towel over to the oak coffer.

'Aye, you're right,' he agreed, grudgingly. 'It would take a proper bath to remove most of this.'

'My hair will be covered with a veil. No one will see.'

To her utter astonishment, Benois dropped suddenly to his knees before her, his brilliant eyes locking with hers. 'No one will be there to see,' he corrected. A rueful expression crossed his face. 'I'm sorry it has to be like this, hurried, secretive, but it is the only way.' His tongue moved woodenly over the words of apology in his mouth; he felt gruff, awkward, too big for his skin.

'I understand.' She smiled up at him, her blue eyes wide, bright. 'I understand that you're trying to help me, and I thank you for that.' She touched her fingers to the slanting sweep of his jawline, feeling the faint bristle beneath her fingers. He reacted with a sharp intake of breath, a hiss, almost, of desire, the grey of his eyes deepening to sparkling jet. In the corner of the chamber, loose coals shifted in the brazier, sending renewed flames shooting up, filling the room with a warm, soporific heat. Her fingers throbbed against his cheek, her heart racing with the realisation that he hadn't pulled away from her, hadn't jerked back. Her fingers moved upwards, sketching over his high cheekbones to the vigorous strands of his hair that gleamed vibrantly in the dim light. His body was rigid, beset with a tension that filled the air around the couple with a dramatic intensity, a sense of being on the brink of danger, of the unknown.

'Tavia,' he whispered, expelling his breath with a whoosh of air. His arms came about her, folding her into his body. He seized her mouth with his own, lips plundering, demanding, obliterating any form of protest she may have had. Protest was the last thing on her mind, as she melted into him, her senses careening upwards in a crazy ascent of desire. Her arms crept around his neck, the downy hairs at his nape brushing against her fingers. The tip of his tongue worked along the seam of her lips and the desire, smouldering gently in the pit of her stomach, ignited into a bright, white heat. The kiss deepened...

The door swung wide open, and Langley stood there, his prepared words fading into the air as he viewed the couple locked together. He had to clear his throat, not once, but twice, to gain their attention.

'Er...the priest awaits you in the chapel.' Langley smirked, trying not to laugh out loud at the guilty expressions on both their faces as they sprung apart. Sabine moved into the room, her arms laden with a colourful bundle of material, bobbing elegantly under her husband's arm that rested high against the door frame.

'You've time for this, yet not time to let this poor maid have a bath,' she stormed at Benois, who rose quickly to his feet, flushing. 'Shame on you!' Sabine marched into the chamber, dropped the pile of cloth on to the wooden coffer before jamming her hands on to her hips, and glaring at him. 'Now, begone with you, and give me a few moments alone with Tavia.' At Benois's reluctant frown, she raised her white hands, shooing him away. 'Go! We'll not be long. Wait for us in the chapel.'

Benois bowed, his eyes flicking over to Tavia. 'Don't be too long, *chérie*.' He smiled at her.

Chapter Nineteen

The rounded domes of the cobbles hurt Tavia's feet as she walked towards the chapel. Her shoes, borrowed from Sabine, were a little too large for her feet, and she had to keep curling up her toes in an attempt to stop the fine leather slipping off. But Sabine's arm linked companionably through her own kept her steady, as the pair drew covert, admiring glances from the serfs and soldiers going about their chores in the inner bailey.

Tavia had been relieved when Sabine had steered her away from the midsummer celebrations that continued with increasing intensity in the fair field; the church was but a short walk away from the main castle building, but, thankfully, in the opposite direction. She still felt sufficiently fragile to not want the marriage witnessed by numerous strangers.

Sabine squeezed her arm in a friendly manner as they approached the impressively recessed archway at the church entrance. 'Forgive me for saying this, Tavia,' she said, halting her step, 'but are you sure about this marriage? I mean, I know I've only known you for a short time, but…'

'Aye, I'm sure, Sabine.' Tavia fought to keep a note of re-assurance in her voice. She knew why she was marrying Benois, and it wasn't for the same reason that he was marrying her. He sought to protect her; but she knew that she loved him, and any marriage, however short, however sterile, would be a symbol of that love. But he would never know it.

'It's just that he's so…so brusque, Tavia. He treats you like one of his soldiers.'

'He's not always like that.' A wonderful feeling flooded through her as she defended him.

'Oh, well, you must love him I suppose, whatever faults he has.'

'Aye, I do,' Tavia murmured, as they moved through the arch and down the wide, stone steps and into the shadowy interior of the church. The exotic smell of incense hit her, assailing her senses with mysterious perfume.

At the click of the latch, the inward squeak of the door, three pairs of eyes turned. Benois's gasp was audible, echoing with surprise through the vaulted church ceiling.

'Oh, my God!' Langley spluttered beside him. 'What a beauty!'

Sabine had done her work well. A flowing *bliaut* of finely spun cream silk smoothed over Tavia's slender form, clinging lovingly to the indentation of her waist, the curve of her bosom. The material, shot through with delicate lines of silver thread, glittered and shone with every movement Tavia made, reflecting magically in the glowing candlelight. The pointed ends of her long sleeves, their shape like inverted teardrops, brushed against the flagstones, whispering with every step. The wide cuffs allowed the tight sleeves of the underdress to be revealed, sleeves fashioned from a pale lichen-green material that accentuated the glossy red of Tavia's hair. A circlet of filigreed silver pinned a short veil to the crown of her head, the delicate folds floating around her like an aura as she walked down the aisle.

Benois reached out and took her hand, as she stepped up to the altar steps, beside him. Her wide eyes of vivid blue searched his face, trying to find the answer to the puzzle that continually plagued her: why should this man put himself out to help her so much?

'Ready?' Benois smiled down at her, squeezing her hand, relieved to see that some colour had returned to Tavia's cheeks under Sabine's ministrations. He still wore the same mud-splattered garments from before: the red tunic carrying the golden lion of Henry II, the brown woollen braies cross-laced with leather straps from ankle to calf.

'As ready as I'll ever be,' she murmured, the pearly cream of her skin drawing his eyes with its ethereal beauty.

Standing facing them, the priest seemed to have fallen asleep, his chin dropping forwards, almost resting on his chest; his eyes were closed. A sudden draught of unknown origin snuffed out a thick candle behind his portly frame, the acrid smoke coiling up behind him, around him, making his slumped figure appear as if in a thick fog.

'Wake up, man!' Langley demanded, his tones unnaturally strident as he pulled at the priest's voluminous sleeve. Slowly, with extreme difficulty, the priest opened his bloodshot eyes, resentment emanating from every line in his body towards the couple that had dragged him away from the midsummer celebrations. He had been enjoying an extremely merry time up to the point when his lord, Lord Langley, had pulled him away to preside over this dubious marriage. She's obviously with child, thought the priest, sneering at Tavia's slim frame trying to detect a slight rounding of the bride's stomach under her gown. Aye, that would be the reason, she's of noble birth and can't bear the shame of bearing a child out of wedlock

The priest stepped forward, clearing his throat, obviously intending to begin the service. 'Dearly beloved...' he intoned. 'We—'

'Wait...!' screeched Sabine. 'I forgot something!' She dashed away, as quickly as her distended figure would allow.

'What now?' Benois twisted his head round irritably, trying to decipher Sabine's intentions. 'That infernal wife of yours, Langley!'

Langley took a half-step forwards and realised he could do nothing, his round, jovial face adopting a look of extreme apology.

The church door opened, then slammed shut once more. Sabine puffed back down the aisle, thrusting a posy of summer flowers into the bride's surprised hands.

'Oh, they're beautiful,' Tavia cried in delight, savouring the fresh, light perfume emanating from the purplish-blue lavender and the white daisies. Against the heady smell of incense that pervaded the dark recesses of the church, this new scent evoked the bright, burnished meadows of high summer. She darted a quick smile of thanks in Sabine's direction.

'Now, can we begin?' Benois growled. The priest, clearing his throat dramatically, opened the heavy Bible that rested before him on a wooden lectern. He began to speak the words of the marriage service, a slow lilting intonation.

As if in a dream, Tavia listened to the cadence of the priest's voice without hearing the words. She almost jumped in shock when the priest lifted her hand and placed it over Benois's, before dutifully repeating the words she had been asked to say.

'And now, if you would like to place the wedding ring on the Bible...' The priest lifted his reddened eyes towards Benois. Benois looked blank.

'Oh, a ring!' Langley blustered from the shadows. 'Here, Benois, take this one.' He began to fumble to dislodge a ring from his left hand.

Benois's fingers tightened around Tavia's hand; a rawness invaded his expression, making him look momentarily bereft. 'Nay, friend—' he stopped Langley's agitated movements with his low voice '—I have one.'

Benois reached into the collar of his tunic, and drew out a leather lace, pulling it over his head. The silver ring on the end spun, twinkling in slow circles, in the mellow penumbra of the church.

'It belonged to my mother,' Benois explained, detaching the ring from the end of the lace, and reaching for Tavia's hand once more.

Her fingers trembled as he slid the cool metal over her fourth finger. The flat edge of the ring had been intricately engraved with small flowers, stems twining across the silver, making it sparkle. His mother's ring! Her throat closed up with emotion, and she glanced up, scanning Benois's impassive face, trying to detect his mood. But his face was set, stern, his hard, granite eyes trained on the priest.

'And I now pronounce you man and wife,' the priest finished the service in a rush of words, hastily covering his mouth to stifle a belch. He closed the Bible between his hands with a snap, dust puffing into the air from the thin pages.

Tavia toed the cold flagstones beneath her feet, feeling strangely ill at ease, self-conscious in her own skin. So this was it. She was married. Married to a man she had known but a few days, days that felt like a lifetime. 'So what happens now?' Her voice wavered with the question.

'Now?' Benois raised one dark eyebrow. 'Now, we wait for Ferchar.'

'And what if Ferchar doesn't come? Then you'll have married me for nothing.'

'Maybe not,' Benois replied enigmatically.

With a small sound of relief, Tavia sank into the hot, steaming water, the heated liquid soothing her aching muscles, allowing her to stretch her limbs to their full, languorous extent. She wriggled her toes, her fingers, her heart flipping as she acknowledged the unfamiliar band around her wedding finger. All that had been cramped and tight, now became supple, pliable, under the effect of the water. Closing her eyes, Tavia tipped her neck back to rest her head on the wooden edge of the tub. Somewhere behind her, Sabine bustled about the chamber; Sabine, whose tireless energy seemed indefatigable, who had asked, nay, told Benois that she was taking his new bride upstairs to give her a proper bath. Benois had barely nodded his assent before Tavia had been whisked away.

The scent of lavender rose to her nostrils; a muslin bag full of the dried flower had been tossed into the water, pervading the air with delicious perfume. The water penetrated the very pores of Tavia's skin, cleansing her of all the dirt of the past few days. Every now and again, a flutter, a niggle, gnawed fleetingly in the pit of her stomach. Had she been a fool for marrying Benois? Would her decision lead to sadness, to heartache? She wished she could know the answer.

'How does the water feel?' Sabine, who had stood like a tyrant over her maidservant, watching keenly as the girl folded the flimsy fabric of the wedding gown and packed it back into the oak coffer, now approached the steep sides of the tub. The tub itself was lined with a thick linen cloth to stop its recipient catching any splinters from the rough wooden sides.

'Oh, like Heaven, thank you, Sabine.'

'No thanks needed.' Sabine plonked her rounded girth on to a low stool next to the bath. 'Especially after what you've been through. It's the least you deserve.' She cast a critical eye over the gash on Tavia's forehead. 'I only wish you'd had a chance to bathe before your marriage.' Her fingers probed gently around the crusting edges of the wound. 'Still, it seems Benois hasn't done a bad job for a man who was in such a hurry.'

'You mustn't blame Benois. He was only worried about Lord Ferchar arriving.' Tavia noted the condemnation threading through Sabine's light tone.

Sabine laughed, leaning forward to clutch at the sides of the bath, her deep brown eyes glowing with intrigue. 'I must admit, I have never seen him this jittery…ever. Most times, he acts with a deadly calm, even when he's about to go into a battle. You must really mean a great deal to him.'

'Oh, I'm not certain about that,' Tavia hedged, wiggling her hips to sink down further, wondering how she could deflect the conversation away from herself. 'How long have you known Benois?'

Sabine rested her elbows on the edge of the bath. 'I don't believe anyone knows Benois well. But Langley and he are great friends, despite the fact they possess completely different characters. I met Benois when I married Langley. But I had heard of him before; his reputation as a skilful knight, a born leader of men, was well known, notorious even.' Her gaze scrutinised Tavia's pale face. 'And now you're married to him.'

Tavia picked up a washcloth, started scrubbing her pinkened skin vigorously. 'He's only done it to help me out. To stop Ferchar from marrying me.' Her voice sounded gusty, breathless.

'Is that what you truly believe?' Sabine rapped out, pushing her upper body sharply upright. The material of her gown pulled taut over her curving belly.

'Aye,' Tavia returned tentatively. 'He's married me out of a sense of duty, of obligation.' She rubbed the back of her neck, her shoulders, the water sluicing down her arms. 'Although I can't for the life of me figure out why…'

'Can't you?' Sabine stared at her in astonishment, drawing her spine straight. 'Has that knock on the head made you completely insane? Benois would never marry someone on those terms. Why on earth would he?'

'So why would he marry me, then?' Tavia ventured in a small voice.

'Oh, Tavia…' Sabine's rose-coloured lips widened into a smile '…because he loves you, Tavia, that's why. I must admit, I had my doubts at first, but having seen the two of you together…he loves you and he wants to protect you. Anyone can see that.'

Tavia crushed the washcloth haphazardly between her fingers, the water dripping into the flat water, causing concentric circles to ripple out around her. 'But I feel as if he's been forced into it…because of Ferchar.' But Sabine was already laughing.

'Oh, you really don't know him very well, do you! Can you imagine anyone forcing Benois to do anything he doesn't want to do? Tell me…can you?'

A stray head of lavender floated on the water's surface, brushing against Tavia's bare thigh, sticking to her wet skin as she raised her knee slightly out of the water. She recalled the intense, unhindered passion of their coupling beneath the magical green light of the forest, the wild, reckless heat of their kisses, and she lifted the washcloth to her face to hide her flaming cheeks. Did Sabine speak the truth? That Benois had married her for love? 'He's never said it, Sabine, he's never said he loves me,' she mumbled through the wet flannel, screwing her eyes up against the memory of his rejection after their lovemaking. Her voice held a forlorn edge.

'Oh, Tavia, you mustn't expect hearts and flowers with Benois. He's a soldier, gruff and taciturn at the best of times, but, oh, if only you could see how he is around you! He shows his love in other ways, in the way he looks at you, cares for you.'

Tavia shook her head, droplets of water cascading down from her hair. 'I've never seen it,' she replied, a helpless, brooding look entering her eyes.

'Just give him a chance, Tavia, give him a chance.' Sabine levered herself up from the stool, indicating with a precise movement of her dark head that she wished the maidservant to bring over some towels.

'Maybe you're right,' Tavia answered finally, wringing out the flannel and hanging it over the side of the tub. She stood up, the water cascading over her naked limbs, her hair plastered wildly down her back, taking the towel that the diminutive maidservant held out to her, horribly aware that her words held no conviction, no certainty. She didn't believe Sabine for a moment. Could she accept this way of life, a life without his love, just to be near him? Would her love for him be enough for the two of them?

Benois stood high up in the darkness on the curtain wall, an undulating boundary of stones that circled Langley Castle. He was alone up here, apart from the occasional patrolling soldier, who marched constantly around the high wall scanning the countryside for potential invaders. Leaning his wide shoulders back against the cold stone, he crossed his arms over his chest, lazily watching the festivities below. Yet while the people of Langley danced and frolicked beneath him, the flames of midsummer fire leaping higher and higher, he couldn't shake the image of Tavia coming towards him down the aisle, and how utterly breathtaking she had looked. Her shining beauty on the outside had matched the kindness and beauty of her soul on the inside, and the urge to hold her sealed within his arms and keep her there for ever had been overwhelming. He had scarce wanted to hand her over to Sabine at the end of the ceremony. She was his wife! The thought swelled within him, growing like a rich, warm aura, a feeling of comfort, of joy, that disconcerted him. After his family had died, he had vowed never to marry, never wanted to inflict his black-hearted soul on any unsuspecting maid, never wanted those complicated emotional ties that love and marriage would surely bring. But now? Now he was not so sure.

'Benois.' The familiar musical tones of her voice drew him, his eyes seeking her out in the dark. At the top of the steps, Tavia paused, the veil covering her wet hair billowing out, a flimsy cloud on the evening breeze. Her loose, damp hair coiled down, dark red tendrils of seaweed. She smiled, tentatively, not wishing to intrude, nerves flittering through her as she hesitated at the top of the steps. 'I'm sorry. Did you want to be alone?'

'Not any more.' He laughed, pushing himself away from the wall, coming towards her in two quick strides. Not now, or for ever more, he thought, cheerfully. Her small hand slipped into his, her blue eyes twinkling in her flushed face. 'Come, stand with me for a while. There's a good view from here.' He guided her along the narrow walkway, bringing her to stand in front of him, his big arm wrapped over her shoulders, pulling her back into the solid warmth of his chest.

'I didn't expect to see you again; I thought Sabine would

have tucked you up in bed by now.' The scent of lavender rose from her newly washed hair, tantalising his nostrils.

'She did try, but I wanted to find you.'

'Why?'

Her hand gripped more securely on to his. 'To make sure it wasn't all a dream.' Extending her left hand out, she watched the silver ring sparkle in the evening gloaming. Why had she really sought him out? To tell him that the marriage was a huge mistake?

Benois sighed. 'It was quick, I'll grant you that. I'm sorry if it wasn't the kind of wedding you had in mind.'

Tavia laughed. 'Benois, I never had any marriage in mind. I was set to be a spinster for the rest of my life. Nobody wants to marry me—my tongue is too sharp, my body too lean for most men's tastes, and the colour of my hair? That's the first thing that men run away from!'

Benois issued a small sound of disbelief, pulling her upper body closer into him. Tavia misinterpreted his gesture, thinking he was trying to comfort her. 'Nay, you needn't feel badly for me, Benois. After witnessing the marriage my parents endured, I was quite happy to remain alone. You mustn't pity me!'

'I don't pity you!' Benois contradicted forcibly. 'I consider myself lucky that those imbeciles didn't see what I can!'

Her brain fogged. Why did he talk in riddles so?

Down below, the beat and tempo of the music seemed to have become louder, faster. The dancers whirled about, the colours of their garments flowing into one another with the pace of their steps. Maids' hemlines swirled upwards, revealing white, shapely calves and bare feet. Men's faces, flushed and grinning, grabbed their partners, swinging the maids around until they threw their heads back with utter joy. Some couples, no doubt fuelled by the alcoholic mead running in their veins, sneaked off into the trees beyond the fire, to enjoy more sensual delights.

'They look like they're having fun,' Tavia said, glad to find an excuse to move the conversation away from that of marriage.

'Hmm, they've certainly had too much to drink,' Benois replied.

'You don't approve?'

'The drink addles their brains.' The regretful note in Benois's voice twisted in her gut. She felt a deep shiver run through his big frame.

Benois smoothed one hand through his ruffled hair, sable locks spilling through his fingers. The ridged scar on his palm brushed against his scalp, a constant reminder. 'It can cause people to lose their heads, do stupid things,' he spoke, his tone low and measured.

'Like your father?' she whispered.

He gathered her close, his arm an iron band around her chest. 'How did you know?'

'You began to tell me once, remember, in the barn at my home.' She fell silent, not wanting to probe, to stir up unwanted memories.

Benois watched the leaping flames below, their red glow lighting up the north wall of the castle, painting the stones a lurid red. 'My father was practically senseless when he returned home that night, the night of the fire. He'd been spurned by his mistress at court, and had drowned his sorrows with tankard after tankard of mead. If he hadn't drunk so much…' His voice died away.

'Then your mother and sister might have lived.' Tavia finished the sentence for him. Benois gripped her small body, luxuriating in the soft, sweet feel of her.

'I loved them so much, Tavia.' His voice was ragged, uneven, as if these words had been locked in a dusty treasure box for years and years before finally being released. 'I loved them… and then I lost them. I never want to go through that again.'

'But you'll never have to, Benois.'

He turned her in his arms then, lifting her chin with one finger. The metallic streaks of his eyes clung to hers, granite fire. 'If I love someone, then the possibility of losing them is always there.'

'If…' she breathed, the tiny word sparkling in the gap of air between them, daring to hope. Her fingers moved upwards, wanting to ease away the hurt and pain in his face.

A soldier's shout, rising sternly above the mêlée of the celebrations, forced them both to turn in unison.

'Hell and damnation!' cursed Benois. 'Ferchar!'

Chapter Twenty

⁂

The solitary messenger, dressed in the green-and-gold colours of the Scottish court, made his way to the top table in the great hall, escorted by a soldier from the gatehouse. There sat Lord Langley, surrounded by a few of his house knights, sharing a cup of mead before they bedded down for the night. A few soldiers, choosing not to join in with the celebrations outside, had paired up for games of merels, their big frames hunched in concentration over the square game boards.

Langley tilted his blond head in expectation as he tracked the messenger's approach. The young squire's faltering step became slower and slower as he climbed the wooden steps on to the dais, and moved towards the table, obviously reluctant to deliver his message. His fingers moved with agitation over the crackling parchment between his hands.

'Come, come, boy,' Langley demanded impatiently, although he said the words with a kind smile. 'What is your message?'

The squire unrolled the stiff parchment with shaking fingers, the red wax that sealed the paper dropping to the wooden floorboards. Benois, pulling Tavia in his wake, reached the boy in the same moment, smartly plucking the missive from the squire's astonished hands. Benois scanned the contents at speed, his expression severe as he met Langley's enquiring glance over the messenger's sandy hair.

'It's Ferchar. He's holding King Henry to ransom, at Marwood Castle.' He frowned at Langley. 'Christ, that's all we need!'

'The castle is but a few miles from here, but the other side of the border,' Langley explained quickly. 'What does he want in return for the King?'

'I'll give you one guess,' Benois growled, the mirror-sheen of his eyes falling on Tavia's petite frame.

Tavia felt the heat of Benois's gaze. 'He wants me, doesn't he?' She scoured his lean features for confirmation. 'He wants you to trade me for King Henry.'

'He can't bear to lose.' Langley's chair legs scraped against the floor as he rose to his feet.

'And he still needs you to gain your father's inheritance; it's worth more than anything Henry could give him. I bet Malcolm and the other Scottish barons won't let him have it.'

'Well, I suppose that's it, then,' Tavia announced practically. 'The end of this charade. If you find me a horse, I'll be on my way.'

Langley and Benois regarded her with identical expressions of disbelief.

'What do you think you're doing?' Benois asked finally.

'Well, it's obvious, isn't it? There's no contest, if the life of King Henry is at stake. He's the King of England, and Duke of Normandy for that matter…and who am I? Just—'

'You're my wife,' Benois cut in, his slicing words truncating her speech.

Warmth rose within her at the possessive nature of his words, but she fought to suppress it, to ignore it, placing a gentle hand on his arm. 'Benois,' she stated calmly, although her heart cracked with emotion, 'I don't expect you to carry on with this…with this parody under these circumstances. You never expected Ferchar to do this, did you?' Her light blue eyes searched his rugged face for some glimmer of understanding.

Benois glared down at her, storm clouds massing in his silvered eyes.

'We could arrange an annulment,' Tavia chattered on, her words tumbling out as she sensed his irritation.

'Bit late for that, isn't it?' His tone, crushing, shredded her fragile confidence. A lock of sable hair fell over his forehead; he brushed it away in annoyance. 'Whoever said anything about this marriage being a charade, Tavia? Is that what you think it is? A masquerade? A sham? Then forgive me, my lady, if I don't see it that way!' Tavia squirmed miserably under the unexpected harshness of his words. He gripped her shoulders, shook her slightly, forcing her in that movement to meet the blistering heat of his eyes. 'This marriage is for real, my lady, so you'd better become used to the idea!'

Tavia recoiled from him as if he had hit her, unsuccessfully trying to wrench her shoulders out from his punishing grip. He stared at the bereft expression chasing across her elfin features and felt like a brute. How could he tell her that he loved her? To speak those words, to breathe life into them would mean that they had real substance, and things of substance could so easily be taken away. He preferred to keep such thoughts hidden, squirreled in the hidden recesses of his heart.

Tavia chewed on one fingernail, trying to collect her thoughts, trying to find the words to explain. 'I didn't mean…I thought…' Her words died under Benois' ferocious glance. She didn't want him to feel trapped by their union, that he was free to go, to leave her. Her dark, spiky eyelashes fanned down over the creamy alabaster of her cheeks; shame washed over her. She had made the situation worse between them, when all she had tried to do was make things easier. She jerked her head up, the silver circlet that held her linen veil glinting in the lowering candlelight. 'I'm sorry, Benois,' she declared finally, 'it's just that I'm very grateful for what you are doing for me, protecting me from Ferchar, and I don't want you to feel you've compromised your position in any way.'

'Let me be the judge of that, Tavia,' he replied, a softness stealing over his face. His hands loosened from her shoulders, smoothing down the sides of her arms, leaving a blazing trail of heat. 'Remember, I'm big enough, and ugly enough, to take care of myself.'

'There must be another way we can extract Henry from Ferchar's clutches,' Langley stated, his jovial face sunk in thought. 'Marwood Castle is more of a fortified manor, and the windows are wide, wide enough for a man to climb through.'

'They'll have put Henry on a higher floor,' added Benois, thinking, 'so we'll need to fire a rope to his window so he's able to climb down. And the only way to do that—'

'Is to use a crossbow,' Tavia finished for him, clasping her hands together. Their eyes met, held, chips of aquamarine clashing with hard granite.

'Nay!' he breathed.

'I can do it! Benois, I can!' Tavia's voice notched upwards with excitement.

Benois ignored her, running his fingers distractedly through his hair, casting his glance around the great hall as if trying to find an alternative marksman. 'There must be someone else.' He looked pleadingly at Langley. 'Surely you must have some good shots in your household guards? Think, man, think!'

Down in the great hall, one game of merels finished in high jubilation, knights coming forwards to slap the winner on the back, before draining the last dregs from their pewter tankards. They wiped their wet mouths on the backs of their sleeves before setting up another game. Distracted by the noise, Langley swept his gaze down the hall, before turning back to Benois. 'I'm sorry, friend, but there's no one. They're all fingers and thumbs when it comes to accurate shooting...excellent on the battlefield, though, can't fault them. I'm afraid it's got to be you, Benois, or Tavia.'

Benois closed his eyes. He knew Tavia was a better shot than he, and he knew that she was aware of that fact. He remembered her remarkable performance in the competition at Dunswick Castle, how she had shot the centre of the target five times in a row. He couldn't beat that.

'You don't think I can do it!' Her sweet voice, fiery, plucked at his senses.

He opened his eyes. The jewelled brooch that held the neckline of her gown together winked blue fire. Beneath the creamy skin of her neck, he could see the beat of her pulse, rapid, strong.

'Nay, Tavia. I know you can do it. You're fast and accurate with a bow. Better than any man I've seen.'

'Then what's the matter?' She inclined her head, her small nose wrinkling faintly in question. 'Why do you want to stop me going?'

He shot her a look of such anguish, such despair, that she took a step closer, wanting to comfort him.

'Oh, God, Benois, what is it?'

In answer, he wound his big arms about her, pulling her close, his tawny head dipping down so his lips brushed the top of her ear. She trembled, her blood careening wildly under his touch, bending into his body like supple willow. 'Because it will be dangerous, Tavia,' he whispered. 'The whole place will be crawling with Scottish soldiers on the look-out for you. I don't want to lose you…again.'

'But you won't lose me, Benois.' Her voice was muffled by the fabric of his tunic. 'I'll stick by your side all the time, if that's what you wish.' Hope fired in her breast at his words.

'Aye, I wish it,' he replied tersely. *I wish it for all eternity,* he thought.

The noisy frivolity of the midsummer celebrations had muted now, the fire subsiding slowly into red glowing embers, great branches of wood shifting, collapsing as they broke in two. Here and there, couples lay side by side on the grass, talking, kissing, but most seemed to have wound their way to bed. Not many people noticed the group of riders clattering over the drawbridge of Langley Castle, cantering off in the direction of the Scottish border.

They rode the few miles to Marwood flanked by outriders carrying flares, rush torches held high, spluttering and crackling their wavering, unpredictable flame in the darkness. Above the billowing shadows of the trees, lumpen clouds built steadily from small froths of water vapour, beginning to obscure the feeble light of a quarter-moon. In the dark patches of sky that escaped the cloud, the first stars of evening began to appear, pinholes in black cloth.

At the front of the group, on a small grey pony, rode the messenger, who kept twisting around in his saddle, his face worried, almost as if he couldn't believe the number of English soldiers that followed him. Wrapped up in a voluminous cloak against the unexpected chill of the air, Tavia was grateful that Langley had insisted upon finding it for her, even if it had meant rifling through one of Sabine's coffers. He had urged Tavia to be quiet as she waited for him outside Sabine's bedchamber; she suspected that his wife would have plenty to say if she knew about their evening trip.

'Ride closer to me!' Benois urged as the forest thickened, darkened around them. He leaned over to clutch at the reins around her horse's neck, drawing her and the animal into him. His booted foot nudged against her outer thigh.

'Benois, careful! You'll have me off!' she protested with a laugh, as his toe brushed against her again.

'Sorry,' he responded tersely. 'I just wish you didn't have to do this. I keep racking my brains, trying to think of another solution to get Ferchar off our backs!'

'Maybe he'll give in once he knows we are married?'

'It's a possibility, but not something we can rely on. I should just kill him.'

'Oh, Benois, you know that's not the way.'

He laughed, dropping his gaze on to her neat head. 'It would have been my way, though. I gave no thought to life, or person, before I met you. I would rush headlong into battle, slashing, burning, killing, with no thought or heed for anyone.'

Tavia scanned his face, marvelling at the sincerity of his tone. 'I'm not responsible for such a change,' she whispered. 'It has come from you, from within.'

'You've brought me back to life,' he whispered, bending down from the waist to touch his lips to her upturned face. Tavia shuddered under the cool feel of his mouth, burning need firing her veins, her heart. She stretched up, standing up in the stirrups so she could wind her arms around his neck, deepen the kiss…until her horse, disturbed by the odd movements of its rider above, stepped away from Benois's destrier, widening the gap between the two horses. Tavia broke away, her lips bruised, sensitive, but laughing, and clutched hold of her palfrey's neck in a desperate attempt to stay in the saddle.

Benois's eyes, sparking with unfulfilled desire, snared hers. 'Later,' he said.

The oppressive nature of the air crushed in upon the riders, making every movement slow, soporific. Thunder grumbled ominously in the distance. Benois ran a finger around his neckline, trying to disperse the beads of sweat that had gathered. He was glad he hadn't worn chainmail; it would have slowed his movements on this sultry night. He could see Langley, riding ahead, was already regretting donning his hauberk. At last the young squire stopped, just as he reached the forest boundary, and pointed out something to Langley who rode just behind him.

Langley hoisted his arm above his head, his metal gauntlet shining, indicating that the riders should dismount, tie up their horses, so they could approach Marwood Castle on foot. Beside Tavia, Benois had already jumped down, before coming round to her horse's flank.

'Let me help you,' he offered.

Tavia swung her leg frontways over the horse's neck. Noting her peculiar way of dismounting, Benois placed both hands on the side of her waist, a grin splitting his features. He held her close for a moment, their faces at the same level, his arms locking her body into him. 'Back there, I almost thought you had mastered the knack of riding. But now I can see you have a little more to learn.'

She giggled, one hand sneaking up to tweak his ear. 'I've not done badly for someone who had never been on horse-back a sennight ago.'

He allowed her to slide to the ground, still holding her. 'Still, I think I'm going to have some fun teaching you.' She frowned, surprised at his words. They implied a longevity, a sense of going into the future, together. She prayed that she hadn't misinterpreted his meaning.

'Benois!' Langley blustered up. 'Listen, let me go down to the gatehouse with a few men, and engage Ferchar in some sort of negotiation. I'll keep him talking as long as I can.'

'I can rely on you, Langley, to keep someone talking.' Benois slapped him genially on the back.

Langley smiled, his skin damp, glistening with perspiration, the nose-piece of his steel helmet obscuring most of his face. 'You and Tavia make your way down carefully; one of my men will give you a crossbow and the rope…and for God's sake, keep yourselves out of sight! I suspect Henry will be in the tower, there's only one, on the north side of the castle. Aim for that. And good luck,' he added, almost as an afterthought.

'He's nervous,' Benois explained, as he and Tavia, having broken away from the rest of the group, began to descend the gentle slope down to the castle. In his hand, he carried a polished crossbow, and on his back, a leather case full of bolts. Tavia carried the rope over her arm, having insisted on carrying something. Nerves fluttered in the pit of her stomach; Benois's gentle teasing on the ride had distracted her from the true purpose of their journey. She glanced warily at the crossbow; it looked heavy, unwieldy.

'Mayhap I should have had some practice.' She licked her dry lips. 'It's a long time since I've shot at a target.'

'It's not much above a sennight, Tavia. That was when I first saw you…at Dunswick Castle. You'll have not lost your skill in such a short time.'

'I pray to God that I haven't.'

'Have faith in your own abilities, Tavia. I know you can do this.'

She followed his assured stride through the waist-high grass at the edge of the pasture. Benois purposely hugged the hedge line, so they wouldn't be noticed by any of the castle guards. The grass tops, feathery seed heads, rasped against her cloak, pulling at the fabric, hampering her pace. Heavy dew soaked through the thin leather of her slippers.

Sensing the broadening gap between them, Benois stopped abruptly, turned, reaching out one muscled arm for the rope. 'Here, let me carry that, it's too heavy for you.'

She hunched her shoulders in protest, despite the coiled rope weighing heavy in the crook of her arm. 'I can manage, Benois,' she tried to insist as he scooped up the plaited flax. 'You're always doing things for me, looking after me.'

'It's how it should be,' he replied tenderly.

'But it's so one-sided. I've done nothing in return.'

'That's not true, Tavia. You've done a great deal.' He reached over to tuck a wayward strand of hair behind her ear. 'More than you can ever know.' Hefting the rope more securely over his shoulder, he resumed his long strides, leaving her perplexed, confused, following in his wake.

Benois halted under the shelter of a small thicket of trees and bushes just a few feet from the north wall. In the faint sheen of moonlight, he raised one finger to his lips, pointing upwards, indicating that she should keep quiet. Tavia raised her eyes to the top of the wall, seeing the glint of chainmail as one of the guards passed by on his patrol. Beyond the wall, the outline of the tower was clearly delineated against the fractionally lighter night sky. The top window was a blaze of light, she saw with relief: an easy target.

'We have to take a chance that Henry is in there.' Benois tugged on her sleeve, pulling her down to where he crouched.

'Keep an eye out, see if he passes in front of the window, while I do this.' He began to fit the bolt into the bow, having already tied the rope to one end.

Tavia fixed her gaze on the lighted window, her vision blurring with tears of exhaustion. From the shadows, the darkness played tricks on her, making her think she had seen things, odd shapes, when in fact there was nothing. Then a shape crossed the lighted space and paused for a moment, looking out into the darkness. She caught the unmistakable glint of ginger hair.

Adrenalin fired her blood: she clamped her hand down on Benois's shoulder as he knelt beside her. 'He's there! I'm sure of it!'

He nodded, a swift assurance that he had heard her, before arming the bow, dragging the sinew line back taut over the notch. 'This takes some strength,' he remarked. 'However do you manage?'

'My own bow is smaller and lighter. The one I had at the competition.'

'How could I forget?' He stroked the soft, downy skin of her cheek, distracted for a moment. He sighed, reluctantly. 'Come on, let's do this.'

'Benois, wait!' she hissed suddenly. 'When Henry climbs down over the wall, how will he avoid the patrol?'

Benois looked up in the direction of the window. 'If you shoot just after the guard passes by, Henry should have enough time before he passes by once more.'

'And if he doesn't?'

'We'll deal with that if it happens,' Benois replied tersely. 'Here, take this.' He handed her the crossbow.

Staggering back, Tavia's arms sagged pathetically under the weight of the weapon. 'It's too heavy,' she cried out. Tears of frustration pricked behind her eyes.

'Shh! Keep your voice down!' Benois knelt down before her. 'Let's work together…balance it on my shoulder. Then you can aim true.'

Resting the bow on top of Benois's wide shoulder, Tavia knelt carefully behind him, knees sinking into the deep, damp vegetation beneath her. Their differences in height meant she was positioned lower than he, putting her immediately at an advantage, as the bow already pointed upwards, straight at the window. Sweat gathered in her palms as she focused her eye down the stock; her heart pounded madly, but her breathing remained calm, regular.

'Are you ready?' whispered Benois.

She took comfort in the solidity of his back, the strong muscular lines of his neck. 'Aye,' she murmured back.

'Wait for my command.'

Her fingers rested lightly on the lever underneath. One squeeze and the arrow would fly, fly across the moat, across the high wall and straight through that window blazing with light. She hoped. The guard's steady pace became audible now, as he approached the point where his gleaming helmet moved directly below the window. And then he was gone.

'Now!'

Eye trained on the window, Tavia squeezed, watching almost in disbelief as the arrow flew from the bow, straight through the opening in the stone wall. 'I did it!' she squeaked with joy. 'I did it!' Her body shaky with relief, with success, she jumped up suddenly, knocking the crossbow on to the ground. Still kneeling, one hand on the frayed end of the rope, waiting for Henry to pull it taut, Benois smiled at her delight, seizing her around the waist, giving her a brief, hard kiss. Desire seared along her veins; a blazing trail of promise.

'Benois!'

At the sound of his name, Benois sprang to his feet,

pushing Tavia behind him, his body and eyes alert, search-ing the darkness swiftly for the owner of the voice. King Henry burst through the thick vegetation, pulling at the brambles that clung to his clothes, closely followed by a panting Langley.

'There you are!' growled Henry. 'You two are devilishly hard to find!'

'Henry?' Benois lifted one eyebrow, puzzled. 'I thought…'

'Ferchar's dead!' Henry announced. 'I'm a free man!'

Midnight was fast approaching when Langley finally managed to gather his men together to make the return journey back to his castle. The thunderstorm that had threat-ened earlier had melted away to the east to be replaced by a fine, clear night, the dark sky peppered with stars. On the brow of the hill above Marwood, just at the tree line, the horses, excited at the prospect of returning to their warm stables, whinnied and jostled, eager to be away.

'Did you really expect me to climb down that?' Henry remarked, his tufted ginger hair tousled by the night breeze as he viewed the long extent of rope stretching down from the tower.

Benois laughed, his teeth white in the darkness. 'It was the only way we could think of,' he admitted. 'You'd have managed it easily.'

'Obviously you believe me to be younger and fitter than I actually am.' Henry grinned. 'But fortune intervened, and when Ferchar collapsed and breathed his last in the great hall, the Scottish soldiers came running to me for advice. And here I am.' Henry ran his gaze arrogantly over Tavia's slight figure, drawn closely into Benois's side, no doubt wondering what in Heaven's name she was doing there. 'Anyway…' he cleared his throat '…it was still an excellent shot, Benois.'

'I wish.' Benois was already shaking his head. 'Tavia took the shot, not I.' Had she imagined the quiet pride conveyed in his tone?

Henry's jaw dropped at Benois's announcement, peering incredulously at Tavia. He let out a long slow whistle. 'You?' His tone bit into her, disbelieving.

'Aye,' she admitted, hesitantly, unable to decipher Henry's true thoughts beneath his fair, ruddy complexion, his imperious tone. She recalled their last meeting, when he had tried to warn her away from Benois. Then, she had believed his words, had broken her promise to Benois. She wouldn't make the same mistake again.

Henry stepped forwards, and bowed low, formally, from the waist. 'Then I thank you, fair maiden, for your help. You have a great skill.'

'It was the least I could do,' she replied, tipping her chin to address Henry with more confidence this time. 'After all, this whole problem has been caused by me.' Benois tucked her more closely into his broad flank, his arm firm about her back.

'That had crossed my mind,' Henry replied casually, his lips curving into a smile.

The night air, cooler now, began to nip in around Tavia's ankles, flirting beneath her hemline with chilly fingers. She tried to suppress a shiver, hunching down into her borrowed cloak.

Benois caught her slight movement. 'I think we should ride back now,' he suggested.

'Aye.' Henry looked up the hill to the spot where Langley and his men waited, Langley holding an extra horse for the King. 'Do you come with us, my lady,' he enquired solicitously of Tavia, 'or do you return to Dunswick, to your own people?' He jerked his head in the direction of Marwood.

'There should be enough Scottish soldiers to escort you back.'

'Nay, she comes with us,' Benois spoke even before Henry had finished his sentence. 'We married this eve, Henry. Tavia is my wife.'

Henry appraised them both slowly, his light hazel eyes keen, intelligent. 'So you've won his heart, maid,' he said eventually, 'and I have lost a good, loyal soldier. I congratulate you, mistress. I believed no one would ever persuade Benois le Vallieres to ever love again.' He wheeled smartly on one heel, striding off briskly towards the waiting soldiers.

A weakness spread through Tavia's legs, eroding the strength in her knees; she slumped against Benois. He adjusted his hold on her, bringing her around so that he could see her face, her beautiful elfin features.

'Take no notice of him,' he said, noticing her pensive look. 'He's a sore loser, that's all.'

'He wants to keep you, Benois.' Her dark lashes fanned around the wide brilliance of her eyes, as she leaned back in the circle of his arms, the comfortable brace of his hands in the small of her back. Her fingers crept up, wrapping around the bunched muscles of his forearms. 'It's understandable. You're a good soldier.'

'Was a good soldier,' he corrected her. 'I'm ready for a different kind of life now.'

The air shivered, held fast, his words suspended as if in a bubble between them. Tavia quivered beneath the light snare of his arms, hardly daring to breathe. Langley shouted down, a sharp tone of enquiry, shattering the tension. A faint look of frustration crossed Benois's face. 'You go on!' he bellowed up to Langley. 'Just leave the horses and we'll catch you up.' A good-natured cheer floated down the hill towards them, Langley grinning broadly before sweeping his arm in a wide arc. Saddles creaked, metal bits jangled in the horses' mouths as the group moved off into the swelling darkness of the forest.

'A different life?' she repeated, her voice cracking a little. A tiny trickle of hope broke through the packed-earth crust of her resolve, gathering momentum as it spilled through her veins. She trembled within his hold—could she dare to dream?

'Aye.' He smiled at her. His eyes held silver sparks. 'A life that involves you.'

Her heart soared with joy. 'But…will you not miss all those—?'

'All those battles, all that fighting,' he interrupted her, teasing. 'Riding out day after day, witnessing countless men lose their lives…nay, I don't think I'll miss it.' He curled his big hands around her face, one thumb rubbing idly over the exquisite skin of her cheek. 'You've changed me, Tavia. From that moment I first caught sight of you, sprawled so helplessly on those altar steps, surrounded by those great oafs, my own soldiers—from that moment, you began to change me.'

She reeled under his solemn words, liquefying heat running through her body, melting her fears, chasing away her belief that there would be nothing for them beyond this night. 'I thought, once Ferchar had been dealt with, that it would be the end,' she ventured, her tone muted, careful.

He shook his head. 'Before I met you, I thought the answer was to throw myself into mindless battle at every opportunity to drive the bad memories away.' Pulling his right hand away from her cheek, he rubbed the scar on his palm with his thumb. Tavia stopped the movement, clasping his hand with her own.

'You've taught me, Tavia. You've taught me that there are other ways to heal the soul. Your kindness, your gentleness towards me has healed my dark soul…and stolen my heart.

Emotion rocked through her slight frame, tears of joy threatening to spill. The restraints she had imposed upon herself since their marriage, fell away, leaving her free, free to love. 'Oh, Benois!' she cried out, reaching up to touch his face, almost in wonderment. 'I can't believe what you're saying to me.'

'Believe it, Tavia, because it's the truth.' He cupped the back of her head, weaving his fingers into the gossamer strands of her hair. 'There's only one thing left to say.' His voice sounded husky, unsure.

'Tell me,' she breathed, her voice a volatile mixture of anticipation, of excitement.

'I love you, Tavia,' he said. 'I love you with my body and soul, with all my heart.'

She shrieked with joy then, raising herself on tiptoe to throw her arms about his wide shoulders, sealing her mouth to his in a kiss that would hold them together, for ever.

* * * * *

MILLS & BOON

Historical

On sale 7th November 2008

Regency

SEDUCTION OF AN ENGLISH BEAUTY
by *Miranda Jarrett*

Lady Diana Farren is used to scandal. Sent abroad and
instructed to behave, she is soon swept away in Italy's passion
– and by its most notorious seducer, Antonio di Randolfo.
With Diana's past threatening danger on the horizon, is
Antonio everything he seems…?

CONQUERING KNIGHT, CAPTIVE LADY
by *Anne O'Brien*

Lady Rosamund de Longspey *didn't* escape an arranged marriage
only to be conquered by a rogue. But Lord Gervase Fitz Osbern,
weary of war and wanton women, will fight for what is his.
Warrior to the bone, he'll claim his castle – and a bride!

HIGH COUNTRY HERO by *Lynna Banning*

Dr Sage West trekked into the mountains with bounty hunter
Cord Lawson to save a life. One river swim and a bare-chested
kiss later, she finally realised that being alive meant *feeling*.
But could Sage survive the heartbreak when her tantalising
tutor resumed his wandering ways…?

On sale 7th November 2008

THE RETURN OF THE PRODIGAL
by Kasey Michaels

From the nightmare of battle…

Being in the care of lovely Lisette, who tended to his *every* need, helped Rian Becket to forget the horrors of war – although his intuition led him to believe there was more to the seductress than she revealed…

To danger close to his heart

If Lisette *was* aligned with the enemy, and endangering the Becket clan, how would he ever bring himself to stop her? Especially when she was beginning to mean more to him than life itself…

The much-anticipated finale to the
Moreland quartet!

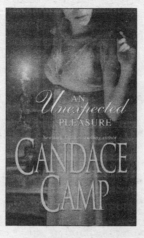

London, 1879

Had Theo Moreland, the Marquess of Raine, killed
her brother? American journalist Megan Mulcahey
had to know. But to find out, she needed to
infiltrate the marquess's household.

The new American governess intrigued Theo. Miss
Mulcahey had come to Broughton House to teach
his young siblings. Now the strange pull of their
immediate desire both troubled and excited him.
But why was this delicious vision snooping around
his mansion like a common thief?

Available 19th September 2008

M&B

2 FREE

BOOKS AND A SURPRISE GIFT!

We would like to take this opportunity to thank you for reading this Mills & Boon® book by offering you the chance to take TWO more specially selected titles from the Historical series absolutely FREE! We're also making this offer to introduce you to the benefits of the Mills & Boon® Book Club—

- ★ **FREE home delivery**
- ★ **FREE gifts and competitions**
- ★ **FREE monthly Newsletter**
- ★ **Exclusive Mills & Boon® Book Club offers**
- ★ **Books available before they're in the shops**

Accepting these FREE books and gift places you under no obligation to buy, you may cancel at any time, even after receiving your free shipment. Simply complete your details below and return the entire page to the address below. You don't even need a stamp!

YES! Please send me 2 free Historical books and a surprise gift. I understand that unless you hear from me, I will receive 4 superb new titles every month for just £3.69 each, postage and packing free. I am under no obligation to purchase any books and may cancel my subscription at any time. The free books and gift will be mine to keep in any case.

H8ZED

Ms/Mrs/Miss/Mr .... Initials ....
BLOCK CAPITALS PLEASE

Surname ....

Address ....

....

.... Postcode ....

Send this whole page to:
UK: FREEPOST CN81, Croydon, CR9 3WZ

Offer valid in UK only and is not available to current Mills & Boon® Book Club subscribers to this series. Overseas and Eire please write for details and readers in Southern Africa write to Box 3010, Pinegowie. 2123 RSA. We reserve the right to refuse an application and applicants must be aged 18 years or over. Only one application per household. Terms and prices subject to change without notice. Offer expires 31st December 2008. As a result of this application you may receive offers from Harlequin Mills & Boon and other carefully selected companies. If you would prefer not to share in this opportunity please write to The Data Manager. PO Box 676, Richmond. TW9 1WU.

Mills & Boon® is a registered trademark owned by Harlequin Mills & Boon Limited.
The Mills & Boon® Book Club is being used as a trademark.